Myriad Lands

Volume 2: Beyond the Edge

Myriad Lands

Volume 2: Beyond the Edge

Edited by

David Stokes

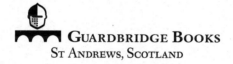

GUARDBRIDGE BOOKS
ST ANDREWS, SCOTLAND

Published by Guardbridge Books, St Andrews, Fife, United Kingdom.

Contents

Introduction

Fantasy literature has traditionally filled with tropes and clichés based on an imagined medieval Europe. Usually, not even real medieval history, which was surprisingly diverse, but the generic pseudo-medieval Europe springing from fairy tales. This landscape is not surprising, given the genre's roots in fairy tales, Gothic literature, and medieval romance. These roots were reinforced by certain giants of the genre, such as Howard and especially Tolkien, who have been much imitated. However, after so many such tales have been told, some of these tropes may begin to feel a bit stale. These overworked story elements have been expertly parodied in works such as Diana Wynne Jones' *Tough Guide to Fantasy Land*. Many of these tropes are also problematic, embodying violent, sexist, and racist ideas. One begins to wonder, is there anything more for the genre?

There is a whole world out there to explore. All cultures have their mythologies, their legendary tales, their sense of wonder. In many cultures, this fantastic realm is more closely integrated into the everyday experience than it is in modern Western culture. These other cultures' tales could provide inspiration for new fantasy stories, if only we would listen. Much traditional fantasy involves conflict between "civilized" people (the heroes), and "savages" (monstrous, swarthy marauders who must be defeated with violence). * But this binary narrative does not reflect the complexity of real societies. Real societies are made of people, not cardboard-cutout enemies to be fought, and each of those people has their own story to tell. Literature that recognizes this fact is richer and, although it might upset our preconceptions, is ultimately

---

* Thanks to Daniel Heath Justice who expresses an idea which I was stumbling towards better than I could in his essay, "On 'savagism' and 'civilization' in fantasy literature...", http://imagineotherwise.ca/creative.php accessed 22 June 2016.

more satisfying. By including the voices of diverse peoples, who were once often stereotyped as savages themselves, we can enrich the world of fantasy storytelling and return the denied humanity to many people of the world.

Fantasy can also expand into realms of the imagination. This genre is perhaps the most free to imagine different social structures, different ways of life. Yet much traditional fantasy remains rooted in the hierarchical, patriarchal systems of kings, priests, and nobles. Yet this is due to historical inertia only: the options available to Fantasy fiction are limited only by our imagination. Fantasy could be used to explore sociological implications of different social arrangements, just as science fiction explores implications of imagined technologies.

The original concept of the *Myriad Lands* anthology was to showcase non-traditional fantasy stories—stories with settings other than the standard pseudo-Medieval Europe. Some would be based on "Real World" cultures, with appropriate fantasy elements, that have been under-represented in traditional fantasy. Others would be original societies that defy the tropes of traditional fantasy to provide glimpses of radically different lands. The anthology would contain a mix of both types, and thereby illuminate many different ways of life, as well as revealing universal themes to which people everywhere can relate.

As stories came in, the collection grew beyond what could comfortably be contained in a single volume. Given the two threads in the remit—diverse real world cultures and non-traditional imaginary cultures—splitting the anthology into two volumes was convenient.

In actuality, the division of stories into two volumes is not as clear cut as the description suggests. The stories of "Real World" cultures actually involve magical analogues of those cultures, sometimes disguising them under fictional names. For example, "Keeper of the Bones" by Daniel Heath Justice draws on Native American culture and history to tell a story that reflects the native experience of colonization, appropriation, and the search for continuing identity, but which changes names and uses secondary-world fantasy so as to make its message more universal. The "imaginary" cultures are often inspired by elements of real cultures. For example, in "Poet-Scholars of the Necropolis", Megan Hutchins combines the dry environment and funerary practices of the Nazca with historical Korean death poems to create an original, but verisimilitudinous, culture. Several stories lie along this ill-defined border, and in the end I assigned them to volumes on other concerns such as balance and tone.

With stories from at least ten different countries and various literary traditions, there is certainly some diversity in the language use among the stories. This presented a dilemma for editing. The editor is originally American, although now resides in Britain. The anthology will be sold in both, as well as several other countries. Do I follow British or American English standards? In the end I did both. Stories from US authors were sent to an American copy editor and follow American spelling and usage. Stories from Commonwealth countries were sent to a British copy editor who followed British standards. For a few authors, English is not their primary language. With these, we tried to edit them to conform to correct English grammar, yet retain some of their less-typical expressions. In all of these cases, this approach serves to best preserve each author's unique voice.

The genre of fantasy is growing. New voices and perspectives are coming to the fore. I hope these volumes can contribute to encouraging that growth. It is important to readers of different backgrounds to see themselves reflected in characters about whom they read. But it also gives us all new and interesting stories to enjoy.

I would like to thank all the authors who submitted stories. There were many more good stories than I could include, and they deserve to be published somewhere. Thank you to Terry Jackman, Melissa Gilbert, Crystal Watanabe, and V. Anne Arden for help with copy-editing and proofreading.

The Truth in Fire

J.W. Hall

"Birds!" yelled the watcher from atop the tower. "The birds are flying to the west!"

Myst raced up the stairs to her window. Black shapes could be seen soaring in the distance, becoming lost in the haze of the dark sky. Below, the Searing Sea rose and fell, as if the watcher's proclamation was strong enough to stir its tumultuous currents. Miles away, Broadbore Tower, rising like some decrepit beacon in the lava, slid out its vessel. Myst could hear the shouts of its crew even from where she stood. They would already have a few miles head start by the time her tower sent their own ship towards the oasis.

"Brim!" Myst ran down the stairs as quickly as she had ascended them. She found her brother in their family's lounge, sprawled out amongst a bed of pillows, perched on his elbows with a book in his hand, his crooked, immobile legs laying to the side of him. He looked even grayer than when she had left him only an hour ago.

"I heard. They're headed west," said Brim, his eyes wide, swimming with a mixture of excitement, sadness, and sickness. He leaned back and coughed, a harsh, cluttered bark. "Probably near Iron

Isle and Crow Spire. They'll be there before we even put our oars into the scorch."

"The captain will beat them."

Brim stared up at the ceiling. "He always does. Captain Trike is the best vessel runner in all the 54 towers. He'll make sure we get our share of the oasis, and give the rest of those lava lickers something to remember Cross Port Tower by, too." He wiped his forehead. "Imagine being out there with them just once? To live their adventures firsthand and not by the text of some book. To taste one vial of fresh oasis water before I—I..."

"Quiet," said Myst. She came to her brother's side and felt his head. The blaze roared within him. It pained her to see him like this when it seemed like only months ago he was outside their balcony, cheering on the *Hell Swallow* as it sailed towards another oasis, regaling her with stories he had read in books about Captain Trike and his crew's great adventures. He always told those stories with such vigor that it made her feel like she was there. But she had never gone, and neither had he. And now, as the sulfur sickness took him, it seemed he would never have the chance to live those dreams.

She looked down at him and already he was asleep, the excitement sapping all his energy. She kissed him on his forehead, and whispered, "I'll see to it you get your wish."

She stood and ran out of the door, the sight of her dying brother quieting any rational thought that had ever prevented her from the course she now ran upon.

"Where are you going?" called her father from their kitchen.

She didn't answer for fear of what their conversation might do to her resolve. Besides, she didn't have much time. She grabbed an empty vial from the cabinet, shoved it in her pocket, and ran.

She burst through the front doors of her family's flat and turned down the hallway. Guards, tasked with patrolling the Upper, nodded to her as she ran by. She darted in and out of the passages, avoiding acquaintances and the councilmen her father would constantly entertain, until she stood looking down Ible's Ladder, the immense stairwell that ran from the upper tower down to the lower regions. Down to the dock.

Never before had she dared the Ladder by herself. Her father's campaigns were the only reason she ever went down, and that was in the sanctity of a troop of guards. It was too dangerous for an Upper to go down by herself, her father had always said. Too dangerous for a little girl.

She took a deep breath and put up her hood. She was down the first few flights of stairs before she realized what she was doing. She was going to the Fry, the portion of the tower who felt the press of the lava the most. The portion who had never had a taste of clean, filtered air like the stuff she and her family were privy to in every breath.

She hurried down, taking the stairs twice at a time. People passed beside her, walking up and down the Ladder in chore or conversation. She began to notice the change in their clothes. The fine black fabric of the Upper gave way to grey and beaten furs, clothes made from the singe rats they raised at such depths. Even the tower began to change. The clean, black ignus bricks of her home began to turn sooty and smudged. Red urlack fungus, spores planted from the magma moisture that beat against the stone, crept up walls like infected veins about to burst. And from the windows she could see the Searing Sea, the vast ocean of lava that was their world, a world created by the opening of the Three Hundred Hells so many years ago.

The sea climbed up to the windows like a savage orange beast bent on swallowing her whole, before receding in defeat. She thanked the Builders then for having the foresight to construct the towers tall and strong, and the gods for giving them ignus to protect against the heat and the soiled air.

Further down, the windows stopped altogether. The heat rose. She found herself barely able to breathe. It smelt of sulfur and sewage, sweat and sour bodies, iron and bile. The few air filters they had did little to quell the stench. She plugged her nose and looked back up the stairs.

This is your adventure. This is Brim's adventure. There's no turning around, she told herself.

She plunged further into the darkness. It didn't take her long to find the crowd of people rushing across the stairwell and into an adjacent chamber. She knew from Brim's stories that when the vessel sailed all the people of the Fry dropped their duties to see it off. It was the only explanation for such a gathering. She followed.

She lost herself in a mob of thin garb and half naked bodies, a style she imagined was adapted to deal with the temperature. She fought to keep up with the press, pushing and elbowing, until at last the crowd came to a stop.

A chant began. "Trike. Trike. Trike."

She could see nothing but legs. She was trapped, but she would be damned if she were to fail her brother and let their adventure stop there. She crawled her way to the front of the line. Little by little she could feel the heat intensify, and soon, the fiery radiance of the lava peeked its face through the tangle of limbs. A few more pushes and she had made it to the sea wall where a hundred children just like her hung halfway over the cooling ignus stone in curious glee. She followed their eyes. The dock had been lowered, and to its side, bobbing in the magma like a giant debris of charcoal, was the *Hell Swallow* and its crew.

Ten of them prepared the ship. They scurried over the vessel, testing pumps and latches, setting up oars and checking various meters. They were like no other people she had ever seen. They wore a collection of strange, metallic looking gear that could all but hide their burnt skins. For upon each of them were bubbly scars that corroded their faces and limbs, like plotted courses of their adventurous lives upon the sea.

And atop the vessel itself, watching it from a half covered cockpit was Captain Trike. His goggles were tied tight against his bearded face. The strange, curved hat that Brim had showed her in his pictures sat atop his head like a crown of authority given by another culture, another time. He pointed and barked orders, ignoring the chants of his name, seeing to the prep of the vessel with such vigor that it was no wonder he had kept the *Hell Swallow* running for such a long time.

Just as soon as Myst had taken in the amazing sights of the vessel was it untying its ropes and pushing away from the dock.

She froze, stuck in a moment of indecision and fear. The Searing Sea rose and fell, stirring up spats of fire that sizzled the deck. Never had she been so close to it. Never could she have imagined the ferocity of it from the height she had lived in her entire life. And the people... Who was she amongst those who had been tried by the sea daily? Those who had lived in the scorch and the smell since they were brought forth into this world afire...

She was a sister whose dying brother needed an adventure.

Myst scrambled over the sea wall and onto the dock. The chants quickly turned into shouts, ordering her back. But she ignored them and ran. Immediately she felt the sea. Its heat groped for her, choking her with its heavy hands, wrenching the sweat from her body. But she did not stop.

The vessel had pushed away from the dock completely now. She came to the edge of it and swallowed. There was nothing between her and the sea any longer. Only the vastness of lava stared back. A few feet stood between the dock and the vessel. A few measly feet between her dying brother's wish and the failure in fulfilling it.

She jumped.

The world seemed to freeze in that moment she was in the air. The lava rose to grab her. The vessel seemed to pull away to avoid her. She reached out and grabbed the side of the ship, her small hands digging into the rough ignus gunwale. She pulled and grabbed, using her feet to scurry herself upwards. She had just about made it over the edge when a man grabbed her by her wrists.

"Stole away!" he cried through a two-toothed mouth.

"Stole away," the others of the crew echoed up to the captain as they continued rowing. Captain Trike peered his head out from his cockpit atop the *Hell Swallow*. He wiped his goggles and sneered. Myst's legs still dangled freely over the magma. For a moment she thought the Captain would order to her to be dropped.

"Pull her in, but keep course."

The crew member lifted her up and over, depositing her under the curve of the bow. He returned to the oars along with the others. The captain emerged from a hatch not long thereafter. Myst's heart fluttered with excitement. *The Captain is coming to talk to me, Brim! Just wait till I tell you what he said...*

"You must be the queen of all idiots." He marched up to her so fast that for a moment she thought he might strike her. She hid deeper underneath the bow as he knelt in front of her. He lowered his goggles and stared. His eyes were dark, like two flecks of ignus. "An Upper? I should have known only someone with smooth skin like yours would be foolish enough to jump aboard. What in the name of all the Opened Hells are you doing on my ship?"

"Its—um—I—It's my brother."

The Captain only stared.

"See, he's always loved stories of you and the *Hell Swallow*. Ever since we were little he would go on and on about your adventures upon the Searing Sea. Your battles with the other towers. How you dealt with fire squids and demon sharks. How you would drain an entire oasis before anyone else could even touch a drop. But those were only from books. He always wanted to go on an adventure with you himself. But a few months ago he caught the sulfur sickness. The doctors say in a few weeks he'll be dead, which means he'll never get to fulfill his dreams..."

"So you thought you would do it for him?" said the captain.

She nodded.

He shook his head, grabbed her by the wrist, and put her on her feet.

"What we got, Captain?" cried a crew member.

"An empty headed Upper who's better off in the burn." He dragged her to the hatch. "Onward. Follow the birds!"

She followed him up a narrow stairwell and into the cockpit. A dashboard full of levers and a small steering wheel occupied the small space. From the vantage point they had a view of the entire ship and the sea it sailed upon. Cross Port Tower shrunk behind them like a charred hand raised in farewell. It looked so small and strange from that view. Like just another tower in the distance striving to survive.

"What's your name?" said Captain Trike.

"Myst Olinglade."

"As in the daughter of Councilman Olinglade, spearhead of the Lower Water Tax and all around buffoon?"

"My father is not a buffoon!" cried Myst.

"No? Why don't you ask the people of the Fry what they think of giving a fifth of their water to the Upper so they may continue to govern the tower properly and further their scientific research?"

"It's for their own good."

The captain threw back his head in laughter. "I see you've got your father's sense of fantasy. You think this is all play. You think this is all an adventure to tell stories about up there in the fresh air, but what you don't realize is that lives matter on this rig. All of them. Not just yours or your brother's."

She opened her mouth to speak back, but Captain Trike interrupted her.

"You're aboard now and we're not turning back to drop off a councilman's daughter just for his peace of mind. There's an oasis that just opened up out there that could quench our thirst for months and I aim to drain it properly. So sit back and have your damned adventure. Just stay out of our way."

Captain Trike turned back to the wheel and yelled out to his crew, "Faster. The current is drifting starboard."

Myst shrunk to the back of the cockpit. She didn't know what she was expecting when she boarded the ship, but surely not a verbal attack.

How could the man say such things? Perhaps if he knew her brother he would understand better.

"He's a good person."

"Who?" the captain grunted.

"My brother. He's smart and funny. Every Rain Season he goes down to the Fry to hand out gifts to the children."

"My mother raised three orphans that lost their parents to the sea. Even gave her arm to the scorch to protect my father when the tide rose over the walls. Does that make her any more worthy than the rest to receive more water? No. Everyone has an ounce of goodness in them. Everyone deserves the equal chance to survive in this damned world should they so choose. Your brother is a good person so he should get his dreams? Bah!" Trike threw up his hand. "Think of the thousands of people who have died of thirst and never had the chance to live out theirs. Open your eyes. This is a mission for life, not the fulfillment of a fantasy."

"Captain! Off the bow!" yelled up a crew.

A flock of birds flew over the front of the ship. A small ridge had risen in the distance, rising from the glowing sea like a brown scab. To either side of it, she could see enemy vessels approaching.

The captain held up a telescope and scanned the purview. "Broadbore and Crow Spire again. Haven't learned their lessons yet. Ready the pumps. Load the cannons. I want both ships towed home this time."

The men responded in a unified yell. The *Hell Swallow* seemed to double in speed. Myst stood on her tiptoes, her fingers gripped on the sill of the open cockpit window, the hot wind whipping her face. Never before had she ever felt such excitement. Oh, she couldn't wait to tell Brim about this. She was already concocting her own story when up from the deck came the cry, "Dire Whales, port side!"

The captain pushed Myst aside and dropped his scope. "Harpoons! Keep them at bay."

She shuffled up to his side and peered out. Four fins dipped in and out of the lava, cutting through the sludgy liquid. Their heads breached the surface showcasing eyes as red as blood, their faces full of horns, their mouth a trap of phosphorous gums. They raced towards the oasis, veering closer to the *Hell Swallow*. Myst had always seen the creatures in the far off distance, frolicking in the magma. Never could she have imagined ever seeing them so close. They were beautiful, majestic things. The captain was wrong. Brim was right. Being aboard the *Hell Swallow* was magnificent and—

"Spray!" cried the Captain. The creatures arched their backs, exposing their blowholes, and spewed a geyser of lava onto the ship's deck.

Most of the crew took cover underneath the curve of the gunwale, but an unlucky few were caught in the scorching shower. Petals of fire bloomed on the exposed sailor's clothes and skin. They cried out, slapping at the flames and their injuries, rolling upon the vessel's floor like squirming fish. Myst saw their faces. The pain. The bubbling flesh. The smears of blood put there by their hands' attempt to silence the burn.

She sunk further into the cockpit, her eyes wide, her heart rattling in her chest.

"Douse them!" ordered the captain.

A few of the braver members dared to dart from their safety under the gunwale to unravel hoses. Someone turned a valve and from it came a spray of water. The burning men whimpered as the liquid met their skin. The crew pulled their injured to safety just as the whales came near once more.

"Harpoons, damn it!" called Captain Trike.

The crew snapped into form. From underneath the gunwale they produced rifles, strange weapons with thick arrows protruding from their shoulder-mounted muzzles. They aimed. For a moment, nothing happened. Only the slap of the sea against the ship's hull and the screech of the approaching whales could be heard.

Closer and closer they came. Myst's hands clenched tighter on the sill. Why didn't they fire? *They're coming!* she wanted to yell. *Shoot before they cover you again!*

The whales breached the surface.

Bam!

The harpoons fired, the report a concussive blast that clapped in her head. The great arrows sunk into the whales' backs in a spurt of magma and blood. The beasts rolled and submerged, diving into the lava, their angry song tossed like a curse back at the ship.

They didn't reappear until much later, further off the bow of the *Hell Swallow*. They were safe.

Myst felt like she could finally breathe, but that feeling did not last.

"Onward!" cried Captain Trike, his scope turned towards the ridge. Below the men scurried back to their posts, even those who had been burnt, holding their injuries and limping to their stations, new scars added to their already marred skins.

"What an adventure," snarled the captain.

Myst looked up. The captain stared down, emotionless. "The men... they're injured."

He put his back to her. "And they'll proudly wear the scars. Ugly badges of honor given for each ounce of water that has ever gone into you and your brother's throat."

Myst gulped.

"If you want to live in this world. You have to burn. You brother never said that in his stories, did he?"

She didn't respond. In the stories the crew always returned unscathed. In the stories, Captain Trike led them to flawless victories against all foes. In the stories, dire whales helped to guide the *Hell Swallow* to the oasis just as much as birds did.

The captain turned his attention back to the ridge. "200 meters. Broadbore vessel. Off the port bow."

The crew echoed his response.

She could see it now, the ridge began to rise out from the magma sea like the spine of a drowning giant. Two vessels were parked at its edge, a black pump slithering out of each, tossed over the side of it like an onyx rope. The *Hell Swallow* veered straight for the one on the left. Dark figures scurried about its deck, pointing at the *Hell Swallow* as it approached.

"Cannons and pumps," called Captain Trike. "And don't stop rowing until the bastards have gotten out of our way."

The crew cheered. They positioned cannons onto the gunwales and bow, huge muzzles that were connected to hoses. Others threw the other end of the pumps over into the magma. Captain Trike steadied the wheel. Like some predatory raptor of the sea, his eyes did not leave the vessel. The *Hell Swallow* cut through the lava, skipping over the small waves. The Broadbore vessel reeled back in its hose and pushed off from the banks of the oasis's ridge. Myst could see the glint of their own cannons being aimed. But they were too slow.

The *Hell Swallow* was upon them.

Myst slunk back as the vessel came crashing into the side of the Broadbore ship. The two metals screamed in a horrific union, barely drowning out the call of the men who steered them. Myst lurched into the back of Captain Trike who held so tightly to the wheel that he barely moved. He made no offer to help her up. So she scrambled up the side of the cockpit to watch the great battle unfold.

But as it turned out, it was no battle. It was a massacre.

The Broadbores had lost control of their cannons, leaving them defenseless. The *Hell Swallow*'s crew wasted no time. They flicked a lever and the pumps turned on. The cannons spat up gallons of lava, upchucking it from the sea beneath and onto the deck of the enemy's ship.

Everywhere the Broadbores burned. Everywhere the Broadbores cried out. At one point someone had undone the valve to their water storage, letting it loose all over the deck. Steam rose into the sky, making a foggy curtain over what happened next. Like demons scurrying out from a gaseous abyss, three men from the *Hell Swallow*'s crew rose from their ship and onto the Broadbore vessel. Myst could see the rise and fall of their daggers like pitch claws in the steam. Screams echoed up to the cockpit. Screams and gurgles and calls of surrender. But none was given. Such horrible sounds were they that Myst had to pinch her ears closed in order to keep the noise from entering her conscious.

"That's it! Every last one of them," cried Captain Trike over the chaotic din, his smile wide and proud. "Make it so they have to scrap every last ounce of that blasted tower in order to brave the seas again."

When the steam finally dissipated Myst could see into the wreckage of the Broadbore ship. Bodies lay sprawled across the deck, its floor a filthy slosh of water, un-cooled magma, and blood. The three members of the *Hell Swallow* stood amongst the ship, victorious.

"Their pump and then hook it up."

A member of the crew flipped a lever. The pump sputtered and then chugged. A dribble of water could be seen slithering down the ridge. They were expelling the water from the ship's bladder.

"Finished!" cried the crew. They tossed a rope back over to the *Hell Swallow* where it was hitched to a clasp on the bow.

A crank was turned. Slowly the Broadbore's vessel was pulled back into the sea, pulled into their possession, a capture of precious ignus to be used to rebuild and repair the tower and the *Hell Swallow* sometime down the road.

"Onto the ridge."

Three more rows and the *Hell Swallow* skidded onto the rocky beach of the oasis. The men gave a muffled cheer, but Captain Trike had no time for celebration.

"The hose, damn you!"

From the depths of the ship the crew unraveled a black hose, each member of the crew inching out the thick, bulky tube. They carried it forward until the crew made landfall. They grunted and groaned from the weight of it as sweat glistened over them like some new translucent outfit.

Myst had never imagined the process to be such hell.

"Imp fish, port side!" called a crew.

All attention swung. A school of fire colored fish had flopped upon the oasis shore. Their scales gleamed like blood against the lava. They worked their powerful fins against the rock, eking their way forward until, flapping their tremendous tails, they flung the one behind them closer to the edge. One by one they gathered and somersaulted. At last a fish climbed high enough where it could extend a long, fat tongue over the edge of the oasis and scoop out water in tremendous heaves, raining droplets onto its family's slurping mouths.

"They're stealing our water," said the Captain. "Wash them away."

Some of the crew dropped the hose and turned the levers of the other pumps. Gouts of lava ushered out, sweeping the creatures off the ridge.

"Move," said Captain Trike, and he pushed Myst out of his way for a better view. Myst was cut off from the frantic action. She was about to push her way back into view when she heard a noise at her back.

Whoosh. Whoosh. Whoosh.

She turned in time to see that another vessel was coming straight for them.

"Captain!" she shouted.

"What do you—" he turned, but it was already too late. The vessel rammed them. Myst tumbled into the Captain and both folded onto the ground as the ship tipped. She grabbed hold of his vest as she nearly rolled out the window. The screams of the crew echoed up to her. She looked behind her and saw a man fall from his comrades grasping hands and into the hellish muck of the sea.

"Pumps!" she heard a foreign voice yell. Something gulped.

The Captain swore beside her. "Spray, starboard! Cover."

The *Hell Swallow* seemed to level out. She clambered back into the cockpit, breathing heavily, her heart thrumming inside her chest.

Captain Trike reached over her and slammed close the cover over the starboard window just as a spit of lava fell into the cockpit.

Myst roared in pain. Her arm. Her leg. Never before had she experienced such agony. She looked down to see drips of molten liquid scarring her skin. It only made her scream more. She went to slap them away with her other hand, but the Captain grabbed it. With his own glove he subdued the fires. Each hit added to the pain. She was sure her skin was gone.

He grabbed her by her chin so hard that her scream became lost in her throat. "Do you want to live? "

Her eyes bulged with in her head. He shook her.

"Do you want to see your brother again?"

She forced herself to nod.

"Then swallow hard and take it." He rose from the ground, and dared to look around the corner of the window. "They're filling the deck," he whispered to himself. From his belt he produced a cruel looking dagger. He beat it against his chest, closed his eyes, and said something she could not hear. When he opened them again, he yelled, "Over the top!"

A cry responded from below. Without another word, Captain Trike slipped out of the cockpit. There were yells. There was the sound of metal upon metal. Though her head rang with anguish, Myst could not stand the mystery of the violence happening at her back. She dared to look out the adjacent window.

A fight had erupted on the enemy craft. Captain Trike waged war against a dozen foes on its deck, while the still standing members of the *Hell Swallow*'s crew clambered over the roof of the cockpit to join him. The lava cannons still sprayed into the *Hell Swallow*, but they were useless against the boarding members. Blood spilled. People were pushed into the scorching sea. It was horrible.

All this, she thought. *All this for water. All this for ignus. All this to keep the tower alive.*

Her eyes fell to the ridge of the oasis standing calm and serene amongst the chaos. It seemed funny that such a thing should blossom upon the always shifting skin of the world. It seemed funny that the gods would give them some respite to keep them alive amongst this hell, a hell she and her brother had never truly appreciated before so high in their roost.

But what did it matter if they couldn't live long enough to have the water in the first place. Then she noticed the hose. It was so close to the edge of the ridge. All it needed was a few more inches of push and it would be over and into the precious resource.

She looked back at the fighting. Who knew who would come out alive. Who knew if they could even stay long enough to drain their share of the oasis.

She bit her lip, and before she knew what she was doing, she was out of the cockpit. She jumped over the lava filled deck and onto the curve of the gunwale, her feet slipped and she stumbled onto the hard ground of the oasis.

She could not believe the texture of it. This natural born phenomena felt so much like the stones of her home. The cries of the fight happening behind her did not let her dally. She ran up the slope. She grabbed the end of the hose and lifted, her burns screaming in pain. It was so heavy. Her body wanted to give up. Sweat poured off of her as if her muscles were sobbing. Yet she dragged it, inch by inch, adrenaline coursing through her blood like magma. At last, she dropped it over the top and looked out over the oasis.

Her jaw dropped. It was a pool of deep blue, a color she had only ever seen in story books and hinted at in a glass of water. It was beautiful. Never before could she imagine so much of it in one place, but clearly it was not enough to quench the thirst of all who took from it. For on the far reaches of the ridge she could see other hoses dipping into the reservoir, the tentacles and tails of beasts dangling in the precious resource for sweet relief. The *Hell Swallow* would get its share before this oasis closed up, but not all of it like the stories claimed. She reached in her pocket, produced the vial, and filled it with the unfiltered water. Satisfied, she dropped the hose into the water and flipped the lever. With a slurp, the tube went rigid, drinking up the water by the gallon.

"Retreat!" came the yells.

Myst turned to see Captain Trike limping over the edge of the enemy vessel, his injured crew avoiding attacks to do the same. The enemies hurried to realign their pumps. They were preparing to spray again, but the *Hell Swallow* was already pushing away, swinging the Broadbore's derelict ship between them. "Cut her loose," she could hear the captain yelling. The empty ship fell away into their attackers, buying them time.

Myst flipped back the lever on the hose and ran. She clambered up the tube, her small feet walking it like a balance game as it slithered out from the water. She clung to the side of the gunwale and hoisted herself up just as the crew evacuated the lava that had filled their deck.

The enemy vessel celebrated in triumph as the *Hell Swallow* crawled away. The crew and Captain Trike stood behind her, watching, breathing, bloodied and burned.

"Damn them," he said. A gash was opened over his head. His goggles were gone. His eyes were as red as fire. "Six of our men dead, and not an ounce to show for it."

"Captain," said a crew from behind. "The gauge is reading the bladder is an eighth full."

"An eighth full? How can that be?"

"It was the girl," said a crew member. "I saw her scramble back onto the boat with my own eyes."

Captain Trike turned to her. He did not smile. He did not frown. He just stared. Then he limped towards her and lifted her arm. He pointed to the burn that had bubbled there. "You earned those badges today."

The crew gave a sullen cheer and called out her name. She knew that deep in her head she should be thrilled that her name was on the tongues of the *Hell Swallow*'s crew and what a story it would make for

Brim, but somehow it felt hollow. There were dead men beneath them that had helped put that water in the bladder. She had seen them die. And those horrible sights stayed with her as the *Hell Swallow* rowed back to their tower.

They were greeted as they had been said farewell to, in a mass of onlookers. Except this time her father and his guards were amongst them.

"How dare you leave this port with my daughter," he began on Captain Trike. "You bring her back burned and nearly dead, I should—"

Myst rose to speak, but Captain Trike stopped her with a rise of his finger and winked. She supposed he had faced much worse than the wrath of an angry father on the Seared Sea. She left them to their debate.

On her walk back up the Ladder, where people gawked at her and whispered behind her back, she saw the hose of the *Hell Swallow* splashing into the well at the bottom of the tower. A huddle of scarred, scrawny children stood beside it, hoping to catch the occasional spray that a hiccup in the pump would cause. Praying like followers to a shrine for a single, unfiltered drop. She looked up the stairs and then back into that gurgling hole. From her pocket she took the vial of water, uncorked it and dumped its contents down the hole.

The kids called her names and swore at her for wasting water, but who were they to decide who received it and who didn't. The water belonged to the people, not to any one person.

She climbed the stairs, exhausted and in pain. When she entered the room, Brim could barely sit up.

"Father said you boarded the *Hell Swallow*," he managed.

She nodded in return.

"Water?"

She shook her head, "But I have something even better."

"What's that?"

"A story."

He smiled and leaned back.

And so she told him of her adventure. It was full of dashing heroes who saved comrades and allowed surrender and flawless victories without burn or injury. Like his books, it was a fine story and nothing else. Something to let Brim see when he closed his eyes and dreamed. Fiction. The real stories she would carry within the bubbly lines of her new scars. There a person could read the truth. There a person could understand the way of the world. If you wanted to live in it, you had to burn.

This story was first released in audio form by Podcastle.
This is its first time in print.

Poet-Scholars of the Necropolis

By M. K. Hutchins

The corpse arrived wrapped and ready for drying atop the necropolis.

"Got a wet one!" Onyo called from the entryway.

Royzca, the other poet-scholar in residence, stared listlessly out the slit-window in her room, watching the porters spiral down the hill road and into the adobe city below. She already knew whose corpse they'd delivered. She'd gotten a private note yesterday.

Royzca's door creaked open. Onyo frowned at her, his furry, white eyebrows pulling together into a concerned line. "Aren't you coming?"

Royzca exhaled and walked through the brick corridors with him, her head down, her throat too tight for words. The narrow windows only let in shafts of light, but her old eyes would have been poor even in full daylight. She trailed her fingers against the wall, letting the time-smoothed bricks lead her.

For all her advanced warning, seeing the body still stabbed needles through her heart. One side of the wrapping was lumped, where the corpse cradled a premature child.

The porters had placed the body atop the necropolis' floating, poem-enchanted board—useful for shifting bodies around. A death poem in the traditional red envelope lay across her chest.

"Do you want me to read it out?" Onyo asked.

"No." She felt like a sandstorm had torn up her throat, but Royzca managed to keep her hands still as she opened the envelope. Squinting hard, she read silently.

The poem opened and closed in the traditional style.

> I go to Paradise—
> Holding my healthy child
> Like my grandmother held me—
> That is Paradise.

Tears blurred Royzca's eyes, turning the page into a wash of white and black.

"Clearly, an amateur poem," Onyo said, looking over her shoulder. "There's a bit of alliteration across the second line, but there's no depth. No clever assonance or figurative language, no allusions to other works to give it resonance."

Royzca's throat tightened. "My granddaughter wrote this." Onyo peered at her, not understanding. "Yula. She died in early labor yesterday."

Reflected grief creased all the lines in his old face. He didn't bother with meaningless condolences—he laid a hand on her shoulder. Royzca let it rest there, heavy and reassuring.

She remembered the day of Yula's birth perfectly—holding the warm babe, watching her eyes flutter open even as the midwife closed Yula's mother's. Joy and sorrow had raged inside Royzca. She could still hear the cheerfully unaware singing of her other children and smell the roasting fish and sweet potatoes.

Yula had grown up with a cacophony of cousins. She loved children. She was eager to become a mother herself.

"I'm going to bless her poem."

Onyo's hand stiffened. Concern bled over his features. "Royzca..."

"Yes?" Royzca stood tall, chin jutted out. She clutched the precious poem to her chest, as she'd once held the child who wrote it.

He sighed. "I know this is hard...but it's still our responsibility to judge her poem. You swore not to waste sacred water on poems that aren't beautiful, on poems that can't become mighty spells."

Royzca glanced at the bulge cradled at her granddaughter's side. Yula knew Royzca would read this. She'd used her poem to send her love. *Like my grandmother held me.*

Hopefully, in Paradise, Yula now had that chance. Hopefully she was playing with her infant, while here her husband and cousins wailed their loss from the rooftops.

"This is the most beautiful poem I have ever read," she whispered. "I'm blessing it. I don't care if it's useful for magic afterwards."

"Royzca..." Onyo pleaded.

She faced him, voice adamant. "Anyone can appreciate an excellent poem. It takes an especially skilled poet to appreciate a poorly-written one."

"Lord-Governor Alyocandro's aunt is coming soon, and she'd grab any excuse to report you to the Guild. If she sees you've blessed that poem, she'll push charges of treasonous misuse. Treason *is* a capitol offense."

Treason or no, Royzca didn't care. Her granddaughter's last words deserved the last blessing she could give. "Then I'll make sure I hide it well."

Royzca helped Onyo navigate the enchanted board up the snaking stairs to the roof. They nestled Yula in the sand next to another dozen drying bodies. A tightly-woven mesh kept birds and bugs away. Filtered through the mesh, the afternoon sun gave everything a white glow. Royzca liked to think that meant the inhabitants had reached Paradise.

"Do you want me to come with you to do the blessing, or should I make supper?" Onyo asked.

"Food." Her soul needed the comfort of a warm bowl. She couldn't find the words to thank Onyo, but after a decade of working together in the necropolis, she knew he'd see the gratitude in her face.

Royzca lit a torch and headed down, first on broad stairs, passing floor after floor of entombments. Her knees creaked as the stairs tightened into a spiral, plunging her into the roots of the hill. Shadows flickered around the curves.

At last she reached the alcove. She placed the torch in its sconce—the uneven light flickered over a broad shelf inlaid with obsidian. A niche held the gold vial.

Royzca spread Yula's poem reverently on the shelf. Yula had been so hale, so flush with life, during Royzca's last visit not two weeks ago. She should have had the chance to hold her child in this world, with her husband and cousins around her. Royzca couldn't give her that, but she could do this.

She opened the gold vial. All the water to touch this kingdom came from mountain run off—all the water except the Guild's sacred spring, a place connected to Paradise, a place known only to Poet-Masters. Royzca was just a poet-scholar, entrusted with a necropolis and a vial of the scarce, sacred water.

Maybe she was breaking that trust now, but she'd held the position of grandmother long before she'd been a scholar.

She read Yula's poem aloud. The alcove echoed the words, reverberated the syllables through the bricks. While the air was still heavy with the spoken word, Royzca sprinkled the paper with sacred water. The paper glowed, then turned a brilliant, uncanny red; its mundanely-dyed envelope seemed pale in comparison. The next time someone read these words aloud, the sacred waters would pull a piece of Paradise, shaped by Yula's death poem, into this world.

Likely, the quality of the poem was too poor to be of any effect. But it was beautiful. Royzca folded it back into the envelope, climbed the stairs with the torch, then wandered the entombments until she found the shelf holding Yula's mother. Royzca tucked the poem under her mummified body.

"I didn't think you'd mind hiding this for me." Royzca bit her lip. "I...I suppose you already know. About Yula. I hope you're holding her, like you never could in life."

Royzca waited there for a moment, as if her daughter could respond. Only silence and the dry-must smell of the dead replied.

Onyo had a vegetable stew waiting for her, warm, thick stuff that seeped into her marrow. He refilled her bowl after she'd emptied the first one.

"So. I've been re-reading Motyono's Epic of the River War. And I do have to conclude that it's the most brilliant poem of all time." Onyo said it with a touch of mischief in his eyes; this was a decade-old debate they'd started on Royzca's first day in the necropolis.

She fell into the conversation easily. "Even better than Pusarla's Odes to Paradise?"

"Ah, that's not *one* poem, it's a dozen."

"While each ode can be enjoyed individually, there's *added* enjoyment in reading them together. I think this is a point in Pusarla's favor; it is good in part and in whole. I cannot read the third portion of Epic by itself with any enjoyment."

"That's because what goes before is crucial, not merely tangentially connected! Even you'll have to admit that Motyono was a master of allusions, carefully building and enhancing his story by drawing on his poetic forebearers."

"And what do allusions matter, when he sacrifices rhythm to squeeze it in? None of his works benefit from being read aloud—especially Epic." She'd uttered that argument a hundred times, in a hundred different ways. She knew how Onyo would counter, and mouthed along as he decried Pusarla's lyricism as less moving than Motyono's story.

Which, of course, moved them into the never-ending debate of what made good poetry. Form or content? Aesthetic beauty, or emotional resonance?

In truth, Royzca liked both poems, but she'd never admit it—she liked the familiar argument even more. It distracted her. It warmed her bones in a way that stew couldn't.

Half-way through a passionate argument about the nature of narrative, Onyo passed wind. He coughed politely. "Ah. Apologies. I dearly wish there was a small child nearby."

"To blame it on?"

"I'm old! My bowels are less trustworthy than they once were. And I'm always cold at night."

"And food burns back up my throat." They'd had this conversation a hundred times, too. Complaining about old age was almost as soothing as debating poetry.

"And my memory's not what it used to be."

Royzca shook her head. "You already said that one."

"I did not!"

"Perhaps your faulty memory is why you enjoy Motyono over Pusarla? It's far easier to keep track of Motyono's broad strokes than it is Pusarla's intricate imagery."

And so the debate began anew, as constant and refreshing as water from the mountains.

Hedrana, the Lord-Governor's aunt, arrived the next morning. She banged on the necropolis door as if she'd been locked out of her own house. "Hello! I won't be kept waiting!"

If Hedrana's shrill, sing-song voice couldn't wake the dead, nothing would.

Royzca was already awake, but she took her time shuffling down the hall, her hip aching as it did every morning. Onyo joined her from his room. "Do we have to let her in?"

"If we're nice, maybe she'll go away more quickly," Royzca said. "She's only here to flatter herself."

Hedrana was obsessed with proving that she was better than the rest of the nobility because she not only had connections and a massive fortune, but also a refined appreciation for poetry. Unfortunately, that meant she insisted on touring the necropolis whenever she visited her nephew.

Royzca turned her face into a polite mask and opened the door.

"About time!" Hedrana blustered, sweeping inside. She seemed too young for this place, with only a few wisps of gray in her hair. "If *I* held a post in a necropolis, *I* would not keep people waiting. I trust the two of you have been dutiful in my absence?"

As if this woman held any stewardship over them. Royzca bowed, back creaking. "Of course."

Hedrana sniffed. "Perhaps you did not know, but I have been attending the Guild Academy."

Royzca doubted there was anyone in the city who didn't know it. There were betting rings on whether she'd threatened or bribed her way in, but no conclusive answers yet.

"And I have just passed their tests." She rolled up her sleeve, displaying a tattoo of a stylized scroll—the insignia of the Guild. It marked her as a novice poet-scholar.

Royzca rubbed her own tattoo under her sleeve. Royzca had *earned* that—and certainly not with bribes or threats.

"Come! I wish to inspect *all* of the necropolis. After all, I am sure the Guild will assign me here as soon as a post is available. Shall we start with the roof?"

"Of course." Royzca barely kept the words civil. She led, patience evaporating. How could Hedrana speak of a post opening—her or Onyo's death—so casually?

"Ah!" Hedrana sighed melodramatically over the bodies drying in the sand. She laid her eyes on Yula. "So fair falls the blossom of youth in bringing forth fruit!"

Royzca gritted her teeth. She didn't care what connections this woman had, she had no right to vomit overwrought verses on her granddaughter.

Onyo shot Royzca a warning glance, then smiled and stepped next to Hedrana. "Truly, your metaphors are as clear and piercing as Gorel's in his Verses of Adulation."

Hedrana flushed. "You think so?"

"Undoubtedly."

Royzca bit back a laugh. Gorel had been a great poet, but nearly everyone agreed that Verses, with its laughable mixed metaphors, was an unfortunate stain in his corpus of compositions.

"You are a poet of excellent taste," Hedrana said, and swept back down the stairs.

Royzca flicked him a thankful glance. He beamed at her, face crinkling down all the familiar lines.

After that, they wandered through the tombs. Blessed and used poems were, by tradition, painted on the walls in blue and green. Hedrana paused often, leaning close with the torch and reciting them aloud.

"You have the voice of Asoyla," Onyo said.

Hedrana nodded, satisfied with herself. Royzca smiled and nudged Onyo with her elbow when Hedrana wasn't watching. Asoyla had been known for her fear of reading publicly; she'd been born with a stutter. Her most poignant verses were about how poetry gave her an elegance her mouth would never know.

After an hour or so, Hedrana's throat tired and she complained of a chill. She promised to return tomorrow.

"I hope she doesn't," Royzca said, tossing another branch onto their clay hearth. The smoke curled out a series of slit window into the evening sky.

Onyo reclined in a chair, peeling sweet potatoes for their supper. "You didn't have a good time? Hedrana's a puffed-up little fox. Scratch her ears and she wags her tail."

"I wonder if she'll ever realize you're insulting her?"

Onyo smirked. "If she's smart enough to figure it out, then she's earned her tattoo, and I won't have to mock her." Royzca smiled at him. She'd first entered the Guild Academy some fifteen years ago, when her husband died. She'd thought poetry could stitch up her torn soul, but she'd only felt loneliness until she met this man with sprawling, white eyebrows.

Conversations. Those had fed her, mind and marrow. How many conversations had she and old Onyo had? Thousands, over the past decade? He knew how to soothe her heartaches. How to make her laugh.

"You're looking at me oddly," he said.

"That's just my rheumy eyes. Or maybe you're just odd?" Royzca offered. She used a pair of sticks to pull a heated stone from the fire and lower it into their clay cooking pot.

"You wound me!"

"Half as much as Hedrana's poetry?"

Onyo paused. "Hedrana's words are twice-deadly. I suppose you're wounding my corpse, then. Don't you feel bad about desecrating the deceased?"

"Not at all!" Her limbs ached from walking and her soul hung heavy with memories of Yula. But here, in this warm room with her fellow poet-scholar, with her favorite conversationalist—she knew she'd survive. "Do you want salted fish or beans in the stew?"

"Ah, perhaps we should save the latter for Hedrana's visit tomorrow. Beans and my bowels disagree with each other; we can blame the smell on her."

That evening, Royzca descended back to her daughter's entombment. She shifted the red envelope out from under the stiff, dried linens.

"I'm sorry to disturb you twice," Royzca whispered. With her bad eyes and the bad light, she could almost pretend her daughter merely slept under a sheet. "But Hedrana's coming this way tomorrow. I need to hide the poem where we've already walked. Sleep well, dear-heart."

She trekked up and hid the envelope under her husband. "Thank you for watching over this. I hope you're taking care of Yula and her little one...but of course you are. You always loved children, too."

Decades of memories swelled through her, stinging. Husband, parents, child, grandchild. Why was she still the living one, in this city of the dead?

"Royzca? Royzca!"

"I'm down here!" She shuffled down the hall, past shelves and shelves of dried bodies. Onyo was puffing, like he'd been running. "What's wrong?"

"I thought you'd just gone to turn the wet ones, but then I couldn't find you and..." He took her hand and squeezed it, grip surprisingly strong. "I thought I'd lost you."

Did he think she'd forgotten her way, or that she'd joined all her family that had gone on before?

Royzca didn't ask. She just squeezed his hand in turn, letting him blunt the pain of surviving so many now in Paradise.

Royzca woke to someone pounding the door. She groaned and rolled off her thin pallet. No light yet shone from her thin window. She didn't care *whose* aunt Hedrana was, waking an old woman before daybreak should be a capital crime.

Shakily, she fumbled for her sandals, then lit a torch. Onyo shuffled into the hall from the opposite room. "Tell me you're making all that noise as a joke in rather poor taste."

"No," Royzca grumbled. The pounding continued, matching the headache in her temples. Sharp words ready on her tongue, she tossed the door open.

A messenger, in the colors of Lord-Governor Alyocandro, stood there. "His Eminence, Lord-Governor Alyocandro, requests a blessed poem of the dead."

"What's the crisis?" Royzca's heart turned over. Some Lord-Governors were reckless, squandering poems on every little thing—but not Alyocandro.

The messenger bowed. "His wife is in labor. And she is dying." They had unused, blessed poems that addressed drought, pestilence, and blight—but only one that spoke of a mother and babe. Royzca turned to fetch it.

Onyo laid a hand on her shoulder. "The puffed-up fox is here. And that..." he refrained from saying *poem* in front of the messenger, "won't work."

"I know." What did she care what report Hedrana sent against her old bones? Her granddaughter hadn't held her child, but she'd want her words to ensure someone else did. Royzca had to at least try the poem. "Wait here, messenger."

She headed down the hall. Onyo couldn't stop her now—the messenger would report they had an appropriate poem, but withheld it.

Onyo's soft sobs echoed down the bricks to her.

The birthing room was beautiful—its smooth adobe adorned with finely-woven rugs and wall-hangings—but it stank of blood. Lord-Governor Alyocandro's wife, Lilinya, lay pale and sweaty on the thick pallet, her arms limp. A half-dozen women crowded around her. Some dabbed her face with cool cloths; some sat back in resignation.

Hedrana lounged on a cushion near the window. "You were so slow in coming, I thought you'd fallen and broken a hip. I hope you have at least half my appreciation for poetry. I would not see mother or child die."

Hedrana projected her words in a childish attempt at a true reciter's voice.

"Perhaps you should go," Royzca said, throat tight. She'd expected trouble eventually; she hadn't expected it to be waiting for her.

Hedrana smiled, something predatory in her eyes. "I would not miss the opportunity to watch a poet-scholar perform."

Royzca's neck prickled. Hedrana wasn't here to see Lilinya healed; she was here to see Royzca fail and report her. A dismissal or execution would create an opening in the necropolis faster than old age.

Royzca exhaled, letting her joints settle into place. She'd made up her mind. Hedrana's presence wouldn't change that.

Her daughter had looked as listless as this woman before she passed. Yula probably looked the same, too. A paper rested on the night-stand next to Lilinya—surely a hastily-scrawled death-poem, just in case.

Royzca pulled Yula's poem from its envelope. The magnitude of its power would depend on her appreciation of the poem. Maybe these poor verses would only ease the woman's passing. She knew it wasn't beautifully written, but her heart still ached to read the words.

Maybe what she'd told Onyo was right. Anyone could appreciate a beautiful poem. A trained poet could appreciate it more. But she was a grandmother as well as a poet, and in that sense, these simple words rivaled Pusarla's for beauty in her heart.

Royzca read.

I go to Paradise—
Holding my healthy child
Like my grandmother held me—
That is Paradise.

Hedrana spluttered. "That is the *worst* poem I've ever heard! You think that's going to save Lilinya?"

The paper glowed, and the letters thirstily inhaled the supernatural red, until the paper was white once more. Yula's dying words, mixed with sacred water. That could allow Paradise to touch earth.

How well it reached depended on Royzca's appreciation of the poem.

The glow faded, leaving burnt-red letters behind.

Royzca traced the words with her finger. Yula would have been a great mother. She should have had that chance. Royzca tried to swallow the brick in her throat. She needed Onyo's heavy hand on her shoulder right now.

A high-pitched wail cut across the room. Royzca looked up. Lilinya's color had returned. She was laughing, crying, as she held her wailing infant. Tiny, perfect nose. Tiny, splendid ears. Red, angry tongue—alive and healthy.

Yula hadn't lived such a scene, but her words had gifted it to someone else.

Royzca wasn't surprised when guards came for her a week later; she was only saddened that it broke up a rather lively Motyono and Pusarla debate.

Hedrana had reported her to the Guild. The Guild requested Royzca's testimony before they ruled.

Testify she did. She admitted to blessing the poem under the scornful glares of the Poet-Masters. But she continued, explaining that greatness in poetry was not an objective matter. A lover of beautiful sounds might find it in Pusarla's Odes to Paradise. A lover of layered stories might find it in Motyono's Epic of the River War.

And a grandmother might find it in the simple verse of her grandchild.

The poem had, after all, worked. It saved the life of Lord-Governor Alyocandro's wife and infant daughter. Was not that the best proof of the poem?

But, as she expected, the Poet-Masters did not stop scowling. She'd blessed an inferior poem and had, therefore, abused her sworn duty. The sacred water, they said, was not to be gambled away on such whims. They named her a heretic, pronounced her guilty of treasonous misuse, and condemned her to a swift execution.

The Guild let Onyo visit her on the day she was to be executed. She ached, seeing his disheveled hair, his ill-kept clothes.

"I disappear for a few days, and you can't take care of yourself, old man?" Royzca asked.

Onyo reached through the narrow window of her cell and clung to her hands. "They can't do this."

"How are you going to stop them?" Her heart burned, seeing him so. She thought this would be easier. She'd lived long. She'd outlived too many. And now Onyo—who was as old as her—would outlive someone he cherished again.

His grip tightened, as if his two, frail hands could keep her rooted in this world. "Royzca, what am I to do without you? They may as well execute us both."

"Ah, so you've heard Hedrana got herself assigned as my replacement?"

His face hardened. "This isn't about her! Royzca, I..." Onyo's words faltered. *I love you.* She could see it in all the ancient lines of his face, in his furry white eyebrows drawn together.

"I wrote a death poem. I want you to have it." It was as close as she could get to *I love you, too.*

"Poems? Royzca, I don't want a poem!"

She gently disentangled her hands and fetched a folded paper from the corner of her cell. The Guild had given her plenty of writing supplies—they hoped to get a good death poem from her, but she'd told them she refused. In truth, she was saving it for Onyo. She pressed the paper into those familiar, heavy hands. "You said this wasn't about you. I ask you to honor that. I want you to bless it and use it."

He obediently took it, without looking at it. His soul needed comfort, just as hers had when they brought Yula's body.

"Do you know why Pusarla's work is best?" she asked. "She'd perfectly capture how horrible your hair is right now."

"And how is an image of horrible hair better than Motyono capturing perfect loyalty in <u>Epic</u>?"

Royzca held his hands and let the old argument play out, until the guards came and took her away.

Onyo laid Royzca's body on the necropolis roof, next to Yula's in the sand. Every grain under his sandals seemed loud as a millstone. He was the only living person in this city of the dead. Hedrana would arrive this evening.

Part of him wanted to lie down next to Royzca and never move again. But he had her poem. And he'd made a promise.

He took a torch and descended to the alcove. He spread the poem across the shelf. There was no one here to report him to the Guild, and Royzca wanted him to use this.

The poem opened and closed in the traditional style.

> I go to Paradise—
> Bones that never chill,
> Bowels that never betray me,
> Free from the barks of a puffed-up fox.
> Knowing you will have these comforts, too—
> That is Paradise.

It was not elegant poetry. It was hastily written. There was no rhythm. But Onyo had no doubt that it was lovelier than anything either Motyono or Pursula ever wrote.

He blessed it with the sacred water, turning the paper supernaturally red. He spoke the words. The paper glowed, the red leeching into the letters before turning the color of burnt marrow.

Onyo flexed his hand—were his joints less stiff, or was that wishful thinking? Royzca's last words deserved to have effect, meaning.

Now he understood why she'd read her granddaughter's poem.

He folded the paper and tucked it inside his shirt. Perhaps it would have been smarter to burn the spent poem, but he couldn't bring himself to do so.

That evening, someone knocked. A youngish man, maybe only sixty, stood behind the door. "I'm afraid Hedrana's changed her mind about accepting the post. One of her children invited her to live on their seaside estate. I'm Anyuso. Her replacement."

Onyo bit back a laugh. Royzca's poem *had* worked. "Well, come in. I've some supper ready. I can show you the necropolis tomorrow. What kind of poetry do you like?"

"I admit I'm partial to Motyono. I lived in his childhood home for some time, and stumbled upon some early, unknown works. I'd just finished transcribing those for the Guild when they sent me here."

"Oh?"

"I made two copies and brought one with me. Would you like to see?"

"Of course!"

Supper was not the same. Pursula was not mentioned. But there was new poetry and warm food.

In the evening, when Onyo curled up on his pallet, his bones didn't chill. Warm from his ears to his toes, he slept better than he had in years. He dreamed of Paradise—he dreamed of debating poetry with a rheumy-eyed, white-haired woman.

Song of the Ancient Queens

Kelda Crich

Odul was at the compound of her betrothed when Emko emerged from the Malicious Forest. Such a strange beginning for the woman who was to become the Sarad's greatest song singer. None go near the forest, except for the burial of those infected with unclean disease.

It was a difficult time for Odul as she tried to convince Akira's family that she'd make an obedient wife. A normal woman will make her home in the village of her husband's family. Odul was not a normal woman. She'd just completed her apprenticeship with Dimar, the royal medicine woman. And the queen had decreed that Odul must live near Sarad Palace a thousand lengths distant from Akira's village in the north most part of the Empire.

Odul and Akira met when Akira, newly initiated into the junior men's cult, came to Sarad to work for six months repairing the great earth walls which enclose the Empire.

"It's not usual for a medicine woman to take a husband," Dimar had said.

"But it's not forbidden."

"It's not forbidden," agreed Dimar. "It's just foolish. You'll make a life of hardship for yourself. And you'll not have time to learn the mysteries of song."

Odul thought of Akira with his silence, with his strength and with his certainty. He'd assembled Odul's bride price by himself, five long years to collect the bags of cowries without help from his family. Their love would overcome any obstacle. "I'll learn the songs, and I'll have a good marriage. It's my chi," she said certainly.

"Then there's no more to be said."

Yet Odul's time with Akira's family was difficult. Each village in the Empire has its own customs. Odul made many mistakes which delighted Akira's mother and sisters. Akira's silence, which had seemed so alluring during their courtship, began to seem like cowardice. But time passed. Odul endured every insult and reluctantly the family agreed that Odul could show obedience, at least under proper supervision. After a simple service they became man and wife.

They returned to the city to the news that old Dimar had taken the strange girl from the forest to be her new apprentice. Odul *had* expected to live in the palace with her new husband, but with the arrival of Emko the queen assigned the newly married couple a plot of land in Odul's family village. Odul was to be the medicine woman responsible for ten villages, nearly four hundred women and children.

"Then why don't I live in Akira's village?"

"Medicine women go where they're needed," replied Dimar, after outlining the long list of Odul's new duties.

"I suppose you'll be busy teaching your new apprentice," said Odul. "I hope she's able to learn."

"She's already accomplished," said Dimar. "Wherever she came from she was taught medicine."

"Wherever she came from?" Odul had assumed that Emko was an escaped slave from Ula, the neighbouring savannah kingdom, fleeing through the Malicious Forest in desperation.

"She doesn't remember. But her medicine is very strong. It has all worked out well. Thanks to Mal."

"I would like to continue learning song medicine," said Odul. Song-singing was a lifetime's occupation. Even Dimar could only move small stones with her voice.

"I'd like that. The new girl is very silent. I miss your chatter."

Odul and Akira settled into married life. Akira was a good farmer. At the end of the first season's sacrifice he had produced three yam stacks, although a quarter of the crop needed to be repaid to the men who'd loaned him seed. Akira helped Odul's father's work his tobacco fields. He worked hard in the maintenance of the village's earth walls.

Odul farmed the women's crops of coco yams and cassava in the company of the village's chattering mona monkeys. She sold the excess at the local market. She concerned herself with the duties of a new wife: fishing and cooking, the production of palm oil which was a community affair, weaving baskets for food storage and fish traps, drying of tobacco, making mats and pots.

She also had the duties of the village medicine woman. Odul oversaw the seasonal festivities of the Mal's twelve daughters and the ceremonies of the seven stages of a woman's life. She counselled on the effectiveness of household gods, choosing from the seventy-eight aspects of Mal. She attended every naming ceremony, every marriage and every funeral in the ten villages. She prepared herbal medicines, especially bird salt which was revered in Sarad. She also maintained good relationships with the twelve priestesses of the Daughters who on occasion could allow traditional enmities to overcome harmony.

Akira was a very fine weaver and had his own loom. Odul bought cotton at market, and he produced the very fine long narrow strips of cloth which always sold well. This was fortunate, as most nights Odul did not have time to weave.

Akira's family visited frequently, because of the unusual circumstances. They often bought food, but it was never enough. And this was a source of discord. Yet the young couple prospered. After three years, Akira took another wife. Odul had her first baby. The baby died within the first month and so was not named, although Odul named him in her heart. Akira's second wife's child survived and Odul performed the rites to welcome her into the tribe.

Odul made her way to the palace as often as she could, because she missed Dimar's companionship. But she had abandoned her ambition of learning song medicine.

"You were right, Dimar. I am *so* tired. From dawn to night my mind is full of duty."

"It's your chi. It will be well. All life is choice and compromise. And you have your handsome husband to console you. And the next baby will come to stay. Children are a woman's jewel."

"That's true." In her youth Dimar had taken many lovers. But she'd no children, whether by design or chi it could not be said.

As the years progressed, Odul made friends with Emko, the strange woman who'd emerged from the Malicious Forest. Emko was almost as silent as Akira. She had no lovers, had no other friends. She was consumed with her medicine and with making progress in the songs.

Odul was pregnant with her fourth child when she severed that friendship. She was emotional and fearful, praying to the Daughters that this baby would live long enough to bear a name. That is perhaps why she said such an unforgivable thing that led to the rift between them.

"You should not drink so much, Emko." Dimar had advised Odul not to let her unborn taste palm wine. Her mouth was dry as dust with the longing.

Emko scooped another horn of palm wine. She drank it deep before asking, "Why not?"

"When you drink, the eyes of your cha burn."

The horn fell to the floor, spilling the white dregs. "What do you see?"

"I'm sorry. I shouldn't have said anything." Cha is taboo. You can never see your own cha, and only people of power can see the cha of others. Cha is the part of the soul that whispers evil. For most people cha is no more than an unformed shadow at the back of their necks. Elders, priestesses, great warriors and medicine workers have more distinct cha. Emko's cha was very unusual, and in truth Odul had longed to ask her about it. Unlike most cha, it was unstable, each day each, each hour it changed.

"Tell me what you have seen," said Emko, her voice low, dangerous.

Odul shook her head.

"Tell me."

Odul had broken taboo. It must be said. "I have seen your cha as a child who smiles. She carries a bowl of severed fingers. I have seen a woman without eyes. I have seen a man with his head turned to face his back. I have seen a woman with her legs stitched to her shoulders."

Emko closed her eyes. "So you know my secrets, Odul?"

"I know nothing. I should not have spoken."

"I see your cha, Odul, as a snake with a woman's head. Its body is wrapped around your womb. It crushes you and your unborn. You try to be two things and you will be nothing. Go and do not speak to me again."

That was the end of their friendship. From that day on, Emko would not acknowledge Odul. A short time afterwards, Dimar died. Emko was appointed as the royal medicine woman. After the funeral, there was no reason for Odul to visit the palace.

Odul's first surviving child passed his sixth month birthday and was named into the tribe. The years passed. A medicine woman died and Odul was given another three villages to minister. She was invited to join the Eighth Daughter's cult, she who was turned to river water due her sisters' jealousy. Odul worked hard to learn the new language in which her secret songs are sung.

Akira took on the duty of collecting the tax that all men pay to the Empire. He took a third wife, a beautiful but petulant teenager, who caused many problems within the family.

Odul heard of Emko's great influence. Men and women crossed the savannah to consult with her. She had mastered the mysteries of song, in a way that had not been known since the Ancient Queens returned to their homes in the night sky. She worked with the palace artisans teaching them to make icons of great beauty, sculpted of glass, but as strong as bronze. These were prized over the land. The Empire grew rich, and the people were happy. And yet the people spoke ill of Emko. Rumour was her shadow. She had no friends. She took no lovers. She was alone. She was as cold as stone. Perhaps she was a spirit made flesh. Perhaps she was a discarded twin that had somehow survived in the forest. Odul squashed these rumours when she heard them, outwardly angry, "Mal would not allow such a thing!" but inwardly she smiled.

The years past, and Odul's cha whispered ill content. All things Emko had, Odul longed for.

A decade after Dimar's death, Emko came unannounced to Odul's hut. Odul was busy preparing a feast for her son's initiation into the junior men's cult.

Without the preliminary small talk Emko said, "There's a problem at the palace."

Odul was still gaping at the size of Emko's cha. It reached the ceiling of the hut. "What's wrong?"

"A man has crossed the savannah. Binwa he's called. He claims to be prince driven out of his kingdom by the Tomb Building King."

"And what does he want?"

"Everything. The queen has already given him a concubine. And she's spoken to me. She wants him as a husband."

Sarad's queen was chosen by merit. That was the Ancient Queen's law. She remained a virgin, consorting only with her concubines, so that no child would have a claim to her throne. And with this law, Sarad prospered and was not beset with the wars of succession that plagued neighbouring empires. "That's impossible," said Odul. "If she insists, a new queen must be chosen."

"Not so," said Emko with a strange smile. "I have consulted the books of law. If Binwa completes a great task, then we'll know that Mal favours him."

"An ordeal? What could he do to prove himself above our laws?"

"In the Malicious Forest there is an old creature named Ush-na-U, a snake imprisoned by the Ancients Queens. His skin is malice. His cha infects the forest."

"I've never heard that," said Odul doubtfully.

"Still, it is true. I have read the secret songs of the Ancient Queens."

"So why are you telling me?"

"I will go with Binwa and his men into the forest to kill Ush-na-U. You will come with us."

From the forest Emko had come, and now she wanted to return. "I'll need to speak to my husband," said Odul.

"Why? You know that you'll come."

She understood everything and nothing. Of course, Odul wanted to go. She craved adventure, the chance to see the things that others didn't see. But why did Emko want her there?

"I speak to my family first," said Odul.

Emko shrugged.

Odul's son was accepting. She was so proud of him. He insisted on teaching her some of the fighting postures he'd so recently learnt is training for the junior men's cult.

"The forest is dangerous, Diwi, but these moves will protect you."

Odul hardly knew how Akira would react. They'd grown distant. Her medicine duties had grown a wall between them. But he had reached for her. "Your chi was always great, Odul," he whispered. "But come back to me."

Odul had thought that the villagers would object to the Emko's scheme. But they were content to let the matter be decided by the great people. So concerned were they with the grains of sand of their lives, they could not see the rush of the boundless ocean.

Binwa was light-skinned, handsome, well-muscled and as tall as a mountain man. He was arrogant: certainly, a man who thought that he could override an Empire's traditions.

He whispered with Emko. He thought he had her under his power. But Odul could see that he was mistaken. Whatever Emko was planning in the forest was not for Binwa's benefit.

Binwa had a company of twenty slaves. Fighting men all, dressed with great clattering armours on their backs like shells and strange swords curved as the tusks of an old bull elephant. Some of them light skinned like ghosts, but all of them as hard as murder.

They entered the forest, though dark trees of mahogany, nutmegs, hackberries, wawas, cloth barks, devils trees, and rising high above the majestic, thorned silk cotton trees. The air was bright with butterflies. The undergrowth was dense. The slaves worked hard to hack a pathway through it.

"One day's travel and we'll reach the elephant track," said Emko.

"Only fools walk in the steps of elephants," muttered one of the slaves.

"Mal will oversee our steps," she replied.

Odul's eye was caught by the many medicinal plants in the forest. She saw bushes of alligator pepper and bird salt; their fruits would be very valuable if sold at market. But a dull atmosphere pervaded all, the gloom and even the sounds of the animals, the cacophony of forest life taking on an eerie quality as if the beasts were imbued with the malicious quality of the forest itself. The chattering mona monkeys seemed to leer at the travelers. Their markings were slightly different from the family that inhabited Odul's village. Fig trees were laden with fruit, but no one pulled the fruit to supplement the rations. Termite nests boiled with albino insects flowing like the froth of milk.

After a half day's walk they crossed an ocean inlet. The ground grew into swamp, with fat crystals of salt on the rubbery leaves. Here butterflies nested and hung great ropes of cocoons strung together like yams in a stack. And the swamp was loud with the call of the yellow throated cuckoo, and forest crocodiles waited with sly eyes for the unwary.

Beyond the inlet the dense forest reasserted itself, resistant to the slashing machete. They were deep into the forest. Odul was lost in the work of finding a slow path forward; almost used to the strange sights she saw when she heard the scurrying sound. The men stopped, covering their noses against the rancid smell filling the air.

"Rats!"

A mass of brown, speckled grey fur swarmed over the mahogany trees. Rats, big as a toddling child, twice as big as the rats farmed for bush meat in the Ula kingdom. All stood marvelling at the rats' size and the dexterity of the creatures, spiralling in furious procession up the trees, leaping branch to branch, advancing quickly.

"Kill them, you fools," screamed Emko. "They are Ush-na-U's guardians."

As if her cry was a signal the nearest rats leapt from the tree, attacking with a fury of claws and biting stained teeth.

When the fighting was over they stood amidst a pile of fifty bodies, but three of the men were dead.

The men began to argue violently that they should return home, but Binwa silenced them with a few words of his own language. His skin paler than usual, hands clasped tightly together, as if to conceal trembling.

"These are unnatural creatures," he said to Emko.

"This is what Mal asks of you, but you will prove yourself worthy."

That night at camp, Odul spoke quietly to Emko. "What are we really doing here, Emko?"

Emko glanced over to Binwa who was engaged with talk with his men.

"Tell me," said Odul.

"Or what?"

"Tell me."

"I did not lie. We seek a monstrous snake, Ush-na-U imprisoned in the bowels of the forest and reeking of corruption."

"I don't believe there is such a creature."

"Oh, but there is. I have seen it. So large it is that we are almost beneath its notice. Yet aspects of Ush-na-U have escaped. Did you ever wonder why the Ancient Queens came to Sarad, Odul?"

"They came to help us."

"I have seen their images carved into glass. In rooms in the palace that are forgotten. They were not women, Odul."

"You're saying that they were aspects of Mal?"

"No. I think not. Something other. I wonder if they knew that there were people in the land when they came here. They came here to imprison Ush-na-U. They stayed and they helped the people form Sarad Empire."

The sound of drums came from the darkness.

"I tell you, Odul. People live in the forest and people worship Ush-na-U."

Binwa came over. "What's that noise?"

"It comes from the villages on the other side of the forest," said Emko. "The sound travels strangely, that's all."

So then Odul was right, Emko was leading Binwa on a fool's errand.

Forest elephants are dangerous animals, always to be avoided. The complaints of the men began again when Emko started on the down their wide track. The murmurs died in their throats when they came to the graveyard. Of all the animals it's the elephant that shows an expression of sorrow at the death. Some years ago Odul had witnessed a herd standing over the dead body of a matriarch in respectful silence except for a calf that mourned his loss in a voice that sounded eerily like a child's cry. The elephants covered the matriarch's body with branches, and stood at the grave for two days before moving on.

A queen's fortune lay in the graveyard, hoards of ivory yellowed by the weight of years. Binwa's men did not restrain themselves. They ran from skeleton to skeleton, shouting to each other as they discovered greater lengths of ivory.

Four of Binwa's men were removing the tusks from a yellowed skull when the shadow of a bull elephant fell upon them, crying its displeasure, enraged that this sanctuary had been invaded. Within moments a man was impaled upon its tusks. The other three men slashed at the bull with swords, while the rest of the party quickly unleashed a volley of arrows. This only seemed to enrage it further. The impaled man was still screaming as the bull charged forward, crushing the three nearest men, advancing towards Binwa who shouted, "Use your medicine, Emko."

Medicine is not to be used for combat, only for healing and worship, but Emko nodded her head. She began to sing and her medicine did not belonging to man or woman but it was the sound of music sung by strange throats. Odul turned away, afraid to witness Emko's terrible face filled with the medicine of the long gone queens.

The medicine thick as sap, tangible, swirled around the graveyard. The skeletons quivered and bones snapped. Shards, razor sharp, flew through the air. The bull elephant lay dead, and so did five more of Binwa's men.

That night as they camped Odul swallowed her pride, "Emko will you teach me the song medicine?"

"It is within you, but you are afraid," said Emko. And she would say no more

The next morning they woke to the sound of drums. It was clear to all that they came from within the forest. Emko was full of bright, nervous energy. She darted ahead following the path of the drums and urging the party forward with silent gestures.

They came to a colossal outcrop of rock. "We are here," said Emko. She led them through a hidden crevice passageway decorated with carvings that must have taken lifetimes to create. Snake of sorts, or many snakes: sinuous and ravelling mouth to tail. The carvings were hard to look at. The eye glanced off them, as if they were depicting creatures not of this world.

Beyond the tunnels was a clearing. Men and women danced in front of an altar of fused stones to the heart beat of the incessant drums. Behind the altar was a hexagonal cave, melted into the rock face. A chill wrapped Odul's heart when she saw that the dancers were all maimed in some way, missing hands, legs cut off at the knee or at the thigh. She glanced at Emko.

"If we couldn't find sacrifices in the forest, then we would use ourselves." Her cha was in the form of the smiling child carrying a dish of fingers.

"You come from here."

Emko nodded. "Here I was born. Here I took part in their obscene rituals to worship Ush-na-U. That is why my cha is so great. I am my cha, Odul. "

Binwa came over. "Work your medicine, Emko."

"This is the place for you to prove yourself, Binwa. I will be at hand if needed."

Binwa assessed the clearing and nodded. He signalled to his men who with vicious war cries ran into the clearing, their swords cutting down the nearest dancers. But quickly the remaining worshippers reached for weapons.

Odul and Emko remained behind, watching.

"You wanted to come here," said Odul. "Why did you need Binwa?"

"I wasn't sure that I could get through the forest alone. I thought the guardians might kill me while I slept."

"Why did you need me here?"

"Watch."

Binwa and his men fought against the dancers. They seemed to have the upper hand, until a woman emerged from the cave wearing the clothes of a queen, her cha massive and malignant reaching to the sky. Like Emko, she was spell singer. Her song moved the vines from the trees that rose up like snakes, engulfing Binwa and his men, leaving them like flies in the web.

"Binwa and his men are dead. It's time," said Emko. She stepped into the clearing to be greeted by a cheer from the dancers.

"All-wa," shouted the queen when she saw Emko. The name meaning, Anointed One.

"Mother, I have returned." Emko began to sing. Her cha reaching past the canopies of the trees, so high, so high it seemed to reach to the sun. The vines which had consumed Binwa and his men, quivered and made their way quickly to the dancers and the queen.

"No!" shouted the queen. She sang, but she was no match for Emko who was as large as the sky. The snake vines swelled like ocean waves to the sound of her voice, until all were consumed and shrouded. Odul ran into the clearing. "It's over."

"Not yet," said Emko. "I still need to deal with Ush-na-U. I must close the door that my mother and my mother's mother opened."

Emko led Odul to the honeycomb cave mouth. They stepped inside together.

"It can only be closed from the inside. As the Ancient Queens did," said Emko.

From the darkness Odul heard the slithering of many snakes.

"They come," said Emko. Her cha towered over her in the form of the smiling child whose eyes were stars.

"I'll help," said Odul. She knew the secret of the song medicine. It drew on the power of the cha.

"No," said Emko. "You have not done the things I have done. You are weak, and I don't need you."

Odul thought about her son and Akira. She thought about the life, how hard it was but how sweet. She hesitated. Emko pushed her out of the cave. She fell sprawling to the ground. "I don't need you, Odul."

Emko sang. Her great voice shining, pulling down the stones of the cave to form a wall which burned red hot, melting and fusing.

Odul watched as the aspects of the snake Ush-na-U moved towards Emko, fastening on her flesh. Emko sang on, her song blending with pain, but still growing, as large as her cha, as large as her anger. Never was there so much anger. And as the cave mouth sealed with the fusion of stones, Odul witnessed Emko's face smiling and unknowable in triumph.

Odul was left alone. She returned to her family. Now she had knowledge and power, and she could acquire what she had always longed for. Her song medicine was strong, although it was a shadow to the power that had coursed through Emko. She became the royal medicine woman, insisting that she build her family's compound in the grounds of the palace. She lived the life of mother, wife and royal medicine woman. It was her chi.

But often her thoughts turned to Emko, who had done great evil, and who had suffered for it. A woman, proud, lonely, powerful, and angry. She had sung the medicine of the Ancient Queens to imprison the malicious creature Ush-na-U.

And she had wanted Odul there to witness it. Odul had been friend to Sarad's greatest medicine woman. And every day Odul prayed that Emko had found Mal's forgiveness.

The Language of Flowers

Adrian Tchaikovsky

Shelony was late for her appointment because of a centennial statue on the Maradesta Bridge. The seven-foot stone figure was making a slow progress up the arch, broad enough with its broken stubs of wings that she could not dodge around it without risking the water below. Its Numer Vitae were carved into its back in a rough hand: '27 minutes/112 years'. It was her poor luck that right now, after over a century of inaction, the thing had woken to continue whatever time-withered errand it had been about when it had last fallen silent.

And of course she could not impede one of the statues, especially a centennial: no quicker way to purchase both bad luck and the disapproval of anyone watching. Everyone was supposed to be very tolerant of the things, as they lived out their vastly punctuated existence in the midst of a thronging humanity that they seldom deigned to notice.

True to the way her day had been going, the statue's 27 minutes came to an end just as it reached the crest of the arch, and it locked into place midway through a ponderous step, ensuring that the narrow Maradesta would be out of commission for the next century and then some. The next bridge was seven streets away and her client would not be taking the delay in good humour. She considered trying to squeeze indelicately past the newly positioned effigy, but the water below was slick and dark, marked by the v-shaped wake of a prowling otter more than big enough to make a meal of her. They were getting bold, the otters, as the light waned.

She had enough of the dawn left to find another path, hurrying through crowded streets in which everyone was trying to get through the business of the day before the gloom set in. So it was that, flustered and out of breath, she found the richly-appointed townhouse of Magister Vollenthall.

The doorman's expression said a great deal about how unsuited she was to the doorsteps of the mighty. Even with her composure intact, Shelony knew she cut a less than imposing figure, stocky and burly-armed as a farmer's wife, her green and silver robes plainly intended for someone of a different build. It was not that the money wasn't coming in, what with her acknowledged expertise, but her expenses precluded a bespoke tailor.

"Madam Astrid Shelony," she was announced, "Floristic Augur."

Magister Vollenthall was a lean man in middle years, his chin fringed with a wiry grey beard. He wore clothes more expensive than her apartment, cut to suggest a martial affectation. His manner sabotaged his dignity: something was eating at him. He looked sickly and shaking.

"What kept you?" he demanded.

Shelony had one of her headaches coming on, so she waved the question away. "I'm here now. What have you got? I want to be out of here long before noon, or you're paying for the lamp-boys to light me home." Being brusque with clients because they needed her was one of the pleasures of the job.

Vollenthall guided her to what must be his dining room, the table laid out from the night before for a breakfast that had never happened. In the centre of the table was the cause of his concern.

It was magnificent. She caught her breath. It was intended as a death sentence for Vollenthall, but she could only admire the effort and the artistry that had gone into it.

The breakfast table was utterly dominated by a vase of flowers, an interleaved explosion of aloes and asphodel, lobelia, marigold and ox-eye and startling sprays of carnations. The entire display was easily three feet across, the flowers set in a jutting, asymmetrical pattern that seemed frozen in mid-leap.

In all her years as a floristic augur, she had never seen anything quite as elaborate as this. Somebody had paid very good money for the death of Magister Vollenthall, for that was what the display meant. The secretive Guild of Arrangers were very serious about flowers. Duly contracted, they had stolen unseen into the Magister's house and left him something that was part warning and part prophecy: the full details of how he was intended to die.

And Vollenthall, being no fool, had straight away sent for someone who knew the secret language of flowers. Not one of the Guild, of course; their assassins were sworn to silence. There were scholars, though, who made the past victories of the guild their study, piecing together the code that connected the display with the final result. It was known that, if Vollenthall could understand the message the Guild had given him, he could take steps to avoid his doom. That was part of their game.

"So tell me," the Magister hissed.

Shelony hedged. "I'll need to check my books."

"I'll have them sent for."

"I'll need to consult my peers."

He bristled. "I had heard you were the best."

"Our discipline is a scattered one. Am I the best? Perhaps. Do I know all? No, I do not. I will need to make sketches. Many sketches." She glanced out of the window. The light was already waning. "Bring lanterns, lots of them, and then leave me to work."

When she had the room to herself she sat down in Vollenthall's own chair and stared at the outlandish display the Guild had left for him. She had never seen anything quite so extravagant. She was not sure she could parse it.

Outside, as the day reached mid-morning, the sky mottled into a bruised greenish-black and swallowed the sun.

She burned the midday oil, working on in Vollenthall's dining room throughout the darkness that eclipsed five hours at the height of the day. One of her earliest memories was of the sun growing dim on the stroke of noon. Now the skies shaded to pitch shortly after mid-morning, and were only relieved by the sinking sun after mid-afternoon. The astronomers confirmed, with their instruments and their science, that the periods of light were shrinking incrementally. Some day there would be darkness from dawn until dusk, and people would long for the night because at least then they could see the stars.

She chewed on the Magister's unwanted breakfast and used pastels and oils to recreate the elaborate arrangement of flowers from all angles. At last, she yelled for a servant and had them bring in the master of the house.

"Well?" Vollenthall growled. "What fate have they set for me? What must I do to avoid it? Can you tell me?"

"No," Shelony said flatly and, at that furious expression she knew so well from her clients, went on, "but I'm working on it, and for now I can give you some securities. It won't be by ingested poison, so feel free to trust your kitchen staff—nor contact poisons neither. It won't be by being pushed, or falling. It won't be starvation or similar privation. These I can rule out."

"Death by water?" Vollenthall asked hoarsely. The dark days had brought fresh terrors to the inky depths of Ashmark's many canals, not least the great otters, which had demonstrated a taste for human flesh. More than one citizen had nightmares about lightless waters marked by purposeful ripples.

"Probably not." Shelony shrugged. "Some manner of violent death seems most likely, although I can't rule out injected poison, so check surfaces for needles and the like. I need to take these sketches and research them. Don't do anything rash, take all reasonable precautions, stay put, and I'll revert to you as soon as I have more information."

Leaving him gaping in her wake, she stepped out into the afterdark, the sun resuming its proper shade as it sank towards the horizon. There was still a distinct pall of green-black to the firmament. Not smog, the astronomers said; not smoke or volcanic particulates in the upper air, but the sun itself, its light become a sickly, radiant darkness that blotted out even moon and stars.

The city had grown more and more afraid as the darkness closed in, year after year. Madness was rife, along with vengeance, tragic love, suicide, all the other burlesques of human behaviour. With the lengthening shadows, the Guild of Arrangers was never short of work. People wanted to settle old scores before the sun turned its back on them entirely.

There was a man handing out leaflets at the door of the Distanced Lovers, the floristic augurs' watering hole of choice. Shelony took one from habit, then made to throw it away as soon as she saw it was a polemic—a caricature of various members of the Sidereal Council engaged in throwing mud at each other. Just as it left her fingers, she spotted an unflattering likeness of Vollenthall himself in the fray and snatched it back. There was no wisdom to be gleaned from the hand-printed pamphlet, though, just a declaration that the corruption and vice of Our Leaders had somehow discoloured the sun.

She slipped into the tavern between the two statues that flanked its door. Today the male was awake, stone eyes bright with life as it gazed with anticipation on the frozen face of its opposite number. The Numer Vitae graven on his shoulder said '103 minutes/19 days'. On the right hip of the stone woman across from him was scratched '27 minutes/61 years.' They had been standing for longer than the tavern that was named after them, never animated at the same time, each waiting always for the other. Were they lovers? Shelony had always fancied they were trying to carry on an argument, but she was not a romantic soul.

There were three other florists in the taproom, in varying states of inebriation. Theirs was a strange path: men and women of learning whose discipline had terrible teeth. They were all that stood between their clients and a merciless but whimsical order of assassins. When they failed, they bore the guilt of those deaths. When they succeeded, all too often their clients began to think that the shadows had been empty of killers all along. All of them spent a depressing proportion of their working time chasing debts.

She showed her sketches to her peers, hoping for inspiration. They were properly impressed at the scale and complexity of the arrangement. Some had leads for her to chase up, others only idle speculation—worse than useless given that a man's life was at stake.

In truth, she got caught up in the drinking as much as the research, but strong, cheap wine was a necessity of the trade. Stare too long at one of the Guild's ominous creations and the image would crawl into a scholar's skull and take up residence there, twisting imagination and poisoning dreams. Such fantasies were soluble in alcohol, however. By the time she left the Lovers, true night was draping the sky, and the Bibliotheca Botanica would have closed its doors. She staggered off home to her cramped garret and tried not to think of the athletic pack of debts that seemed always able to keep up with her income.

The next morning she opened the door on one of Vollenthall's staff, whose expression of supercilious annoyance suggested he had been knocking for some time. Astrid Shelony was only a morning person because noon had become untenable.

The Magister wanted an update.

"Tell your master I'm working on it." Astrid gathered her notes and began to stomp off towards the Bibliotheca in the hope that some journal or annal would hold more clues to decoding the floral message.

"My master is gravely concerned that the Guild will act before you finish your researches," the servant told her sharply, keeping pace. "He is not interested in you perfecting your scholarship over his corpse."

"I've already told him everything I can with certainty. I need to do some reading."

"My master was persuaded that you were an expert."

She stopped and glowered at him: a youth who had barely a shadow of a beard on his chin.

"I'm all the expert you're going to get for the money," she spat.

"He feels he must take other precautions," the servant called at her back.

"And I told him," she yelled back, "do nothing. Wait to hear from me. I'm working on it." But she stopped and sighed hugely. "What is he doing?"

For a moment she thought the boy wasn't going to tell her, which would have been unwise given that he was within shoving distance of a canal, but then he redoubled his arch look and said, "When younger, Magister Volelnthall was quite the duellist. If he is to fear assault, as you intimated, he feels he should return to his former associates and the protection of steel."

"If he thinks a few toffs with smallswords can keep the Guild off his back then he's barely worth a fistful of dandelions, let alone that grand display," she snapped. "Tell him to do nothing."

"He is not a man who can do nothing, when he is roused," the servant returned sharply, and at last she saw that some of his hostile manner was rooted in a real concern for his master. But she had no more words for him. All she could do was hurry herself to the Bibliotheca as quickly as possible.

Ashmark was not short of libraries. Generations back the city had pillaged the world for its lore, and every trade and profession maintained its own jealously-guarded archive. Often these were sufficiently occult that even those who had every business entering were treated like book-stealing arsonists by the staff. The Bibliotheca

Botanica had a single human librarian, a grey-haired woman named Madam Kersenna whose face was so stern and still it might have been worked from cold iron. Her frosty vigilance ensured that Shelony spent most of the morning attempting to establish that she was a paid up member of the Augur's Society, and the rest of it scraping together sufficient loose change when she was at last revealed to be in arrears. Only then was she permitted access to the reading room.

She wrote out a list of half a dozen volumes and posted it through the slot in her booth. Like most of the archives, the Bibliotheca was crippled by lack of space. The storage shelves below her feet were pressed so close together that no human agency could have wormed through them to retrieve so much as a sheet of parchment. Instead, Kersenna relied on tribes of educated mice, denizens of the stacks for countless rodent generations, who would scurry up and down, and ball together in great squirming masses of fur and tails and hand-like paws to haul the required volumes to her table.

She always remembered to bring cheese. A good tip ensured quick service the next time. The mouse families had long memories and bore grudges.

Surrounded at last by six of the most authoritative guides on the secret language of the Guild of Arrangers, Shelony got out her sketches and tried to fill in the gaps. Out across the city, Magister Volenthall was no doubt winding himself up tighter and tighter with fear of the Guild, and with good reason. She could only hope he kept her advice in mind and did nothing rash.

The language of flowers was complex and many layered. Hidden in the precise choice and positioning of blooms, in the numerology of petals and stamen, was not only how Vollenthall was intended to die but for what reason, at whose bidding, a whole revelatory text if Shelony could only read it. She leafed through the tomes, squinting in the artificial light at the faded ink, at all the marginalia of those who had come before.

She had identified the threat of a physical attack already; she saw a cluster of carnations that spoke of ruptured skin. There was no suggestion of mechanisms or traps—whole volumes of the florist's lexicon could be ruled out. Deception, she saw, but the precise trick that was to be played remained hidden. She delved deeper.

She found precise flourishes of wild thyme that spoke of grudges long held in abeyance, an enmity from long years ago. The single bird's foot trefoil at the heart of the array was a sullen symbol of rivalry. Who were Vollenthall's rivals? Other members of the Sidereal Council?

No, Shelony thought. Who were his rivals, long ago? Who has saved up this grievance? The dried aloe spoke of past grief, the broken almond of failed promises. She cursed herself for letting herself get distracted. The Magister cared far less about who his enemy was, than about how he was intended to die.

She focused on the deception, noting how the thorn-apple flowers led the eye inward, finding cherry blossom for learning, laurel leaves for renown, winged sycamore seeds for a message. But surely the whole display was a message...

Deception brought about by the message of a renowned learned individual, she considered.

Moments later she was pelting past Madam Kersenna for Vollenthall's house, praying that, of all the advice she had given him, he had obeyed that last piece most of all.

When she arrived at his door, the same servant met her. Could she see his master? No, she could not?

"My master has despaired of your help," the youth told her flatly. "He has gone to seek more material protection from the duellists."

"Which society?" she got out.

"The Locust Eaters."

Needless to say, their preferred haunts were halfway across the city, back the way she had come.

She never found just what dark secret lay in Vollenthall's history, that had bred him such an enemy. To pay the Guild of Arrangers for such an artful summons would have bankrupted a wealthy man. In their sinister wisdom, the Guild had predicted everything; they had baited a trap of which Shelony herself was a component. The surface language of the display had been plain enough that she had put the idea into Vollenthall's head to fear attack. Being an impatient man, while she had wrestled to uncover the true death written into those flowers, he had gone to seek protection from the society he had once drawn sword for.

And there he had met his end. There, a lean and leathery old soldier had come to him and called him out. Before the eyes of all those duellists, Vollenthall could not have refused. And he had fought, for the first time in decades, and he had died.

When she got there, it was to see his ruptured body sprawled in the chambers of the Locust Eaters, as officials of the society explained to the civic enforcers that the whole affair had been entirely legal. The flung limbs, the bright darts of spattered blood: she looked on dead Magister Vollenthall and could have mapped him, angle for angle, drop for drop, onto her sketches of the Guild's extravagant display.

Shadowslain

Alter S. Reiss

All manner of degeneracy found root in the city-states south of royal Edras. Beyond the borders, punishment for even the darkest crimes could be avoided by leaving one town for the next. Murcen's target, the renegade Kellim Ardak, had burrowed into the heart of Tapur, the worst of the southern cities. The manors of Tapur had high walls, and despite the wealth of the residents, few beggars or peddlers dared the streets. To Ardak's north and west, the streets were watched by sharp eyed guards; to the south, his walls touched those of a wealthy merchant, whose defenses and depravities matched his own. On the east, there was nothing beyond his walls but a narrow verge of trees and grass, and the rolling brown course of the river.

High amongst those trees waited Murcen the Knife, as still and silent as a gecko on a wall. He faced across the water and watched the fading light of the sun touch the tops of the trees in the forest beyond, and saw twilight spreading like a cloud. He watched and waited, and prepared to die.

Kellim Ardak had been among the royal sorcerers of Edras. He was as dangerous as a wounded tiger, and would know the King's Knife for an implacable enemy. Worse, a dull green stone that Murcen wore at his wrist had become a dull gray stone. A thing of sorcery was coming for Kellim Ardak, and Murcen had to stop it to have any hope of getting what he'd come for.

As the shadows moved across the river, Murcen picked out a patch that was darker than the rest; darker than the mere absence of light. When the army of Shu had come across the border of Edras, their campfires had glittered like a field of fireflies, like the stars in heaven. The royal sorcerers sent their own shadows against that army. A hundred and fifty thousand men had laid down to sleep on the banks of the Candras, and fewer than three thousand woke to see the dawn.

Ten shadows had walked that night. There was only one coming across the Anhasa, and Murcen had been given the best protections and weapons that the royal sorcerers could devise. But it wouldn't be enough. Kellim was one of the few still living who had cast his shadow at the army of Shu, and Murcen had gotten no chance to learn what the renegade knew before the shadow had come.

The shadow touched the shore, and Murcen dropped from the tree in which he had been waiting, his knife crackling with blue lightning. There was no more time for thought; now, it was fight or die.

Alendar was a full cousin of the King of Edras. Alendar had left a life of pampered luxury to become a general and a sorcerer in the service of the crown, and when Murcen came for an audience, Alendar still carried himself like a prince. But the audience was not in a palace or a pleasure garden; it was in the chamber of light in the Seanest Shrine, a border temple where Alendar was somewhere between a prisoner and a guest.

Murcen had been told what to expect of the chamber of light, but words had not done it justice. It was all illuminated; light poured from the stones of the ceiling and the tiles of the floor, from wooden tables and brocade pillows. The air itself had a glow to it, so when Alendar opened his mouth to speak, it was lit from the inside, as red as raw meat.

"Has my sentence been decided, King's Knife?"

He was sitting at a table of inlaid wood, white in white. There were tea and pastries on the table, and a courtesan standing behind him; an older man, tall, straight-backed. Murcen gave the man a curt nod, and the courtesan bowed deeply and left, taking with him the scent of lemon and cloves. The monks who stood guard outside the door were not there solely for Alendar's protection, but if the chamber of light was a jail, it was as pleasant as any Murcen had ever seen. He sat down opposite Alendar, and poured himself a cup of tea. Murcen was not showing Alendar the deference due a prince, but Alendar didn't seem moved.

"In the past week," said Murcen, "three of the royal sorcerers have been killed."

"Three?" asked Alendar.

"Yes," said Murcen. "The last of those who served during the invasion from Shu. Killed by shadows. It seems the research that you destroyed has not been completely lost."

Until that point, Alendar had sat like a stone; he had been utterly calm when he asked if Murcen had come to kill him. At that suggestion, there was a flicker of reaction, quickly hidden. "This is not a rediscovery, King's Knife. These are the shadows we cast, returning home."

Murcen raised an eyebrow, drank his tea.

"Why do you think that I have enchanted this room the way I have?" asked Alendar.

"Because you fear that one of your enemies will use a shadowcasting to kill you," replied Murcen.

"No," said Alendar. "My enemies would strike with poison, or a whisper in the king's ear; nothing that I can defend against. I have made a room where there are no shadows because I fear the shadow that I cast against the armies of Shu. That is why I destroyed the research, as I have said. All those who cast the spell cast their own doom as well. We knew this, though some shut their eyes to the facts; it seems that their eyes have now been shut for them."

"I see," said Murcen, swishing the tea around in his bowl. Even the tea seemed to have a luminescence of its own. There were no shadows in the chamber of light, not beneath the tea-bowl, not within the teapot. Shadows must travel through darkness, and there was nowhere in that room they could find purchase. "You believe that the shadows that you cast have come back to you?"

"Yes," said Alendar. "They are... they came from within us, you see? They were our shadow selves, and we rode with them to do the killing. You have killed, I am sure, Murcen the Knife. But never so many as we did that night, and never with such joy. It came from our shadows, I think, the joy in death, and it doubled and redoubled with every life we took. If the spell had not broken with the dawn, we would have killed the world."

"The version that the others tell was that the shadows came apart in the light of day, and the spell was broken."

Alendar shook his head. "With the dawn, we no longer rode with the shadows, but all that broke was the connection between the caster and the spell. The shadows we cast found places that were dark by day as well as night. Now, they are coming back, as I said they would."

"The attacks on the royal sorcerers were well planned," said Murcen. "In one case, the victim was lured out of his wards through his obsession with religious relics. If this is magic rebounding it would seem—"

"It is not magic rebounding," said Alendar. "We cast our own darkness against the armies of Shu, gave it breath and blood. All the royal sorcerers of Edras gave birth that night to things of blood and destruction, and now our children are returning."

Alendar shook his head, drank from his bowl of tea. "I am going to die, Murcen the Knife. Perhaps by your hand, or by the hand of another servant of the king. But if you do not kill me soon the shadow I cast will; already it haunts the eaves of the temple and drifts past my door in the dark hours. It is clever; it will find a way. It was a terrible spell we made, and I cannot regret destroying the knowledge that I destroyed. This spell destroys its casters as surely as it destroys its targets."

There was more talk, but it was in the same vein. Once he was done at Seanest, Murcen took a fresh horse, and headed for Feshlaar. Whatever his reasons, the work that Alendar had destroyed would have saved years in the development of counterspells. Now, even the king's person was not safe, and the armies of Edras were as vulnerable as the armies of Shu had been. Aside from Alendar, all those who had worked the casting against the army of Shu were dead or renegade.

A royal sorcerer fleeing his post happened so rarely that the army and the knives had not agreed as to what was to be done about the two who had left. The trail of Kellim Ardak led to the far south, and Lesser Nesadi seemed to have vanished into the slums of Feshlaar, at the heart of Edras. Murcen had urged restraint; that they should be left alive despite their crimes. The time had come to see whether or not he had been right.

Little of the knowledge that Alendar had destroyed had been regained, but the royal sorcerers made every effort to prepare Murcen for battle with the shadows. The knife he carried was the culmination of their efforts.

It didn't work.

When he stabbed, the shadow ignored the blade, rippled around him, rejoined behind him, and vanished up over the wall. Murcen swore, turned, and leapt. The wall was a high one, built to keep out thieves and assassins as nimble as he was. The enchanted blade cut deep into the stone; he pulled himself up by it, used it as a step to propel himself up and over the wall. It meant leaving behind a fortune in magical effort, but it was the quickest way over, and that was more important than any failed weapon.

There was no point in drawing another blade; he had nothing else that would help. He leapt off the top of the wall and landed, inside the shadow.

There was a miasma of rage and a fearful joy, and he staggered back. The stone at his wrist, that had warned of the shadow's approach, had become as dark as the shadow itself. Inspired, he grabbed it, punched with it in his fist, and this time there was a faint shock of magic, and the shadow shrank away.

Meanwhile, his own intrusion had not gone unnoticed. There were guards running up the marble paths of Kellim's garden, as the shadow slipped on ahead, like a cloud racing past the sun. Even though it was dark, Murcen saw the shadow—that spell, at least, worked as it was supposed to—but the guards couldn't. There was no time for explanations, even if the guards would listen. The shadow was moving, and Murcen followed, ducking under a spear, driving his closed fist into the soft space just behind a guard's jaw.

The guard's head snapped back, and she fell to the ground. Possibly dead. Not his concern. Murcen vaulted the body, followed the shadow as it flowed towards the mansion proper. A guard behind him was yelling, and there were another two ahead. Murcen drew a blade. He did not have any more time to waste.

This time, the shadow did not slip past the guards. It touched them, and they fell.

Murcen could not keep pace with the shadow. If Kellim Ardak was going to live, it would be through the strength of his wards.

The shadow went through them like a rock through glass; flickers of power broke apart and curled off, but it barely slowed. What was left did not slow Murcen as he followed.

It had been less than a minute since the shadow had gone over the wall when it slipped in a window, and Murcen crashed through behind it.

There were oil lamps along the walls, with wide swaths of darkness between. The shadow moved in darkness, and Murcen followed. The stone had barely hurt it; there was no way he could hope to defeat it, but he could not let Kellim Ardak die without learning what he knew. The shadowspell had been the greatest weapon in Edras' armory. It had promised to take the place of armies, to establish the line of the kings of Edras as secure for all eternity. Now, it was being used as a weapon against the sorcerers who created it. Alendar wanted to believe it was the magic, rebounding against itself, but no one else ever thought that likely. If those shadows had been cast by a foreign power, once the last of the original casters were dead there would be nothing to protect the king or the country from the shadows.

Lesser Nesadi was born to merchant parents. Despite her talents, she had to fight to gain a place in the sorcerer's academy due to her class and her gender. Once there, she had fought to get the education her skills deserved, and the recognition she had earned. In the king's service, she had never stopped fighting.

Murcen found her in a free kitchen, not far from the banks of the holy river Candras. The temples for the rich clustered at the northern end of Feshlaar, where the pilgrims would immerse themselves in the sacred waters, with guards on hand to drive off the crocodiles. As the river passed through Feshlaar, the waters were no less holy, but were mixed with the effluent from dyers and tanners and three quarters of a million chamber pots and sewers.

The kitchen where Murcen found Nesadi was in one of the shanties beyond the southern city walls, where the water was too foul for crocodiles, and only vast catfish, blind and ulcerous, prowled the channel. The smell of the river there was as inescapable as the poverty of the shanty.

"You are Lesser Nesadi," he said, as she rolled dough into discs, dropped them into the frying oil.

"No," she said, not looking up. "I was Lesser Nesadi. Now I am Nesadi. Did you want food? There is no charge here."

Murcen did not laugh. There was a steel in her voice that precluded it. "You fled the council of sorcerers," he said. "It would be well for you if—"

"You are not here to kill me," she said, scooping the puffed bread from the oil, and putting it to the side. "You are here to talk, but I am busy. Unless you have other business, I would suggest that you leave, or, if you are hungry, take some bread, some red lentil paste and eggplant. There is no charge here."

Murcen considered. There was a line of those who needed food; lepers, those too old or too young to work enough to eat, men and women who were maimed, or whose faces simply showed a tired emptiness. Nesadi was making bread, a monk was spooning lentil paste onto it from a pot, and beside them a woman wearing a pilgrim's robes was frying eggplant.

"It seems that matters would progress faster if you had someone to cut the eggplant for you, so that none of you need to interrupt your other tasks," he said. "And perhaps we could talk while we worked."

Nesadi hesitated, then gave a cold smile. "You are, I am sure, very skillful with knives."

"Thank you," said Murcen, and began working at the chopping block. The cleaver was dull, but not too dull, and it had sufficient weight to get the job done cleanly.

"Of those who cast the spell, none who remained in the king's service are still alive," he said. "It is believed that the shadows killed them."

"So," said Nesadi, "Someone else has made the same mistake." She shook her head. "I wonder how long before the armies come."

"The shadows have not moved against anyone other than the wizards who cast the spell," said Murcen. "Prince Alendar is of the opinion that the shadows have returned to kill their creators."

"Is he?" asked Nesadi. "He always was a great believer in justice. But I do not think that the world is so fair a place."

"You feel that killing the army of Shu was unjust?" asked Murcen.

"Not exactly," said Nesadi. "It may have been just for them to die, but I cannot say that it is just for me to live. In either case, that is not why I left. Before the night that we cast the shadows, I would not have scrupled to kill. I had not scrupled to kill in the past, in the king's name. I do not think that you would understand, since you have not cast your shadow, but that spell showed me who I was."

She paused, and for a time, there was nothing other than the working of the kitchen, the thunk of the cleaver, the crackle of the bread in the oil.

"The shadows that we unleashed," she said, so softly that Murcen could barely hear her, "they came from inside of us. Everyone has a darkness inside of them, a terrible darkness."

"You left because of what you found in yourself?"

"In a way," said Nesadi. "I left because I had not known that it was there. I could not remain the woman I had found myself to be."

Nesadi put the lump of bread she was rolling out to the side, and turned to face Murcen. "The king of Edras held a weapon that could break armies; that could end whole nations. The shadows can kill a city in a night, and leave its treasures for the taking. Perhaps he does not have the darkness in his soul that I saw in mine. But what of the next king; of the next royal sorcerer?"

She picked up the bread again, turned back to her work. "But Alendar is wrong; if shadows are killing the sorcerers of Edras," she said, "they are not the ones we loosed. Those burned away with the morning sun."

"They cannot survive in the day?" asked Murcen.

"If care is taken, they can last for weeks. But care was not taken, and weeks are not years."

"It is always the way of violence," said the monk who was ladling the lentil paste, "to return against its source."

"And you think this is just," said Murcen, not turning aside from Nesadi.

"Just or not," said Nesadi, "it is. I cannot stop it, and I will not forge a more terrible weapon to counter it. If you feel the need to execute sentence, you know where to find me, King's Knife."

The last of the eggplants had been cut; the line of those coming for free food was dwindling. "Thank you," said Murcen, and left.

Nesadi had been looking down at the bread she was making, and Murcen's lips were hidden by his mustache. The line of those who had come in for food had been moving quickly enough, and was far enough away that he did not think that they would have heard the conversation, and even a lip reader would not have gotten more than the occasional snippet. The monk and pilgrim, on the other hand, would have heard most of what was said.

Decisions like that one, matters of state, could not be decided by emotion. The monk... if he was killed, Nesadi would know why, and would never again help the crown; she would have to be killed lest she turn against it. The monk would live. The pilgrim, though, could not be allowed to return from whence she came. There was little chance that she was a foreign agent, but she now had information, and there was the chance that she might sell it. With the same logic, the monk would not be allowed to outlive Nesadi.

It was not right. It was not just. But it needed to be done. Murcen signed the orders for the murders of monk and pilgrim before heading out to find Kellim Ardak, the last of the ten who had cast their shadows.

The shadow rippled through Kellim Ardak's estate, and Murcen followed, along carpets and polished wood, through sleeping quarters and wine balconies, past chambers dedicated to pleasures more refined. Guards and courtesans, serving maids and musicians fell when the shadow touched them, life leaving them like riffles of wind on still water.

The wards on Kellim's chamber were stronger than those which had guarded the outside of his house. They blazed up, full of power, and the shadow shrank back from them. It was Murcen's chance, and he struck, the stone in his fist. Again, the faint shock of impact; again the feeling of his soul coming loose from its moorings.

The ward on Ardak's door was in the shape of a great wheel, with a dragon staring out from the center, and demons and arcane symbols all around the edge, the whole thing crossed and over-crossed with lines of power, a perfect and beautiful shield. Murcen leapt forward, to take another swing at the shadow, but it wasn't there. There was, instead, the tiniest blot on Kellim's ward. There had been a gap in the lines of light, and between those lines, there was now a shadow. Murcen tried to close in, get his stone in contact with the darkness, but the wards pushed him back, held him in place.

The dark spot spread, pushing the lines of light aside, pushing until they broke; the ward came apart, and Murcen was free to move, free to follow the shadow into Kellim Ardak's inner chamber.

There were fine woven rugs and golden vessels, tapestries and furs, water pipes and a lotus pool, instruments of pleasure and pain. The sorcerer stood with a glowing orb floating above his head, and a thousand spear points of light flying from between his fingertips.

The light of the magic showed the decay in Kellim: the pallor of opium, the pouched cheeks of lotus leaves, the red nose and ears of alcohol, his whole body showing the marks of constant, exhausting, abusive pursuit of pleasure. He was slow; his fingers fumbled as they directed the spearpoints of light; there was a hesitation between his spells.

The shadow sped between the spearpoints of light, flowed up towards Kellim. Murcen wrenched his stone loose from the binding in which he wore it, threw it.

No. The foremost tendril reached out, touched Kellim's left nostril. Then, the whole thing was gone, and Kellim looked at Murcen for one brief moment. He tried to cough, could not, the shadow bubbling up in his throat, bubbling out from behind his eyes. He died as Murcen crossed the room. His mouth had been suffused with shadow, his eyes clouded, but the look on his face was one that Murcen had seen so often before that he could not fail to understand the rage and reproach.

Murcen grabbed up the stone, prepared to do battle again, as the glowing orb that had flown above Kellim Ardak turned gray, fell and shattered. The shadow left the body, but did not turn to fight him. Instead it fled, in a dozen directions at once.

Outside of the chamber there was yelling, and the sound of a great many footsteps. Murcen sighed, replaced the stone, and loosened another blade from its sheath at his back. He had failed, but there was still work to do to win free of the estate of Kellim Ardak.

When he reached the nearest outpost of Edras, battered and bloodied, there was a report waiting for him. The shadows had taken Lesser Nesadi three days after he had stopped at her free kitchen.

Murcen had much to think about as he wore out horses in a race to the Seanest Shrine.

The monks still stood guard at Alendar's chamber of light when Murcen returned, long spears at the ready, and light still poured from every surface of the chamber.

Alendar was alone this time, seated behind his low table, and once again, there was a pot of tea, and tea bowls. Once again, Murcen poured himself a bowl of tea.

"I need to know why," he said.

"I don't understand," said the prince, stone-faced. No, not entirely stone-faced; Murcen could see the reaction in his eyes.

"There are two reasons why I know what you have done," said Murcen. "The first is a question of timing. Nesadi was killed three days after I arrived in Feshlaar. Kellim was killed three days after I arrived in Tapur. A strange coincidence, unless the shadows were using me to help find their prey."

"No," said Alendar.

"The other was what Kellim Ardak told me." There was a sudden wild light in Alendar's eyes. "No, not with words. With the look he gave me when he was killed. He blamed me for his death, and when I saw that, what was clear to Kellim Ardak became clear to me as well."

Murcen looked away from Alendar, into the shadowless depths of his bowl, and drank. "Finding the sorcerers in the king's employ was easy enough. You had sat in that council chamber with them, you knew where they could be found, and what defenses they had. To find Kellim and Nesadi... that required an expert, a King's Knife. It was cleverly done; now I should like to know why."

"I don't understand—"

"No," said Murcen, not raising his voice, not shifting his position, but with enough authority to quiet even a prince. "You do understand."

Alendar allowed himself a small smile. "Say I did understand," he said. "Surely, the wizards had given you a device that would tell you if a shadow was near. I cannot—"

"Very good," said Murcen. He produced the stone from within his shirt, laid it on the table, where it glowed a vibrant green, as bright as everything else in that chamber. "It is, in my understanding, a sort of tuning fork that resonates to the same frequency as the shadows. That is why it detects them, and why it was useful as a weapon—the shadow did not enjoy the resonance. But a spell can be covered by a stronger spell."

"No," said Alendar. "No, this is all wrong. These men, these women... were my friends. We lived closer than brothers, than any husband and any wife. Why would I kill them? You think that I produced the shadows, that I sent them on your track? How could I, in this chamber? The shadows would perish in the light as soon as they left my fingertips."

Murcen nodded, took another sip of tea. "The first question—why—that is what I have been asking. The second, Nesadi answered for me, though I didn't realize it. 'There is a darkness inside all of us,' she said. It is true in a metaphorical sense, perhaps. But it is certainly true in a literal sense. Where could you have hidden it? I recall that there was a gentleman here with you—the shadows could have gone from the darkness within you to the darkness within him, and never had to cross the light."

Alendar was not a young man. He had not been a young man when he had started his service as a royal sorcerer, and that had been more than a decade before. But there was a youthfulness to him, despite the gray in his hair and in his mustache, or at least, there had been. "No," he said. "You are very clever, but no." He stood suddenly, upsetting his table, the teapot and bowls shattering, tea spilling on the floor. "I am as much a victim," he started, and then he could speak no more; the shadow was coming out from inside him, swallowing his words, pouring from his eyes. He fell back, dead, and it came for Murcen.

Murcen had the stone in his hand as he rolled clear, threw it at the center of the shadow. The thing recoiled from it, but it wasn't necessary. It could not hold together in the clear light of that room. It fell apart like a dream on waking, and Murcen the Knife was left alone with a corpse.

There were times that the King's Knife reported to his lord in open court, where his words were recorded in the royal archives, and where the actions he had taken were judged by the king, by his chancellor, and by the nobles of the court. This was seldom the manner in which important business was conducted, and this matter was important. Murcen the Knife walked with his king in the royal gardens. Night had come, and the lanterns cast pools of light on the marble and the flowers.

It was not the first time that Murcen had reported a failure, and while he had come at the truth too late, the situation was better than they had feared when he had been given his task. Prince Alendar had been behind all the attacks. No foreign power had learned the secret of the shadows, and neither the king nor his ministers nor his generals were in immediate danger.

Not that it was likely that the king had ever been in danger, as Murcen took care to point out. "Prince Alendar," he said, summing up, "was attacking the shadowcasting spell. That people were killed was incidental. Alendar made war against a spell, and he defeated me."

The king leaned forward to smell the red honeysuckle that grew in a torrent down one of the garden's railings. "A spell is an idea," he said. "It is difficult to win a war against an idea."

He looked away from the flowers, and at Murcen, who was standing two steps back, arms behind his back. "Tell me," he said. "Were you tempted to give your story a different ending?"

Murcen tried to answer, did not.

"My cousin Alendar died trying to convince you that the spell he had cast had come back and destroyed him," continued the king. "Were you not tempted to tell me that it had, that it had been the spell that had destroyed its casters?"

Murcen knelt before his lord. "I have never betrayed you," he said, "and I have left nothing out, I swear it. Yes, I was tempted to hide the truth. If you wish to replace me as—"

"Stand, Murcen," said the king. "You are not going to be replaced for disloyal thoughts. But tell me; why were you tempted to carry on Alendar's deception?"

"It is too perfect," said Murcen, rising to his feet. "Knowing that the attack was coming, the best I could do did not even slow it. Your majesty knows that there are those who seek your life, and who are thwarted by the army and the blades. A weapon like this... it seems that Lesser Nesadi and Kellim Ardak did not want to see you dead. Can we be certain that the same will be true of the next sorcerer who becomes a renegade? It is too perfect a knife; if we use it, it will cut us. It would have been better had Alendar been telling the truth."

"I see," replied the king, and he walked for a time in silence, Murcen two steps behind. "And why did Alendar wage his war against this spell?"

"I do not know," said Murcen.

"Your concerns are those of an assassin," replied the king. "Alendar was a general, a prince; how would he see it?"

Murcen considered. The same logic did apply, and at a grander scale. "Our armies..." he said, and trailed off.

"Not just armies," replied the king. "As Nesadi said, it could slaughter cities, and leave their treasures for the taking. It is a terrible thing, this shadowcasting. There are those who suggested putting other pressures on Prince Alendar, to convince him to share what he knows, but the sorcerers were against it, and not solely out of respect for my royal line. They fear this spell, and would not dare trust anything he said, regardless of the pressures put upon him. It would be best if it could be forgotten, but we cannot ignore what we have done. Shu knows what happened to their armies, and rumors have spread far beyond the borders of Edras and Shu. What one man has learned, another may copy, even from a tissue as fine as rumour."

The two walked together for a time in silence. "Prince Alendar thought the spell killed its casters," said Murcen, finally. "Perhaps he was right. The only evidence I had that it was he who killed Kellim and Nesadi was the timing; perhaps that was a coincidence."

"Timing," said the king, "and the look on a dying man's face."

Murcen nodded.

"Hm," said the king. "Yes, perhaps Alendar was correct and you were mistaken. Even if the shadows return to kill their casters, we shall have to continue our researches, and see what counter we can find—Shu might count the loss of a dozen sorcerers a cheap payment for all of Edras. And, perhaps, in times of need, we will need to turn once again to this weapon, if we can find any willing to use it."

They walked again in silence, for a time. "In all honesty he was right, even if you were also right," said the king. "Alendar was destroyed by the spell he had cast, and not just in the purely physical sense. As were Lesser Nesadi and Kellim Ardak, and the others who had performed the working." He shook his head. "You have killed perhaps a hundred men in my name, Murcen, have you not?"

"One hundred and forty-three," said Murcen. "Not counting those who I injured but who may not have died of their wounds, and not counting those who I killed indirectly, by giving orders."

"There, you see? I ordered these deaths, but most of them I have forgotten. If I had seen the faces of all those killed at my orders or in my defense..." he trailed off, looked out into the darkened garden, and listened to the chorus of frogs and night insects.

"Guilt?" asked Murcen.

"To some degree," said the king. "But not only that. It could be that in this spell, the sorcerers in my service caught a glimpse behind the curtain—that they faced a thing which must be avoided by any who wish to rule. It might be that Nesadi made herself into someone better, but the Lesser Nesadi was destroyed by the spell she cast." He shook his head. "Or perhaps you were mistaken, and Alendar was correct."

The king and his Knife left the garden. Behind them, the lanterns cast their pools of light against the encroaching shadows.

Life for Death

Amy Power Jansen

Sensilia revelled in her escape.

As the boat paddled, Sensilia leant against the railing. This was so much better than being cooped up in the council chamber, negotiating interest rates and repayment schedules.

And she was convinced, so much more effective for their cause.

The river widened into the estuary as it reached the island's coast, reflecting the planted terraces, the forests above, the glittering black beach below, and Mount Cracatorius looming over all.

She stretched, and breathed in the warm air, the mix of freshness and decay that typified autumn; an endless cycle continuing. Then she turned to check on Gerten, still searching for the 'mechanism' that moved the boat forward.

Ever since he had arrived, the emissary from the Necracian Death-Mage Council had been shunted from one serious meeting to the next. If Sensilia hadn't been a powerful member of the Life-Mage Council, he wouldn't have had a single glimpse of the lighter side of Cracatorian life.

Now, look, she thought. *He's laughing and enjoying life.*

Others on the Life-Mage Council had expressed dismay at his youth and lack of magic, worried the Death-Mages weren't taking their appeal seriously.

But Sensilia had made enquiries, via her sister's trading network, and found out he was heir to the most important trading family on Necracious. And amongst the Necracians, trade mattered more than magic. A potential long-term ally, if only they could seize the opportunity.

And she was young too. And the most powerful of the Life-Mages.

He was young. She was young. She smiled, watching taut olive skin ripple over his athletic frame. So finely-honed, so different.

"I give up," he said, flinging himself down next to her.

"So soon," she raised an innocent eyebrow. He had been relentless in all the negotiations thus far.

He nodded. "So, tell me, minx, how does this boat run?"

She pointed to the aft-deck, where the captain of the boat crouched behind the wheel, sunk in the slight stupor he'd allowed himself. "Can you see the captain's legs?"

Gerten squinted, lifting a hand to shade his eyes from the afternoon sun. "No. Should I be able to?"

"No," she said. "He doesn't have any. Not right now, anyway."

She leaned back against the railing, watching confusion displace disgust on Gerten's face. *Surely, he had seen magic worked before?*

"He's a mage, like me," she said. "Right now, he's joined with the boat, his legs the propellers."

"But..." Gerten sat straighter. "But... why? The boat could run without him. Then he could do other work."

"Because he loves the river. Look how happy he is."

They rounded the bend in the river and tinkling laughter diverted Gerten's attention to the hustle-bustle of the market. If she squinted, Sensilia could make out her sister, Petra, busy behind her palm-roofed booth.

"See, we get things done, just *our* way," she said. "My people enjoy themselves. This is... life."

Gerten shook his head. "Not as I know it."

"Well, while you're here," Sensilia shifted closer to him. "Why don't you live a little?"

When Sensilia returned to her villa, she found Frieda, the leader of the Life-Mage Council, in her sitting room, perched on a hand-carved stone-chair set beside her fountain. Her very own fountain. She'd grown up in a comfortable trading home, but nothing compared to the luxury given her as a Life-Mage.

Frieda looked as angry as Sensilia had ever seen her. Sensilia sighed. *Why can't they see longer than the ends of their noses? We could get so much more out of this.*

Frieda glowered. "I hope you have a good reason for slipping off with the emissary like that."

"Oh, Frieda, the negotiations are all but done and he's barely seen the island."

"He doesn't need to see the island. We need to agree the terms of the loan so they can send a Death-Mage to silence our volcano. We can't spare a single day. And you have already wasted too many with your unscheduled excursions."

Sensilia sighed, sinking into one of the woven chairs. "We could get better terms if he sees us as potential allies."

"We don't need better terms," Frieda said, back ram-rod straight. "With that volcano silenced, we can end this cycle of debt that we've been trapped in. We won't have to go with begging bowls to re-build every time it erupts."

"It isn't just the debt. Until we clear the loan, we can only trade through them, which makes it even harder to repay. As long as we have to deal exclusively through them, they control us."

Frieda placed her hand to her forehead, closing her eyes. "Sensilia, that's not what matters. You're too young to remember the last eruption.

Even your parents couldn't have been much more than children. But I do. Not just the eruption, not just losing everything, but the camps after. And the re-building. Knowing it would just go on and on. This is our chance to be free, if we act fast."

"Free?" Sensilia said, staring off into the distance, listening to the splashing of the mountain. *How can she even imagine that this loan frees us?* "Not so long as they give us such unfair prices on all our goods."

"I understand, I do. You grew up in a trading family. Even with your parents retired, your sister is a trader. You see everything through that frame of reference. And it is important. I agree. But nothing can be allowed to slow down getting this loan and quieting that mountain's rumbles."

Sensilia bristled. "This isn't about my family. This is about our people's future. We need to stop making every decision out of fear."

Frieda stood. "I am still the head of the council. Tomorrow we agree the terms of the loan and Gerten goes back to send us the Death-Mage. Interfere again and—I'll suspend your membership of the Council."

Sensilia sprang to her feet as Frieda walked out. "You can't do that."

Frieda didn't look back. "I can and I will. Don't try me in this."

Sensilia crouched by the side of the ferns she'd planted, soft, dark earth caked over her hands. *If I could only get these ferns to take without magic...*

She rocked back on her heels. The heads of the ferns remained curled, but she could see the green rushing back in, the yellow retreating from their tips. *Why won't they grow on their own?*

After her last visit to her parents, high on the slopes of the mountain, hidden amongst dense forest and mineral baths, she'd brought a handful of clippings back with her. It would be a fresh challenge. She'd mastered the network of life rushing through the Island years ago, but transplanting pieces was much trickier, requiring far more subtlety. Most had already died and what remained held on due to magic. She couldn't get the mountain ferns to connect properly with the life flowing lower on the island. *Can't even get a bunch of ferns to do what I want.*

Her loose gown billowed around her as a slight breeze caught it. She stretched, trying to enjoy the sensation of air over her sweaty skin. Autumn had always been her preferred season, a respite after the cloying heat of summer and before the biting cold of winter.

But even that didn't seem to help. Frieda had gotten the end of her precious negotiations—at the cost of onerous terms hastily agreed to. It had taken forty years to pay off the loan from the last eruption, but Frieda was worried about a few days.

She'd sent Gerten back. But even for that, she hadn't trusted Sensilia, and she knew Sensilia was the strongest flier.

If she wanted that Death-mage so quickly, why did she send someone slow?

Sensilia took a steadying breath, and scented...

Ash. Sensilia came to her feet abruptly, searching the gloom for the distant peak.

The ground lurched below her and Sensilia found herself sprawled on the tiles as a sharp pain pierced her skull. It was a warning, echoing not only to her, but right across the island. The volcano!

A sense of dread clawed through Sensilia. Then instinct and long training took over.

She scrambled to her feet, running down the stairs. As she ran, the warning sirens started to wail, echoing across the water. This was it; this was not a drill. The volcano was erupting.

She set off for her evacuation point. The paths were well-tended and Sensilia was grateful for that as she stumbled along in the dark. As she neared her launch point, she had to push her way through the growing crowd.

As she was recognised, people cleared the way for her and she climbed gratefully to where the gargantuan basket waited at the centre of the clearing. As the most powerful of the Life-Mages, she had the largest allotment of people. She tried to summon a reassuring smile for those around her.

I can't believe this is happening.

"Sensilia." Someone grabbed her arm. She looked back to see her sister, Petra, her husband carrying their swaddled babe behind. "It isn't a drill, is it?"

Sensilia shook her head, swallowing down the feeling of dread that threatened to envelop her.

"Mom, Dad," Petra said. "They won't make it, will they?"

"No." When their parents had retired to the live on the slopes of the mountains, they had known: resources had to be focused on saving the strong and the young.

Petra stayed at Sensilia's side until the community-wardens confirmed everyone had arrived. Sensilia climbed up to her nest at the top of the basket. She strapped herself in, leaving only her arms free, the wind goose-pimpling her flesh. She drew on her magic, feeling it course through her veins, then focused on the basket, threading the power between her arms and her feet. Her body softened and transformed.

Eagle wings extended, growing until they could support the enormous weight . Below the basket, claws extended as Sensilia's feet shimmered into nothingness. Then she leapt into the air, carrying her people with her.

As she climbed, she could see the dark ovoid of her island below her, lit by a lurid glow. And there, in the distance, where the mountain rose up into all its height, tongues of fire spreading their way down the steep slopes. So slow, she could barely see it move. But inexorable, unstoppable, it would swallow her home.

Sensilia squelched through the camp's mud. It plastered her shoes and the tops of her bare feet. The organised Necracians had laid out the camp, put up the tents, set up latrines and gathering spaces for feeding and healing the refugees. Not the first time they had done this. Though it had been a while.

She clutched the blanket doubling as a shawl as she skirted past the hushed circle of tents where the rest of the Council lay. She was the only one with the strength to face the Necracians. Some of the Council, including Frieda, would never regain their magic, having drained themselves to the dregs. Others would only ever experience a thin trickle for their rest of their lives.

They'd been Life-Mages; now they were nothing.

But Sensilia, exhausted a few days before, could feel her power building again, even as she felt her hope for the future seeping away. Everything had changed and so fast. So many had died. She'd thought she'd understood, but she hadn't. And those that had, like Frieda, would likely never recover. *If only... I can't think like that. I have to stay strong. I have to fix this.*

She traversed the edges of the camp, up to the observation deck positioned to the side of the tents, wrinkling her nose at the thick smell of antiseptic wafting up from the latrines, and the earthier smells hidden below it. She didn't know which bothered her more: the dank reality of their current lives or the Necracians' attempts to tidy it up.

From the observation deck, she could see the huddled nodes that made up the camp. A structure perfected over so many disasters. And beyond it, the Necracian city. In all its deliberate glory. Straight streets marching to the centre, spirals all around. The occasional splash of green breaking up the glimmering buildings, never too high, never too crowded.

Once, there had been a slum of disordered streets beyond it. But no more. Where the slums had once been stretched the Valley of Death, a dark slash gouged into the ordered landscape.

While the city itself might be ordered, to her both it and the slash beyond it radiated lifelessness. Wealth was the island's only life-blood. Without it, they wouldn't even be able to feed themselves.

The camp had been strategically placed, not too close to the city, not too far for it to be serviced. They wouldn't want the Cracatorians to stay any longer than necessary. Reports suggested that the volcano had already started to settle. A short eruption, but no less devastating.

And when they returned, everything would be gone. Their island had never had the structure nor the slums of the Necracians. It had had order. Terraces for living and for growing. Wide open spaces. Preserved jungle and stretches of agricultural land. A jumbled order; a fertile order; their order. Gone.

Everything would be different. They'd have to start from scratch. With a huge loan to bear and no end in sight.

"There you are," her sister Petra said, as she climbed up behind Sensilia. "You need to get ready for the Death-Mages' Council. Can't have you looking like..."

"A beggar. That's what I am. What we all are." Sensilia tried not to sound bitter, but Petra's expression confirmed her failure.

The gargantuan glass sphere that housed the Death-Mage Council squatted in the centre of the city. The whole structure, completely dead to her Life-Mage senses, unnerved her. Especially as she stood there in what ragged robes she had and in bare feet, having had to discard what little footwear she had to the mud. Cold seeped up from the tiles and through her soles.

The Death-Mages on their circular platform towered around her, their expressions grave. *Is their sympathy even real?* They'd got their hold back. The cycle had been restored. Once more the Life-Mages would be in their debt. If only she could stretch their credit far enough.

The Head Councillor was a tall woman with not an ounce of fat on her. Her greying hair scraped tight back along her skull. She peered at Sensilia over the edge of her beaky nose. "I'm sorry, Councillor Sensilia. We simply don't think we can extend such a large loan. Especially at this time. Considering your lack of collateral, your ability to repay."

Sensilia took a deep breath, ready to try and force the point one more time. "Never before have we had a completely clear record. Even with the additional loan to have the crater drained, we would still not be any more indebted than we have been after any of the previous eruptions."

The Councillors glanced at one another, then the Head spoke again, her voice, unmoved. "We could hardly have refused to extend credit under those circumstances. It would have been... unneighbourly. However, we always registered our dismay at the size of the loans. At this time, there is no reason why we should expose ourselves to such a high level of risk."

"It wouldn't be a risk. If one of your Death-Mages drains the crater, there would be no reason why we would be unable to repay our debt."

One of the Councillors to her left, an older man already developing a paunch, cleared his throat. If she remembered correctly, he wasn't a Death-Mage but some kind of merchant. "And if we did this, what reason would we have to believe your people would work to repay their debt? Your island's reputation for... pleasure-seeking is well-known. Without the need for future credit brought on by the threat of eruptions, you would lack the incentive to clear your slates again."

Sensilia stared at the man, feeling her gorge rising in her throat. "For how long have you made money off our pleasure-goods? You pay us next to nothing for them, and then charge the earth to those you sell them to. And you claim that you take the risk, that you add the value. We grow, we give life. You trade."

The man leaned forward, his eyes narrowed. "If it's so easy, why don't you do it?"

"We choose a different life." *And because we have to trade through you as long as the loans last. One day that will change.*

"Then why deny us the profit?"

"You profit off our deaths, off our blood."

"No-one forces your people to live there."

"Then you would let us stay here?" Sensilia stepped towards the man. "Who would feed you then?"

The Head Councillor intervened. "No-one is suggesting your people leave their homes. We will, as always, help you re-build."

Sensilia tried to appear calm as she waited in the sitting room. The ride in the metallic contraption from the Council to Gerten's home hadn't been long, but it felt like it had. He lived in one of the better districts where houses were allowed to sprawl. Even in the city itself, everything smelt too clean, sharp instead of soft. She waited in a room full of dead furniture, crafted by machines, instead of magic or human skill. She couldn't bear to sit on any of it.

The door opened to admit Gerten. He looked different here, all smooth and pressed. And he smelled different, of that strange alcohol Necracian men insisted on splashing themselves with.

"I'm so sorry."

He sounded sincere. She tried for a smile. "I... I've been to the Council. They've refused to extend the loan far enough to drain the crater."

"I know."

"We need to drain it." The arguments died on her lips. She'd summoned them so many times already. "Can you help me?"

He put a guiding arm around her. "Why don't you sit down?"

She pushed his arm away. "I don't want to sit down."

"Sensilia, you're over-wrought. Just sit down."

She bit her lower lip. It didn't seem worth fighting. She sat down on the nearest piece of furniture, a double-seater overlaid with a thin layer of cushioning, so thin her sit-bones could feel the structure beneath. He took a seat across from her.

"I can't... I have to... There has to be a way," she said.

"Maybe, in a few years... once you've started repaying."

"No, it has to be now. Once we're in debt, we can't negotiate from that position."

"You can't negotiate from this one. You already owe us."

She nodded, a tear trickling from her eye, betraying her. "The camps." She put a hand over her mouth, holding in the cries trying to escape. "What if we don't take the loan, just stay there? Refused to move until they helped us. Just stayed."

"You don't want to do that."

She looked up at his tone, so grim. "Why? Wouldn't it work? You've got so many people. You're terrified of refugees, of migrants. There's no space here. And if we stayed, wouldn't they have to give in?"

He looked away from her, tension furrowing his forehead. "I need to show you something."

Sensilia stood at the centre of the scoured valley, staring up at its crumbling crust bending around her. When she knelt and placed her hands on the dry, cracked earth, she could feel no trace of life. Emptiness. Above and below. Even the air tasted thin and nauseatingly clean.

No birds flew over. Nothing grew beneath.

To do this to a volcano would be one thing, but to do this to land where people had once lived seemed unthinkable. This valley would not support life, not for hundreds of years. The damage they'd done was so much worse than she could have imagined.

"How could they do this?"

"The slums didn't fit into their vision of our city."

"How many died?"

"Enough."

"And you'd do this to us?"

"I wouldn't. But the Council might. There are ruthless people on it. And the site for your camp was specifically chosen so that if this were repeated... we wouldn't lose valuable land."

Sensilia stared at him. She almost laughed. "So that was your only regret... you killed all those people, and all you regretted was the location."

"It wasn't me."

Sensilia covered her face with her hands, marshalling her thoughts. Then she took them away in one swift movement. "So what you're saying is that you can't help me? That's the long and the short of this little excursion."

"I'm sorry."

Tortill, Frieda's successor, sat across from her in the tent set up for their Council meetings. The other council members had heard her report and gone. The old man's shoulders already looked too weak to hold the burden.

"I didn't really expect that they would extend the loan that far," he said, at last.

"But I had to ask," Sensilia said, holding the tears at bay. Was she the only one who saw? *We came so close, we can't give up. Not now.*

"Maybe this is how it should be. There have always been those that thought bringing Death-Magic onto the island would be a mistake."

"Why?"

He shrugged. "In the old days, our people believed the volcano was our protector, our benefactor. That it gave us life, our magic and every so often it asked for something back."

Sensilia stood. "That is an old superstition. My parents were not some sort of sacrifice. I refuse to accept that. I will find a way. I will."

"You do what seems best to you, Sensilia." For the first time, she heard anger in his voice. "You always have."

Sensilia had waited until Petra could use her contacts to summon up a fresh set of robes. She needed to impress the Death-Mages, and she couldn't do that covered in their dirt. The remnant of her Council might have resigned themselves to the Necracians' decision, but she held her own status, and more than that, she had her power. Which is more than could be said for some.

So she stepped alone into the gaze of the Necracian Councillors. Their fake sympathy had all but disappeared, and their irritation at her return rippled through the room. She stood even straighter. The Head waved to acknowledge her. Sensilia took a breath and began. "I have a proposition for you."

"We're listening," the Head Councillor said.

"I would like one of your mages to drain our volcano, silence it once and for all."

"We have refused the loan, and you have no way of paying us."

The Councillors looked away, shaking their heads. One or two sneered outright.

"I do." Sensilia ignored the faint titter that went through the chamber. *This is it—one last throw.* "I can revive your Valley of Death."

The laughter stopped. She'd caught their interest. She withheld her smile.

"So what?" said the heavy-set merchant, his eyes narrowed.

"So you could grow your own food."

"We buy our food from you."

"And that's what you want, forever?"

The merchant looked ready to argue, but the Head Councillor raised her hand to stop him. "You could do this?" she asked Sensilia

"Yes."

The Head Councillor narrowed her eyes. "If it's possible why have your people never offered this before?"

"It would take more strength than most Life-Mages possess."

"And you have this strength?"

Sensilia indulged a thin smile. "I do."

The Head Councillor shifted in her seat. "We will consider your proposition."

Sensilia stood with Petra at the docks as the last of their people were loaded into the boats. The debates had lasted a day, but the Necracian Council had agreed to the deal. Her people would travel back, in conveyances provided by the Necracians, along with teams to help them reconstruct. And a single Death-Mage who would drain the crater when word came that Sensilia had been able to complete her part of the bargain. They had it all in writing, in one of the Necracian's precious contracts.

"You don't have to do this. You know that. No-one would blame you," Petra hugged her.

"I know." *But I would blame me. I've always believed it was about the future. I have to stay true to that. No matter what it costs.*

"What if..." Sensilia could feel her shaking.

She put an arm around her sister. "Hey, hey, I'll be okay."

"What if you over-commit yourself? You could die. I can't lose you, not now. Not after..."

Sensilia turned her sister to face her. "You'll be fine. You will be. If I don't come back, you will be. You promise?"

Petra nodded, blinking back tears.

"Good. It could all be for nothing. But I have to try. And if I succeed, even if I die, that's a price worth paying."

Sensilia stood overlooking the Valley of Death, a gaggle of Death-Mages hanging back behind her. If it were possible, it horrified her even more than it had before. For even dirt to feel dead. No cycle of worms to replete it. No water to relieve it. Nothing.

She had taken up her position beyond the dead area itself, where some greenery struggled to grow amidst the rocks. She would use that to anchor herself. In her mind's eye, she summoned a picture of her island as it had been before, reminding herself of what patterns of life were meant to look like. Then, she brought her attention back to this island, this valley.

Dead. So dead. Was this why the Death-Mages had chosen the island, this absence of life, or had their magic caused it? While the island as a whole supported life, its resources were very close to collapse, leaving her very little to work with. It was even worse than she'd thought. And she needed what magic life there was in it to anchor this new work. She needed to revive this dead space. What if it wasn't enough?

She forced herself to relax, allowing her power to trickle out through her feet and into the ground beneath. As she felt its flow quicken, she fought the urge to grab for it, halt the process. Instead she knelt, both in a gesture of surrender and because she knew that she couldn't remain standing while allowing herself to be drained to such a level. Closer to the ground, her magic would drain from her even faster, the empty earth gulping it down.

As her magic sank into the earth, she focused on reaching out to gather what few strands of life she could find.

The first time the pattern slipped away from her, she felt her body go limp. She heard the distant voices of the observers as they crowded around her.

"Is she dead?" one asked.

Cold fingers fumbled at her neck. "No."

I can do this. I can be strong.

Sensilia forced her mind back to her task, groping for the strings connecting her to her magic, to the island. She focused on building a ring along the perimeter of the dead area, to bring in what she could from the outside, to maximise what she drew both from the island and from herself. Once she'd laid it out as best she could—by then the evening cool had settled on her skin—she pushed tendrils of life into the dead area. Felt it resist, pushing off her imposition. But she pushed back, reforming the network.

Then she pushed into the heart of the dead valley, forcing brittle channels open. Her body began to convulse as her own life-force entered into the pattern. Steeling her will, she pushed again, re-anchoring herself. The network closed. All she needed now was one last push, to make it resilient. She summoned all her magics, all her energies and pushed all her reserves into it, holding nothing back.

Sensilia woke on a hard bed, her stomach churning. She threw up twice before she opened her eyes, supported by someone. She didn't recognise the small room, but she knew she was home. She could smell the life in the air. Normally the winter air seemed lacklustre compared to the summer. Now she could make out every evergreen, and it was so good.

She lifted her head to see Petra. "Hey," she said.

"You did it."

Sensilia relaxed back into the cushions, closing her eyes. Part of her wanted to wait to check, but her mind sought her magic. All gone. Not even the smallest base for it to build back from. A wave of exhaustion threatened to engulf her. She'd never do magic again, never lead her people.

She felt a cool cloth on her forehead. "The Death-Mage has drained the crater. No more eruptions," Petra said.

Sensilia tried to smile. This was what she'd wanted, why she'd done it. She knew it was worth it. It had to be. She forced humour into her voice, "Good, then I can retire." Like an old woman.

"You'll have to wait till we've rebuilt."

This time, Sensilia did smile. She would wait. Her people would rebuild. And this time, they could build to last.

From the world of the novel *The Moon King*.

Darkday Night

Neil Williamson

Club Comedia was a Darkday myth. A rumoured peripatetic pop-up parlour that manifested somewhere in the city of Glassholm every month end to provide entertainments of the most dubious reputation. Scandalized whispers circulated around the city. Everyone had heard some story or other that someone's colleague or professor or sleazebag brother-in-law had been seen furtively crossing that threshold. Bet had never known anyone who'd actually admitted to seeking the place out before, but Megan's new café friends were full of such insinuations. The tales they told were crammed with such lurid details that it was hard to not believe that they were talking from first-hand experience. *You wouldn't believe... There's this man who... And then, right there on the stage, they actually...* But they were only stories. No place in Glassholm could be so awful. Not even during the dark of the moon.

The nadir of the monthly lunar cycle, when the never-setting moon vanished for one terrible night and plunged the city into communal depression, was always difficult enough but lately it had been proving harder and harder. When Megan and Bet had first got their little Dockton apartment, made it nice together, they'd spent the low end of the month in each other's arms, whispering comfort and drying each other's tears like every other couple in the city. But lately the flat had proved too small a space to contain their Darkday despair. They'd needed somewhere else to go for the night, but their family homes were too antagonistic, the Promise Centres too earnest, the artists' parties in the Rottens too stuffy, and Bet had begun to worry that what was *really* dissatisfying Megan was Bet herself. She was so sceptical about Club Comedia's existence that she expected the search for it tonight to be a monkey chase, but had agreed to try out of something approaching desperation.

The dense alleys of Dockton met the low-rent houses at the foot of Garton Hill at a place known unofficially as Chicken Town. Chicken Town had not been part of the Lunane's original design for the city, but it had thrust itself up between the cracks, squeezed into the crannies, nevertheless; a haven for the destitute, the deviant and the Dark-destroyed. Something that Glassholm appeared to require, regardless of the King's intent and numerous attempts down the years to raze it. There was no mistaking when Bet and Megan passed into its environs. The first thing they heard was a dog's whine; frantic and short-lived. The first thing they smelled was the greasy odour of meat. The first thing they saw was a woman in a nightdress, clutching a stationery spike and hissing: "Sasha?"

Bet pulled Megan into an alley. "How far now?"

"I don't know." Megan peered at the lumpy brickwork. "The streets don't have names here. We're looking for a sweetshop."

"A *sweatshop?*" Bet tried not let the brittleness of Dark and the stupidity of this whole palaver turn her tone as snappish as Megan's, but only partly succeeded. "There are no sweatshops in Glassholm. Not even in somewhere as benighted as Chicken Town. The Lunane ensures a fair wage—"

"A *sweet* shop. Though who would come to this filthy place to buy candy, I can't imagine."

"Oh. You mean like this?" While they had bickered, the cottonish clouds had teased apart and a splash of starlight now revealed a deep-set door. There was an awning above it and faded cartoon bon-bons pasted to the wood. Megan raised an eyebrow and tried the handle.

The door opened onto a long room that was thick with heat and the smell of burning sugar. The shop's counter was a street, candles lined up like lampposts—if lampposts had ever taken the shape of crude, flaming erections. The trays the candles were planted in held melting slabs of toffee and shattered boilings. At the end of the counter there were stairs leading downwards, and from there came the sound of voices. It seemed Club Comedia was not a myth after all.

"For a secret club they don't seem very security conscious," Bet said warily. She wanted to say more: *I'm frightened, I want to go home,* but Megan tugged her on. The stair took them down, every fifth or sixth step sprouting another of those foul candles. A muffled roar of laughter rushed up to meet them. *Laughter,* on Darkday. The noise sharpened into focus when Megan tugged aside the heavy curtain at the bottom, resolved into a wave of coarse emotion. In the grubby cellar beyond the curtain, a crowd assembled on a scavenged assortment of chairs brayed and yelled and spat invective in the direction of the "stage". If a tacked-up glittery backdrop had not grandly bestowed that title on the platform constructed from boards laid on top of crates, the woman tottering around on it in a pearlescent shift and a pair of ridiculous heels surely would have.

The woman was younger than her slumped shoulders and sea floss hair first indicated, but her spiderleg lashes, rouged cheeks and lascivious lipstick still made of her a cartoonish grotesque as she strutted the stage, urging the audience to clap in time with the crackling gramophone music and pausing frequently to bend low and flash her cleavage. "Go on, get them out," someone shouted, sparking another round of laughter. The woman needed no further urging. The straps of the shift were shucked off, and the material slid down to reveal that her breasts had been painted to look like cartoons of the moon, complete with the Lunane's face. Then she began to jump up and down. "Put them away again!" That got an even bigger laugh, but there was still a round of applause when the performer finished her act and left the stage.

Megan was, of all things, smiling. "Sky, but it's good to hear people having a laugh. I want a drink. You want a drink?" She indicated a clot of activity around the makeshift bar in the far corner. "Find us a seat. I'll get them."

Bet found a sofa near the back. It was torn and lumpy, and the view of the stage was restricted but she felt that might be a distinct advantage. There'd been little to admire in the artless striptease and she did not expect the quality of the entertainment to improve.

A tall man was next up. His ashen hair fell to his collar and a poor attempt at a beard and moustache emphasised the thrust of his bony features. He unfolded a sheaf of yellow paper.

"Sonnets," he declaimed. "For The Lunane."

"Oh, for goodness sake." Bet glanced around in case her exclamation of dismay had aroused attention, but it had gone unnoticed amid the half-hearted cheers and jeers. Really though, the last thing she needed right now was a paean to the glory of their immortal king setting Megan off on one of her rants about the Lunane, the city...the *bloody* as she called it. Its narrow definitions and unbending constrictions for anyone who might stray the tiniest bit from the norm. Bet's misgivings, however, were quickly allayed. The poet's recital turned out to be an acid appraisal of the many ways in which the Lunane's promise to always care for his people did not quite meet expectations. In some ways, the poems were actually quite funny and Bet felt guilty for wanting to laugh. It was wrong to make fun of the King at the time when you were supposed to need his solace, feel his comfort, the most.

She did laugh, she couldn't help it. She tittered at the King's random method of Halfday arbitration that attempted to satisfy everyone but ended up pleasing no one at all. Then she snorted at the Palace's stuffy obsession with process and order and tradition. The only people who Bet had heard dare be quite this critical were the artists in the Rottens, but they were always so deadly earnest and confrontational about it. This fellow made the absurdities entertaining. And laughing at them was liberating.

"Having a good time?" She looked up, expecting to see Megan with the drinks and found instead a man perched on the arm of the sofa. How such a heavy-set fellow could have settled there without her noticing she couldn't fathom, but here he was in his antique suit with the shiny cavalry stripes down the legs and three bone buttons on each cuff, his once-white shirt and mildewed velvet bowtie, his patent shoes and silk top hat, all dusty as if unearthed for this occasion after years of disuse. The man grinned, yellow teeth in a face that had been daubed white over a day's growth of beard. From within the dark circles that could either have been intended to represent eye sockets in a skull or the moon's craters, horrendously bloodshot eyes nevertheless managed to glitter with humour.

"It's...all right," Bet managed. "So far."

The man slapped his leg as if her response had been hilarious. "Oh, it gets better," he said. "Or worse, depending on your point of view." He slipped off his perch. "I'm the Host, by the way." He extended his hand with a rattling sound. Around his wrist he wore a bracelet of shiny black things that Bet realised with horror only as she shook his hand were the beaks of the Lunane's favoured white crows.

She snatched her hand away. "The Host?"

"The Host of the cabaret, dear girl. Every show has to have one. See you around."

The poet on the stage departed and, as the audience stood up to stretch their legs, the Host vanished among them. Looking around the crowd Bet was surprised to discover that far from being the collection of creeps and dangerous weirdos that she had imagined they all looked very normal. United perhaps by their pallor, a certain fragile glaze over the eyes, a strain at the corners of the mouth—it was Darkday after all—but otherwise unremarkable. Many had come on their own, sitting quietly and avoiding eye contact, but there were some couples too, even a few larger groups, friends who apparently made this their monthly arrangement. In many ways the place was not unlike a Promise Centre, except instead of congregating for comfort, here it seemed they gathered to laugh. It could certainly have been a lot worse. All the same, Bet was relieved that there was no one here that she recognised.

"Sorry, sorry. I can't believe it's this busy." Megan had two enamel mugs brimming with something pink. Bet took one while Megan lowered herself onto the sofa. "This is absolutely not what I expected."

Bet sipped her drink. It was even sweeter than it looked and had an aftertaste that could not she thought be wholly attributed to the detrimental effects of the moon's current phase. She grimaced. "Me neither."

"You're okay with it?" In that look Bet saw that Megan knew she'd been pushy tonight. Now she was asking, belatedly, for approval.

Bet made herself smile and against her better judgement sipped again. "Yes, it's fine." Megan clasped her hand in that strident, confrontational way that she always did to show people that they were together, ready to stare down anyone who so much as glanced askance at them. Concerned with their own preoccupations, no-one did. For once Bet didn't feel like pulling away.

Their relationship had been a struggle from the beginning. But then everyone had told them it would. The Parks, where Bet had grown up, were conservative even for Glassholm, and for her mother having a daughter move to Dockton was embarrassment enough. To do so to live with another woman... There was no Lunane's law against homosexuality—the King cared for all his subjects equally, after all—but their lifestyle wasn't *traditional*, and throughout the Constant City, tradition often carried more weight than the law. Things were difficult in a myriad of ways that, on their own might seem inconsequential, but mounted up. The income from Megan's Foundry job was meagre and they had to do without the allowance that Bet had once taken for granted too, although her dad—a Garton boy himself, originally—slipped her a little something from time to time, but they'd managed to find a place to live among the immigrants and the workless, where the neighbours more or less ignored them and some of the shops at least served them without fuss. The man at the bakery on the square even added a couple of extra rolls to their dozen from time to time, and shared a wink with the rosy, befloured man who baked them. The artists were more open about who they loved of course, although for them *love* never seemed to be the actual point. So, there was little solidarity, and even less help in their chosen life, but it was worth it. *They* were worth it. She'd always believed that.

"Tombola time! Tombola time!" As the shout moved from the back of the room towards the stage the audience retook their seats. A beer barrel had been placed on the platform. It sat on a cradle and was painted with stripes of red, white and blue. The man who had identified himself as the Host wheezed up onto the stage, and he now had a luck monkey on his shoulder.

"Well now, ladies and gentlemen," he bellowed. "Are we all having a fabulous Darkday? Are we?" The reply was a lukewarm, sarcastic cheer undercut with an air discomfort. For the first time, Bet realised that despite their bravado most of the audience were as uncomfortable coming here as she was. "Well, not to worry, we've several more excruciating acts to lift your spirits before the night is done. But now..." With a knowing grin he tapped the barrel. It rocked, rattled. "It's time once again to say *Fuck You To Luck*. Yes, it's Tombola Time. Thanks to all of you for your kind donations, and all the very best to those who wind up on the receiving end." He crossed his fingers with a mugged expression of trepidation. "So, without further ado..." The Host made a theatrical show of spinning the barrel. Its contents rumbled and thumped, and when he stopped the drum Bet thought she heard something inside snap.

The man opened a hatch in the side of the barrel then turned to the monkey. "Go on then, do your bit." When the monkey chittered reluctantly the Host growled and the scrawny creature shot down his arm and disappeared inside the barrel. After a few moments it reappeared with something silver clutched in its paw—a policeman's whistle. The crowd responded with an *ooh* of nervous anticipation.

Megan craned her neck to see. "Are those...*luck gifts*?"

Bet shook her head in disbelief. "I think so."

"They're *redistributing* unwanted luck gifts. They've actually trained a monkey to do that?"

Bet didn't share Megan's enthusiasm and, watching the monkey looking around the audience as if unsure who to deliver its prize to, she didn't think the animal was entirely happy either. When a luck monkey brought you a token it was *yours*, for good or ill. There was no giving it back if you didn't like the look of it. The monkeys were as natural a component of Glassholm life as the cycle of entropy and bloom that matched the moon's phase, as the communal rapture of Full and the awfulness of Dark. And quite aside from it being against the Lunane's Law, it was well known that any attempt to influence the scabby little monsters could only ever result in the worst luck.

The audience were wary, enjoying the transgressiveness of the game but still unwilling to invite the risk. They flinched as the monkey jumped down to the floor, shuffled their feet out of the way. Bet and Megan couldn't see whose lap the monkey jumped on to, but they heard a man's groan. The Host was already spinning the drum again, and the little ball of fur scurried back to the stage. This time the gift was a crab claw and it went to a young woman who proudly showed it to her friends. Their cheer to bolster her fragile bravado was unconvincing.

"Two lucky, lucky winners," the Host brayed. "Shall we have one more?" The monkey returned again to the spinning drum and this time whatever it produced was too tiny to be identified. The creature took off at a mad run. Chairs scraped, folk squirmed out of the way. Bet turned to Megan to ask if she could see it, and that was when she felt the weight landing on her thigh, the fingers needling through her skirt. She looked down and saw the little face nimbussed in orange fur, the huge eyes. The monkey held its paw out, revealed the gift: a creamy, glittering pearl. Attached to it was an antique hoop that indicated it had once been part of an earring or perhaps a bracelet. The monkey thrust the thing at her again, demanding that she take it. The whole room watched.

"Do I have to?" Bet said.

"Oh, come on scaredy-cat." Megan's tone was edged with something. Excitement? Envy? She reached across. "Here, I'll take it for the both of us."

The monkey bared its teeth and squealed a warning. Megan withdrew with a scowl.

"That decision is up to you, young lady." The Host had appeared beside the sofa again and he ignored Megan, addressing only Bet. "Most would. It's the convention after all, but our motto here at Club Comedia—our *raison d'etre* you might say—is to stick two fingers up at convention. Here we say *Fuck You* to luck." Taking up his cue the crowd began to chant the words: *fuck you to luck, fuck you to luck.* Louder and louder, their eyes all on Bet. She snatched the pearl out of the monkey's fist and while everyone cheered, slipped it into the pocket of her cardigan as the Host returned to the stage, taking the audience's attention with him.

"Fuck *you*," she muttered, though she was not at all certain to whom.

"May you all enjoy your newfound, second hand fortune," the Host said, then grinned. "Or not." The crowd laughed nervously. "And now, I think it's time for another brave performer, don't you?" He half-bowed and left the stage to whoever would follow him. Bet had the feeling that he neither knew nor cared exactly who the performers were. Judging from the amateurishness of the performances so far, she was becoming certain that they were in fact merely patrons like everyone else here. Ones who had something specific to get off their chests.

The two girls who took his place were so alike they must have been sisters. Both had straight hair that hung down their backs. Both had moist eyes, pink cheeks, sullen mouths. Both wore pinstriped trousers from which bare feet peeked and matching waistcoats over bare skin. Their pale arms were marked with welts like ugly stitchery. The one carried a viola, the other carried a razor. They matched each other stroke for delicate, sawing stroke. The spectacle was harsh. The music, harsher.

"Are you enjoying this?" Bet said it to have a distraction, but Megan had also been sullen quiet since the luck gift. "Is it what you were looking for?"

"I wasn't *looking* for anything." Megan's tone was snappish again. "It's a change though, I'll give you that. At least here people are prepared to think differently and not just go along with it like everyone else. This city, Bet. It's so *stifling*. We're all supposed to be good citizens and play our allotted part, but for the benefit of whom? It's not the people." She raised her mug and tossed back the contents.

"Why are you so angry?" Even with her mouthy poet friends, Megan was never this vocal. This environment had clearly knocked loose some impediment in her. "Sure, things are a little difficult sometimes," Bet went on. "But if we didn't practice conservation we'd lose everything within a dozen Darks. The Lunane does his best for the city. He always has done. If it hadn't been for him we wouldn't even be here."

"I'm angry because the Cataclysm, the Founding, all that, was *five hundred years* ago. We don't need rescued now. We don't need to procreate to survive or all pull together. It's just become...habit. And still we all have to live these tight, tidy little lives. No risks, Bet. No rewards. Not for us anyway." She tossed the cup back again only to find it empty. She thrust it out. "Your round."

It was an old argument. Bet was constantly surprised at her own willingness to engage in it, to defend a way of life that contorted who she was out of shape, squashed it down until you could hardly tell by looking that she was any different from her neighbours. She took their mugs and joined the queue at the trestle bar. She'd hardly touched her own drink, and wondered if they'd have something else that wasn't booze. Tonight was proving difficult enough without both of them getting drunk too, which at the rate Megan was knocking it back seemed inevitable. And the last thing anyone needed was a Darkday hangover.

"You can always just bring it back next month." The Host had an uncanny ability to appear unnoticed. "Your token. There's a good chance that the luck was used up anyway. If you actually believe in that stuff."

"Well, the monkeys..."

"There must be a reason for all their scampering around giving things to people?" The Host's smile softened into something that almost looked genuine. "Maybe. Hey, at Comedia we don't mind what you believe. If you believe that a monkey's going to change your life one day, fine. If you don't..." He shrugged. "All we care about here is that everyone feels free to express themselves. Be the person they really are. More than they normally can, you know...*outside*."

Bet nodded. Club Comedia had turned out entirely differently from her expectations. "I'm not very sure who I *really* am."

"Then I hope being here helps you work that out." The Host inclined his head to the other side of the room where Megan slouched on the couch. "Both of you."

"Oh, Megan has no reservations about being who she really is."

The Host made a face. "She has no issues with projecting the person she'd like to be seen as, certainly. Ooh, *so daring*. So, *provocative*. But that's hardly the same thing now is it?"

Bet was too astonished by his presumption to reply. Instead, she changed the subject. "And who are you," she said. "On the outside?"

The Host leaned close enough for her to smell the mothballs from his suit. "Why, I'm the Lunane, my dear," he whispered, then put a finger to his lips. "But don't let on." The Host raised his eyebrows and then swivelled slowly away from her, whistling nonchalantly. It took Bet a few moments to recognise the schoolyard tune: *The Lunane is every man, and every man is he.* The myth that the King occasionally came down from the Palace to visit among his people wearing whatever face suited his purpose was a thing told to children to keep them in line. Bet found the joke patronising.

"That's not going to last long is it?" Megan frowned into the mug when Bet handed her a judicial half measure, but drank it anyway. "What did he want?"

"Not much." Bet rubbed the pearl in her pocket. "Just telling me about this place. Some people bring those old luck tokens back every month."

"Well, we'll not be coming back next month, will we?"

"Won't we?"

"Of course not, because..." Megan's scowl couldn't contain all of the disaffection she clearly needed to express. "Because, okay, no—this place is not what I was *looking for*. I wanted somewhere daring, somewhere dangerous. But such a gathering obviously doesn't exist in Glassholm, does it? This? This is...a neutered *sop*." As her diatribe rose in volume, people looked over. Megan stared back until they looked away.

"You know, maybe if you were able to express a tiny bit of community spirit instead of pushing against everyone all the time," Bet hissed, "you might get on better." Megan looked stung and Bet immediately regretted speaking her mind. This place really had a knack of loosening tongues.

"How can you say that?" Megan's whisper was shocked. "What is so *fucking* wrong with wanting to be who I am?"

Bet didn't have an answer and she was saved from having to find a response by the advent of another act on the stage. The satirical playlet on the subject of childbirth managed to lampoon both the stuffy infirmary nurses and the eccentric Church Of Women while the comically, heavily pregnant woman who had sought their advice just wanted to be allowed to give birth. It was witty enough in places but Bet no longer felt like laughing. Megan disappeared half way through to top up her mug again. When she came back she drank in silence.

The acts that followed were of a similar mode to the ones that had gone before: cheap and amateurish, but heartfelt. Comedia allowed its patrons and performers to say things that would have caused riots elsewhere, exercise feelings that they'd had to keep bottled up. It might have been cosy, but it had to be healthy, didn't it? What did Megan want, short of all out revolution?

Bet didn't notice the singer at first because the woman had made no effort to stand out: a plain sweater over a long skirt, a practical haircut, no make-up. She could just have walked in off the street: a factory worker or a waitress or a cleaner, one of the classes that were the tiniest cogs in the Lunane's great machine. But what a singular voice she possessed. Another time of the month it would have been pure and clear, but tonight the ragged throatiness suited her song's melancholy and embittered sentiment perfectly. The song was a rising howl of frustration at having to live one's entire life in a city that never changed, under a king who never aged. *Like a moth frozen in a moon beam*, she sang. *Drying up to dust*. On the last utterance of that line she pulled her hands from her skirt pockets and showered the audience in grey grit.

The front row were still wiping dirt from their eyes when the Host ambled back up. He had changed into an outlandish get-up that very loosely approximated the Lunane's official attire. A woollen balaclava for the cowl, a dressing gown for the robes of state, a pair of hobnail boots for the ceremonial shoes. He plonked a wooden stool on the stage and sat down heavily.

"Ladies and gentlemen," he declaimed with put-on pomposity, "the night is nearly over but, as is the Club Comedia tradition, we have one last piece of business to attend to." The audience hushed. "Yes, it's time for the Lunane," he indicated his attire and got a laugh, "to dispense his wisdom to you lucky people. Now, as you know, on Darkday we don't bother with all the rigmarole and ceremony of petitioning for a few seconds of his moonship's attention. No, here he just gives it to you straight. So, are you ready?" Without waiting for a response, the Host affected a comic gurn, face strained, eyelids fluttering. Then he pointed at a woman in the front row. "You, Imelda Cochrane. Don't give your brother any more money. He'll only blow it on the boxing." The surprised woman made a sound of protest, but he interrupted her. "You know it's true. Time to put your foot down, girl." As he spoke his tone gentled until the exchange was more like friends sharing confidences. The woman began to cry. The audience responded with a murmur that was half way between embarrassment and awed sympathy.

"Oh, come on." It was the first thing Megan had said for a while and the words were slurred. "It's a trick. Obviously, he knows her."

"The Lunane knows everyone, doesn't he?" Bet whispered back.

She pretended not to hear Megan's, "Oh, fuck off."

The next one went the same way. After another bout of gurn and eye-flutter the mock-Lunane identified a lanky lad among a group who had been the source of the room's swagger all night. This time he came down off his perch to sit beside the lad and spoke quietly to him. Whatever was said was missed by most in the room, but the boy quickly turned pale and when the Host left him his friends gathered round to offer him comfort.

The Host may have been lampooning the Lunane, but he was doing the job exactly right. He toured the room, picking people out randomly and dispensing advice that was sometimes funny and sometimes serious, but always, it seemed, true.

Megan snorted. "Let's get out of here."

"Not yet."

"You're not telling me you're falling for this?"

Bet whirled to face her. "It was *your* idea to come here, remember?"

Megan got unsteadily to her feet, grabbed her coat from the arm of the sofa. "And it's my idea to leave."

"Don't be stupid. You can't go out onto those streets on your own."

Megan was already moving towards the door. "Then I guess you'd better come and protect me."

Bet swore. Loudly enough to snag the attention of several audience members who stared at her with annoyance. For a moment she was tempted to sit right back down and enjoy what remained of the night, letting Megan fend for herself out there, but her conscience intervened. She slipped her coat on and headed for the exit. She had her fingers on the velvet, ready to pass through the curtain when she felt a hand on her arm, a warm voice in her ear. Words of wisdom from someone who seemed to know her better than she knew herself.

"He didn't say that." Megan was half-incredulous, half-angry.

Bet kept walking. They had already passed from Chicken Town into Dockton but even here she didn't want to stop and have an attention-grabbing argument. Not on Darkday night, not any time. "Believe me, he did."

"Politicized...*what* was it?"

"Politically-motivated attention-seeker who brandishes her sexuality like a protest flag." Bet quoted the Host's words as if he'd only right then whispered them.

"What utter bullshit. Of course I protest. If no-one protests, how can we expect anything to change?" Then, as if it was an afterthought, "And I do so know the meaning of the word *love*."

Bet kept walking. It hadn't felt like bullshit. It had felt like listening to a voice inside her that had been yelling for her attention for months. Only, with every step she took the certainty of that voice leaked away. Soon, they'd be home and there'd be hugs and soft words and they'd wake up in the morning ready to struggle through the new wax as if nothing had changed.

She needs taken in hand, the Host had said. *A strong word from one who loves her, to smooth out her life and yours. The founding principles of this city are conformity and compliance. They're the only reasons we're here.* She felt in her pocket, found the pearl, the luck gift that, if she had faith in their society's mystical mechanism of co-dependency, might promise a chance of change.

"Well, *isn't* it?" Megan grabbed her arm. "Babe?" Bet kept walking, rubbed the pearl, felt its solidity. When they reached the door of their tenement Megan stopped. "He wasn't the King, you know? It's all a con."

Bet stopped too, finally turning to face her. "It doesn't matter whether he was or not. Megan, this city isn't going to change, not ever." It was the truth, they both knew it. People who visited from other nations might bring stories of societal progress, but Glassholm's cycle was eternal, a machine in which all the pieces had to bend to fit. "He said something else too. That there's always a stage at Comedia if you need it. That's what the club is for, and I'm going back next month end, with you or without."

And what about me? she'd asked the man who wasn't, couldn't be, the Lunane, but nevertheless gave her the comfort she had always sought.

You? And all the care in the world had been in that smile. *My girl, you're a good citizen of Glassholm, is what you are.*

Everyone knew that the Lunane never left the Palace, but if he ever was to decide to don a disguise and visit the neediest of his people on Darkday night, then Bet thought that tonight would have been a perfect example of his care for his community. Those who needed cheer got that, those who needed solace and comfort got those too, and those who needed to let out their deepest frustrations got that chance there as well.

That's what she told herself anyway as tried and failed to find sleep in the unforgiving silence of Darkday night. In which she was forced to acknowledge one more thing.

If, during his hypothetical ministrations, the King were to encounter anyone who happened to be in need of a coward's escape, they would be fullish in the extreme not to have taken it.

The Last Great Failing of the Light

Samuel Marzioli

Solis had commenced and the Festival of the Forever Sun was well underway. Ever since dawn's light first peered over the horizon, townspeople had crammed the streets of Magtagal in honor of longer days and shorter nights. Even children joined the gaiety, laughing and chanting as they waved golden streamers in the air.

As for me, I had no time for festivals: for drinking and dancing; for the singing of raucous songs; for food carts and trinket sellers; or for the evening feasts where they wheeled in roasted hogs with their throats slit and their insides hollowed out. Since I had been born in distant lands, Solis days meant little more to me than extra light and extra time to bleed and sweat and toil.

While I'd woken early with all the others, I spent the brunt of the morning peeling wood from my neighbor Amado's rooftop. By noon, I managed to isolate the damage he had suspected. It was a patch of dry rot three meters long and half as wide, a simple fix even with the meager tools I'd brought. But as I carved away the feeble timber from the rafters, the light began to waver and an airy roar melded with winds blowing from the north. Clouds appeared, thick and black as smoke. They sailed across the vault of heaven and, once they reached the opposite horizon, day descended into dusk.

The townspeople drew together for comfort, staring up at the spectacle; others watched from windows or through open doors.

"Is it a storm?" a young girl asked, tugging on her father's arm.

I turned to face the crowd below me. "No, it's worse. This is dayglow!"

Some began to tremble. Most stared on in confusion, having been born too late to remember the Great Failing of the Light and the destruction that followed. A time that nearly brought our people to extinction.

"It means that abomination, the Kivranmak, has awoken. The Iblis have returned. We must flee before it's too late!"

This everyone understood, and panic swept the streets.

The Kivranmak—a giant ball of flesh—tumbled through the sky like a moon let loose from the firmament. A horde of Iblis monstrosities swarmed across the western scrublands and in the ocean to the north. While some townspeople waited for the Datu's orders, the rest of us hurried to our homes to prepare for evacuation.

It didn't take long for me to assemble my provisions. I loaded three packs with blankets, clothes, food and water, and a barrow full of wood for fires. No sooner had I opened my door than the crier's voice rang out, backed by the steady thump of men on horseback.

"By the Datu's decree: wives and daughters, barricade your doors. Fathers and sons, arm yourselves and gather by the shoreline."

My heart shuddered as I stowed my things out of sight and went to greet Bayani, the leader of the maharlika. He and over fifty men were organizing the assembly, already wearing the deep red baros of their battle dress. Men and boys waved to their loved ones, their faces grim or sodden with tears, as they settled in a line behind them.

"Be reasonable, Bayani," I said. "If all the remaining powers of the world united, we still couldn't defeat the Iblis. Let us go. If the Datu wants to save this town, he can guard it on his own."

He cantered closer and regarded me with tightly knitted brows. "We have our orders, Marden, and so do you."

I leaned in closer, lowering my voice. "Then consider I'm not from here. I have no roots, no wife or children. For years, I've labored for the good of Magtagal, but in the end I fight and die for no one."

He glowered and tossed me a sword, still in its scabbard. I caught it and hefted its foreign weight in my hands.

"Coward. You've enjoyed our town in times of peace, now defend it in our time of war," he said.

"There won't be any war today, just our extermination."

Bayani nodded, his expression resolute, as if he already knew it.

We stood four hundred strong when all were accounted for. At the farthest edges of our perimeter, we lit bonfires, a measure known to ward off smaller Iblis. Five heavy cannons were spread out to face each advancing front. Behind them loomed the maharlika on horseback, armed with swords and flintlock rifles. The rest of us—fishers, metal smiths, weavers, merchants, servants, carpenters and farmers—crowded in the rear. With weapons drawn, we stared in fear and awe as the Iblis horde drew nearer.

The Kivranmak arrived first. Once it settled over town, a hush fell and every face turned toward that quivering mass of flesh. Far from a mindless brute, a look of cunning filled the many eyes strewn across its body. Each of them returned our stares as if probing, counting, determining our fate. Silence gave way to a rumble of terror that spread throughout our ranks; I used the confusion to steal away.

After collecting the provisions from my house, I slipped back into the streets. A faint wind ruffled golden streamers, their tail ends slithering in the dust, supple and alive. Cries from wives and daughters leaked through the walls of their hiding places, and I imagined them as bleating carabaos, awaiting the coming slaughter. Once I reached the edge of town, I fled toward the plains beyond the southern border.

"Marden!" a voice shouted from behind me.

Malea stood buried in the shadow of the Kinvranmak, an arm wrapped around her son Lawin. I'd known her for many years: a wash maid during working hours, but something more to the rich merchant Danilo at night. She'd always been a frail thing, but with the blackness of her hair framing the borders of her sallow face, she looked almost cadaverous.

"Go home and hide," I said. "It isn't safe out here."

"Take us with you," she said, dropping to her knees, forcing her son down next to her. "Please!"

"You may come," I said, cursing the words the moment they spilled from my lips.

A blur of motion on the outskirts of town caught my eye, as if something had loosened from the ground and bounded in Malea's direction. However, when my eyes rested on the spot I found nothing but dust and empty shadows. We ran from that place with all our might. Shouts grew and merged with the sporadic crack of gunfire and the tremulous boom of cannons, but soon the Iblis' wicked howls absorbed all sound, save the chorus of screams that followed.

Three miles south we turned to gauge our progress. Before, the Kivranmak had swung in patient arcs; now its body made violent rotations, as if spurring on its Iblis horde. Directly beneath it, Magtagal lay wrapped in squirming darkness, everything from the houses lining its borders to the tip of the central temple's steeple.

Forty years had passed since I'd seen a sight like this before, but I felt no different than I had then. My body shook, and my insides screamed for the lives lost—first my parents all those years ago and now the neighbors I'd left behind.

"Are we safe?" said Lawin, his voice quivering.

"Yes, we're safe," said Malea, hugging him close, wiping the tears from his eyes.

"Do you promise?"

"Yes, I promise. Nothing can hurt us now."

If I could have peeled my eyes away, I might have shouted at her for the false hope she gave her son. Fleeting comfort was no excuse for careless words. While our greed for life had impelled us toward the mere chance of refuge, in truth there was no safety left—except for those already dead and rotting underground.

We continued on for some time. Lawin's child-stump legs slowed us to a plod, and Malea wasn't much better stooped under the weight of a single pack. By the time we stopped for rest, we'd only added another four miles between us and home.

We camped in the barrens, spotted by clumps of withered grass left over from the rain season. I'd heard it had once been a thriving route between cities, where merchants lugged their wares to and from every corner of the continent. But trade had dried up along with the Great Failing of the Light, leaving it abandoned—except for us and wagon tracks pressed into the earth like remnants of an ancient civilization.

I set up a warding fire while Malea and Lawin laid out our bedding. They drifted off soon after, leaving me to keep watch alone. A curtain of night descended around us. Earlier, I'd seen a ridge of hills to the west, and to the east a grove of mahogany, withered and charnel. Now the world bled black too thick for human eyes to pierce.

In the silence, I thought about the movement I'd seen in the shadows before we'd left Magtagal. So much more threatening now that I was in a calmer state of mind. Briefly, I wondered if we'd been followed, if even now the Iblis were converging on our position, ready to burst into our midst and finish what they'd started. Though it may have been a product of my idling brain, I couldn't shake the feeling that the darkness gathered in, watching us and waiting.

The next day we woke and assembled our gear. Dayglow remained, reducing the sun to a faint crimson ball. To the north, the Kivranmak hung above Magtagal, throbbing like a beating heart. It could only mean one thing: the town had fallen. Malea wept in swells when she saw it and Lawin, too young to interpret the tidings of that sky behemoth, held her hand against his cheek.

"Don't cry, Mommy. We're safe, remember? You promised me we're safe."

Despite myself, I laughed. Somewhere far off I thought I heard the laughter caught up and echoed by another voice. Baleful, deeper toned, quiet so that it filled only the narrow cracks of silence.

"Let's go," I said, eager to press on.

We swung east to collect more firewood. Up close, the mahogany grove appeared no larger than a lake, with trees spread wide, as if each preferred their solitude among the collective. Focused in the center clearing, bones lay jumbled among the dust and litterfall, laced with the fragments of wagon tarps. No doubt the vestige of some previous Iblis awakening.

"You two stay here," I said and rolled the barrow in.

I collected fallen twigs for kindling and tore branches off the brittle trees. Once I replaced what we'd used the previous night, I hurried out—noticing movement only when I'd rounded on the barrens. A carabao skull was seated on a pile of bones, its lower jaw hanging wide, its blackened sockets fixed in my direction. I took another step to test my suspicions and, sure enough, it swiveled and caught me again within its line of sight. It had to be an Ibli, and now it had my scent.

"I see you," I said, pulling my sword from its scabbard.

"I see you," it said, its voice coarse, flapping the carabao's lower jaw as if to mock me.

The skull's sockets wept gray and its mouth vomited the same. The runoff collected in a pile and hardened like a scab. Compound eyes emerged across its body. Tentacles bloomed from its torso and a beak extended like a spear from the center of its face. I barely had the time to lift my sword before it was upon me.

It flailed its appendages like whips, darting away from the inelegant swing of my blade. I managed to sever a plot of its eyes, but the wound mended before it even bled. I wasn't so lucky. Blood streamed from the gashes it slapped into my arms and side, making my hands slick and wet, weakening my grip. After it ensnared my leg, I fell to my knees. It wasted no time surging forward, stabbing me in the chest with its beak, thrashing its body side to side to force itself in deeper.

To my surprise, I felt no pain. My mind drifted to better days, long before the word Iblis held meaning. Back to a particular night when my parents had put me to bed at the end of a blazing, Solis day. "You're safe. We'll always protect you," they'd said, as earnest and false as Malea's promise to Lawin.

With that, I collapsed to the ground, lost in a roiling cloud of numbness.

"Martin? Martin, what's wrong?" Malea said, standing beside me with a hand upon my shoulder.

Her clothes had changed, no longer the mishmash brown and white stripes of a peasant. Now she wore a clean silk baro and matching skirt, swirling with shades of yellow, the color of—

"Sunlight," I said.

I looked up. Tucked into a corner of the sky, the sun burned fierce and unrestrained. I reached a hand out toward its warmth, laughing, clapping, chanting, "Dayglow is through! They've gone to sleep! The Iblis have gone to sleep!"

Malea took a step back. She folded her arms, unsure, as if I were the fool that didn't understand.

"Malea, don't you know what this means?" I said.

"It's Maleah," she said, the end of her name punctuated by a hard "h." She cocked her head. "Martin, you're acting so strange."

"Marden," I said in the same admonishing tone she'd used.

As quickly as I spoke, I knew I was mistaken. In that moment I became aware of this new world, with sprawling cities that spanned the continents—the kind of civilization that could only arise if the Iblis never were. My whole life flashed before me. The enduring peace of it. The simplicity that came without the constant threat of monsters. But more than that, I saw my time with Maleah: our courtship, our wedding, the birth of our son Heath, who was different from Lawin in that his eyes were green, not brown. Here, I hadn't merely endured; I'd lived and loved, and even made a family.

I shuddered, not from fear, but because of the intoxicating joy I felt. Caring only that blessed daylight had returned at—"

Dried old mahogany. Stunted dayglow. Staring at the desiccated earth level with my eyes.

"No," I said, pushing myself from the ground, wishing I could rip the unwelcome sight away like a veil from my eyes.

From what I'd gathered since the Great Failing of the Light, there were two kinds of Iblis: those that devoured flesh and those that consumed the minds of men. When the Kivranmak came for the city of my birth, my parents hid me beneath the floorboards of our house. I watched through cracks as the Iblis ravaged them and ate them piece by piece. Besides me, two others survived that day. Whatever they'd seen had driven them beyond insanity, to a place where self-harm was their only source of comfort. Since I was alive, it wasn't hard to guess which kind of Ibli I had met.

"Where's that Ibli?" I said, my voice croaking.

"Gone," said Malea. "It grabbed your sword and slipped back into the grove."

"Are you injured? Where's Lawin?"

"He's fine. We're both fine. You're what matters now. We saw you fall and believed that you had—"

"Not yet."

Shifting to a seated position, I lifted my baro to inspect the wound, bracing for the worst. But no puncture or scar marred the skin of my chest. The sigh that escaped my mouth would have made the winds blush with envy. After Malea bound my arms and leg with strips from her skirt, we headed south again, fully stocked with wood.

Most of my life I'd walked in silence, my mind left open to impressions made by my surroundings. This time I tried to forget that hallucination, or dream, or whatever it may have been. Yet try as I might, I could still feel the warmth of sunlight and knew that for a moment, one perfect stretch of time, I'd found true happiness at last.

Five miles onward, the barrens gave way to a meadow dotted with orange poppies and the occasional oak. The range of hills I'd seen before formed a barrier to our right. From our vantage point, I couldn't tell how deep they ran and, with the way I'd been favoring my right leg, I hoped we'd never have to find out.

We rested under a thriving mango tree. There we ate more than salted meats and dried rice. Malea and I were ambivalent for the reprieve, but Lawin munched his share of mango like a special treat.

"Do you like them?" I said to Lawin, offering him another.

He looked at me, stunned, and took it from my hand without a word. I returned his stare with the same confusion. After all, I'd never spoken to him before, nor had I ever wanted to. So why now?

From then on no one said a word, save for Lawin's happy chatter as he lay, poking insects on the ground. Malea took out a comb and began unraveling the tangles of her hair. As for me, that other place dominated my thoughts. The years of Martin's life remained stark and fresh within my mind, as if they were true memories.

Malea must have sensed something was wrong because she asked, "What's the matter?"

"I'm just thinking," I said.

"About that Ibli that attacked you?"

"Not exactly."

"Then what?"

I almost huffed and turned away like I'd done to her so many times before, both on this journey and during our various encounters in Magtagal. But when I looked into her eyes, the mirror reflection of Maleah—save for her slumped posture and the many wrinkles etched into her skin—the anger didn't come.

"Do you believe in other worlds?"

She winced. "The ones we go to after death?"

"I mean something much like this one, but for a single difference. Like a place where the sun is blue or grass is red. Or a place where the Iblis never existed."

She smiled, but it quickly slid into a frown. "No. Do you?"

"Would it be so strange if I did?"

She chewed the words in her mind, narrowed her eyes, and said, "Yes. It sounds much too hopeful and you, Marden, have never struck me as a hopeful man.""

Sometime before nightfall, the Kivranmak floated over us, its motion punctuated by sporadic jerks. Already we could hear the Iblis, their ecstatic moans lacing the wind, low as the rumble before an earthquake. We turned east, entering a broad dale, and managed to bed down before the hidden sun slipped below the horizon.

Before I settled in, I scanned the borders of our camp. For a second I thought I saw a few pinpoints of light beyond the fire's range and I imagined the Ibli from before, its compound eyes glaring at us through the darkness.

"I see you," I said.

There came no response, but I had every intention of keeping the fire strong until dayglow returned. I lay down, facing stars that would not twinkle, and a moon that would not shine, pretending Maleah was by my—

I returned to that sunlit world, now standing in a garden behind a house I knew was mine. Malkohas clicked and warbled from the branches of the surrounding trees. Across the way, a white cat skirted the edges of a trunk, measuring the distance between itself and the lowest branch. What's more, the air tasted fresh, bearing the sweet scent of plumeria, and the grass felt thick and soft beneath my bare feet. While I knew this had to be a dream, nothing in it struck me as false.

A familiar voice said, "Are you sure you're alright? You've been acting strange for days."

I spun around and found Maleah, her expression pinched and worried.

"Yes. I'm fine," I said.

A flutter filled my chest and I swallowed deep to loosen the lump building in my throat. Then I remembered that, here, I was Martin and Maleah was my wife. The nervousness I felt melted away at once and I embraced her, taking in her warmth, her scent, the feel of her body pressing into mine.

"What are you doing?" she said, sweeping glances left and right. "Someone may see us."

"It's not wrong for a husband to hold his wife."

She laughed and my insides stirred. "Some might call it unseemly."

"Let some call it what they like. I doubt I have much time left and I don't want to waste it worrying about the opinions of prying neighbors—I had a thought. Let's have a picnic, just you and me and Heath. We'll go to the beach, enjoy the sunlight—"

She eased herself from my grip. "I can't. I have business to attend to and Heath is coming with me. In fact, I'm late already. I only came to check on you, but I really should be going." She lifted herself on tiptoes and kissed my cheek. "I love you, Martin."

"I love you too," I said, and I realized I meant it.

I wasn't surprised when I woke lying in a bed of grass, but the frantic scream that had roused me from my sleep struck me senseless. Malea was huddled next to Lawin, crushing him in her grip while rocking back and forth, his name pouring from her throat in shrieks and wails. I didn't have to see him for myself to know that he was dead.

I threw myself beside Malea, wanting to console her, wanting to hold her like I'd held Maleah moments before. But I couldn't. When I saw the state of Lawin's body, it took all my strength to twist away and keep myself from vomiting.

Lawin. He could have been my son, but for the Iblis. Could have been my friend but for the hate inside me, born of four decades worth of misery. I'd treated him like nothing—nothing—and now I could never make it up to him.

"Show yourself!" I yelled between cupped hands, rising to my feet and glaring into the distance.

There came no response, no sound, except for the gentle hiss of wind blowing through the grass. As I staggered back to Malea, the echo of laughter from days before returned, still baleful, still low, hidden in the cover of silence like a shadow in the dark. We tarried in that place for hours. Malea huddled over Lawin while I dug a burial hole. I started by using the flat end of a branch to scrape the ground, but in the end, it proved easier to use my hands. Besides, the dirt and stones that wedged between my fingers and nails felt comforting, a token sacrifice of pain to honor Lawin's memory.

We laid his body inside the groove I'd made—careful to assemble his parts into their proper place—and covered him. Malea smoothed out the rough edges of the mound before collapsing on top of it for one final, tearful goodbye.

"Any last words?" I said.

She looked up at me. "You and I spoke before about other worlds. I only hope they do exist and that, one day, I'll join Lawin there."

"I believe they do. One way or another, we'll both see him again."

She rose to her feet and hugged me, kissing my cheek several times before falling into my embrace. I kept silent, allowing the solace of the moment to linger.

We traveled on much slower than before. The wounds of my leg had worsened, reducing me to a hobble, and Malea went no faster in her grief. Before long, the darkness took us by surprise, forcing us to build our fire in a hurry. Once we set out our bedding, Malea rested her head upon on my lap. I raked my fingers through her hair, humming ancient songs of comfort that my mother used to sing to me. She fell asleep still crying.

As I watched her slumber, it pained me to see how weary she looked. So frail a blade of grass might snap her bones. And yet, it didn't detract one ounce from her beauty. Now that Martin and I were one, in some way Maleah had also merged with Malea, and the feelings I had for this woman of soft snores and tear-stained cheeks surprised me with its suddenness and depth.

"My love," I whispered, and the words felt natural on my lips, as if a void had always been there, waiting for her to fill it.

Somewhere southwest of us, the guttural cries of the Iblis strengthened, too near for me to feel at ease. I wondered what town or city they ravaged now or how many more would fall before their thirst for blood was quenched. But more so, I wondered how much time remained for Malea and me, two travelers on the open road to nowhere.

When daybreak came, we spotted the city of Karagatan arrayed beside the coast. Though distant, we savored the thought of their future hospitality and the hope of restoring our supplies. But during the early hours of our trek, the Kivranmak glided past us and settled above our destination. The Iblis couldn't be too far behind.

In our panic, we quickened our pace, glancing around to discover the route the Iblis had taken. For a while, all seemed calm. I began to hope they'd been waylaid by the maharlika of some other city, long enough for us to make it through the dale. That hope didn't last for long. The Iblis' moans drifted in from the west and we turned to find a swelling line of black devouring the landscape.

"What do we do?" said Malea, eyeing the Kivranmak and the Iblis in turn.

The dale hedged us in along the north and south with rampant hills too steep to climb. But farther east, I spotted the means of our escape.

"See there?" I said, pointing to where the northern ridge petered into hillocks.

"We'll never make it," said Malea, already panting.

"We have to try."

I shoved the barrow aside and ran, pushing through the pain, dragging Malea by the hand. When we fell, we helped each other up. When we stumbled, we pulled each other straight. Yet despite it all, the Iblis horde drew nearer.

By the end of the first mile, their cries intensified into roars. By the end of the second, their roars became deafening screeches. The black line of their advancing front broke into a herd of silhouettes, each with thrashing limbs and scrambling feet. By the third mile, the Iblis further clarified. Most were humanoid, but others crept on all fours, and others still were so twisted and twined within themselves that they defied description.

Finally, my leg gave out and I collapsed, too heavy for Malea to lift. Nevertheless, she tried and each time ended up on the ground beside me.

"It's no use," she said.

"No, it can't end like this."

"But—"

"It can't!" I shouted.

I wouldn't give up, not with everything at stake: a life with someone I loved and cared for, who might someday learn to love me too. So long as I breathed, we would crawl to safety. And that's exactly what I did, inching along, pulling the hopeless Malea against her will.

We gained ten more feet before the Ibli that had murdered Lawin pooled above the surface of the soil. It collected and solidified, staring through its outcropped eyes, shifting to block our path in whatever direction we tried to crawl.

"Let us pass!" I screamed.

The Ibli chuckled, that same baleful laughter from before. I realized then that it had been following us from the beginning, that it was the source of movement in the shadows at Magtagal's edge. For what purpose, to what end, I couldn't guess.

"You spared my life this long, so spare it again. What use will I be to you if I fall into the hands of your bloodthirsty kin?"

The Ibli sprouted tentacles, one on each side of its bulbous body. "Sleep," it said.

My body locked. I fell to my side and the world drained into a void.

When I found myself again in Martin's garden, I crumbled to my knees and faced the sun, taking it in until my eyes burned and watered and my vision blurred. I prayed to every power I could think of, every god or demon who had ever been said to concern themselves with the fleeting world of man. And then I waited.

"Malea," I said, clenching my fists so that my nails cut into my palms. "I'll come back for you. I'll come back and save you, somehow."

The promise rang false and hollow even to my ears. Nevertheless, I meant them and vowed to make them true. From then on I braced myself, trying not to think about what I would find upon my return. Or what would be left.

I opened my eyes and looked around. Our packs had been shredded into fine strips of leather too small to ever be of use again, and our supplies were crushed and scattered in the dust. A glance at Karagatan confirmed the Iblis had already passed me by, but I could find no sign of Malea. Not a scrap of cloth, a strand of hair, or a drop of blood. And so, I turned to the one thing left by my side.

"Why? Why me?" I said to the Ibli.

A sound like gurgling emitted from its mouth. "I liked your bitterness, your cowardice, the taste of your pain. I wanted more."

"This is the end. The end of everything," I said, staring vacantly at the Iblis horde laying waste to Karagatan.

"Yes."

"So what will happen to me now? Will you kill me too?"

"If you turn west."

"And east, to Karagatan?"

"Whether you die by my hand or by my brethren is of no concern to me. So long as you die."

I nodded, more out of habit than a desire to respond. But I couldn't leave quite yet. I had one more question that needed answering.

"Tell me. That world you sent me where the daylight never fails and the Iblis never were. Was it real or a figment of your creation?"

"What would make you suffer more? Being where you could never stay or craving what could never be?"

"Either way I'm ruined."

With that, I hauled myself to my feet and stumbled off to greet my fate, to meet the Kivranmak a third time. For a moment, the Ibli watched me go and then sunk beneath the ground, disappearing from sight. Only then did I allow myself to smile.

Toward the end of our encounter, I'd painted my face with sorrow to let it think it won. But after forty years, I'd found the reason behind the promise my parents had made to me, and the one Malea had made to Lawin. It was hope, a belief that even in the face of all this suffering better things would come, and what is dreamed and what is real would both someday converge.

So now, at the end, this was hope to me: that I would fall asleep before the Iblis found me and go again to that world of light, where the spirit of Malea and Lawin lived on. Once all bonds to this place were severed, and my body died, there I would remain the rest of my days, with a family this nightmare world had never allowed.

Maybe it wouldn't happen that way; my mind accepted that possibility. Nevertheless, as I headed for Karagatan, it wasn't a march toward imminent destruction. I went to hope, borrowed from Martin, refined by love, strengthened by the memory of sunlight, and sealed by promises that I finally, finally understood.

Firebird

By Nitai R. Poddar

One night, the Emperor dreamed of a firebird. Its wings were flame and its tail a trail of smoke. He summoned his physician and described the dream to him.

"The August Emperor has witnessed a Firebird," said Zhao. "The Firebird knows not the pangs of death, being reborn through the same fires that destroy it. The portent is auspicious to the person of the August Emperor, and predicts a swift recovery from the pernicious affliction that troubles his spirit."

"Find it," said the August Emperor. "Capture the creature, lay it upon your surgical tables and sever from it the secret of immortality. Eternal life is the purview of man and God, not bird and beast."

The next morning, amid streaming banners and the call of bugles, the August Emperor gathered his hunting party and departed for the Endless Mountains, which were said to be the abode of the Firebird. The August Emperor rode in the splendor of his palanquin, bedecked with the colors of the Imperial House, and accompanied by his three sons: Jin, Yin, and Tong.

In his palanquin rode his daughter, Meilin, born to him by his favorite concubine. Meilin inherited none of her mother's courtly grace and effortless charm; being plain and ungainly, with hair and eyes the color of iron, she resigned herself to attend upon the August Emperor as a servant.

"You ought to let the old man fall asleep and stay asleep," said Tong. He had developed a habit of riding beside the palanquin to keep his sister company. They spoke through the veil of scarlet that separated the palanquin from the world. "And do open the curtain sometimes. Let the sunlight reach his face, for once."

"Our August Father dislikes the sunlight," said Meilin. "Daylight implies night, and reminds him of the passage of time. It makes his melancholy worse."

She touched the silken curtain. Tong drew it aside. He wore an expression of profound distaste. Meilin had crouched to one side at the palanquin's corner, her legs drawn up and her chin resting upon her knees. Her hair was loose and long in iron-dark locks that tangled at the ends, and dark rings encircled her eyes. Beside her lay their Imperial Father, his white beard smeared across his face and shaking with his breath. Meilin frowned.

"What did I just say?" she said.

"He isn't the man I remember," said Tong. "Do you remember when he'd return in triumph from his campaigns? Seven white horses at his vanguard, caparisoned in silver and shining like the Pleiades. Captives by the thousands. War chests filled to overflowing."

"I don't," said Meilin. "I was not allowed to attend the triumphs."

"Ah," said Tong. He averted his eyes, embarrassed. "So, Firebirds. Great, blazing things that circle the sky and live forever. Personally, I think it's…"

"Mmmh," said Meilin. Her fingers smoothed through her hair. Her eyes glanced out beyond Tong's shoulder. Brought forth from the palace for the first time in her life, she watched the world roll by, enraptured. Forests greener than the silks of palace courtiers; trees straight and tall, arrayed like the spears of an army, piercing the summer sky; mountains in the distance, their range endless, peaks crowned in mist.

"...the slow onset of senility. Ridiculous, really. Sister, are you listening?"

"I'd like to come with you," she said. The words came slow and dreamy, and for a moment she wasn't sure if she'd spoken or imagined them. Tong raised both eyebrows, closed his mouth, opened it again, laughed. "I'm quite serious," she said. "I can use a bow. I can ride a horse. I have been taking lessons."

"To what end?"

"I must be useful for something!"

"You are useful to our father."

"He has no end of handmaidens. Let me come with you."

Tong paused. He regarded Meilin. Her face was impassive, her eyes iron. "Ask our father," he said, "when he wakes. And—after he's done babbling about flaming poultry that grant him eternal life."

That evening, the hunting party of the Imperial Family set up camp at the foothills of the Endless Mountains. Banners of yellow and scarlet rose to salute the wind. Tents sprang up in the clearing. A bonfire followed, and wine flowed. The Emperor remained in his palanquin, having woken when the sun dipped behind the mountains and wreathed the camp in twilight. Braziers smoldered with sandalwood and coal, prescribed by the Emperor's physicians, to exorcise the temple of his mind of the demons of mortal dread. Meilin brought her father a plate of steamed rice and tea. He waved her aside.

"Come now, father," she said. "You have not eaten since last night."

"When I was a young man, I crushed the rebels at Scarlet Bay on an empty stomach," he replied. Meilin sighed. The moods of the August Emperor flowed in predictable patterns. She'd come to recognize the onset of melancholy, manifested first as wistful brooding, and then guilt, and then anger, and then long and sullen silence punctuated by barbed hostility.

Here it comes, she thought.

"I took lives as a hunter takes trophies," said the Emperor. "My armies returned to the gates of the Imperial Capital with the heads of their enemies slung over their shoulders. The wheels of my chariot plowed the earth; I sowed fire, harvested glory."

Meilin sighed. She put the plate of rice and the cups of tea on a nearby tripod, and sank to the grass beside the palanquin, her arms wrapped around her crossed knees. Years of service had taught her the futility of opposing her father during his darker moods.

You are growing old, she thought. *But you aren't the only one.*

Campfires sparkled across the clearing, guttering in the wind, spitting forth showers of sparks that rose, swirled, vanished. Meilin heard her father grunt, rise, stretch. He creaked like old timber.

"Jin leaves at dawn. Remind him," he said.

"Your son is aware of his duties."

"I sense the whiff of opprobrium in your tone, daughter."

"That is just the sandalwood from your ointments."

The Emperor laughed without mirth. "Where are my physicians," he said. Arching his back and setting his shoulders, he walked toward the encampment. Soldiers rose in his presence, parted to make way for his path. Meilin rose, followed him.

"Allow me to accompany my eldest brother tomorrow," she said.

"I forbid it," he answered, without turning, and without hesitating.

Then the August Emperor entered into the company of his black-clad physicians, who were many, and who flocked around him like dipping corvids. Meilin ate the neglected rice, drank the cold tea, and practiced her archery by the woods' edge.

At dawn, Jin, the eldest prince, led his hunting party into the Endless Mountains. Yin, the second prince, followed him. Tong, the third prince, lingered behind until noon before following the trail of banners that marched in serpentine formation up through the misty forests to disappear into the clouds. All day the August Emperor remained in the company of his physicians, to whom he leveled philosophical questions pertaining to the nature of mortality, and from whom he received answers both obsequious and vague. Meilin attended to her father; his manner remained listless, enervated by apathy.

He came alive when she asked about the firebird.

"What does it look like?" she said.

"Bright," said her father. "Bright as the sun, so that I do not know where the rays of its brilliance end and its wings begin."

His eyes shone as he spoke, and his voice had a feverish tension to it. Meilin believed little of the firebird's existence, but nonetheless appreciated the spark of vitality in her father's graying eyes. Delusion or otherwise, the pursuit of immortality had rekindled his ambition, a faculty Meilin knew to be essential to her father's spirit.

"Its cry parts the clouds. Its tail is sometimes a plume of smoke bellowed forth from the mouth of a volcano, sometimes a trail of incense smoke encircling the horizon, sometimes the tail of a falling star slashing across the sky like a blazing wound."

Then Meilin would offer him tea and rice, and being thus roused, the August Emperor would drink and eat, and speak of the firebird who haunted his dreams. When evening fell, and the Emperor rose from his tripod to walk among his physicians, Meilin would ask him again:

"Please allow me to accompany my noble brothers in the Endless Mountains, so that I may have the honor of bringing you the firebird you so desire."

And whenever she asked, her father would reply: "I forbid it."

Days rolled by like the wheels of a cart. The hunting camp grew restless, and with each passing day Meilin's stratagem returned diminishing results as her father grew more restless, more impatient for news of his elusive prey.

"Tell me about the firebird," she asked.

"Be gone. I no longer desire your company. Why did you not learn courtly grace, as your mother had?" he said.

And Meilin left him to his brooding and his physicians, and practiced her archery at the edge of the forests. Her arrows riddled the trunks of trees.

Then, on the seventh day, the banners of the First Prince were seen descending from the mists that encircled the Endless Mountains. They were tattered, and their bearers moved in a broken formation. Jin returned with his men. His face was haggard and pale, a mask of exhaustion. Meilin greeted him at the forest's edge.

"Jin. Did you find it? Did you find the firebird?"

He laughed. "The firebird? The firebird is native only to the interior of our heavenly father's imperial skull. For seven days we searched." He sighed, shook his head, ran gloved fingers through his matted hair. "Leave me. I will speak to our father over supper. My men are hungry."

"Jin, I've made a decision. I'm joining the hunt," said Meilin.

Jin paused, regarding his sister with a hint of a supercilious smile on his lips, as if the notion of Meilin making a decision was alien to him; but after seeing her straight-shouldered and square jawed, with her iron-colored hair drawn into a knot, and her hunting bow slung over her shoulder with a quiver of arrows, Jin's smile presently faded. He sucked air through his teeth.

"The hunt," he said, waving his hand toward the men at his back, "is finished. As I've told you, there is no firebird. We are all here entertaining our divine father's delusions, because we are dutiful children who humor him in his dementia—"

"I've made my decision," Meilin interrupted him, and immediately regretted her words. "I have never been beyond the palace. I have never seen the mountains. You and our brothers traveled with our father on his campaigns. I have a bow. I borrowed arrows from the soldiers. I can defend myself."

"There is no secret to immortality, sister. Death is the debt we owe to life, and our aging father dreads the collection. The firebird is a fool's errand, but a good prince behaves like a fool while the crown rests upon his father's head."

Meilin said nothing, being well accustomed to the pleasure with which the men of her family lectured her.

At length, Jin relented. "Take my horse, then. Yin and Tong have yet to return. I expect they are lost. If you are fortunate, you will meet them on the mountainside."

"Father will be disappointed in you," she said.

"He will learn to accept his disappointment. Only children believe they live forever," he said.

"What should I do if I find a firebird?"

"You will not."

"Yes, but say that I do."

"Shoot it from the sky. Present it to me."

"To you? Why?"

"If it exists, then the secret of immortality should go to one who is not suffering from senility."

Meilin thought about this. "But it doesn't exist."

"Indeed," said the First Prince, and returned to camp.

Meilin had taught herself to ride horses, but only ever within the confines of the Imperial Palace. Here the forest was trackless, but the horse was surefooted and clever, and Meilin guided her mount between the high pines shrouded in perpetual twilight. There were no trails here, but signs of her brothers' passage provided Meilin with an improvised route. She followed them up through the foothills.

It occurred to Meilin that she had never experienced a silence like this. The forest was heavy with quiet. She heard only the breath of her horse and the crunch of its hooves against the earth; the wind through the pines; the murmuring of streams; the creaking of her own saddle. Instinct seemed to propel her, and for the first moment in her life, she savored the silence.

Hours passed. The shadows deepened. The wind brought a chill to Meilin's face, and night draped its cloak over the foothills of the Endless Mountains. Her horse shuddered. She stroked its flank, dismounted, stretched her legs. She was in a clearing, and the air smelled of wet earth tinted with acrid smoke. Meilin washed her face, her hands, and her hair in a nearby stream. She drank from her cupped palms; the water was cold and sweet. At length Meilin curled on a bed of pine needles at the root of a great tree, wrapped herself in her cloak, and slept.

The sound of horses woke her. Meilin stirred, found herself staring up at the burnished masks of Imperial soldiers. They were crouched around her, some armed, some bearing torches. She saw a familiar face behind their ranks, made ghastly in the firelight.

"Why were you riding our eldest brother's horse?" said Yin. Meilin shielded her eyes, scrambled up to her knees, and felt the trunk of a pine tree at her back. Her head was throbbing.

"Yin? Brother said you were lost."

He shook his head. "He lied. Come, get up. There's shelter nearby. We've roasted deer. There may be a few scraps left for you."

"He lied? What do you mean?" said Meilin.

Yin mounted his horse and signalled his men. They surrounded Meilin in a wall of spears, and marched.

"Oh?" said Yin, glancing once over his armored shoulder, "No, I suppose he had no reason to tell you. We found the Firebird. It exists. It is quite real."

They marched through the night. Meilin could not see the sun rise, but felt the heat of day prickle against her neck, and the balmy wind rush under her cloak, bringing with it the scent of ash. By daybreak, the hunting party of Yin, second son of the August Emperor, arrived in a the ruins of a village of thatch and wood at the center of a great clearing. Yin noticed his sister's apprehension.

"Don't worry," he said, and passed her a wineskin. "The village was long since abandoned, purged by our divine father during his Northern Campaigns. Only their ghosts remain, and even they shield themselves from my hunting party."

Meilin gazed at him, bewildered. She turned her head, refusing the wineskin. Yin shrugged and quaffed a mouthful. "I don't understand," she said. "I met Jin by the forest's edge last morning. He told me the firebird—"

"—was a fiction? Yes, sister. That's because he is clever, whereas you are simple. Don't make that face. Your simplicity is endearing."

"I want an explanation," she said, chin lifted up eyes gazing at her brother with an iron sternness she inherited from her mother. Yin relented, opened his mouth as if to speak, but Meilin interrupted him. "In private, treated with a little dignity, if you please. I do not like speaking to you from inside a wall of spears, while you sit on your horse."

Yin shrugged, and with a wave of his hand, dismissed his soldiers. The wall of spears receded, parted, and Meilin marched through them. Yin dismounted and led her down the single dirt road dividing the ruined village, and into a cottage. This one had most of its roof intact. Light poured thick through broken windows, bearing motes of dust in its slant. Yin tossed himself into the iron frame of a chair and swung his legs over one arm. Like the rest of the village, the cottage had been abandoned, and its previous occupants left behind them the evidence of their lives. A mattress overturned, wooden plates rotting on a stone sink, bottles gathering cobwebs in a lightless corner—Meilin felt like an invader. Yin noticed his sister's discomfort. He took another long swallow from his wineskin.

"Are you drunk?" she asked. His posture was slack and his eyes dark. He had treated her with a degree of blasé disrespect she found surprising, even from him, and now she wondered if he'd been drunk when they met within the forests. Yin cocked his head to one side, as if listening for an answer.

"What else is there to do? I'm a husk of a village at the end of the world," he said. Meilin drew up a chair, sat herself opposite it and planted her arms on its frame.

"Why don't you start with an explanation?" she said.

"After three nights' hunting, our scouts witnessed a falling star low to the horizon by the light of the morning. Giving chase, our three hunting parties followed the star until we arrived in this village, or what remains of it. There I saw the creature with my own eyes, as did our brothers. Its wings were an inferno, its tail a tongue of fire, and its cry the cracking of thunderbolts."

"So our father's premonition was right?" said Meilin. "It does exist?"

"Indeed," said Yin. "We pursued, but the bird retreated into the mountains, where the roads are too narrow and dangerous for three hunting parties. Now we make camp in this village, and should the creature circle into our skies..."

"I don't understand," said Meilin. "Why lie to our father?"

Yin scowled. He set aside his wine and leaned over his seat.

"Use your head, sister," he said. "Say our father marches his men into the foothills, surrounds the Firebird, captures it, and wrings the secret of immortality from it for himself? And then do we suffer eternity under the rule of a melancholy old man? The purpose of an heir is to pass on the legacy of the father through the son; what use are heirs to the man who lives forever?"

Meilin gazed at him askance, with an expression that combined vexation with disbelief. "You are," she said, in a slow and measured voice, "quite mad, brother. If you and your men saw the creature with your own eyes, then yes, I will believe you. But what is this nonsense about immortality? Supposing the creature lived forever, how do you intend to inherit that power? Do you drink the blood of a tiger to inherit its courage?"

Yin sniffed. "The physicians seem to think so." Meilin rolled her eyes. He pressed his point. "Once we have it in captivity, we may by methods of natural philosophy understand its secrets. And," he said, shrugging, "if not? Then we spare our father the embarrassment of failure."

Meilin rose from her seat.

"Wait!" said Yin. "Where are you going? I won't permit you to return to our father. My soldiers—"

"Ridiculous," she said. "Why would I want to return? This is the first time I have stepped outside our father's domicile, the first day I have spent without any duties. I do not want to return to serving him his rice and his tea, applying his ointments and salves, or listening to him mutter fearful things about his own mortality. Today is the first day I have taken a horse out into the woods, or watched the light of day fall through the tops of trees. I," she added, slowing her tone to enunciate every word, "want to see the firebird with my own eyes."

"Alone? You will be burnt alive."

"You and your hunting parties survived, did you not?"

"We were at a safe distance."

"I want to see it, Yin. I have made up my mind."

Yin dragged his hands through his hair, tugging with his fists. He grit his teeth in consternation. "Tong said the same thing. The two of you are too alike in blood. Go then. Follow the village road into the eastern mountains, and look for the falling star."

Meilin never looked behind her when she left Yin's cottage, the ruined village, the royal huntsmen who watched at her with equal parts suspicion and bewilderment as she fetched her horse, mounted her saddle, and followed the village road up into the mountains. The mountains loomed over her, violet peaks clothed in green and smeared with the fading mist of morning. She rode through the afternoon, until the beaten path broke away, and the road faded into rough grass and passages too narrow for a horse; so she said goodbye to her borrowed mount, gathered her bow and her arrows, and proceeded on foot.

Now she walked above the forest of spears, and her path curved along the mountain's face, ever rising. The trail was narrow and treacherous, but the air of the mountain filled her lungs, brighter and sweeter than any incense of the palace. To the west, against the canvas of sunset splashed with violet and scarlet, above cream-colored clouds smeared across the horizon in thick brushstrokes, shone a single point too bright and too near to be a falling star. It gleamed and flashed like the beacon of a lighthouse in the center of a sea of stone against which marble waves broke. A tower, black against the sunset, its summit a pulsing blaze. Mei felt her breath catch in her throat, her muscles taut with excitement, exhaustion, and the strange sense of freedom that compelled her.

Dusk faded into twilight, and twilight into night; stars emerged, arranged in radiance behind the blazing tower like the jewels of a diadem on the head of a queen.

Her legs burned from exertion, and every breath filled her lungs with gusts of chilled air that settled and froze in her chest. The ache in her body burned like smoldering coals. Sweat matted her iron-dark hair to her neck and her face, but she had arrived. At the summit of the tower burned a blazing pyre, too bright to behold; Meilin averted her eyes, approaching the tower by the sight of her shadow.

The interior: stone floor, stone wall, stone stairs spiraling upward; firelight poured in from high above the stairs, casting the interior in a warm glow. There, on a bench beneath the staircase, lay a figure wrapped in a cloak, with a cloth over his eyes. He turned his head at the sound of her entry.

"Who is it? Yin?" he said.

Meilin's eyes spread in recognition. "Tong!" she said.

"Sister! Why are you—is anyone with you? Did you come alone? Oh, for Heaven's—" Tong muttered, sat up from his bench, knocked his skull beneath the stairs. His blindfold slipped from his eyes. He grimaced, squeezed his eyes shut. Meilin approached him, finding her way into the tower by running her hand along the stone walls.

"No," she said. "I'm alone. What are you doing out here?"

"Hunting our illustrious father's golden goose. At least I have an excuse. What's yours?"

Meilin sat on the bench beside him. She told him of her departure, of meeting Jin on the forest's threshold, of her confrontation with Yin, of the ruined village. Tong listened.

"You shouldn't have come," he said.

"But I have," she said.

"Why?" he said.

"To see it with my own eyes," she said.

"Hand me my blindfold," he said. She did. He tied it around his eyes, gingerly sat up on the bench. "I saw her with my own eyes. My vision has not yet returned to me, but the sight of her is properly burned into me."

"Her?"

"Yin spoke the truth, being, I suspect, too drunk to lie. We did indeed see the firebird three nights ago. I followed on foot, alone, likely on the same trail that brought you here. I saw a tower with a blazing crest like a beacon in the darkness.

"Drawing my sword, I climbed the stairs to confront the creature, and saw instead a woman with golden eyes and golden hair. When she turned her gaze toward me, it was as if I were staring into the heart of the sun."

Meilin listened. The way Tong spoke had a certain quality of awe and wonder, which did not escape her notice. "Come," she said. "The three of you have had a grand adventure, but it is time to return home. Let me escort you back to camp."

"First," he said. "Food. No more groping around in the dark for my rations. My pack is by the wall beside the door. There are dried meats and fruits, and a skin of water. Don't light a fire. My eyes haven't recovered."

Meilin rose. She found the pack. She brought him food.

Tong ate and spoke some more. He talked to her about Yin's ambitions and Jin's sense of arrogance, of how it felt to lie in the dark beneath the tower, so close to his goal and unable to capture it—an ideal symbol for his life and his lot: close to the throne, close to the kingdom, close to his brothers, and yet not close enough. Then he spoke of the firebird, and the awe and wonder returned to his voice; he spoke of his theories, of the indigenous people of the mountains who worshipped a goddess of fire and dawn before the armies of the August Emperor arrived; in that moment his voice bore the same quality of feverish wonder that had infected her father when he spoke of his dreams.

It occurred to Meilin that Tong had not thanked her for her help, nor yet for the food, nor inquired about her well-being, and it was not until he'd fallen asleep after an hour of talking that she, in the silence of the tower, realized the thoughtless automation with which she fetched his food and listened to him ramble. She did not regret it, for of all her brothers, Tong alone made some effort to reach out to her. Perhaps they shared a certain understanding—she, being the daughter of a concubine, and he being forever overshadowed by his siblings.

In the last two days, she had been acting rather strange, she realized. There was a curious headstrong irrationality to her actions, plunging forth on an adventure that had not belonged to her nor welcomed her, for no desire for reward or recognition. She'd felt it the moment she sat astride Jin's horse and rode out away from the circle of firelight that spread from her father's camp and into the clouds and the mist, the trees and the brooks.

Beside her, curled on a stone bench, Tong slept with a blindfold over his eyes.

Meilin's eyes traveled up along the winding stairs. She slipped her quiver over her shoulder, gripped her bow, and marched up the stairs. The air from above smoldered like an oven. She walked. She reached the top of the tower. She found a hatch of solid stone, outlined in the glow of fire. She climbed to the top of the tower.

There sat a woman dressed in gold. Her hair was gold and flowed to her waist. Her skin was burnished bronze, and the silk that covered her body moved and flowed like molten iron. Her radiance filled every crenellation, every inch of the tower.

The Firebird turned her eyes toward Meilin. Meilin saw her face, and in that moment knew that it was her own.

She dropped to her knees and pressed her forehead against the hot stone, her hair spread before her, her arrows rattling out of her quiver to scatter against the ground like so many flowers offered upon an altar.

Meilin did not know what it was that compelled her to kneel, as if she were kowtowing in the presence of the August Emperor, but neither did she raise her eyes from the ground. Out of the edge of her vision, she saw the woman's golden hand reach down toward a fallen arrow. Then followed the sound of rushing wind, and a blaze of light that filled her skull with redness even as she squeezed her eyes shut. Then there was silence, and darkness, and Meilin atop an empty tower with a wind that played with her hair.

On the ground before her lay her arrows, and a single arrow she did not recognize as her own, fletched with the feathers of a bird the likes of which she knew not, glowing with its own strange pulse, as if it were breathing in the darkness, exhaling light; as if it were a living thing. With care, she reached for the arrow, and found it cool and smooth in her hand; presently its brightness multiplied, and its radiance made her shadow long.

The wind played through her hair.

Meilin turned toward the west. She saw the sea of spears that were the forests, and the clearing where Yin and his hunters waited, and the edge of the woods that became the glade upon which the August Emperor and his hundred physicians; his countless entourage; his soldiers and his hunters; his horses and his ladies-in-waiting; his imperial palanquin; her brother Jin, festooned in the armor of his office; the braziers alighting the camp, billowing out incense smoke in great heaps as if to drive away the demons of doubt and dread, fear and mortality; the bowls of rice, the cups of tea; her father, the August Emperor, restless in his old age.

Meilin drew her breath. She nocked the arrow. She drew her bow. She let the arrow fly.

It curved into the sky, gaining brightness in its passage, radiance in its velocity, becoming a shooting star with a tail of fire, a bird with wings that scorch the sky, and a cry like the sound of lightning.

From the world of *Tales from the Flat Earth*.
First published in *Realms of Fantasy*, June 1998.

I Bring You Forever

Tanith Lee

*Did the sages not say, in Jeshlah, each human thing is but a
little place of life, surrounded by the desert?*

*Just so, the palace lowered upon its rock like the back of a
lion, and all about, the town, pinned to the Earth by towering
trees and stems of water. But beyond—beyond, the great lakes
of dust, whose close hot breath is the desert wind. Gardens
falling like green steps. A fountain that sprinkles, by night,
the water drops of the stars. But beyond, beyond, the hot white
Moon that has the face of the skull of the gazelle. There are
bones under the dust. And bones in Heaven, too.*

When she was a year old, the king saw his daughter for the first
time. He had been at war, triumphed, and come home. Three beautiful
wives had already given him several strong sons. But his favorite wife,
the fourth, had borne during his absence a female child. The woman
approached, her soft hair falling to her waist and filled with tiny golden

bells that made a placating noise. Her lambent eyes were downcast. (A nurse held the child sidelong, as if to hide it.)

"Forgive me," said the fourth wife.

"I shall only," said the king, catching her to him, "not forgive you for thinking me such a savage. Forgive you for what? For bearing me another such as you, to charm the hearts of men like music?"

Presently he took the girl child, who smiled and waved little fists, trying to snatch his jeweled earring. "See, she wants this." The king removed the costly earring, broke off the sharp hook by which it had held to his ear, and gave it to his daughter. "She must have everything she wants," he said, warm with victory, homecoming, lust, and simple happiness. "Always."

They had not named the child, for fear he would not want it to have even a name.

So the king named her Zulmeh, which in that tongue meant Diamond—the gem she had reached for.

The diamond child grew up. A clear child, like cool water slenderly poured. And her hair was like dark copper, and her eyes a smoky green, like jade.

As she grew, so grew the town of the desert king. Long channels were made to conduct the water of the oasis, enamel roofs arose, and towers and lions of white stone.

By the day she was, Zulmeh, 10 years of age, the king was called Great King. And by the year she was 13, he was dead. A tomb was built for him that the desert people said was a wonder of the earth, and traveled far to see. Pillars and stairs raised it up to Heaven, showing it to the sky and the gods above, as if to ask them, What have you done?

But the Princess Zulmeh was only 13. What was death to her? It was true she wept beautifully as she followed the king's bier among the flowers of his weeping women. But it was only that the sad songs made her cry. She had scarcely known him. He had always been away at war, and in the end war had claimed him utterly, with the spear that pierced his vitals.

Her mother had died too, somewhere in those years. But her mother had not meant very much either. Her mother belonged to the Great King.

Only one thing Zulmeh knew for sure. That whatever she asked for she was given. How strange, perhaps, she never thought to ask, as another child would, for her father or her mother. She must have learned very early, perhaps even that morning in the arms of the king, that she would be given bright and shining things, valuable things, mystical and longed for. Hard, too. Hard as diamond. But nothing easy. Nothing that was hers—by right?

It would seem then she was a demanding child. Not so. She learned also, and quickly, to choose with care what she would have.

At seven years, asking for a particular beast, which she had been told of, she saw a caravan dispatched for a foreign land, to fetch it. One year later they returned, those who that had survived the dreadful trek, and they brought her, stiff and stuffed, the animal she had wanted, since it too had perished on the journey. One more lesson. Hard lesson. Diamond lesson.

When she was 15, Zulmeh's brothers fell to fighting among themselves for the crown of Great King. Their armies clashed out in the desert, and from a place high on the city walls, one might see a flash of swords and arrows, over and over, and the dust rising like a purple column to uphold the indifferent sky.

The victor presently returned. His name was Hazd.

He swept the city like a broom, and settled on the golden lion throne, and called them all to admire him there. He asked who the girl was, the royal girl with dark red hair. They told him. Hazd said he would marry this girl, to uphold his claim to his father's throne. They were only half brother and sister, he and the Diamond, and Hazd was a bastard.

Strangely, again, for one taught she might have anything she asked for, Zulmeh must have known not to ask to be spared her half brother. But then, he was ebony-skinned, with corded hair that fell to his knees, lion-strong, a warrior and a poet. And she had never known him as a brother, as she had never known, let us be exact, father or mother.

They were wed, and he led her to a pavilion high on the palace roofs, and from there he showed her the enormous desert of dust in the settling dust of evening.

"What do you see Zulmeh?"

"The Great Sands," she answered.

"No, you see my kingdom. Soon that absence of life will be covered by the life of my city."

But then they sat drinking sweet wine, and he played a melody for her on a lap-harp of ivory. He sang a song he had made for her. It compared her to the Moon, now lifting over the desert. But Hazd did not say the Moon was a skull. No, it was a young girl, whose eyes were green, if only one might see them. Of all his fine songs, this was, at that time, the most beautiful.

Zulmeh listened. Perhaps she thought, if she had not already, "I want and must have this man—"

At midnight, colored birds were uncaged above the roofs of the palace, where, behind the highest lighted windows, the city knew that Hazd and his bride were mated and made one.

Their love was glorious. He told of it in his songs, carved into the stone pylons of the city, beside his lion songs of war. But Zulmeh left no record of this love. For some reason she did not conceive his child. He would have assured her not to mind it. He had plenty of women who could do that in her stead.

Was there ever a night or morning then, standing in the high place, when Zulmeh invoked magic from the stars or those strange otherworlds, the planets, or the gods, or the Sun or the Moon, saying: I want and must have the child of Hazd—I—I—No. There never was.

She had learned her lesson, had she not. No father nor mother. No child. And, at last, no lover-husband either. Zulmeh was 17 years, when one brother returned across the desert, a true son of their father. His name was Hroor. He slew Hazd in single combat, before the gates of Jeshlah. Did she see? Yes. But she was high up on the walls. Such little figures—so far off. Did she ask the gods for his life? Perhaps she thought of the exquisite living animal brought dead and mummified and laid before her. Perhaps she asked a moment too late—even as Hazd fell, dying—but by then her request would have been only a denial, Oh let it be not so. A prayer must always be framed, the sages tell us, in the positive mode. Never do not, but only Let it be so.

If she thought she would be given to Hroor, the victor, with the other wives, she was correct. But Hroor was not a man for women, and did not trouble any of them. Also, not being a man for women, he was kind to them. Seeing Zulmeh stand alone, white as ivory in her red hair, dry-eyed green among the wailing queens of Hazd, Hroor asked who she was.

Then, "Ah," said Hroor. "The Diamond. I remember well my father's decree. Take heed, all of you. Give her always what she wants."

She never wept when others were by, not for grief, she who had always softly and publicly wept at melancholy music.

She sat alone, high up in the women's courts, in her own luxurious pavilion, which Hroor had not taken from her. She gazed away over the desert. Once or twice someone will have asked Zulmeh what she desired. She will have answered, "Nothing."

Hroor ruled three years.

One warm evening, with a Moon like a bow in the sky, the faction that had risen against him took their omen, and shot him full of arrows.

He lay unburied in the street, flighted like some old dead bird, while the sections of Jeshlah fought together. When the fighting was done, in the hour before dawn, men came to Zulmeh's pavilion.

They kneeled down to her.

"You," said they, "are the last descendant left living of the blood of the Great King. Only you, our Diamond, are fit now to rule."

She saw their smiling, crafty, blood-streaked faces. She would be Queen, but they would rule through her, for a woman was only an ornament, as the Moon only gave light.

But it was not a time to argue or declare what instead one wanted. She acquiesced meekly.

So Queen Zulmeh took the throne of Jeshlah.

And sages tell us, wisdom comes with the years, as with pain. We are scourged in the school of life that we memorize the lessons. To rule, even as a puppet and a woman, was dangerous, and so Zulmeh now encouraged, secretly, her own faction, those who revered her true royal blood, or were struck by her beauty and her sorrowful widowhood. Those too who liked power, but preferred it second-hand, the natural captains of a king.

When the fruit was ripe, Zulmeh the Diamond addressed them. It was a night of feasting in her private apartments. Cloth-of-gold, velvets strewn, tame birds with long tails of amethyst that stalked about, perfume playing in the fountains. The gold cups were raised high to praise the Queen and the gods.

Zulmeh spoke. "Never compare me to Heaven. They are perfect and eternal, and I have only my little span of being, which any moment may be wrenched away."

Then they cried out that they would serve her with their very lives. What did she wish of them?

She said: "I want safe rule in Jeshlah. I want the crown of Jeshlah and not its shadow. I must be rescued from those who, today or tomorrow, will cast me down, and all you with me, in a grave. I must have their heads."

The color crimson was on the room, crimson, purple, and gold. Before the lamps failed, on golden trays they brought her, her faithful men, 24 severed heads, dyed in their own red-purple blood.

Then Zulmeh truly was Queen in Jeshlah. And she had been given what she wanted.

Seven years passed, and the city grew like a natural thing, until it filled the horizon on four sides. Then Jeshlah was called the Great City, and the Queen of it, Zulmeh, the Diamond, the Moon of Jeshlah. Whatever she wanted, she was given. A thousand towns and cities paid tribute to her. From the four corners of a horizon beyond the horizon of the Great City, came the merchandise of the world. Silk and sandalwood, precious jewels and priceless stones, trees of resin and cedar, baths of oil and wine. Men came there too, mighty soldiers and princes, musicians and poets, acrobats, magicians and scholars. All to the white wheel of the Moon of Jeshlah, wrapped in her copper cloud.

Feasts and shows of great extravagance were continually arranged. Here men fought to display their skill rather than to kill each other (although, quite often, kill each other they did). But also sorceries were worked of incredible kinds, to thrill and astound. And there were competitions for music and the making of songs. Jeshlah was civilized. Towers of books stacked scroll on scroll, volume on volume, the height of many tall men. Instruments that made a hundred ravishing sounds.

Zulmeh was in her 30th year. Among the poor such an age was a crone's age, but among the royal kindred it was not much.

A competition there was to be at which the best songs of all the world, as the world was known, were to be sung before her. Judges would award the prize not to the singer, but to the poet who had made the winning song.

As Zulmeh was carried to her stadium of music, she glittered flawlessly on her people. She had earned her name, they said, she blazed so bright with her riches they could hardly bear to look at her. Her face too, might have been cut from diamond, they said. So pure and radiant. (So hard?)

She sat and heard the songs. If her mind wandered now and then, no one could be sure. If she wanted anything, everyone might see it, a cup of wine, green figs or honey, the breeze of fans, and these things were given her at once.

Then a whispering began all about that did not quite center on the Queen. If she had been thinking of other things, this noise recalled her. A man waited below, tuning a little lap-harp modestly. Presently he sang.

His voice was fair, but it was the song which held the stadium.

The song told how a poet had seen a woman, and thought her at once a harp of ivory, but strung with his own black hair. By herself, this harp could sound him, as if he had been will-less. Yet without the strength of her strings, these long black strands, her music must be dumb.

When the song ended, the world seemed itself made dumb.

Zulmeh inclined her head, on which an uncountable fortune flamed and spangled. Who could miss the flash of these fires, like swords at work in the desert far away.

She was not unloved, but the love had come with her station, the accessory of her rank. Doubtless what they had devised had been meant to please her, honor her, to be, even, kind. When finally the judges rose, the sky was red. But if any other songs had been sung, Zulmeh at least had not heard them. There was no deliberation. Naturally not. The judges declaimed their verdict to the stadium, which roared back its approval. Perhaps it truly was the best of all the songs, for Hazd had made it for Zulmeh, in the first year of their marriage.

It was the custom at such a festival, after the announcement of the winner, for the victorious poet to be called by a herald, three times. Nor did they omit this custom.

Loudly the name of Hazd was called, once, and then again, and then again.

And then all that stadium packed with people cried aloud for Hazd, and the noise rocked the sky, as if it were one huge bell of ruby glass.

Yet after the tumult, a silence fell, profound and terrible. The silence of a grave.

The Queen alone spoke softly, and none heard her. It was a silly childish thing she said. "He cannot take his prize. He is dead."

Darkness swept over the stadium. And all the kindled lights became little hopeless wisps beneath it. Anything might snuff them out. And nothing light up the black of the sky but the careless stars.

Zulmeh raised her face to these stars, and the tears glinted on her cheeks, and were, of course, taken for yet more jewels, by the crowd. It must be said, if they had heard what she uttered, they would have taken the words for the moistureless wit of kings.

But if they had thought to please or honor or be kind, they failed. They had only taught her one more lesson. For though she had known in her mind for 10 full years that Hazd was dead, only now did she know it. So long it took the message to sink home, like a slow, slow knife.

All that night she walked about the palace's high places. She touched the birds upon their gold stands, so they trilled or spoke, the leaves of exotic shrubs, so they gave off a myriad scents. She looked through the magnifying lenses of her mages, and saw the stars more closely, tinted rose and sapphire and bronze.

Later she whispered, "But even the stars go out."

And she gazed to the edges of the city, to the desert that surrounded all things.

Her counselors were anxious. They stood in anterooms, puzzling, planning, not yet plotting.

At first light she came back among them all.

She had no appearance of madness, rather she was implacable, as some had seen her father, the Great King. They bowed to the ground.

"Now I will tell you," said Queen Zulmeh, the Diamond, "what I must have. What I will have. What you must get for me." Never had they heard her so clear, so sure.

They waited in instinctive terror.

They were wise.

"Bring to me," said Zulmeh, "immortality."

Only one year passes now, perhaps more swiftly than all the others. Experiments of all sorts took place in Jeshlah, acts of magic and religion, of devotion, of cruelty, elixirs, mythology, drugs, philosophy, poison. Men died, so that the Diamond might learn how to live.

Yet she did not learn. None learned, save only a few old tales which none could credit. All lessons require canny teachers.

Of her punishments for failure little is recorded. Possibly she was merciful. Only her looks of disappointment killed.

At the year's end, the city stood in its magnificence, yet about it hung a kind of smoke. And this inchoate thing towered up to the sky, like a pillar, a tomb. As if to ask the gods, What have you done?

"Oh Great Moon," cried the girl, casting herself down before the Queen, "someone has come to the palace."

Zulmeh lifted her head, she stared, her green eyes fixed as a hawk's upon far distant prey. "Who now?"

The girl replied rapidly. "An old man, from the desert. But he says that he has heard of your quest—and has the remedy."

It was the hour of lamp-lighting. But the slaves stopped still and the tapers blew out in their hands.

"Bring him to me!" cried the Queen.

She rose up, thin and white and gleaming. Hard, hard, hard. Diamonds last, but they scratch scars on things, even merely by looking from their burnished eyes.

And the appalled girl rushes away, and then returns, with the man from the desert, evenly flanked by 12 guards. (Strangely. One for every full year since the death of love.)

Others had come, of course, to Jeshlah, promising they could find the way to get the Queen what she wanted. Perhaps none had said so decidedly that he possessed the goods already.

He was a tall old man, narrow as a stick, but straight and strong, sunburned, with a life carved on his face. Much scarred by years, he seemed unwary of the Diamond's scratch. But he was anomalous. So ancient a creature, to hold the secret of ageless eternity?

His clothes were ragged hides. He had no adornment but for his silver hair and the blackest black of his eyes. Such as he wandered the deserts, living in caves, feeding on sand, and drinking the dew. So poor a beggar to hold a secret that might have made him rich as any king?

"Kneel, old man," said the nearest guard. "On your knees before the Moon Queen of the Great City of Jeshlah."

At this, the old man smiled. Then he knelt with surprising agility on the tiled floor.

"Are you of this land?" asked the Queen's steward.

"Am I of any land?" asked the old man.

"What is your name?" frowningly asked the Queen's steward.

"What is a name?" smilingly asked the old man.

The steward indicated that the guard might strike the old man. Who laughed. And Zulmeh spoke to prevent the blow.

Then she ordered every one of her people from the room, and stayed alone there with the old man who kneeled, smiling, on the floor. One so old and so poor and so arrogant and so unafraid must hold some secret, after all.

Then a while passed. A fly might be heard crawling on the wall.

At last the Queen herself instructed the old man: "Speak."

He rose, and his smile was gone. He looked into her eyes and said, "I bring you forever."

It seemed to Zulmeh then, that all the lights that had been lit faltered and went dark. But a moment after, they burned up again, bright as before. As if time itself had blinked.

"What must you do," said Zulmeh the Diamond, "to make this so?"

"What indeed?"

"Tell me," she said.

"I have told. And I have done."

"Is it done then? But—is this all?"

"It is everything," said the old man.

He had stepped farther off, although she had not seen him do so. Maybe in that moment of the blinking of light and time. He seemed in shadow now, and the black of his eyes was almost violet—or red, a red-violet burning through the fabric of him, from within.

"Well," said the Queen, "you shall remain as my guest. There must be trials made, to see."

But across the room a curtain turned to a wind and blew, and he was gone in it, gone away, gone out like a lamp that did not rekindle.

The Diamond stood alone, and touched her face with her smooth fingers. (And how smooth they felt.) Am I changed?

The Moon of Jeshlah ruled in her city. "She is the Diamond," they said, "see how smooth and burnished-bright she is, graceful and slender, her metallic hair and expensive eyes. Not a mark on her. Always the same." But they squinted as if also they beheld that now each day was for her like each previous day. And each night all other nights. One eternal day and one night of forever.

Time unravels, samenesses, changes...

All the days and nights the same. Where do they go to? Changing into what?

Zulmeh left her bed early, and her women brought her a cordial of roses and mint. As she drank it, she saw them changed and changing. There a pale young girl, but now more sallow than pale. And there a voluptuous girl, whose figure drooped. And there, and there, a thread of gray in the silken hair, or hair too colorful, dyed to hide the gray.

When they laughed or sulked, Zulmeh saw the cracks time made in their enamels.

They clothed her and brought her jewels. Their hands were not so deft as they had been. Their perfume not so fresh.

Zulmeh gave an audience. Gnarled hands on yellowing papers... chipped voices... Now Zulmeh walked in her gardens. On the green steps, places opened slyly in the arbors. The white marble of the seat, as she sat admiring it, realizing that it had lost its glow. Flowers had burned themselves out. The vines were ancient and the grapes, that hung to be plucked, no longer tempting. Green droplets of juice shriveled to raisins.

Zulmeh looked aside into the palace courts. Children had become stubborn adults, and moved grumbling and fussing there. Already their shoulders were bowed. Their tones coarsened.

The sun rushes to the apex. She was left behind it.

She re-enters a great pavilion—

She ate a meal in one of the great pavilions, among her nobles and captains. The gray is creeping in their hair. Rheumatic hands, old wounds that hurt them. The dogs were thin, with filmy eyes. Young dogs stand up on wild ungainly legs—steadied, and began at once to stiffen like the beautiful dead mummy brought her once across the world.

The lilies that had been wound in the garlands crumbled away. The bread has a taste of mildew.

Zulmeh gives another audience. Over the floor, feverish ambassador, the Sun hurries, moving so fast.

Old men paraded before her who had entered the palace young men. The tribute of sparkling veils spread for her delight were fraying at their edges. Only the hard jewels dimly shone.

Soon the palace and the city slept in the heat of afternoon. The Queen prowls like a panther up and down.

Over the Earth the Sun now shuffled. The Sun was old, and surely has lost some of its light. The sunset burned out like the dullest flower.

Zulmeh bathed once more and was dressed once more. Morning? Night? Old women tended her, she sees the bones behind their faces, their breasts are fallen empty bags.

The tiles in the floor had been rubbed almost clean of their pictures.

Time flew, flies, has flown. It flew, flies, had flown, over and over, circling the dish of the world. Like the blinking of the lamps, the sunrise and sunset, the flicker of the black-blue eyelids of night.

A dead bird lay on the terrace. It always lay there, lies there, or another bird. No more songs.

Zulmeh looked out to the four corners of the horizon, and her powerful city was laid like a carpet before her. But the wind and Sun had pared away the colors of the city. The old trees leaned or had fallen or been cut down. An axe strikes. There, another will fall, falls, fell.

At last, one day, some day, Zulmeh has them bring her carriage, and was carried through the streets. She watched the elderly people bowing to her, painfully, and the children stand taller and gain their first true balance—and stiffening there at once to statues of pallid wax. She watched the lights die in their eyes already long ago, heard their shrill bright savage voices tamed to monotonous regret.

Dead flowers littered the carriage, thrown in alive. Thrown in, yesterday, tomorrow?

"How wonderful is the Queen-who-is-a-Moon," she heard the fissured voices croak, "she has not aged one hour." Or do they only mutter against her, that she is a witch?

The guards marched by the carriage, and their breathing rasped, their footfalls rang heavy, exhaustedly.

Now the buildings of the Great City of Jeshlah are and were partly ruinous, with stones fall-fallen out. The inhabitants crouched in hovels made from bits. The dust of the desert had come in and covered everything it could, thick as yellow flour.

There was a huge gateway, a gate of triumph inlaid with blue lapis, and guarded by two lions higher than the towers around. But the lions had lost, one, his forepaws, and the other his head. And the lapis rains out of the doors. Had rained out of the doors. Here and there a blue petal of lapis lay and lies, in the dust. One petal that would not fade. Already fading.

Zulmeh left the carriage.

The ancient men in their tarnished armor stared at her with half-blind eyes. When the Queen said that she would walk a little in the desert beyond Jeshlah, they remonstrated, but feebly.

"Rest," said Zulmeh. "Rest a while."

She thought that when she turned back to them they must be skeletons, fallen or propped on their shields and spears.

It seemed to her she moved like a slim white knife and cut a way through dust and age and time, and as she cut, her own cutting made her sore. And conversely the rush of everything toward death, leaving her behind as did the Sun and the Moon and the stars, rubbed on her, grazed her. But a Diamond is polished finer by abrasion. So they say and said.

When her feet, in priceless sandals (of which now the straps gave way) met the flame-harsh grit of the desert's back, Zulmeh paused a moment.

"This I know," said the Queen. "For you are made by the grinding up of all else, as now, it seems, am I."

So she walks among the sloping dunes.

The racing hound of the Sun ran more slowly yet, aging, losing ground.

Zulmeh stared after its bled-out shape, all wrapped in a distant storm of dust. She would, then, outlive the Sun? She would outlive the world? She, and the desert.

The frayed veils of dust, the desert's tribute, furled over the city, which seemed finally like a mirage. Soon every tower would drop down. Every wall collapse. Jackals would howl among the wreck—for a moment, only for a moment. The Moon would set behind the Sun and darkness would come, but not the dark of night. Night too will have died, with all the stars, for she has said before, the stars go out.

Zulmeh walked, and the Sun came and went, comes and goes, and night likewise, and she reached and reaches a little place of life surrounded by the desert.

Two trees rose above a pool. A deer was drinking there, and seeing the blown white brilliance of the Queen, the deer sprang away. But as it touched the Earth again, it lost its vivid momentum. Through the flesh, Zulmeh saw its Moon-skull stare at her.

The Queen of Jeshlah sat down by the pool of the oasis. She thought she must be thirsty, and so cradled some water in her hands and drank it, before the pool should dry up and shrink away.

From two trees spread a shade that seemed cold, and almost still. Zulmeh sat down there. But, as she spread her hand in the shade, the shade seeps off, as soon, surely, the pool must do.

Zulmeh sat beneath the trees, and the shade came and went, comes, goes, the cool of it, never staying long, the heat. Somehow the pool was replenished from some fountain under the ground. She thought achingly of Jeshlah. But Jeshlah must now be dust. A place of bones.

"Time moves so fast," said Zulmeh to the desert, "but only adds to you, and never diminishes me."

Winds blew, hot as the sting of scorpion, and burnished the Diamond more.

"I wish," said Zulmeh, "how I wish I do not have forever. How I wish that I am dead." (The denying prayer that does no good.)

Then she lay down in the moment of the shade under the trees, to sleep. For she seemed not to have slept at all, for many hundreds of years. And after she had slept, this once, she might never sleep again. Although, when she woke, she knew the Earth too might have vanished, will have done, dashed and rushed down into the bottomless abyss of nothing. Opening her eyes, she would find only the desert and the darkness left, and the cry of the soulless winds of immortality, the music of unforgiving forever. (No more songs.)

But, even so—even so, she slept, she sleeps.

Zulmeh dreamed. For the sages said, even the eternal gods have dreams.

A man was walking over the sand, in the dream, and Queen Zulmeh got up and followed him. He was changeable, this man. First he was black as her lost lover, Hazd, or blacker perhaps, but his hair was not black. Then he seemed goldhaired, but also grayhaired. And then he had no hair, his head was smooth as a brown nut. And then his hair was black, and then silver. And then his hair was a wave or a wind which blew the world sideways.

However, changeable as he was, he did not dash only one way, toward the pit of silence and dissolving.

Halting, Zylmeh thought he was, after all, the forever-bringing man from the desert, who must be a mage, and so quite capable of constant change.

"I will give you all I have," said Zulmeh, no longer running at his back but standing deadly still, "if you will take your curse from me."

"Did I curse you?"

"Yes. With your venomous blessing."

"I only gave you, Diamond," he said, "what you wanted."

"No one," said the Diamond, "ever gave me that."

Then he laughs, and turns and faces her. She cannot see at all who he is, for he is all shapes, all colors, coming and going, chaotic, elastic—terrible. Yet, his voice is like a song.

"My father," said the Diamond, "gave me a gem in place of my mother. The animal I loved they brought me made into wood, with cold hard fur, and eyes of vitreous. They gave me the heads of men in a pond of blood. They gave me the heavy crown of Jeshlah. Only one thing I never did ask for, and that was my marriage to my husband. And this was the only thing I ever wanted. Yet I did not know I wished for it till he was by my side."

"Hazd is gone," said the whirlwind upon the sand.

"Hazd is dead. I wish for death."

"You asked for never-ending life. Wished for and wanted it."

The Diamond said, "Did I not tell you. It has always been my way to ask for and receive that which I do not want?"

"You are a fool," said the thing before her. "Go back to Jeshlah."

"Jeshlah has fallen," said Zulmeh, "I have lived on, and centuries have passed. I have felt every one of them drag over me as it went. It has been centuries."

"Fool," said the thing which had given her forever, "it has only been 30 days. The number of the years of your little human life."

Zulmeh opened wide her eyes. "Then have you not—" said she, "made me an immortal?"

"I gave you forever in 30 days. I did not promise you your wish, but its remedy."

Zulmeh opens wide her eyes once more, and this time wakes. The night is spread above, black and still, the stars fixed in their places, each sparkling hard and enduring as any diamond.

They say, it is true, that Zulmeh returned to her city, over the desert. She was very strong and not old. But the rumor of her journey, and her brief (it had been brief) sojourn in the waste, became a legend of that land.

When she came near the city, peasants at a well saw her walking toward them, and knew her as the Queen. They brought her milk in a clay cup, and she clasped their hands, those of young and old alike, laughing like a girl, so they laughed too. She petted the goats of their wild herds as if goats were quite new to her. The herders said, never was there a king like this.

But for Zulmeh, what? The frantic race of time, which she had only imagined, or been spelled to see, or spelled herself to see, had ceased. What she had witnessed in her sensation of eternity, the line beside the mouth, the fallen stone, were those intimations that all men, and all women too, will notice now and then. But not as she had done.

For had she ever noted a gray hair in the black harp-ropes of Hazd? No, never. But they were there, since he had been many years older than she. Had she thought the Sun ran across Heaven? Never, until she was given forever. (The remedy.)

Nothing is forever, unless, like the demon creature in her dream, it changes. Youth to age. Age to death. Death to birth to youth—

Re-entering the gate of her city, it stood high as Heaven, and full of its blue petals, the lions proud, their paws and peerless heads only a little worn. While on the avenue her soldiers raised their spears in salute, young men, mature men, strong and valid. And beyond, the people called for her, and the children timelessly played, and roses fell, firm and fragrant, the color of a sunset that was not blood, nor decay, but like a young girl's blush. And in the city, the towers and the walls, they soared up. And in her private rooms, her lovely maidens welcomed her, peaches, jasmin, with teeth like pearls.

Zulmeh had seen what immortality might entail. Now she saw again what mortals see, dancing together on the floor of life, whose tiles are whole and perfect. Yet never would she forget her vision, her 30 days in a wilderness, static, and about her the whole wheel of time revolving and revolving. Poor child, she saw what men should never see. Wise child, she learned, and left it and came away, and lived. Hard lesson. Last lesson, perhaps.

In Jeshlah, Zulmeh the Diamond raised a pylon, which at midday held the Sun upon its tip. She would watch this phenomenon through a lens, a third jade eye. It always took the proper time. By night she traced the measured progress of the planets.

Also, in her 31st year, she married again a prince of another land. He was not black, but the color of honey. She bore for him, and for herself, three children, who ruled the city when Zulmeh's mortal time was done.

Long, long before that hour had struck, one night, near dawn, there was a shooting star. It flashed like a jewel across the firmament.

Zulmeh's lover-husband kissed her, and he said, "If you wanted it, I would give you that brilliant thing—if I could. I cannot. But I will love you forever."

The Diamond said, as the sages record, "We love. But nothing is forever, as forever is nothing. Forever is this moment. The world in a grain of sand."

Incense Shrine

Terry Jackman

The slender body cannoned into Serak as he crossed the temple yard. His mind had been entirely focussed on the Judgement; now he felt the disapproval from the supplicants around him. Not of him, of course, but of this girl, because she'd touched him. There were mutterings. She didn't seem to hear them. Soft brown eyes stared up at him; confusion marred them.

She was... lovely. That thought jolted one who never noticed such externals. Serak stiffened; watched the soft face tighten too. He knew the second that she really saw him. She looked frightened, but then wasn't he the Judger, pure and sinless? He released her arms and swung away—the crowd drew back—and strode across the ancient paving to the dais where his priests were waiting. What was it she'd seen, a young man or a legend? Maybe both, first one and then the other? His mirror told him what they usually saw, an image carved from holy visions. Every Judger through the ages looked as he did. Blue-black hair swept back then down to frame his milk-white features, pale as his heavy tunic with its dull black shoulders. White skin never touched by all the fierce sunlight round him. Always different. When he faced the crowd again his blue-black eyes were stony as the walls around them. At his back the sun rose from behind the Tower of Testing.

From up here he could watch the heat and light sweep over all the upraised faces. This year they had filled the barren triangle of ground, at least a hundred, bodies jostling to see him. More priests stood around the walls, but it was hope and fear that controlled the crowd. The three great towers that linked the walls loomed over all, in silent witness.

He had stood like this for seven years now. To his left he saw the grandest arch; the Arch of Supplicants, its round white tower higher than the others. They had passed its frowning statues as they entered, in their search for healing and forgiveness. To his right, the Arch of Incense stood, built lower, plainer; almost disappointing. And behind him loomed the Arch of Testing. Waiting for its victims.

Many of these supplicants wore orange strips upon their clothing, warning of an unclean status. Some were 'cleansed' at birth by over-righteous families but every year some survived till they were old enough to try for absolution, hoping, praying that the Tree would heal them.

Overhead, these foreign priests had started chanting. In the crowd stood Meren, still unsteady from that brief encounter. All her thoughts had been on Dayan's illness, not on what was happening around her. When this crowd recoiled a flailing arm had flung her forward, right into the man they'd all made way for. Thankfully the close-packed bodies had forgot about her once this chanting started. Meren listened to the priests sing of forgiveness and the other supplicants sing promise of atonement. *Yes. Me too!* She sent the thought out fervently. *I cannot ask, but I will gladly beg, and suffer.*

Serak felt himself grow colder, distant, as he should have been before this started. Not for him a sense of contact with the people. It had been a foolish whim, to walk for once across a corner of the courtyard rather than emerge like magic from the walls behind him.

No more foolishness. He raised his head. The chanting stopped. He felt the burden of their faith. To them he would appear a living statue, handsome features carved in marble. His words struck cold upon the warming air, to crack the nerve of some who waited. For his promise every year was a harsh one. "Know that those who reach the Incense Tree may win what they desire, but for such a gift there must be payment. Some will not survive their Testing." Movement stilled. Across the open space the air itself had frozen as his empty voice continued, "Know, all, once you take the path there is no turning back, and you must find the Tree before the sun sets or you perish. If you doubt then go no farther. If you still believe then take the tunnel. May your faith sustain you." Hard-faced, Serak gestured to the Tower behind him, and its tunnel, three stone steps above the courtyard. Here, instead of carvings they would walk past faded frescoes, arcing images of pain and death entwined in sinuous black branches.

Serak stood in silence. One by one, some scurrying, some halting, supplicants came up the steps, bowed low to him then headed down the tunnel. Not all came. A few backed off and scurried for the grander entrance as their courage failed.

Was that girl among them? Had her fear won?

No, she was coming forward now. He watched her footsteps slow as she drew near, as her resolution wavered, then she trod the steps, head lowered. Scared to look at him? She'd touched the sainted Judger after all. Outside the temple she'd have been attacked for that by these around her. Worse, she wore an orange sash, she was unclean. That was the law, that all contamination, even human, had to be destroyed or labelled, to avoid contagion. Yet... her face, a golden oval, was no mirror of a mind unbalanced or unfit to reason. And her body looked quite perfect.

What? He almost backed away from her. He didn't see such things as that; he was the Judger. Had the contact with her damaged him as well? But she was level with him now and still he could see nothing sinful, he who saw much more than others. Then she raised her head.

His dark eyes caught her, like a rabbit mesmerised by torchlight, and she started shaking. Serak felt his face grow stiffer. Moistening her lips she wrenched her gaze ahead and stumbled quickly past him, almost running. Had she feared he would refuse her passage? That at least was spared him. Still expressionless, he turned to those behind her.

Within the temple there'd been early warmth. The air had smelled of herbs and incense, clean and wholesome. So it was a fearful shock when those who braved the painted arch stepped through into a burning wasteland. Meren saw the awestruck faces round her staring at the transformation; saw the fear she herself was feeling, but she took the three steps again down as they did.

They'd emerged above another stone-paved walk. More priests attended here, further up the line, to offer every supplicant who passed a water bottle and a small, clay pot, both black with pale leaves drawn on them. Each supplicant in turn gave what they had, in payment. Meren prayed they would accept the only gift she had, the ring that Dayan gave her.

There was a stir among the crowd, heads looking back. The Judger had arrived out here, behind them. Meren peeked at him as well. His bleak expression made her shiver but his gaze had fastened on a youth ahead of her. At once two priests stepped in to block the way.

The youth looked startled first, then angry, then he wheeled, head raised, perhaps to protest. Meren looked as well, and gasped. The Judger's eyes were glowing! Crying out, the youth pulled out a hidden blade and flung it to the ground, as if it burned him. The Judger looked away, across the line. His priests stepped back again. The youth sprang forward to catch up, then faltered. Past the priests two whitened obelisks marked out a boundary. Beyond them lay another, harsher path, through barren land, and mortal danger.

Scavengers. She'd seen such creatures on her journey here; criminals or mutants, branded, cast out from the righteous. A ragged, filthy pack had come here too, to crouch in wait beneath the meagre shelter of the stunted bushes. They would surely also lurk in hidden fissures in the rising ground before her.

The youth stared wildly round then lurched toward the archway, falling to his knees. The living statue gestured once; the youth ran past him to the tunnel. Meren understood now. No one was allowed to take the test unless they went defenceless. Well, she was. And he had warned them that not all would live to find this Tree they spoke of.

The supplicants ahead were stepping through the obelisks by then, and setting off along a dusty, stone-edged track, the painted edging all that marked it from the land around it. Scavengers in sight were shifting restlessly across the slope. One darted forward, clawed hands stretching for a chosen victim. Almost there, the creature jerked away instead in obvious pain, and skittered crablike backward, shrieking wordless anger. Others hopped and cackled and began to climb the rock-strewn slope, but kept their distance from the whitened markers. So they couldn't breach the path?

The other supplicants ignored them; very well, then so would Meren. There were hardly any other women here but she raised her chin and passed the boundary, pretending not to see the way the scavengers' attention clamped upon her. Her shoes would be too thin for this terrain, but she'd ignore that too. The path was at her feet and that was all she'd need. She took it, gaze fixed on the markers.

Time passed. When she looked up again she was above the highest tower of their temple, on a path become uneven and already steeper. She was climbing more than walking now and grey dust rose at every step to choke her. Far below, that tunnel was a black mouth in the temple's whitened face. The priests had gone inside. Except for one foreshortened figure. So their Judger liked to watch them struggle? Meren shivered in the baking air then straightened slender shoulders. Let him scowl at her, she'd find this Tree of his, despite him. He couldn't stop her now. But oh, she wished she had a voice, to mock him, though it would be laughable to stand here and defy a man who neither knew nor cared how much he'd scared her. And would waste her precious time and energy on nothing. Drawing in another dust-filled breath she turned and went on climbing.

She had halted, turning back. Regretting her decision? It was too late now, but she was surely far too fragile. Frowning horribly the Judger strode back through the painted tunnel. All who wished had long departed. Now, they must be Tested.

The hill dragged at her feet. When an eerie, reddened sun was at its highest Meren found a tiny patch of shade among the rocks and rested briefly, sipping from the painted bottle. There was very little water in it; she was scared of being greedy even though her throat felt dry as parchment. She had seen no other supplicants for hours, as if she was the only one. But she had heard things; stifled noises she had closed her ears to. When she rose and climbed again the sharp stones cut her fingers so she tore her tunic's hem to wrap them then climbed on. The heat, still rising, shimmered off the rock. It made her head ache and her throat feel even drier. It became an act of will to put one tender foot before the other, and assure herself she didn't need—not yet—the final dregs of water in her bottle.

Still she climbed alone. She seized on that as a distraction. Where were all the ones before her? Had they given up, or fallen to the scavengers who dogged them? Every one? Or had she gone astray? She would not even think that. *No*, she vowed to Dayan, *I am on their path, I haven't lost it. I won't fail you.*

Her feet turned raw, unused to such uneven ground. Her shoes were rags but still she didn't falter. Squinting in the glare she struggled upward, always upward, fixing on the narrow, white-rimmed path that beckoned. Sometimes it showed dull brown stains. She realised the stains were blood when, glancing back, she saw her own was adding to them.

Pray for me, Dayan, if you can? She winged her prayer to him who lay so helpless in that greedy town. *Give me your love to help me through, as always. There is nothing stronger.*

Her trousers were torn and dirty where she'd slipped, her headscarf and her tunic coated with the dust she stirred. She couldn't see the way the reddened sun struck fire in her hair but sensed the scavengers' attention, heard the rattling of stones, and catcalls. She refused to look but sometimes still caught glimpses of the bent, contorted bodies, like a dark tide lapping at the mountain. Told herself their distance had to mean she'd kept the pathway.

Her foot slipped. She lay winded for a moment, then swung round in panic at a wheezy voice. "Take care, girl, or you'll break an ankle."

Meren breathed again. An old man stood above her, dressed as poor as her, but she could see a painted bottle sticking from a shabby pocket. Though he didn't wear that telling strip of orange. He was breathing hard but had a staff to help him and he looked determined. Not as ancient as she'd thought at first, she reasoned, standing up. There was a pallor underneath the dust. From illness? He was here for healing then, as she was. But he'd see her orange sash now she was standing up, and shun her.

But instead he waited till she caught him up, and climbed beside her; unexpected comfort.

Soon came something more, the gurgling of running water. Up ahead a tiny stream ran down the slate grey rock then vanished back into the mountain. Meren darted forward. She could drink her fill and even fill the bottle.

"Wait." The old man caught her arm. "There's only one way to the Tree, remember?" Meren's only thought was: *water.* "Go that way and you will fail, girl. Look closer."

Meren swayed. The path. It didn't reach the spring as she'd assumed, it veered, as if afraid to touch it. She had almost left the path. She stood, for what seemed hours, then turned to join her saviour; turned her back upon the chuckling stream and clambered onward.

"Keep the path," he panted. Meren couldn't answer, but she nodded. She could hear the water laughing. Eyes too dry for tears, she picked her way between the jagged boulders, taller now than her, until eventually the sound retreated.

Another turn. Another challenge. Now a steep face waited, scarred by tiny cracks and fissures. Almost vertical this time. Not far away lay bones. She swallowed then she drank her last few drops of water, set the bottle down, made sure the pot was safe inside her sash and started climbing. Her slender fingers hooked in cracks, her smaller feet found minute ledges. She could do this. Meren fought for strength, and purchase, slipped, caught hold again, crept on. Then suddenly the world of rock gave way to sky, a blaze of pink above her reaching fingers.

It was then she heard the old man whimper, such a sound, defeat and sorrow. Clinging to the rim, she peered back. The man was balanced on a narrow ledge, in sight of winning. But he couldn't find another hold, the cracks she'd used were smaller than his swollen fingers, and he clearly knew it. Meren looked, then pulled herself to safety. He said nothing. But he gasped when she turned round, head hanging past the rim above, her hand stretched out to help him.

He couldn't reach. She mimed the remedy. A nod; he raised the staff he'd slung across his back till she could catch the top and wedge its curving head onto the rim, then grip it. Now he too could continue. Not long after, lying side by side and out of breath, they grinned like errant children.

But the light, so fierce before, was fading fast. With Meren's help the man regained his feet. Their path led downward now, between rock walls, and took them to an opening: two tall white pillars, pale sky and deep red sun beyond them. Almost sunset. Almost out of time. She longed to hurry but the old man couldn't. Greatly daring, Meren held a hand out. He accepted it. He even smiled as he took what slight support she offered. Past the pillars steps descended, proper steps carved out of white-veined marble, leading to a sheltered bowl below the summit. Here at last she saw the Tree they worshipped.

It was old, so old; thick-limbed, with many spreading branches. How could such a thing survive up here? Its bark was glossy black, its heavy, cream-white leaves were veined with purple. Roots like sinews curled across the stony ground and split the rock beneath them.

They hobbled down the final steps. Once there, she watched the old man tug the clay pot from his tunic, offering it to the laden branches. She could see his hands shake and she thought his lips moved. Then she saw. Her cracked lips parted, bleeding, but the Tree was giving up its lifeblood too. Black sap was trickling down the leaves into the old man's pot. It had a heady perfume. But the old man trembled harder at the sight, the pot slipped from his swollen fingers, hit a root and cracked. The sap began to soak into the ground; his test had come to nothing.

Quickly Meren knelt and pushed the two clay halves together, held them out to him and nodded urgently until he took them. Swallowing, she pulled at two fat leaves until they parted from the Tree then stripped the bloodstained cloth from round her fingers. Mopping up the fallen sap she held the leaves against the breaks then wrapped the cloth around them in a bloody bandage. The old man looked astounded but he turned the pot to help her. Meren tried to smile but a dreadful fear consumed her. Would the Tree be angry? She had stolen from it. Short of breath, she held her own pot to the rustling branches. If she had no voice to beg her eyes spoke for her...

To Serak, those eyes stared right into his. He sat now, in his high-backed throne beside the temple's hidden altar. Ansem stood behind him, oldest of his priests, the witness of his vigil, one hand on his shoulder. Touching him, the older man could see what he did. Earlier the hand had tightened when that 'old man' warned the girl to keep the path. But she had never spoken. Serak wondered what her voice would sound like; he'd have liked to hear it, even once. He sighed then memorised the face before him as the sap flowed, all she could have wished for. But a second later he was leaning forward, black brows rising, and his priest was frowning.

The sap had flowed and filled her bowl, so fast this time it left her gaping. The rags around the old man's pot had stiffened too; the sap had hardened quickly. *It will hold*, she thought in triumph, then her smile faded. *But his pot is two thirds empty.* Very carefully she tipped her own, transferring sap till both were level. *This is right*, she tried to tell him with her eyes. *We two have helped each other.*

He raised his head from staring at the pot, his blue-black eyes serene, and glowing. "Oh, well done." And then... he faded into nothing. Meren's breath went with him. Clutching at her precious pot she sank onto her knees, eyes wide. The sap scent whirled around her.

Her back was set against a wall. The temple courtyard? And the sun was rising now, not setting, washing out across the flags toward her. There were others here but the crowd had shrunk to maybe twenty, strewn across the yard like autumn, stirring now as she was. Priests, above, watched over them again but this time smiled.

Was their Testing over, or was this another? Dazedly she watched as one by one the others who had somehow made it here were waved into that smallest tower. Till she was the only one still out here. Stumbling, she gained her feet and followed, down a simple, rough-hewn tunnel to a cavern high and deep. The furthest end held restless little lights, amid the larger shadows.

"I have waited for you." It was still the voice she'd feared before, yet now... so changed. Much softer. No, much weaker. Treading forward, Meren found the Judger shadowed by a high-backed throne beneath the flame-lit altar. Clay pots sat on narrow ledges, burned their perfume to a graven image of the Tree. The effigy rose all the way from floor to ceiling but the white-clad figure, frightening before, seemed dimmed this time, half lost in darkness. Meren hesitated.

Serak beckoned. "Meren? Come."

He knew her name? Afraid of going closer, fearful not to, she crept forward till she almost touched him. Close up, he looked older now, his features hollowed and the blue-black eyes... Were now serene, and glowing. Meren trembled. Knowing how he'd Tested her at last, she knelt and offered him the incense.

"Burn it at the altar, Meren. It will cure you."

Scampering away from him, she shook her head in panic. How could she explain?

"Come. Back." The voice was weak but when she knelt once more he pulled her closer, fingers shaking even more than on the summit. Then he kissed her, on the lips, though nobody had ever dared to touch her since she'd worn the orange. "Now, what is it that you want from me, if not a cure?"

"My lord, to heal Dayan. Oh!" She stared.

His fingers fell away. "This Dayan," he said dully. "Where is he?"

"In, in the town, lord." She was *speaking*, for the first time ever.

He was frowning. "You are meant to seek your own atonement, not another's."

Meren hung her head. "My brother brought me here to do that but he has a fever, lord. They say he's dying." She dared a look. "And he deserves it so much more than I do."

Serak's voice was lower. "If I should cure him instead, what happens then to you?"

She tried to smile. "Then I will vanish, so he thinks I failed your Testing. There's a girl he covets in our village but her father wouldn't let her join our household, not while I was in it. Dayan swore he'd never turn me out. He brought me here. He hoped your cure..."

The Judger studied her. "So you will give your prize away and leave. You would no longer be protected. Would you... stay here?"

Meren stared then whispered, "Lord, whatever you command."

He stared at that, then raised his head, as if he saw some far-off vision. Then he gave a strangled laugh. "Don't fear, I'll grant you what you fought for. Take my kiss and pass it to your brother." Leaning back again, he closed his eyes.

Meren hesitated for a moment, then she left.

The Judger's eyes flew open on an empty cavern. Wearily he leaned to light her incense at the altar, watched it burn as Ansem's voice came from the darkest corner. "Does her flame burn higher than the others, lord?"

"Enough for both." The Judger went on watching.

"Why?"

"Because she did not ask." He sighed. "Because I too was Tested this time, wasn't I? And now, they will go back to where they came from."

"Oh?" The old priest's voice was full of laughter. "Leave, when your dark eyes have held her? I don't think so." Serak only stared into the flame. "I've never seen you look so, at a woman. You could tell her what you feel."

"No. She fears me. If I commanded she might stay, but if I asked... No, she would run from me in terror, as they all do." Serak's voice was fainter. "But she has her voice, the only gift that I can give her." Ansem shook his head and left him. Meren's flame flared higher, she had reached her brother. Serak slumped, exhausted, drained; recalled the day the Judger who had trained him hadn't woken from the Testing, leaving him to feed the altar and to pay for these atonements. One day, he supposed, he wouldn't wake up either.

"My lord?" The blue-black eyes jerked round. She saw the effort in the movement. "Lord, my brother's well again. You healed us both. We had no right to that." She ventured forward, surer this time. "You asked if I would stay."

"There is no need. Go home, be happy."

He was so quiet her heart turned over for him. Kneeling by his chair she said, "Now I have thought, I think it would be better if I stayed here in your temple. If you please, lord." When he stared she laid a hand upon his sleeve. "You were as powerful as the Tree you worship. Now you are as helpless as the man you showed me on the mountain; weaker even. When you healed me with your kiss I saw your face go paler. You give your own life, don't you, as the Tree gives up its sap to those who reach it? That's why we are Tested first, because each year you die a little every time you help us?"

Serak's hand lay limp upon the chair arm but she smiled and touched it. "I was frightened, but I'm wiser now, and stronger. Stronger enough to help you. If you'll let me?"

Serak didn't have the strength this time to lean toward her but his hand curled slowly, round her fingers.

The Rounds

Tom Fletcher

You got to get the round done before the sun comes up or it all goes rancid. The days sure are hot. The nights are humid but the moonslight doesn't itself have any heat in it, so you can keep the stock in water and it'll be okay as long as you get the round done before the sun comes up. Look; I use barrels made out of Gutwood trees. The wood's a nasty grey and full of swirly faces but the customers don't see it, so... The wood's good strong stuff. I wear these goatskin gloves to handle it, see—I never used to, and the Swamp got into my skin what with me handling the barrels all the time. Now I keep the gloves on to protect myself, and also to cover my manky hands up. The coopers live in the Gutwood trees; their own houses look like barrels. They coop their own damn houses. Like big grey barrels caught in the tree branches, suspended above the Swamp. I don't go down there much. Who can bear the Gutwood but Gutwooders? You should see how it changes them. Who can bear the Swamp but Swampies? Not I. But I did go down there a good while ago, to sort out the barrel contract. I can't tell you the relief you feel when you're picking your way through the Gutwood and you come across them barrel tree houses, warm light shining out of them little round windows. I didn't think I'd be coming back up until I saw that light. But anyway.

So I get the barrels from the Gutwood coopers, and I get the water from—well yeah, it does seem like a lot of water just to keep the milk cool! But I sell all of that too. Don't worry yourself unduly. I waste not a thing. So as I was saying, I get all of the water from a well that goes deep. Like, mysteriously deep. *Weirdly* deep. I'm not going to use the word magic. I'm not going to say it's magic. I'm not going to imply the presence or influence of innate magic or actual genuine magical activity. Because I don't know if the well is magical or not. But the water is crystal clear, icy cold, and fresher than any other water I've tasted across the whole of Gleam. And I've been all over Gleam, believe me. But what I'm saying is, when was the last time you saw any ice? I've never seen any ice. That's why this well is special. Yeah, you'd better believe I'm keeping it a secret. I mean the maintenance gnomes'll know about it, I'm sure. But nobody but a gnome speaks gnome.

And the milk! The milk itself! That comes from the Goatherds. No great surprise there, probably. Good fresh goat milk. Good for fermenting with a little bit of potent fungus—you've never known dreams like the dreams this cheese brings on! They don't call it Soul Gold for nothing. And nobody but me can sell it to you! But the milk, yeah—good for the little ones, good for your hot drinks, good for the rotten stinking mornings after those Dog Moon nights, especially with a fresh snake egg cracked into it. Good for what ails. And delicious, it should go without saying. I've got a lot of loyal customers. And that's a sign of good product. That's how you get loyal customers. Product.

But I'm not here to make a sales pitch. Not exclusively. I mean if I've piqued any of your interests then I'd be glad to come to some sort of arrangement after the tale-telling. But I'm having a night off. I'm here for a drink and some hot food and some company. The thing about being a milkwoman is you see a lot of folk, you see a lot of places, you pick up a lot of stories. So today I got to thinking, well. Milk in the mornings, stories by night. Why not?

The story I want to tell tonight is—it's something that affects all of us. All of us who deal with bugs that is, and that's all of us, right? Yeah? No lichen-licking transients in this tavern tonight, hey? Glad to hear it. Don't understand why a body would just float around, hand to mouth, when there are so many ways to make a quick bug or two. Seems lazy to me. Betrays a dull kind of mind, to me. But I don't want to get side-tracked. I want to talk about the bugs themselves.

Look at these. Let me get a good handful. Look how lovely they are. Look at the many colours in their shells. We all know Gleam's crawling with beetles, some big bastards amongst 'em, but none of us have ever seen one of these beauties alive, have we? They're extinct, right? There are only so many. Pass them around. I want them back, of course I do! But I want you to have a real good look at them. When did we start to use them to buy things? Generations before our time. There are always treasure hunters, and they never find any more. They're all in circulation, and the beetles themselves are extinct. Right? As far as we know, right? But that's the basis here. That's how we work. Good thing Gleam is so damned dangerous, or there'd be too many people for the bugs to go round, right? It's almost like there's a system at work, something beyond the grind and the slip and the fall and the cut and the thrust. So that's the basis.

Well, I was on my rounds. All my stories are going to start like this. I was on my rounds out towards Tanglepipe—there's a rooftop village over there, mostly full of old folks, by the name of High Nest. It's nice and horizontal for them, with plenty of air and sunlight. They're tough, though. I mean of course they're tough; you don't get to that kind of age in Gleam without being tougher than peach pits. And they look after each other. You don't get close unless they know you. They know me. It's where I do my own buying; it's a safe market, and the prices are good. So I was up there, dropping off bottles. And it was payday. The day I knock for their bugs. So I was knocking, saying hello, having a little chat. They like to talk, you know. Payday, the round takes twice as long. And there's one old man, he opened the door to me, and he looked *bad*. He could barely stand up. I asked him if he was okay and he tried to answer but his voice was so quiet and his lips so slack, I couldn't make out a damned word. His skin was wet with sweat, and he had that acrid sweaty smell about him. He raised his arm, shaking it was, and dropped the bugs into my hand. And then he slid down the wall and just kind of quietly lay down on the doorstep. I knelt down and he was dead. He was dead. Now we've all seen dead bodies before. Milkpeople probably see more than their fair share. But that was the first time I'd seen a spirit leave its shell. And by Green, it hit me. This was an old man I'd seen almost every morning for four years. A kind, friendly, respectful man. Not a groper, not a peeper. Just died right in front of me. I dropped all my bugs and started wailing like a Swamp wisp, this dead feller in my arms. His neighbours were there straight away though, and a couple of glasses of mint tea later I was feeling better, and they were dealing with his body. Death isn't a stranger to them, of course. Like I said, they look after each other. In death as in life. So I picked up the bugs I'd dropped and kept going.

The next customer was a new fellow. He'd built a little wooden shanty house in the corner of a lovely cool, shadowed courtyard a couple of weeks previous. The first time I saw it, I shouted out—whoever was there was on my route anyway, so I'd be damned if I wasn't going to try and squeeze a little extra custom out them—and he appeared. He was a spindly thing. Handsome, if you like your men tall and thin. But too young for me. Anyway, I told him what had happened at High Nest, and he invited me in. His hut was full of skulls—goat, human, lizard, bird—and braziers, burning all kinds of herbs. Thick air, despite all of the gaps in the wooden walls. He had a table covered in dead beetles. At first I thought he was just being friendly, but he started asking questions. You know when a body starts asking questions, and at first you think, y'know, you're having a nice chat. But they just keep on asking questions, and you realise that they're not really interested in you, as a person, but just what you know? His line of questioning proved a little too intense. What *exactly* were the symptoms? Did they say anything before they died? Were they in obvious pain? What *exactly* did their sweat smell of? How many died in the shade, how many in the sun? Had there been any incontinence before death? What about afterwards? He gave me the willies he did, in the end, and I got out of there. I realised afterwards that I hadn't picked up his payment—it had been laying there on the windowsill, and I'd just gone and left it.

The next day, three more High Nest oldies had died. Just like the old man, they'd suffered from a sudden weakness, a sudden lethargy, a terribly odorous and voluminous perspiration. And then a quiet collapse. The villagers were distressed, as well you might imagine. The day after, three more. The day after that, another four. They stopped letting me in.

"There is a sickness here," the swordswoman on the gate told me. "And you, who goes from place to place, you cannot catch it." I started leaving all of the deliveries for the village with her.

Then there was a death at Tanglepipe Junction. And not an old person, this time; a young woman. Then a man. Then another man. The last one not in Tanglepipe, but—you understand, yes? The common factor? It was me, of course. They were all my customers. Of course, I worried about my product; was there something in the milk? In the water? Was the power of the Swamp poisoning my stock? But I was living off it all myself, and I had exhibited no symptoms.

Not until a night or two later. That night I had a dream. Now I'm not a big dreamer; the getting up early, and all of the physical exercise that comes with being a milkwoman—by the time night rolls around, I'm ready to sleep the sleep of the dead, and that's what I always did. A lovely black nothingness, that's what sleep has always been to me. But that night, I dreamed vile things, the likes of which I'm not going to go into, but suffice to say the dreams involved a lot of sickness, a lot of pain, a lot of bodily malfunctions. And the creatures that accompanied me in that dream, that pressed me and whispered to me... the thought of them makes me want to be sick, friends. Let me tell you. I cannot describe them. That is description in itself. The most skilled artist could not draw them. The sky was all billowing colours. I felt it was the end of the world, friends, in a strange interior way. Like something inside me had broken loose and was laying waste. My bones had grown and split me open and fused together in a cage around the world. Not that, but... it is difficult to describe, and that's part of the point. Now this may not seem like anything much to those who dream, but as I've said, I do not dream. I'm not a dreamer, friends. I'm a practical type. I like to get up early and work hard and make some bugs. Who's with me? Ha ha, that's right. Who's got another drink for your tale-teller? This is my kind of tavern. Where are my bugs? Yeah, they're pretty pretty, right? Prettier than your usual bugs? Do you think? Are they really discernibly different? I think that's the drink talking, friend. Bringing the sheen to life.

So I didn't get much sleep that night. The next day there were more deaths. The following night I had more dreams. You know what it's like when your sleep is corrupted. The days take on an unreal quality. By the time I got to the beetle man, as I thought of him, I was not myself. It was payday, but his bugs were not on the windowsill, so I knocked on his door. There was no answer, so I pushed it open. He was not in the room, but a scabby rug that had been on the floor was rolled back, and there was a hole in the stone floor. Red light came up out of the hole, and skittery, chittery sounds. I could not help myself, of course. I went and looked.

The hole was deep. A ladder clung to one wall of it. There was a room directly below, but the shaft extended through the floor of that room too. I could see the corner of a great glass box, with uncountable black forms crawling around inside it. Beetles. So he collected living beetles as well as dead.

I descended. Of course I did. There were more beetles than I had realised; more boxes, more breeds. I went deeper than that though. I kept on going down the ladder. I put it down to my state of mind; I've always been the type to ignore that which I don't understand, or that is no business of mine. But I was thinking, *he owes me this week's bugs.* Maybe you are putting things together now? Where are my bugs at? Haha. I think some of you have had too much to drink. Anyway.

Deep, deep, deep down. I found the beetle man. You know Gleam: you can always go deeper. We are surface dwellers, but there is a whole world of empty rooms beneath our feet, and who knows what lurks down there. Beetle man had found something interesting. He was in a room too big for me to see the sides of, lit by torches placed around him. He was crouched over the edge of a pool of black water.

"Hey," I said. "You owe me a week's bugs."

I startled him, and he jumped back. I'd left the sound of the beetles behind long ago. We were deep. Deep into Old Gleam, into the original structure.

"I've got your bugs," he whispered. Then he started to laugh. "You like bugs?" he asked me.

"Sure I do," I said. "Who can't use more bugs?"

"Look at this," he said. He gestured towards the water.

At first I thought—I'll tell you what I thought. I thought, I dared to think, that he'd found *living bugs.* Some kind of breeding ground, or natural habitat. But no. He'd found a slick of some kind of mysterious liquid. He was dipping his dead beetles. And they were coming out looking like—that's right. Like real bugs. Like—yes, thank you, I'll have them back—like *these* bugs. In fact these are the very ones. Almost indistinguishable, really. It's just the sheen. The sheen is in the liquid, and it remains on the matt black shells once the liquid has dried and gone. He'd been paying me with them, and I'd been using them at High Nest. They were in circulation. And the sheen is incredibly poisonous. Fatally so, if you touch it with your bare skin, which of course I don't. He did. He died just this morning.

None of you look well. I know you want to hurt me now, but trust me; you are too weak. You have an hour or two to live, and then I'll clean out your pockets. And your hidey-hole, barkeep!

I still have the bad dreams, but I'm learning to live with them. It's worth it. The bugs are worth it. It turns out they don't need to be alive to breed. I'm going to walk out of here with my pockets bulging. Bugs can make bugs from beyond the grave. That's the lesson. Death is not the end, my friends. Take solace in that.

Backgame

Lev Mirov

On the last day of my life, the necromancer and I played backgammon all night. I had come to discuss military orders, the latest consultations of the dead, who she would summon, and what information my superiors wanted, but we had long wandered afield: to literature, the magic we both studied, music—anything but the war and my impending death with the rising sun. We drank arrak until we both slurred our words, me only partially to keep my courage up. But our escape from the siege could not last, and I had one more appointment, the one there was no delaying.

I shook hands with my necromancer, paid the military bill, and then, discarding professionalism, hugged her tight. Over many games of backgammon, paid for by the military's desperate need for the secrets only dead soldiers knew, she had become a better friend than I had admitted, even to myself. But when I had to choose who I would visit at the end, she was the top of the list. I wanted the last face I saw to be friendly, and call me by my true name. Of all the necromancers in the city, she was the strangest and the oldest, the very best at her work, deserving of her terrifying reputation. She had frightened away many of the military sorcerers, but we had taken to each other immediately. My strange fate, worn on my skin, nakedly visible, didn't bother her—she had called me by my true name on first introduction, and I had felt more at home at her table than almost anywhere else.

"When you are dead, I shall summon you from the dark sometimes," she said, which is how other people say they will write or call. I promised her I would come and play a board, as if speaking of a teatime visit.

There was no desperate talk of trying to escape my fate; we were professionals, and both of us knew better than to bother with such false hopes. Since I had been born, and the midwife's fortune-teller had predicted I would never be at home in my body and thus doomed to a short life, I had been expecting this. I had not struggled, as expected, with the curious detachment of spirit and bone that comes with dangerous magic, but with the certainty my body was shaped wrong for my spirit, an ill-fitting vessel. Sorcery and good tailoring had given me glamours to change my face and the shape under my uniform, and even the army had gotten on with using my true name after some fighting, but I had never felt true relief from my relentless need to be more like my brothers.

My parents, driven hysterical by my ill fortune, had imagined my body would cause my early death, frantic to stop my inevitable demise by bringing me back to the name and the life they had chosen, as if staying away from magic might save me, but destiny just is. The hour of my departing had only recently been revealed, a party trick gone horribly wrong with the other wartime sorcerers, confirmed by my grim mission orders, but there was a cold comfort in knowing at last my parents had been wrong. The war was a cruel enough executioner, more than sufficient for me.

She watched me from the window amidst the falling ash—I looked back three times, but she did not come out or call to me, not even to give a final goodbye. I circled the city, passing by my favorite temple, the towers quiet tonight, the shuttered, shelled out restaurants, and tried to remember what things had looked like before the siege, thinking of happier days when the city had bustled full of life and noise, the smell of frying oil and the cries of sweets sellers.

Still thinking of the ancient imperial gates decorated for long-abandoned parades, the street markets and their cold hibiscus tea in summertime, I came under the bombardment, and there met the most final of all my deaths, as my destiny had foretold.

It took her some weeks to revive me, but she kept her word. The cannons rumbled on, steady as a heartbeat, as constant as the day I died. She called me back in the old bath-house, among the calcified remnants of one of the pools, the half-ruined walls a shield to hide her from prying eyes, though the stars of the rare clear night came through the ruined roof. Chthonic wine lay on the snow as dark as blood, and bone char streaked her hair from the goat fat she had burned to summon me. Behind the necromancer's mask, her eyes were wild and dilated, round as saucers. Her voice sounded like the smoked out ruin where she had done her magic, like she was speaking for the mineral waters that had once bubbled from under the broken tiles. "Hey," she growled, then coughed, weak from work.

Being back was not entirely welcome, despite what I had presumed before dying happened to me. I squinted through the stinking bone haze. Smells were new and overwhelming. I felt sick already.

"Why did you bring me here? What do you need?" New life was sharply uncomfortable, skin and bones pinching me like an ill-fitting corset I had forgotten how to wear. Something was different about physicality this time, but I could not quite pinpoint it yet.

"It's complicated," she said, as if that was any answer. "I think the world is better with you in it." She held her hands out to me over the low fire, inviting me to step across, the final step to make this resurrection stick. Her dark brown skin was painted with ash, intricate bones to make herself like a corpse, as if our places had been exchanged and she was the one buried beneath a heap of rubble a half-dozen streets over where the old theatre had been.

"But I died," I stammered, my voice lower than I remembered. Some terrible thing, just on the edge of memory, bit at my thoughts, a shape I could not outline. Lightning-white pain, cold smothering snow, and so much darkness. "What have you done to bring me here?"

She did not withdraw her white stained hands. "What's done is done," she said defiantly, no answer at all. Every moment I lingered, my ability to see things bigger than myself was shrinking. The shape of what she had done was leaving me in flashes; lightning, a doorway, something green, something red. Something dark and heavy that smelled of her rose-oil perfume lingered on; that scared me the most. "Are you coming or not?"

I came. Resurrections are hard work and you don't turn one down without good reasons. Her hand was solid and real in my own, and I was already corporeal enough to smudge the paint. We crossed out of the circle together. She threw salt in my wake to close the door to death, which was when I collapsed and my legs wouldn't move.

She fed me honeyed wine until my new body fit me about as awkwardly as the last one had. It was, for the first time, the right body, the one I had always needed and never had before dying, angular and flat-chested, like someone had drawn my father as a younger man and slid me inside. I no longer looked like my mother, no longer slid awkwardly in clothes I struggled to make fit me as they would have fit my brother. I was not exactly handsome, but I was myself, high-cheeked and broad-lipped, eyes deep-set and hooded like I remembered, at last fully my father's son with his olive-brown skin, my own rough hair as black as the indigo and glamours had painted it. How she had managed to fix that, I feared to ask.

Being alive wasn't exactly wonderful. Nightmares tormented me. Specters leapt out of the night to eat away at me. I felt them chewing over my bones, sucking the marrow out of me, but I was outside it, unharmed by the hideous pain. Every night she would rush in like a billow of silk sails, nightgown flying like a pennant, her curly hair all tangled, trying to soothe my horrified screams. I drank tinctures of forgetfulness when offered but the dreams lingered on. Whatever I forgot, it wasn't her face, twisted with guilt, or the biting pain that took hours of wakefulness to shake.

She said little, drained by her labors, and I was too ill with recovering from death to question much. I had expected I would have a lot of questions, but getting used to being corporeal was hard work. She shuttered her doors and closed the windows and didn't answer when military men like I used to be tried to knock the door in. Nobody was stupid enough to try and barge into a necromancer's home. Somehow they figured out what she had done, because one day I looked out and there was a sign that said 'Danger of Dead – Keep Away'. We were the epicenter of a contamination zone, magic hemming us in, not that there was anywhere to go.

The army had written me off now that I had a body that fit me. I wasn't even useful to my old commanders as a source of information about enemy movements or good for spying on rivals inside the walls, as I might have been as a ghost. Now I was a danger, unable to be cut down, at the mercy of the necromancer who had raised me. In a way, being abomination, too dangerous to be let out, hardly felt like a new sorrow.

Together, we summoned the energy to hide the house as a ruin, as if it had been a victim of the shelling, full of trapped spells and too dangerous to be crossed. Surely the other sorcerers would find what we had done in short order, especially if scavengers came looking for something to eat or barter. But we hardly need have worried—the siege seemed to intensify, and the sorcerers were busy with other tasks, more important than one necromancer and one revenant, now out of sight, and, perhaps, out of mind.

We often sat around her table in total silence as she fed me. It took time to work up the energy to ask questions as I puttered around her house on awkward feet, learning how to pick things up and sit on the low furniture without falling through it. Corporeality came in fits and spurts; sometimes as easy as eating a winter currant, sometimes an exhausting as a tearful fight with a spoon that was supposed to carry bone broth to sustain me that I could not quite bring myself to grasp or lift.

"When are you going to tell me why you did it?" I asked, two weeks into my recovery. "Bodily resurrection is called the hardest magic of all. It must have cost you things I cannot count to bring me here like this."

She sighed tiredly. The ash paint had washed off long ago but I still saw the white bones smeared across her black body when I looked at her just the wrong way. Other times, her face was only half there, gruesome and cut open. I didn't quite know how to mention it. "I don't need a reason," she said defiantly.

"I need one," I insisted. "You broke the necromancer's oath to bring me here. We're trapped, the city is even smaller for us than what the siege has left. If I ever show my face, no one will dare acknowledge me, even my own parents would rather die of shame than have a revenant child. For what?"

"Your parents hardly acknowledged you anyway," she said, as if this diversion would distract me.

"Tell me," I insisted, the loudest I had ever been since dying. It wasn't very loud at all.

"I missed you," she replied, as if I would be content with a child's answer.

"It was three weeks!" I surprised myself by slapping my hand on the table and hitting it solidly. "It must have taken you the entire time to prepare! Did you even wait for my corpse to be recovered before you started in on the ritual purifications?"

"No," she admitted, almost smiling. "No, I didn't wait. I started as soon as you left."

"Oh." Loudness left me as the wind passed through my lungs, which always seemed to be the most insubstantial part of me. I could never quite catch my breath fully, as if the air had become heavier than my body. "Why?"

She rolled her lip between her teeth and took her time. I waited. "All my friends die," she said at last. "The war kills them all. But I thought—I don't know. If anybody could get used to being dead and alive at the same time, it's you. You said you used to feel like a ghost in a borrowed body anyway, like your body never fit you right. Why not give you more time, a better suit?"

"Why me? Why not a lover?" I asked uncertainly. Her list of gone friends was long; everyone's was. The siege was into the ninth month and we mostly ate magic, exhausting to produce and exhausting to eat. Nothing would have grown under the magical snow they bombarded us with constantly even if we had space to grow it. It had never snowed like this before—many people had died from the unending cold. I had figured death would be a relief from army food; it almost had been.

She laughed. "What lovers? I needed a backgammon partner and you were the best. I had the most fun with you."

We stared at each other for a while, neither of us speaking. I could not count my own questions: how long would this new body of mine last? When would I die again? What kind of life was I going to have as her pet revenant? The stories said that revenants were little better than slaves, that the army outside had revenants in its midst; when would I find out what she planned to do with her command of me? Should I give up these awkward attempts to sit at her table, and flee, spirit-form? Where was there to flee to? I could not remember where I had been.

But instead of speaking to what hung in the air, she pushed a cup of tea at me. I fumbled to pick it up with my awkward, corporeal hands. I wondered, if the stories were true, why she did not simply command me to drink. But that had never seemed her nature, and I wondered if the stories of necromancers and their dead bone-armies of helpless slaves had it wrong.

"Please stay," she said softly, no fire to the request at all. A hundred games began this way; please stay, just for a little while; please stay, share some wine or a nargilah with me. Please stay, I cannot stand the sound of the enemy's thunder alone.

The tea tasted of smoke and lemon against my tongue. Sharp like death, but sweeter, too, the bright citrus I remembered at festivals from summers before the war. "I will for a while," I said at last, not sure if I had any choice in how I came or left. But I found I did want to stay. Where else was there to go? Who else would even see me now?

She smiled, but her eyes were sad. For a minute I saw her as she really was; still so young, so scared, unchangingly young despite long years in the business that aged everyone. She was haunted by something, a magic whose shape was so vast I could barely even see it, a shadow I had never even begun to see before I had died. "I'm so glad," she said, as soft as her vulnerabilities.

We played backgammon until the early dawn, drinking tea as I learned to be solid, listening to the distant sound of the war that had killed us both. The enemy snow fell so thick and heavy that it buried the sign that hedged us in. When she smiled at me over the board, I thought I might be really alive after all.

Hollow

Benjamin Jacobson

In the light of a fading star, the Hollowmen wrestled. Crowskin watched, perched and ready for his moment to come. The vision of the creatures, a hundred-foot tall, but still human in form, grappling in the twilit wasteland, had become a common one. It had a dark beauty, like the taste of blood or the cry of a motherless orphan. He breathed deep and inhaled the dust of the land that had once been a city, now rubble beneath their feet. Crowskin checked his oil supply. He had precious little. If he failed to recover some today, he may not survive to see another fray.

These two had fought before and often. The Statesmen, as Crowskin called the taller one, generally won, if winning meant standing your ground and taking fewer hits. The Statesman had folded paper skin in the places that weren't torn. Every joint was marked by a seam that made him appear to be assembled out of parts. Cerulean stripes crossed the seams on his legs and arms adding regality to the tatterdemalion. Another stripe ran down his otherwise featureless face. He stalked with the gait of a great ape. A mighty clawed slap landed across his chest and a stream of oil spewed forth and began to rain to the ground.

The Cathedral, the other Hollowman, reared back from his successful attack. Cathedral's torso was all points and spires. A lucky blow could detach a spike and make him bleed oil; this had kept Crowskin nicely supplied in the past. Today, Cathedral's vigor had turned the tide against the usually dependable Statesman. Yet the Statesman faltered only momentarily and an open hand strike landed on Cathedral's chest. A bounty of riches tumbled to the ground, enough to keep Crowskin safe for a year, if he could get to it.

The scavengers would be coming soon. He wasn't the only one who needed the discarded treasures of these giants. The other Hollowmen would come. The small ones, startups, some as short as twelve feet, would not ignore him, would not let him feast at their feet. If he wanted what he needed he had to go now.

Crowskin ran his fingers over his feathered cape. His hand came away thick with the flame-resistant salve. He rubbed the deposit on his cheeks, coughing at the strong smell, and then looked to the behemoths. For a moment he was taken by their apocalyptic majesty. As the sun set, their silhouettes filled the sapphire sky. Their blows were quiet as rats' feet over broken glass; their screams whispers on the wind. Why shouldn't they be, for they were the Hollowmen, the final fate of humanity? He donned his thick gauntlets and threw his pump over his back. Stave in one hand and siphon in the other he made his way to the battleground.

They'd tussled enough that the sight of first blood lay a hundred yards from their shuffling feet. A smile crossed Crowskin's lips as he stood at the edge of the oil pond. A last column of sunlight drew a rainbow at his feet. He took one look toward the horizon for scavengers before dropping his stave and dunking his siphon in the pool. He'd churned up a good half gallon when he heard the scream.

The high-pitched, guttural cry marked it unmistakably as a Wholeman. Though it drowned out the dry-grass shuffling of the combatants, they paid it no heed, but Crowskin turned in time to see the kid burst upon them.

"Look upon me, Monsters! I am a Wholeman and I have come for you," the kid shrieked.

The scene was comical. The kid stood at barely five feet, a cockroach to Cathedral at whose feet he stood. Crowskin would have found it hard not to laugh if he didn't fear this intrusion would spoil his bounty. He grabbed his stave, threw his pump around his shoulder and cautiously headed toward the kid.

The kid continued, "Ignore me at your peril, for my wrath is righteous."

Crowskin snickered. Whichever movement had indoctrinated this boy, they'd taught him all the right emotions and none of the right responses. Crowskin double-stepped to reach him, afraid that before he did the Cathedral might step once and end the kid's impotent protest. Only as he got within twenty yards did he notice the treasure in the kid's hand. Steel. A sword, an honest to goodness, forged weapon. The risk/reward ratio on this adventure had just gone up.

The kid hacked at the toes of the Cathedral. This close, Crowskin couldn't comprehend the movements of the giants, but the placement of their feet suggested that the monsters were in a hard grapple and they had a few moments to escape. The kid's face had turned red as he flailed helplessly at the creature. Nothing boils the blood faster than being ignored by your tormentors.

"Kid! Come this way! You're going to get killed." Crowskin called with outstretched hand. That got the kid's attention. He looked up. His piercing blue eyes stood bright against his red skin. He paused only for a moment and in that moment Cathedral's foot rose beyond their sight line. "Now!" Crowskin said.

The kid swung his sword. With an unnatural twist Crowskin parried the spontaneous blow with his stave, only to have it break in two.

"I will not join you, Hollowman! Keep your petty tyranny."

Crowskin ducked another swing and grabbed his stave-halves. "Do I look like a Hollowman to you, Kid? This is not initiation. It's an invitation to get out of here."

"I come to fight; if you've come to stop me then you're one of them." He swung a third time, a tired swing. The tip of the sword barely cleared the ground.

"I fight them, too. Believe me! If I thought it would do any good, I'd clip their toenails all day. You're not killing them. You're not even hurting them. These ones, they're too big to fall. You have to get them when their young. Come with me and I'll show you."

The sword tip touched the ground, but before a decision could be made Crowskin noticed the eclipse of the sky. He launched himself at the kid and tackled him to the ground, taking care not to impale himself. The foot fell softly just beyond their legs. A puff of air and dust flew across them.

"Do you believe me now?" Crowskin said before getting to his feet. "Come with me and I'll show you how to hurt them, yes, even kill them, but come now, before it's too late." The kid was confused, but if Crowskin couldn't get him to leave before the scavengers arrived they'd both pay the price.

"Okay?" he said as if asking himself, "okay! I'll follow you. Death to Hollowmen!"

"Yeah," Crowskin said, "of course. Death to Hollowmen."

Adjusting to his new status, Crowskin calculated what he could salvage. He took a few steps and the kid thankfully followed without further instruction. Back at the oil pool he stuck his siphon in, but kept the pump on his back.

"Lesson one, Kid, if you want to fight a Hollowman you need oil. See that lever on my back, start pumping and don't stop until the gauge says full or I say run." The kid took instruction well and pumped like a pro. Crowskin scanned the dark horizon of the twilight kingdom. This was a push, he knew. The kid would slow him down and he'd already stayed too long, but without the oil, they wouldn't survive anyway. Darkness fell.

That the Hollowmen could stalk so quietly amazed Crowskin. Cathedral and Statesman's ruckus could barely be heard just a few hundred yards away and they were gargantuan. It was the nature of emptiness, he supposed, and some element of the magic that transformed men into monsters. The smaller variety could approach in near silence especially when sound was obscured by the working of a manual pump and the strained breaths of a young man.

Between the idea and the reality of their ambush, Crowskin struck the flint and stone concealed in his gauntlet and held it to his staff, already pretreated in oil. The flame leaped into existence and the shadows of the scavengers fell long on the ground. Three Hollowmen.

Crowskin recognized the largest, a ten-yard crag-faced maniac he'd named the Rock. The other two smaller assailants were the Clerk, a miniature, if fifteen feet can be thought to be miniature, version of the Statesman, and the Fighter, a scrappy ten-footer with a missing hand courtesy of Crowskin. He lit the back half of his stave and handed it to the Kid, who'd stopped pumping.

"Time for Lesson Two. Only one thing can hurt a Hollowman. Fire. They're stuffed. Walking effigies. You can light them up real good, but right now, we have to get out of here. One-on-one is barely a fair fight with these monsters and they will kill us. So whatever bravado you still have, stuff in your scabbard and listen to me. On the count of three, I'll go left and you go right. Wave the torch behind you and do not stop running until you hear my next direction. Do you understand me?"

A flash to his right was the torch in the hand of the kid being flailed erratically in the face of the Fighter. The monster flinched, but Crowskin knew it wouldn't last. It was a mistake to fight Hollowmen like animals. They were men after all and smart enough to learn and to strategize. Fire was only an edge, like a sword in a knife fight, but plenty of men had died with a two inch blade in their gut. Distracted by the kid, Crowskin heard only a shuffle of wind as he found himself seized by the Rock.

The Rock squeezed his chest, not enough to stop his lungs, but enough to force his breath out. He feigned fainting. Truth was the Hollowmen wanted the oil. Men were a distraction, a nuisance. Get out of their way and they'll rob you blind and leave you helpless, but as a rule they didn't want to kill you. The Rock cast him aside. Crowskin struggled to get his air back while falling but lost it all again on impact.

The torch had gone out in the melee. He checked his canister by hand. It had been dented, the lever broken. The only light to see by came from the kid's frantic battle. Crowskin smiled. The kid had courage and little else. Crowskin remembered himself at that age. Ready to take on the Hollowmen, to save the world. Had he been stupid or noble? Both, he guessed, like this kid. Still he'd spent so much time in their shadows he'd almost stopped thinking of them as the enemy. He barely even hated them anymore. He hated them like he hated rain, but this kid still burned with the fresh wound. This is what we made of the world? These are my choices, join the Hollowmen and live as a part of a consumption machine, or refuse and eat their scraps?

The knot in his gut tightened, reminding him that it had always been there. When you fight a losing battle, you forget your purpose, so you don't have to face the failure. Here he lay, playing dead on a battlefield, scared to lose the few scraps the Hollowmen had left them. The Rock and the Clerk had moved to the puddle sucking up oil through their proboscises. They ignored the plight of their compatriot or rather used it to their competitive advantage. The kid was giving a good showing. Keeping the Fighter at bay, but not really doing any damage.

It would be an easy thing to take the Fighter from behind. Give him a singe on his backside then grab the kid and run to the hills with the oil. It's what he should do, to be safe, to keep living. It's what he should do.

He clicked his fingers, relit his torch, and raced to the pond. The Hollowmen, lost in their gluttonous repast failed to notice the torch fly into the pool. The fire erupted, engulfing their heads in flame. Crowskin felt the heat wave suck the moisture out of his salve. The fiery tendrils reached out to caress his face. He threw his cape around himself. The crackle and whine of fire drowned out the subtle screams of the Hollowmen.

Swaddled in his cape Crowskin coughed at the dark cloud that also hid him. A tingle of pain on the back of his head turned to a pinch, then a punch, and finally a rush of agony he couldn't ignore. He reached back to find he'd left his hood down. His hair was on fire and, when he brought it back around, so was the back of his gauntlet. He held tight down cradling the flame in front of him and cowering below the one all around. A few more seconds and the heat would subside. A few more seconds...

The Rock grabbed him again, but this time with a flaming hand. The creature, eyeless like all Hollowmen, nevertheless stared him down. Its face was smoke and cinders. The remains of his proboscis hung lewdly over a paper frown. Crowskin's feathers sizzled in the grip. When the creature opened its maw to let out a whimpering roar, Crowskin flung his still burning gauntlet down its gullet.

Instantly Crowskin was dropped to the ground. The Rock gripped its throat, flailed about and then fell into the pool of fire. Death to the Hollowmen.

The Clerk had buried its face in the stand, extinguishing the damage done by the initial assault. Weaponless and injured, Crowskin decided, with one dead Hollowman, that he could take this victory and run. He looked to the kid who, incredibly, had engaged the Fighter to a standstill. He fought the instinct to run to the boy, a useless gesture, instead listening for the shuffle of giant feet he headed into the dark. As he approached the titans he noticed the stars disappearing and reappearing behind their giant forms. He slipped through an oil slick he had not noticed, but recovered enough to find his feet.

The only light was the now distant flailing of the kid's torch and the shifting starlight. Somewhere the Clerk stalked him, or perhaps had run to the hills licking his wounds, he couldn't know in the darkness. Crowskin checked the flint and stone in his remaining gauntlet. Click, click, spark. Enough. He pulled his pump around to the front of his body and jammed the lever into position. It resisted at first, the dents of his impact not wanting to give way, but he leveraged it against its casing and pop. He was ready.

With siphon in hand he triggered the release. The oil shot out in a stream. He did his best to soak the foot of the Statesman. The monster, as usual, ignored him. He waved the hose back and forth, thinking for a moment about how much oil he was wasting and if he would have enough to make another assault. Then he looked to the kid, still vigorously defending himself. He held his fingers below the stream and snapped.

Flame erupted from the pump. The flash blinded Crowskin. He took his sightless moment to throw his hood over his head. His fingers grazed the fresh burns there and he flinched at the sensation. As his vision returned he saw the massive form of the Statesman aflame from foot to thigh. The Hollowman danced hysterically: raising and lowering its massive legs, its arms akimbo. The big ones acted slowly, but always in their own best interest. He wondered how long it would take before the Statesman decided to drop to the ground to extinguish the flame. He knew he needed to be gone before then. The Cathedral had departed and anything that could spook a Hollowman should also make a Wholeman wary.

Crowskin discovered that the pump had expelled all its fuel. He dropped it to the ground and turned to run. The burning man lit the whole landscape like midday. The kid stood staring past him at the spectacle, while beyond him the Fighter had wisely decided to flee.

As Crowskin reached the kid he shouted out, "Death to Hollowmen!" and for the first time in a long time it felt like more than a slogan. "Now come with me." After a moment of silent contemplation of the burning Statesman, the kid turned and followed.

The kid ate hungrily from the cured meat Crowskin had given him. They hadn't spoken on the entire return voyage and now that they sat, in Crowskin's forest hideout, the time for silence had ended.

"Who are you?" Crowskin asked.

"My name is—" the kid replied.

"Stop," Crowskin interrupted. "I didn't ask for your name. Your name is just a leash your parents hung around your neck to pull you around by. When the Hollowmen come, they take your name first. I asked who you are."

"I don't know what you want?" the kid said.

"You don't know and shouldn't care." Crowskin internally chastised himself for giving an argument when a conversation was needed. It been so long since he'd talked to anyone, let alone someone who agreed with him. "Tell me about your life. What brought you to the middle of the desert to kill Hollowmen?"

"I hate the Hollowmen," the kid said. "I come from the Valley of Dying Stars. My village was pledged to a Hollowman we called Sweeney. Sweeney protected us, blessed our fields and kept our beasts fertile. This is the way it was in my mother's time and on back. Each fall as the harvest was collected Sweeney would take our strongest leaders into itself, so they could become part of it.

"Then the drought came." The kid's eyes turned down as he spoke. "We could not supply what Sweeney demanded. He began to wither before us, to writhe in pain and to beg in his whisper voice for more. He spoke in the voices of the past.

"We argued and fought. To feed Sweeney was to starve ourselves. My mother and a few others protested. The elders argued that we couldn't survive without Sweeney. That it protected us from worse Hollowmen and also blessed our village. My mother said that Sweeney had never blessed us at all, that our prosperity belong to us, those who had worked for it, and that we would never know what lies Sweeney had told until we lived free of them.

"Despite her protest it was decided to feed Sweeney. As Sweeney was filled, so were we emptied. The elderly died first, then the children. By the time Sweeney had recovered even the strongest of us, even my mother, was weak with hunger.

"Most of the elders had died in the feeding. Unencumbered my mother confronted Sweeney, who had become fat on our sacrifice. She took this sword." He grabbed the hilt of his weapon and gripped it tightly as he spoke. "With it she demanded that Sweeney return his blessing to the fields and the river, so that we may live another day to serve it.

"Sweeney agreed and departed to the fields, as it often did." A moment of hesitation in the kid's practiced tale. He swallowed hard before continuing.

"He never returned, nor did our water, nor our beasts." Another pause.

"My Mother died with one hand holding this weapon and the other on my cheek. Just before she passed she swore me to vengeance against Sweeney. I agreed heartily and that is the path you found me on. I know now they can be killed, and I intend to kill every last Hollowman. Death to the Hollowmen."

Crowskin leaned back. "It's a familiar story," he said, "I have the same one. Details changed perhaps but the narrative remains. This is humanity's story now. Rats in the tombs, crows in the graveyard."

"I owe you something," Crowskin continued, "When I saw you fight in the wasteland, it reminded me that although we have no chance of destroying this pestilence we brought upon ourselves, we can still fight. We can still kill. While there are a few wholemen left we can resist, until we are all dead or taken. It is the most pathetic victory, but a victory none-the-less."

"You will help me then?" the kid spoke through a gnawed-off hunk of cured meat.

"I will, as you have helped me. Come." Crowskin lead him through his lair. A knotted collection of nets and trees. After a short walk they came to the armory, a great twisted oak. From a low branch Crowskin grabbed an old cloak and handed to the boy.

"You may have this." he said. "It's a rat's coat, much like my crowskin. You'll notice the salve upon it. It resists the heat of flame. Bathe it in water before going out." He handed to the kid but the boy was distracted, his young eyes locked on a sphere of nothingness they couldn't even see.

"What is it?" asked the boy, reaching out. Crowskin grabbed his hand.

"Don't touch." Crowskin looked at the hole in the world with fresh eyes, though it was more a sensation than a view, the feeling of emptiness, his treasure and his captor. He took a deep breath, knowing the time to tell had come. Whether the kid knew or not taking him into his confidence marked the moment of inheritance. "This is a hollow."

"A hollow?" asked the kid.

"The promise of the Hollowmen. Back before me and before you, we were just people, human beings. When we had to come together, we did it through argument and debate and compromise. It was a messy, ugly thing. It rarely worked. People would rather fight than be wrong, rather kill than let others have what they lacked. We had war then. Wholemen would fight each other for resources, for power, but mostly for their own righteousness. Then the hollows came.

"Holes in reality. Someone made them. Broke the universe for the power it would give. And it did give power. Watch."

Crowskin plucked a leaf from the tree and dangled it above the hollow. He released it and it glided down until, impossibly, it froze in mid-air. The kid leaned in, looking for the trick, but Crowskin put his arm across his chest.

"What does a leaf want?" Crowskin asked.

"What? A leaf doesn't want."

"That's a hollow view to ascribe desire only to yourself. The leaf has purpose and therefore desire."

"A leaf wants sun?"

"You learned something in your village." Crowskin grabbed the claw that hung just below the hollow and reached in with it to grab the suspended leaf. "Put out your hand."

The kid did so and Crowskin dropped the leaf into it. A glow grew within it, but beyond that the sunlight streaming through the netted roof turned to find the leaf, pulled into its impossible gravity. Smoke rose as the leaf burst into fire. The kid yelped and pulled back his hand. The leaf incinerated before it hit the ground.

"Amazing, right? Horrible though they are the hollows are a gift. To turn an object toward its ultimate purpose. It could have been our salvation, but humans have their own purpose.

"At first they were another bauble to fight over. Fair enough, there had always been plenty of those. With the power of the hollow one could recreate anything, but we mostly made weapons to make our wars more deadly and our leaders more righteous. Until one day a Wholeman entered a hollow.

"This is how the Hollowmen were born, a soul deprived of flesh and wrapped in the ideology of its own convictions. The power went inside them, they could take it with them and they could bring others along. It cost only their doubts, their empathy, their consideration. When you become a Hollowman, you leave substance behind, shape without form; all things fall to your power. There is no longer a need to doubt. A shell of a human with a desire only for righteous might. Like that leaf, the Hollowmen are the ultimate expression of our desire."

The kid reached his hand out again, stopping himself short of touching the hollow. He drew his hand around it as if stroking the invisible surface. "Do you know? Can you kill it?"

"You cannot touch a hole nor destroy an absence. The world is falling apart piece by piece. We cannot kill them. Even the Hollowman I destroyed in the wasteland is recovering now, a fragment of the soul inside reconfiguring itself in that hollow. You can join the shredders or fight to keep the quilt from buckling, but there is no win for us. Everything falls apart."

"Will you fight with me, Ratscoat?" again Crowskin held out the garment this time as a baptismal gown. The kid took it, but without looking away from the hollow.

"We'll never kill them?" he asked.

"The best we can hope for is to slow them down, a whimper in the wind."

The kid, Ratscoat, said nothing, but donned the garment, a patchwork cloak of rats' skin.

Ceremonial discussions aside, the fatigue of Crowskin's journey caught up with him. They'd taken a few short respites on the road home, but not nearly enough to recharge his aching muscles or rest his burnt head. He showed Ratscoat to the hammocks, slung between two dogwood trees. He flipped the lower one, dumping a random collection of scavenged goods to the ground and offered it to the kid.

"Work begins tomorrow," he said as he scaled the tree to reach his own perch. Within a moment of lying down, he fell asleep.

The howl of the coyotes woke Crowskin. It was twilight again. He hopped down. The kid slept. Crowskin let him. It may be nothing and only by letting him sleep could he get his hands on...

The sword was beautiful. Crowskin coveted it. He'd spent so many years piecemealing weapons and tools. Building a life from the remnants of what came before, but never had he come upon such a find. He lifted the scabbard and pulled the sword out partially. It shined. He ran his finger across the sharp of the blade and came back bleeding. He licked the blood as he felt the weight of the weapon.

Could he trick the kid, or ask for it? He wasn't used to the subtle negotiations of Wholemen. He'd become a bit hollow himself, hiding alone in the woods fighting an unconscionable, obvious evil. He lived in the shade of the twilight kingdom.

Silence surprised him.

The coyotes had been howling, but one-by-one they'd stopped. That's not the way of coyotes. He climbed his look out tree, only when he reached the top did he realize he hadn't put down the sword.

Over the limbs of a nearby grove he saw them, the Clerk, his face still singed, and the Fighter. Their direction was unmistakable. Somehow they'd followed him, but it was the view on the horizon that frightened Crowskin.

The Statesman and the Cathedral and a half dozen more of the titans coming for the forest. He'd lose his home and he'd lose his hollow. He slid down the trunk and landed hard at the bottom, almost falling over. He looked to his hand again to the sword, a weapon with a purpose. Without pausing, without as much as a whisper, he headed to the armory.

He thrust the blade into the hollow. With a slow pull he unsheathed a demon of a weapon. The blade had become solid, blue flame, flickering yet constant. Poised eternally between potency and existence. A smile crossed Crowskin's face. Maybe he could kill after all, maybe there was a way.

He couldn't reach the Hollowmen fast enough. He pushed his way through the woods, hopping over roots and jumping onto boulders. When he found them he paused, just for a moment, lifted his blade and screamed.

He went for the Fighter first, slashing and spinning, a dervish of destruction. The monster's limbs separated like paper, falling in ribbons. The merest touch of the blade littered the ground with pieces of Hollowmen. In a moment it ended. Crowskin stood, sword-up, in mountain of slivers.

Crowskin thought he could see fear in the Clerk's emotionless face. It was a precious-sight, priceless in a world with so few victories for humans.

"Death to Hollowmen!" he cried before running sword first toward the Clerk.

The Clerk's maw gaped, his broken jaw unhinging. In a single forward thrust he deep-throated the blade and Crowskin's hand. The hollowman was toothless, but his jaw was powerful enough to wedge the blade away. Crowskin escaped with his fingers, for the moment. The monster swallowed Crowskin's courage along with his weapon. Suddenly helpless, he looked behind him, hoping to see the kid, but no. He'd left him sleeping and the hollowmen were just wind in dry grass. If Ratscoat couldn't be his savior he'd at least be his legacy.

The broken maw opened again. Crowskin froze. A shadow fell.

A confusion of flapping and the field cleared. Crowskin looked around. A new hollowman had arrived, hard, on top of the Clerk. He'd never been lucky or religious, but this circumstance opened his mind. No time for reverie, he turned to hoof it back to his hideout. He couldn't resist a look back.

The new hollowman slashed at his competitor with vigor and violence. Hollowmen were careful, thinking creatures by nature, but this young thing was wild. He recognized the kid in that moment, the same unrestrained fury. He'd taken the hollow. He'd crossed the line.

Crowskin's gut twisted in pain as he watched the kid eviscerate the Clerk. He came back to that beauty. Maybe tragedy was the only beauty to find. The kid could no more resist the hollow than he could resist the sword. Victory in a pretty bow for those willing to take it and the only cost was your soul.

The Kid roared as he stood over his defeated foe, but it came as a whimper. Crowskin did not run. He had nowhere to run to. He approached the Kid.

The Kid sniffed at him, like a whisper on the wind a voice came to Crowskin.

"Join me," it said with outstretched hand.

Crowskin thought a moment. The war was lost long ago. He could only delay the inevitable at best. What little chance he had as a wholeman was nothing compared to what a hollowman could do. Maybe it was time to change, to accept his fate. To become what he most feared. Maybe there were no wholemen anymore, only broken men and hollow men in Death's twilight kingdom.

Crowskin looked at the corpse of the Clerk. He saw a glint of blue inside. Crowskin's own betrayal. The Kid watched as he walked over and pulled the sword, still strong, still vital from the shredded remains of their enemy. The Kid's featureless face crunched together in recognition. His head tilted like a dog. He groped the ground and avoided speech.

Crowskin was hollow either way. He knew that now. He'd become a stuffed man long ago, when he put all else aside. Emptiness was his only concern. He never thought of filling the holes. He was a *hole*man. With a single slash he took the Kid's head. It rolled on the ground like a tumbleweed in the wasteland.

This is the way the world ends, he thought.

Night Child

Mame Bougouma Diene

It was the dusk of her eighth day, the eve of her ninth night, her very first sunset, and her last.

"We gotta push forward, Jaydaan," she said, her breath short. "There has to be an entrance somewhere."

To her left, her brother maintained the steady but futile pace north to the subterranean magma fields of home. They had hours at best, no more than a full waking cycle, before night dropped like an axe. Still, with a little luck they could reach ancient forays into the region, shade themselves from the temperature drop, and with more luck than she had earned make their way back to Nyand'La.

The sun lingered in the sky, beating down on them as if it weren't his last cycles as well as theirs. Theirs had more finality to it, but the biting light denied the imminence of death. Everything was different in the dark. Ghosts come alive in the dark, a grain of dust on the air schemes and bites in the dark. She could run all cycle long in the sunlight, but she needed the haunted dampness of the tunnels when the dark came.

"See anything?" she asked between breaths.

"No," Jaydaan answered. "But we don't even know what we're looking for. No one's mapped this region properly for decades."

There were bound to be some. There had to be. The Tunnel Wars were a thousand-year-old nightmare, and most of the former infiltration tunnels had been decommissioned, but a few were still accessible in this region. At the height of the fighting, when the pits clogged with bodies and disease, there was no telling how many more had been dug, nor where they led. The ice changed the topography. There were new hills every season. They could be running over an entrance right then, and never know it.

In less than a few hours, sooner maybe, the planetary terminator would become visible, slicing day into night across the hemisphere. There would be no twilight, no endless stream of purple clouds. If you had told her so she would have asked you what twilight meant. There was either light or no light at all.

They'd had little time to ponder over their predicament. They'd gone to sleep comfortably, woken up, and, six hours into the waking cycle, swarms of mountain-gliders in the thousands came screeching down from the western plateau, their powerful membrane wings pounding the air close overhead. The banshee-like marsupials were fighting in their flight. The sky was wide enough for all of them, but they were used to small numbers and tight formations. They couldn't coordinate a thousand squadrons, and none of them wanted to be left behind.

Mountain gliders were the last to cross the plains before night sealed half the planet in ice. They should have had several full cycles before the murder of beasts were a smudge on the clouds bordering the western continental plateau. Time had slipped somehow, and now they dropped out of the sky, their mangled wings bloodied by their siblings' claws in desperation.

They had gathered their water, meat strips, dry bread and their weapons hurriedly, ran and hadn't stopped since.

Something ruffled in a nearby bush. They slowed their run to a halt. Her brother pulled a short diamond-tipped spear from his quiver.

"Hold on," he said, holding up his hand.

She relaxed immediately. If he had sensed a large animal he would not have used his short spear. He was ready for the kill, but not worried about it.

"I'll be right back."

He slipped behind a bush.

Her own broken solar lancer hung at her side, hardly any good for hunting, but in its contracted form she could weld it as a knife if need be. Her brother's short spear had been a stun stick and a lightning trap until the crystal core melted. It was still the better weapon. She glanced at the ruffle in the bush, and took a step ahead and out of the thicket, grateful to catch a breath.

Small, rolling hills spread north ahead of them. Behind her the short brownish green brush grew steadily thicker, greener, and bigger, turning into a forest of giant baobab trees a little under six hundred kilometers south.

The ground was rough between the hillocks; small bushes and thorny trees dotted the healing landscape, often in clusters, conspiring against the gravel to take the land away from it. Patches of yellow-brown grass grew between the bushes, sometimes tall as two men, mostly thinner than a week-old beard. The sickly grass was as healthy as it was ever going to get, but then it never had much water. The grasslands and the forest drew all the surrounding underground water sources to their roots. Even at this distance, the filaments sucked the land near dry.

A small, blue-green water lizard peeked his head through a hole in the ground, and looked about in the shadow of her thigh. It lunged at her for a bite, and she picked it off the ground by the tail. You could squeeze enough water for yourself from the bushes and the long grass, but you had to reach deep, or you could squeeze the lizard's abdominal pouch and drink the water it stored there. You could. The lizard was not poisonous, but the water inevitably came in contact with its internal fluids, and those were rancid and purulent.

She threw the small animal ahead of her and took a sip from her leather flask. The lizard tumbled mid-air, opened the thin skin flaps around his head and shoulders, glided to the ground, then skittered off towards the border.

The border was only a short distance south: the absence of any indication that marked the no-man's-land leading to the forest. Any closer than two hundred kilometers, and the reflection from the trees would burn through the retina; closer, and the radiation would cause organ failure, shutting the body down one step at a time.

From where she stood, she could see beyond the border to where the bush started thickening, opening on the plains spreading to the horizon towards the high altitude plateaus and the semi-desertic mountain regions ahead of the Eastern and Western Rims. South, over the vast flatland, the first of the mountain-sized trees glowed faintly across the horizon even against the blearing sun: an impossibly long wall, four thousand feet tall, running along the equator from one continental plateau to another.

The wall was an illusion; the trees were far apart enough for thousands of species to blossom between them. She looked up at the forever midday sky. The strong northward winds carried pungent drafts of the distant underbrush, where the smaller life forms growing alongside the mammoth baobabs shriveled on themselves in the day season, opening their pods to gulp down the radiation from the trees, and fed on it during the night season, in colors that had no name—a microcosm that kept the forest alive through the night.

The wind was warm. Jaydaan's hand landed on her shoulder.

"Thinking about the forest again?" he asked, dropping a dwarf boar in his pouch.

The animal's frontal tusk caught in the fabric and ripped a hole through the side of the sack. She caught a glimpse of one of its missing eyes where the spear had hit it. The useless appendage was the reason the baby boar, and even its larger parents, made for easy prey, getting caught in everything low enough for it to claw into. Where they migrated to or from it must have served a purpose, out there in the plains, but here they were like angry little berries on a bush.

She nodded.

"Yeah. Haven't you?" she answered, her eyes drawn back to the distant glow, undulating against the heat, like the steamy breath of a giant on a cold cycle. The woodland always sent her imagination running, but since they'd woken up it was tugging against their stampede, like a lasso around a horse-badger's neck.

"All the time," he said, shaking his head. "Even now, I feel like I should be heading towards it. It looks nice, doesn't it?"

"The most poisonous things look nice, Jay," she said absently. "That's their catch. The same goes for people."

Jaydaan barked a laugh. It had been cycles since he had, and it broke her heart to hear it, knowing they would die. She had always wanted to get a glimpse of the night, to get a feel of true cold, taking these trips south late in the season, beating the closing gates by a few seconds. Even as a little girl, the giant metal doors looming behind her tiny frame, the sirens ringing, and fellow Nyandi streaming in from the nomadic day settlements running and laughing, blue-brown horse badgers carrying loads on their backs, their two extra arms nudging children playfully, pulling them close and licking their faces with their rough tongue, the sun high in the sky behind them, and chains of trucks hauling last minute supplies of grain and game clearing a path through the throngs. She would stand there until they dragged her in fighting, hungry for the unknown.

"Alright, we gotta pick up pace," she said, refusing to give up, "and keep our eyes open for anything. Anything Jaydaan. Piles of boulders, if you catch a draft where there shouldn't be one you—"

Her brother spun suddenly, crouching, and facing the opposite direction. Something much larger was creeping behind nearby bushes.

She froze, one hand on her knife.

Whatever the creature was, it didn't seem to care for them. Yet. It didn't stay behind one bush but moved around, still several yards away, without trying to come closer. She couldn't discern it, not clearly, but in the shadow of the small hills it looked as if the little light there was..., was bound to it. The air appeared darker around it, as if sucked dry, a stygian ring outlining its shape against the sunlight.

Jaydaan lay on his stomach and crawled backwards towards her, pulling her down as the thing passed behind a bush, moving down the same line over and again, pacing. They crawled back further and slipped behind a bush of their own. She turned towards her brother. He was kneeling head down, holding his head in his hands, trembling slightly. She reached for him, but he held his hand up, stopping her, and took a hold of himself.

A branch snapped loudly a few feet away. They bounced backwards and up, landing knife and spear in hand.

A very tall and thin albino stood in front of them: somewhere between eight and nine feet tall, bald with red stripes painted down his head and face and over his eyes that spun unfocused in their sockets. She had the distinct feeling the man was blind. He seemed otherwise unarmed, dressed in only a loincloth, a stack of ropes rolled around his shoulder. She corrected her assumption; sharp claws dangled at the end of those ropes, possibly a throwing weapon, maybe a tool of some sorts. He didn't look like a hunter, but in her knowledge those things were usually both.

Up close, the halo disappeared intermittently around him. He might be an albino, but his skin was covered in a type of pulsating fungus. It grew from him, covering his already pale skin in uneven, white, and wrinkly blotches. The fungus released a negative light; a thick, black ooze with a hemoglobin-like inner glow, contracting and expanding an inch or so around him, drawing light in, toying with it, and releasing it before pulling it back in short angry bursts. Against his absolute stillness, he looked surrounded by crackles of tiny black lightning.

He opened his mouth, but nothing sounded. He stood there leaning slightly forward, focused on them, his jaws open on pearly white teeth sharpened to a tip. The pulsating stopped and the darkness closed in on him with intent.

Besides her Jaydaan trembled again, *kneeling in a circular field somewhere in the baobab forest. The field reached to the horizon in every direction; on either end of it the side of the trees facing the clearing had been trimmed down, scrapped clean of their bark, and painted a deep black so the sun didn't reflect from them. The field was wide enough that even the blast of radiation from the tree tops was too far away to harm the thousands of crops growing along the meadow. Looking up, the light from the tree-wall formed a circular dome of sunshine several thousand feet above the ground. Her people had taken centuries to clear the trees and...* She gasped for air and looked ahead, her vision slipping in and out of focus. The horizon appeared closer; she felt the ground build a wave beneath her, sending her stomach into her spine. Her mind reeled but Jaydaan was kneeling there, groaning, his eyes bulging in and out of their sockets.

Taking a deeper breath to clear her mind, an unsteady step towards her brother *sent her over a root, rolling into the long translucent grass of the field, the sap flowing through the foot-long blades a multicolored hue, sometimes deep blue and purple, then slightly green to yellow and red. The blade crepitated as her shadow reached over it, and the sap started glowing faintly, the plant confusing her shade for night. She picked herself up...* running into Jaydaan. This time he let out a yell, convulsing against the gravel. She kicked the spear out of his hand before he stabbed himself, and bounced backwards and turned to face the stranger.

The man had backed up a couple of steps, his eyes spinning counter clockwise, red irises appearing and disappearing in regular cycles. He was from somewhere in the forest. There was no doubt he planted those visions in her mind, and was driving her brother mad. He was trying to turn them into him, into thinking they were him, and had for cycles, but what was he doing here and why? He was too far to make it home. Perhaps..., the harder she tried the less she could hold her thoughts together. She opted to let them go.

The albino turned his face on her, she felt the grass change between her bare toes, *and something wet, multi-legged and pulpy ran over her foot,* and pushed the intrusive thought away. The creature tilted its head. It was impossible to read his expression with his eyes rotating in their sockets, but she sensed an amused, mild-interest in his poise, just as when an adult finds that a playfully fighting kid was not fighting playfully, and holds his head at arm's bay, while he punches away at nothing.

Something large cracked in the distance. It couldn't be the dizziness this time. Even against the northward gales, the blast knocked her off her feet as all over the planet, forty thousand square kilometers of land and water froze in a flash, contracting with a sonic boom-like crunch, sending tremors all the way to the eastern plateau.

Where the ice began, night mowed across the surface. She had seen circular saws used all the time in the deep caves. Every Nyandi was a smith, though it was never her favorite task, but perhaps it looked the same from space, a searing axe of darkness freezing everything in its path.

Now she knew what death sounded like as another ripple rocked the surface with the ground crushed under instant glaciation a hundred kilometers west. In Nyand'La, the cave doors will have been sealed by now, the anti-quake devices will absorb the shock while night closes over the fields and ruins of her people before the war. The great forges will hum. Their mother will cry. The turbines will pump air into the network. And the Nyandi will sing for one waking cycle and one sleeping cycle, and pray for a soundless night and a bountiful day.

The creature had dismissed her entirely, and if he felt the blasts he gave no sign, stepping forward, leaning deeper in towards where Jaydaan wreathed around, bleeding out his ears and nose, choke holding himself.

The terminator was less than fifty kilometers away. The planet felt dwarfed. She felt gigantic. She leaped up from where she stood, just as her brother's head made a sound like exploding fruit, spraying bone fragment and brain matter against her leg. She bounced off a small boulder, threw her knife, rolled over forward, and using her arms to push herself up, she propelled herself kicking upwards towards his chest with a roar.

He deflected the knife and threw one end of the rope in her direction. The claw missed her by an inch. She rolled over to her left, but the rope twisted and lashed at her leg. A weak hold, the claw caught in a cluster of stones cut her forward motion, but she kicked back at the man's knee.

His leg didn't move, the fungus started oozing the strange black light, and his leg bent around her foot like rubber. The black tendrils were all around him now, a foot long and creeping down her leg where she had aimed and missed. He spun on his other leg, lashing out with both ends of the rope, his head floating over the ooze. The claws struck in rapid volleys, the rope undulating and snapping like an enraged snake.

She pushed herself up, crawling backwards, only narrowly dodging the blows. The blasts were getting stronger, more frequent, bouncing over each other in waves. She should have been tossed around like a toy doll, most of her bones crushed, but to her and the albino the air was steady. Caught in the glowing tar, a bubble shielded them from the elements.

Immediately in front of her, the rope and claws billowed at such intensity she could see the man clearly behind them, and behind him an immense black curtain revealed the universe.

She had never seen stars before. The sky arm-wrestled between night and day. Night leaned heavily on the wrist, its elbow digging into the table and thrusting its shoulder. With every second, more stars appeared against a translucent, warped halo blending the two forces.

The rope caught her leg. He pulled her backwards and up, grabbing hold of her ankle, lashing her left and right as if she were the rope. The land raced back and forth beneath her eyes. She could hardly catch her breath; the sun appeared intermittently but she could not tell where it was from the ground.

He threw his arm back.

Her body flew upwards, high over his shoulder, letting her dangle head down behind his knee, and facing away from him into oblivion. In the fight she had lost track of sound, but in that instant the thunderous glaciation burst through her eardrums, only meters away. Beyond it, the bushes, hills, and grass were shinning white, catching some of the last sun rays breaking faintly through the formidable darkness and penetrating cold.

In these last moments she could hear everything around her distinctly, the ice crepitating on branches, the albino's almost nonexistent breathing, and the tidal wave of arctic death bearing down on her. And impossibly far in the distance, the baobab forest glowed in the night sky: multicolored hues pigmenting its base, the top of the organic fortress wall fading into darkness, a curtain swaying between the world and the night.

The scenery accelerated suddenly. Her body twisted into an arc as he threw his arm forward. The night crept ahead, only a few feet away from them. She felt her hair freeze, the tingle of cold burning infinitely slowly through every strand as the temperature dropped two hundred degrees in an instant.

The cold touched her skull, spreading in waves over her skin. For the briefest of moments, she saw the world through the ice covering her eyes, shimmering in prisms, and exiting the stage slowly as stars won this battle with the sun. They would learn their lesson soon enough. They always did. She blessed her ninth night as her eyes exploded under the pressure. She was a night child.

The land stood frozen from horizon to horizon. Somewhere in the farness, no one heard the rumble of frostbite announcing the long night.

Except for the ghost of the forest floating away, you may not notice much difference between the ice statues carved from lonesome trees among the swirling towers of ice rising randomly across the land, but on a hill you could see what might appear to the persnickety observer like a giant about to smash a smaller being against a boulder.

Inside the battle-shaped ice carving, a dark glow grew steadily, pulsating gently, lighting the ice a dark, reddish hue against the otherwise starlit night. The glow grew until it delineated only the taller figure clearly to its fingertips.

The glow intensified, dark black and blood red, and the ice burst outwards. The smaller figure still encased in ice shattering on the ground, its diamond-like dust blown away by the wind.

A bare foot shrouded intermittently in reddish-black darts crushed what might have been an arm. The albino shook off what was left of the ice and turned south. He looked to where his rope lay frozen, stuck to the ground and rested a hand on it. The negative light enrobed it, the ice not melting but peeling off the cords. He freed it, wrapping it around his shoulder.

The ooze pouring out of the fungus solidified, creating a slick, skin tight armor isolating him from the sub-arctic drifts. He looked around. Surprisingly most of the Nyandi girl's skull remained intact. He knelt before it, laying his hand on it as he had his rope and hummed powerfully into the night.

The missing ice grew back, taking on the features of the young girl down to her flowing hair. She had been quite pretty, brown haired and dark brown skin, radiant purple-grey eyes, full lips and a fair fight.

They would have been home cycles ago if he had not caught their thoughts and delayed them. Somehow, she had managed to withstand his hypnosis at close range, and he could not read her mind entirely when she attacked him. The *Shedu* could have used her; she'd had the makings of a fine demon. If only they'd been more malleable, they would be on their way with him, their minds at peace. The others *had* to have been luckier than he. The war with the Nakkam loomed. They needed all the minds they could use.

He turned towards the misty rainbow of the forest, leaving her head to melt at dawn, a smile on her lips. *A night child indeed,* he thought, and walked away southbound, the beating, sanguine light, disappearing into the darkness.

Venom in the Cloud Forest

Katherine Quevedo

Sweat crept down Acoti's left temple and tickled his eyebrow as he stabbed his knife into the tree bark. He withdrew the blade and used it to smear the thick, sanguine resin against the wound in his neck. His skin burned as he rubbed it in with his finger. He knew the resin of the dragon's blood tree would help heal his wound, but he feared it couldn't counter the poison.

Why had he been targeted? He hadn't seen the person who'd blown the dart, only heard his attacker sneer, "You poisoned me first," before disappearing among the mist and leaves.

Now Acoti knelt, dug his fingers into the soggy dirt, and yelled, "I never poisoned anyone!" His voice echoed off the mountainside. The cloud forest around him rustled in apparent mockery. The constant mist at this altitude sent beads of water sliding down the tree trunks and pooling on the orchids, like his sweat from the poison fever.

He heard footsteps approaching. His friend Pamba appeared through the mist clutching a jar with both hands, her stone bracelets clacking against the hard clay and her dark hair swishing. She spotted him, gasped, and rushed over, sloshing water over her wrists as she ran.

"Acoti, you're so pale," she said. She set the jar down against the tree trunk and tried unsuccessfully to help him up. The cool water on her hands felt soothing against his fevered arms. "I heard you yell," she said. "What happened?"

He pointed to the puncture wound in his neck, which the resin had temporarily stained a muddy red. "A surprise this morning."

Pamba gasped and sank to the dirt beside him.

"But whoever it was," he said, "picked something very slow-acting to put on the dart."

"You didn't see who blew it at you?"

"He hid himself well. When I heard him run off, I didn't have the strength to follow him."

"I'm surprised you had the strength to get here. You should have gone straight to Cuadelo." She stood up and tried once again to pull him with her. "What good is a curer if you don't go to him when you're hurt?"

Acoti had been hoping to avoid Cuadelo. He thought back to the last meeting with the elders, where he had worked up the courage to ask why, whenever Cuadelo read and interpreted the petroglyphs for them, the carvings always agreed with everything the curer said. Cuadelo had glared at him, then laughed and tried to brush the question aside, but some of the elders had watched Acoti with great interest.

Now Acoti fought against the obvious conclusion, hoping it was nothing more than a product of his fever. Could the curer have poisoned him?

"I've never so much as pointed a blowgun at another person," he said. "How could he think that I poisoned him?"

Pamba, thinking he still spoke in general terms about his attacker, said, "Let's go see the curer first, then you can worry about that. Come on. Dragon's blood is good for cuts, not poison. You should know that."

He did. It had just been wishful thinking. He debated telling Pamba of his suspicions, but he knew how much she admired the curer's medicinal knowledge.

Pamba helped him stagger toward Cuadelo's hut along the riverbank. On the way, she snapped a twig off a branch and instructed Acoti to chew on it to slow his fever, since the dragon's blood had done nothing to help his symptoms. He chewed the end, gagged at the taste, and tucked it away next to his knife.

Soon they arrived at the section of the riverbank where Cuadelo lived, where the mist always seemed thinner than in other parts of the cloud forest. In front of the hut, Pamba lifted her hand to knock on the door, when it swung open suddenly. There stood the curer, tall and gangly. Cuadelo wore a collar of blue hummingbird feathers, a flap of fur from the spectacled bear around his waist, and the brightest orange feathers of the cock-of-the-rock around each of his thighs. His silvering hair indicated he was far from young, although his calves were as taut as ever.

He took one look at Acoti and motioned them both inside. There, a small fire crackled below a pot that filled the windowless hut with salty scents. Suddenly Acoti imagined that the crackling was coming from his hot forehead and that the saltiness was emanating from his sweat. He shook his head.

Pamba set her jar down by the door. "He's been poisoned."

"So I see. I'm so glad you brought him to me. Now run along."

"Please, curer, I'd like to make sure he's all right."

"That won't be necessary." Cuadelo ushered her out of the hut so briskly, she didn't even have a chance to retrieve her jar. She managed to cast one look of concern back at Acoti before the door shut behind her. Acoti wished she could stay. One of her homemade remedies sounded far more comforting than being here with the curer, even if it meant chewing a hundred more of those bitter twigs.

Cuadelo led Acoti to a chair of wood and braided grass, made him sit, and examined his neck. "A dart wound. You tried using resin of the dragon's blood tree on this?" He clucked his tongue. The red-brown stain was a sure giveaway. "That will do nothing for your fever. Very rarely do I see this kind of wound when we're not at war." He released

Acoti's neck and stepped back. "Or perhaps we are." His eyes searched Acoti's.

"Someone out there thinks I deserve this," he said, hoping it was the answer Cuadelo was seeking.

The curer ignored this statement. "Did you try drinking directly from the river?"

"That was the first thing I did."

Cuadelo paced around the chair, his bright feathers fluttering. "So even the great river could not purify you. The very source of all our life. How does that make you feel?"

"I might be more concerned if it weren't for the fact that someone deliberately did this to me."

Cuadelo took Pamba's jar and emptied the contents into a pot. Then he hung the pot over the fire next to the one with the salty smells.

"Can we open the door?" Acoti asked. He wiped his forehead with his hand.

Again, Cuadelo ignored what he'd said. "Acoti, it is carved in the sacred petroglyphs that sometimes the health of the many thrives on the sickness of the one. But for that to happen, the one must be isolated. Do you understand?"

Acoti shook his head. Somewhere between his throbbing, burning head and the curer's cryptic words, he was struggling to concentrate.

"Consider our surroundings. The clouds float through our forest and let our trees and ferns and mosses strip the very moisture from the air."

Acoti nodded.

"Now, suppose those clouds became tainted, poisoned. What would happen then?"

A cloud of venom? Acoti had never heard of such a thing.

Cuadelo answered his own question. "The venom would collect on the plants and trickle down into the soil. It would penetrate the roots and poison the very plants we rely on for food and medicine. You see, it would poison us. It would be our undoing."

"I'm not sure I understand, curer."

"Ideas are like clouds. They drift by, and some bits here and there catch on." Cuadelo leaned forward. "Acoti, your ideas are a venom. A spider bite to the mind."

All this talk of clouds, venom, and spiders made Acoti's head swim with fever. The hut seemed to be growing and shrinking incessantly. Cuadelo danced in Acoti's vision, the orange feathers blurring until the curer's thighs looked as bright as a ripe naranjilla.

"Venom spreads if it isn't contained or removed, Acoti. Can you think of no one you may have offended?"

The curer's voice sounded small and distant. Acoti commanded his mind to focus, and he thought of the penetrating look Cuadelo had given him just moments ago when describing the puncture point as a wound of war. He recalled receiving that look once before from Cuadelo, in front of the elders not too long ago.

"You," Acoti said, his own voice sounding fuzzy now too.

The curer had stopped pacing and loomed over Acoti, tall and swaying like an avocado tree. "Did you ever stop to think that, when you tried to discredit me in front of the elders, you got it backwards? That I say what I say because I've already read it on the petroglyphs?"

Acoti closed his eyes to block out the throbbing room, the blurry orange and blue feathers. He pressed the heels of his palms against his eyelids and felt sweat gather around his eyebrows, but he couldn't tell if it was from his palms or his temples. He opened his eyes and saw Cuadelo crouching next to his chair.

"These people have entrusted me with their health," the curer said.

"Then why are you keeping me sick?"

"Poisonous words!" Cuadelo sprang up. "You are crazy with a fever. No one will listen to you now and soak up your venom. You see, I have protected their health. And as for yours, there is an antidote. But you're going to have to earn it."

Acoti shut his eyes, wishing the so-called curer's words could stay small and distant, but now Cuadelo's voice seemed to resound through the hut.

"Tomorrow, Acoti, you will go before the elders. You will tell them that your ideas poisoned you and that only I could cure you. The dragon's blood will have healed your wound by then, and the stain will be gone." He tapped his lip. "Your friend knows about your wound too, doesn't she? Well, she will have to keep her mouth shut about it too. I'm sure she wouldn't like to wind up with a dart sticking out of her neck."

Ordinarily this would have made Acoti's blood boil, but his body was already too feverish for him to feel any difference. His gaze swept the hut for Cuadelo's blowgun. Nothing. But of course the curer wouldn't leave such proof lying out in the open.

"Just cure me," Acoti said, his voice thick.

"Swear it first."

Acoti stared at the bright orange feathers around Cuadelo's thighs. Even though the curer stood still, the feathers seemed to rustle and flap of their own accord, like butterflies. Cuadelo was right; he was too delirious with fever to have any credibility, and for all he knew, the poison was fatal. "I swear it."

"Very well." Cuadelo rose and busied himself at the pots over the fire, using Pamba's water to make a tea.

Cuadelo kept his back to Acoti while he sprinkled dried herbs into the pot. Acoti noticed him cast one guarded look back as he grabbed an animal skin pouch and produced a stick from it. Was the old man planning to poison him for good this time? Acoti half-closed his eyes to feign fatigue so that he could observe. Luckily, the old man's back was too skinny to block everything from view. Out of the corner of his eye, Acoti saw him move the stick in a typical stirring motion, but without immersing it at all into the liquid. Acoti caught glimpses of two orange and blue butterfly wings attached to the bottom of the stick. Clearly this was no typical stirrer.

What Acoti glimpsed next, he assumed was a product of the fever. The tea rose slightly above the rim of the pot and twisted in the air, making shapes like curlicues before sinking back down. Then Cuadelo grabbed a stone spoon with his free hand and ladled some of the steaming tea into a cup, still moving the butterfly stick with his other hand. When he was done ladling, the spoon looked misshapen, as if the liquid had carved it up in places. He quickly put away the damaged spoon and closed the stick back in its pouch. He turned and held the steaming cup toward Acoti.

Acoti didn't take it. "How do I know this isn't a stronger poison?"

Cuadelo lowered the cup a bit, still holding it within Acoti's reach. "Don't be so dramatic. That girl knows you're here; there's no use in her knowing that you came to the curer and then didn't leave here healed. But more importantly, I need you to go before the elders like we agreed. Now drink. This is your antidote."

The cup was the first thing Acoti had touched all day that felt hotter than his own body. The tea tasted bitter—like the old man, he thought with a cold inner laugh. Cold. That word had seemed so foreign to him just a moment ago, but he could already feel his body cooling. By the time he had gulped all the tea down, his mind already felt clearer.

His thoughts turned to the butterfly stick. Had it actually warped the stone spoon? Was that the only stone it could warp?

"Tomorrow at midday," Cuadelo said. "The elders and I will be meeting at the petroglyphs. Come alone."

Acoti nodded. As he stood to leave, he feigned grogginess and asked Cuadelo to hand him Pamba's jar. While the curer's back was turned, Acoti snatched up the pouch with the butterfly stick and hurriedly swapped it with the twig from Pamba. He threw the pouch down just before the curer turned back toward him with the jar.

Outside at last, Acoti refilled Pamba's jar at the riverbank—it was the least he could do before returning it to her—and turned to leave, when through the lack of mist he spotted her crouching near the curer's hut, hugging herself. He waved and motioned her to join him silently.

She rubbed her nose with the back of her hand and reluctantly stood, avoiding his eyes.

Only when they had moved well out of earshot of the hut did she speak. "I was waiting outside to get my jar back, and I heard everything. I never should have brought you to him."

After a few steps, he said, "If you hadn't, I would still be wondering who did this to me. You wanted to make sure I got healed, and I wanted some answers. We both got what we wanted."

Her voice regained some of its spark. "You're not healed. He may have taken down your fever, he may have given you his antidote, but he caused it all in the first place, and now he's hurt you even more. You're not healed." As though reminded of how weak Acoti had been earlier, she snatched her jar from his hands. "Thank you for getting this for me. I should have intervened! What a terrible man, that so-called curer."

Acoti shrugged. "He may be corrupt, but every village needs a curer."

"I'm sure I could do his job well enough," she grumbled.

"But could you do it without this?" Acoti pulled out the stick with the butterfly wings.

"What is that?"

"I think it might be a wand. While he was making my antidote, he used this to move the water around, and it left impressions in his stone spoon."

"I can't believe you managed to get this from him. Won't he find out?"

"He keeps it in a special pouch. I don't think he uses it very often."

"What are you going to do with it?"

Acoti had been so caught in the extremes of fever to health, he hadn't thought that far ahead. "I think this controls the river water somehow."

"One way to find out."

She set the jar on the ground, and Acoti swept the stick over it. The water inside trembled. Nothing else happened at first, but then gradually it rose as if he were pouring more water in. Rather than spill over the sides, the water gathered around the rim. Then it recessed back in, leaving the rim warped with ridges where it used to be smooth.

Both their mouths hung open.

"I'll bet this isn't the only thing it can change," Pamba said. "Maybe you were right about the petroglyphs, how they always conveniently agree with what he says."

Was the curer using magic to rewrite history and sway the elders? Acoti glanced at the sky. If they hurried, they could make it to the petroglyphs and back before dark. He and Pamba descended into the lower regions of the forest, where the mist passed through less often and the trees grew taller and thinner, as though trying to reach the higher elevations and their more abundant moisture. The petroglyphs stretched along the riverbank at the edge of a grassy field.

"Look." Pamba pointed to one section of the carvings.

There, a small boulder protruded from the river with designs etched into its dry upper facets. Butterflies with familiar half orange, half blue wings fluttered around it. Pamba and Acoti ran to the river's edge. More and more butterflies drifted toward the boulder as they approached. Acoti decided to wade in after them in case he had to be close to the rock for the magic to work.

The riverbed felt jagged under his feet, which were used to the squishy soil of the cloud forest, but he waded as close as he could to the boulder. With water rushing around his knees, Acoti held out the wand and traced with it above the rock face. A thin layer of water rose from the river and covered the boulder like a shroud. It lingered there for a moment, making the rock look like a giant rough gem, and then the water flowed back to rejoin the rest of the river. Suddenly the zigzags on the boulder had become square spirals and the sunbursts had morphed into concentric circles.

He and Pamba stared at each other.

The next day, when the sun slid into its zenith, Acoti and Pamba walked together into the petroglyph clearing, where the elders sat in a semicircle in front of Cuadelo. When the curer saw Pamba, his eyes bulged. He glared at Acoti and made him feel as if he had just been shot at with another dart.

"You owe me your life," Cuadelo boomed, "do you not?" His ribcage expanded and contracted in abnormally quick breaths. "Tell the elders what your treacherous ideas did to your mind."

The elders muttered and turned their weathered faces to Acoti.

"Tell them," Cuadelo continued, "how you learned, all in one day, how quickly a poison can spread and how thoroughly it can be cast out. Tell them how the river's healing powers rejected you until I intervened."

Pamba interjected. "One doesn't thank a jaguar for attacking and then letting go. Show them, Acoti. Show them the one thing the curer keeps that's more harmful than his poison darts and blowgun."

Again the elders muttered.

Acoti stared straight into Cuadelo's eyes as he withdrew the wand from a pouch and lifted it toward the riverbed petroglyphs. The water rose and formed its chrysalis over the rock, scattering the butterflies momentarily. A collective breath sounded from the elders, as if that quiet utterance was the most shock they had the energy to convey. By the time the water had died down and left new markings in its wake, the elders sat in silence.

Finally the eldest stood up with some effort and shuffled forward, her long, white hair fluttering in the breeze. Her head barely reached Cuadelo's armpit, but she spoke to him with such authority that Acoti saw the curer flinch. "My grandmother helped carve these rocks for her generation. How could you take away her voice like this?"

From where he stood, Acoti could see sweat trickling from Cuadelo's temples.

"You steal voices," the eldest continued, "like an illness. I no longer know now whether it was your meddling or our ancestors' true voices, but the petroglyphs say that the health of the many can sometimes thrive on the sickness of the one."

"But the one must be isolated," Acoti added.

She turned to him while the rest of the elders mumbled their approval. She smiled. "Of course." She shuffled over to him and held her hand out for the wand. Acoti handed it to her, and she promptly snapped it in half. Immediately the orange and blue butterflies dispersed from the river into the meadow and forest.

The eldest called to Cuadelo, "That stick may as well be your body if you're ever found near this village again. I will see to it."

Acoti saw Cuadelo's leg muscles tightening, like a jaguar ready to pounce. When he lunged, Acoti managed to intercept him and shove him backward several steps.

"First you poison someone," the eldest said, shaking her head, "and now you're attacking outright? We won't let you be both our sickness and our cure."

Cuadelo's gaze swept around the group, but he found no sympathy. He glared at Acoti, but with one glance down at the strap holding Acoti's knife, Cuadelo's face fell, his bony shoulders caved, and he slinked backward to the river. He waded through it, ruining the feathers around his thighs, and dashed into the trees on the other side.

"Now," the eldest said as though she had done nothing more than throw out a rotting avocado, "Acoti, isn't it? I hear you are handy with a knife but not so fond of butchering. Perhaps you would be willing to use your talents instead for carving our own voices into the rock?"

Record the voices of his people? "It would be an honor."

"And you," she said, addressing Pamba, "are said to have a way with plants. Pamba, correct?"

She nodded.

The eldest placed her frail arm on Pamba's shoulder. "I daresay this solstice will bring us not only a new harvest, but a new curer as well. Perhaps you would be willing?"

Pamba looked at the elders watching her. Acoti knew it was one thing to carve petroglyphs, but another thing entirely to be entrusted with a whole village's health.

"I'm really not as knowledgeable as I should be," she said. "But if the elders find me worthy, then of course."

The eldest patted Pamba's shoulder and gestured with her other arm to the petroglyphs extending well beyond the river's reach. "Not everyone's voice was stolen. You have plenty of others to guide you."

Two weeks later, Acoti was engrossed in carving the great mystery of his people's existence in the cloud forest, when his knife slipped and cut his finger. He sucked on the wound while checking his work. Just a few more marks, and he would have captured as well as he could the strange situation of living in a world constantly invaded by clouds: the mist obscured his people's surroundings while also enabling them to thrive. They had learned to embrace the uncertainty. Well, all but Cuadelo, whose attempts at control had weakened him far more than any fever ever could. No one had seen him since his disgrace in front of the elders.

Acoti's etchings were still rough, to be sure, but every day they resembled more and more the untainted carvings of generations before him. He hoped he could say the same of the ideas he recorded.

His cut stung only slightly, but he remembered being told not too long ago that he should always go straight to the curer. This time he looked forward to it. In fact, he could already feel the soothing tingle of dragon's blood on his skin as he approached Pamba's hut.

Winged

Emily McCosh

The sea eventually calms tonight. Half-frozen waves lap at the shores of the City of Stone for hours before setting into glassy, moonlit calm. I lean against the smooth cold of the balcony railing and enjoy the sight. No one has come to bother me in my assigned sleeping quarters—my evening meal appeared on my doorstep, empty tray disappearing when replaced. Although some may find it rude, I enjoy the solitude.

Of course, I'm not entirely alone. Other people just can't see it.

After replacing the empty food platter, I keep the three linen napkins, tossing them to the floor near the foot of the bed. Now, invisible hands rearrange the forget-me-not blue fabric into folded patterns, becoming more intricate as they learn exactly what is between their fingers.

"Aurora," I ask, "what are you making me?"

The napkins float to a crumpled heap on the floor, reflecting white-blue in the polished wood surface as little feet creep away with a feather's weight.

"Aww, don't be like that."

I crawl along the floor on my hands and knees to avoid stepping on her, searching for a glimpse of the phosphorescent light she exudes with any sort of restless emotion.

Water streams from the washtub in the attached room. Over the noise, her gentle cooing echoing through the door—she wants to play.

"Where... did... you... go?" I ask in a sing-song voice, creeping to the washroom.

The washtub is built into the floor, water spouting from a bronze spigot. It redirects upward, bent by Aurora's glass-like hands, shooting in a perfect arc towards me. I roll sideways and only catch stray droplets, opening the door to the large cupboard, flinging out perfectly folded piles of fluffy, paper-white towels to slip inside and close the doors. Wood-dust fills my nose, echoes ringing loudly as Aurora sprays the door.

When I stay still, remaining silent and dry, the water shuts off and she pads away. I follow, snagging the pillow she directs my way and flinging it back. The vibrating hum she emanates is laughter, and her humanoid form becomes more pronounced in flecks of light. The napkins on the floor fold into the shape of a swan, neck bent gracefully.

"Thank you," I say, letting her drop the bird into my cupped hands, careful to avoid the brush of her fingers.

Her lights flicker like the auroras I nicknamed her after. She bounces toward the balcony, bending over the edge and humming to me. I join her, watching the self-drawn coach glide into the lower levels of the palace. Through the glass of its windows, I catch just the slightest glimpse of a slim, hooded figure before it vanishes.

My study subject.

Aurora swings on the railing, dangerously high over the city, but she won't fall. She never falls. I lean on my hands against the rail and let my eyes drift downwards. The seaside city crawls up the slopes of the jagged circle of mountain range, surrounding it like a nest. The walls of the houses below me are gray and smooth like dried clay, each roof a varying shade of slate blue. Floating paper lamps glow with sydar, the people's magic, gently illuminating the sleeping cobblestoned streets. Some make their way to my level of the palace—a tall, slim piece of architecture with rooms of shelf-like slits along the rising tower, a scabby stem of a flower. The room perched atop it resembles the half-opened bud of a rose. On the outer layers of petals, each of the fifteen mages has their own private room, and in the center of the flower they meet when necessary to discuss issues of their lands. They are all elected by the people and work together as a single entity although they represent different sections of the world.

Above me, I can just make out the reflective waters of the skysea among the cold fire of the stars. The floating islands and sparkling sea surrounding them drift above the city like a second skin, only accessible through the sky ships and their tickets so expensive I can't possibly afford them. It's where my parents are. Where they are waiting for me.

The skysea is a recent discovery, and the mages took the best and brightest up on those expensive ships to explore and colonize the new land. My parents were among the first, but the mages had no use for me when my talents had not yet become apparent. Mother and Father did not go willingly, and no one returns from those floating lands. After all this time, the only choice is for *me* to go to *them*.

My eyes burn with unshed tears, and Aurora senses it. She tugs on my arm, her small hands burning and cold at once. It's not unpleasant, but I pull away—I don't like to be touched, even by her. Still, I follow her away from the balcony. The skysea's where I'll be going when this is all over. And if I can gain the trust of my little friend, I'll be taking her with me.

I know my study subject's name before we are even introduced—before I'm even given a chance to see the face he was hiding within his cloak last night. One of the assigned assistants for my project, a middle-aged man with a blotchy morning shave, hands me a sheet of freshly-pressed paper with the man's information. And so I find his name is Psi. I've never heard that name before, not even when I lived on the undersides of the mountains. It's unique.

The rest of his information is vague, and by the time the doors to the study room slide open, I know nothing more about this man than I did last night catching a glimpse of his form through the coach windows.

He enters the room alone—I'm expected to carry out my studies unaccompanied. But I know the mages are keeping an eye on me.

He walks with a stiff gait and hunched favoritism of his left arm, as if it pains him. Still shrouded within the midnight blue cloak he was wearing last night, his age and expression are hidden. The only part visible is the bottom of his chin, skin tanned to a lovely shade.

Despite his shady appearance, Psi shuffles from foot to foot, nervous and younger than I expected.

"Hello," I say, feeling unprofessional in my own youth, "my name is Elza. We'll be working together on project... " I have to check my papers, "...thirty-two."

His hand twitches. I did not offer mine up in the traditional greeting, and it seems to have put him on edge. "Um, Psi."

He has a lovely, thick accent but isn't happy to be here—it drips in his voice. Truthfully, I wouldn't want to be studied either. I don't want to be here now, but it's the only way to get to the skysea. I'm talented, and the mages still want people like me for the skysea. When I prove my worth, they will deliver me into the new land, and right into the arms of my parents.

So I grit my teeth and force my face to smile again, making this work.

"You can remove your cloak," I tell him, organizing papers nervously. He pushes his hood back, keeping the rest draped over his slim form, and my mind blanks. "Holy earth and sky, how old are you?"

"Um." He blinks, taken aback. His black eyelashes are unusually long. "Fifteen."

I mentally kick myself. "Right, fifteen, sorry. I just—"

"Thought I'd be old?" he questions.

Older than me. "No, I guess not."

"But you're just a kid... "

"I'm fifteen," I say. "I'm—I was born with a better natural knowledge of sydar than most people. It's a... thing."

He stares at me, and I notice how blue his eyes are. Not normal blue.

"There are just some papers we need to fill out, then we can get started." I gesture for him to sit on the examination table.

He doesn't. "What are you getting out of this? Or are you just a *skia*?"

Skia. One who studies mythological creatures. "I am a *skia*, and I'm also getting transportation to the skysea."

I don't mention my parents, especially when the mages might be listening. My disgust with them over taking me from my family is only dampened by the knowledge that I'll be joining my parents soon. Still, I don't want them to know anything about my life. Psi stares at me with blatant dislike, eyes roaming over the examination table. I close mine and glance away, spotting Aurora in the corner playing silently with a roll of bandages. She must have followed me in.

"Okay," I say, compromising. "You can sit wherever you want, or stand, I don't care. I need your... full name, year and month of birth, and... ages of your parents and any siblings you might have."

His eyes snap to mine, expression twisting into one of full hatred. I instinctively take a step back, shocked into silence.

He doesn't yell or rage or even open his mouth to speak, but turns and strides back to the door. Aurora sees him going and glides up the wall to hang over the door, and, too quickly to be stopped, reaches her feather-weight hand down his cloak to pluck something as he storms through, slamming it behind him.

She scurries to me and places a downy feather the size of a fingernail in my palm. A feather. And the same, strange black blue color of his eyes. I sigh down at Aurora.

"Well, I don't suppose anyone's going to tell me what I did wrong?" I ask the empty air, still sure the mages are listening.

No one answers, but I never figured they would.

I trudge out of the study room in defeat on my very first day. Aurora follows, cheerful and puppy-like.

It is winter here, and the days consist of only a few hours of sunlight. I make use of it by going to the palace library to find something matching the feather Aurora plucked. I know what it is, but I'd like to cover all the myths before I go about asking Psi anything.

The library is cool and quiet, and I find a nice corner to read in but soon run out of material. I already know all of this. I glower at the book I'm holding, Myths of the Sky, and drop it gently on the floor.

Useless.

With books and the limited sunlight exhausted, I return to my room to find dinner waiting. Nibbling at pheasant with blackberry sauce, I form a shimmering silk of sydar around the feather and trace the bloodline. I'm not entirely sure this is allowed, but my curiosity was always a bit on the wild side.

A glossy family tree appears before me, focusing in on Psi and his direct relatives.

Orphaned. His parents died when he was a small child—he and his younger brother have been under the care of a children's home since then. His brother is still alive, less than a year younger than him, and I pull up his picture. He resembles Psi, but more human. His hair is dark and brown, eyes blue, and skin tanned.

I erase the research, putting the feather in a drawer. I feel guilty, but I was only asking the questions the mages put on the paper for me.

I wonder if they know.

So Psi is magical in some way—that's the only reason he'd be here. And he's letting some strange girl study him. He's going to end up telling me what he's hiding.

I look down at Aurora. I might as well return the favor.

I would more than understand if Psi didn't show up this morning. But he does, shuffling in right after Scruffy the assistant finishes the daunting and unnecessary task of organizing my papers. He looks disheveled, as if sleep evaded him the night before.

"Hello Psi," I say, still not reaching out to touch. "Have a seat."

He still keeps standing but stares at the ceiling when he speaks in an exasperated monotone. "One of the mages informed me that apparently I was rude to you yesterday and I have to apologize."

He peeks down at me, and I offer a smile. "How about this: you don't have to apologize and, if you tell me what you are, I'll show you a trick with my sydar."

I wink, trying to communicate more than just a little trick. He's quick, and I can see I've piqued his interest. He rocks from foot to foot again, something ruffling in his shrouded left arm. He looks vulnerable today—not so frightening.

And he relents.

"I'm uh—I don't know what I am," he says, crestfallen.

"Alright," I put my pen and papers down, "would you like to show me?"

"I have to."

"That's not what I asked."

He finally looks at me and scoots up onto the examination table, waiting. I undo the ties on his cloak and, careful not to skim his skin, pull the soft fabric from his shoulders.

The downy feather Aurora plucked doesn't even begin to cover what he is. His whole left arm, about a hand's length longer than the right, is a partial wing, shimmering with glossy, full grown feathers the black-blue color of his eyes. Each is long as one to four of my hands stretched out, patched with small, scaly ones. They stop just after his shoulder socket and a little farther past his armpit, fading into scaly blue-black skin, eventually turning regular, soft and tan.

I circle him, fascinated. The rough midnight skin extends along to the center of his left shoulder blade. Back in front, I bend over to look at his hand. It resembles a bird claw—a bird of prey, thick and muscular, but not too terribly different from his right. Long, deadly black claws sprout from the tips of his fingers.

I circle him like a fascinated child—mouth open and partially smiling.

"Do you... ?" Psi asks.

I start. So enthralled with the wing-arm, I've mostly forgotten the person it's attached to. I blink up at him. "Sorry, what?"

"Do you... know... what it is?"

Ah. So he's here to find out what he is. It must be difficult to be born with strong sydar and not have your parents to explain to you what's happening—what you even are.

"I think," I begin, returning to examining his clawed hand, "it looks partially like the wing of a *rox*, but I didn't even know that extended to humans."

"What's a *rox*?"

"It's a mythical bird-like creature. Part human, part bird. There's really nothing to know about them because they've never been seen."

Psi looks defeated, so I change the subject. "Which room are you in? I'll come over tonight and show you that thing I was talking about."

He brightens just a bit. "One twenty-two—"

"Hey there!"

Psi and I both jump, startled. His wing ruffles violently. Out of the corner of my eye, I see Aurora dive under the examination table.

I'm lost as to how they got in here, but a boy and a girl stand at the side of the examination table, hands folded in front of them, grinning cheekily. They're twins, each with nests of blond hair and sea-green eyes, they look no more than ten years old. Judging by their clothes, they must be children of one of the mages. They are far too smug for the situation.

"Hi," I say. "How'd you get in here?"

"We're shapeshifters," says the girl.

The boy continues. "That is to say we can shape shift other things—"

"So we just shape shift each other—"

"It really is a lot easier than people think—"

"And fun."

"Yes, definitely fun," the boy says. "I'm Benny."

"And I'm Bletz."

"You can call her Z."

"And you can call him B."

"No one likes keeping track."

They stop, looking at us expectantly, and Psi sniggers. When I smile at him, he only laughs harder.

"Nice wing," Z says.

Psi nods as if saying, 'Sure, thanks'.

"Benny! Bletz!" a voice hollers from outside the doors, infuriated.

B says cheerfully, "Uh-oh."

Z continues, "Time to go. Bye!"

Simultaneously they turn to each other, their bodies melting and compressing into two small shapes that eventually become recognizable as bluebirds. They swirl around our heads and fly out the open window. Their clothes are in a heap on the floor.

"Wow," I say, and Psi grunts in agreement.

A disheveled hand-servant pops his head into the door, looking around frantically before seeing the clothes and turning to us.

I tell him, "They flew out the window."

The man groans, gathers up the clothes, and shuffles away. Psi and I grin at each other; he looks nice when he smiles.

We have a few hours of daylight still left, so I grab some paper and a soft measuring tape, holding them up in question.

Psi nods and smiles.

Aurora skips along behind me to Psi's room. It surprised me that she agreed to this, but it gives me hope. If this can work, maybe Psi will trust me. And maybe Aurora will accompany me to a new life around the skysea.

I knock, and Psi cracks the door, stepping aside to let me in. He's back under his shroud, and a chair has been pushed against the wall, sloppily covering what seems to be claw marks in the wood. His talons are dangerous. I never suspected for a second that they wouldn't be.

At least his hood is down.

His eyes travel over me once, eager to see what it is I have to show him. I take a seat on the floor, gesturing for him to follow. He steps through Aurora to sit opposite me.

"Do you know what the *letyz* are?"

He shakes his head, glancing around.

"They're small creatures with glass-like bodies and expert hiders. They only show themselves to a rare few if they decide to like them. They're not particularly magical other than that, but they're undetectable. You just walked through one a second ago."

Psi blinks and whips his head around, curious but unafraid.

"You can see them?" he asks.

"One so far. Her name is Aurora... well, I named her that. I don't really speak her language."

"Can I see her?"

"We shall see."

I turn to Aurora's shimmering form and Psi's eyes follow, trying to grasp something impossible for him to comprehend. This little *letyz* trusts me; she begins to hum and Psi yelps and rises to his knees, startled by the now undeniable closeness. She waves at him, a gesture learned from me.

"That's," he stumbles for words, finally settling on, "beautiful."

Aurora hums at the compliment, drifting off across Psi's room, already losing interest.

"She has a short attention span, sorry."

He continues to stare at her. "Are you taking her with you, to the skysea?"

"I hope so, but it's hard for her to leave this land—frightening."

He nods and turns back to face me, expression still blank as he takes it all in. Absentmindedly, he mutters, "I wish I could leave like you."

I don't ask why he hasn't already. The answer is too obvious—he can't afford it. Even the rich cannot always. Instead I ask, "Why don't you come with me?"

He rolls his eyes, but not after the briefest shock slides across his features. "The mages won't pay for me to go. I'm not talented. You don't have enough money."

He gestures toward me, a simple action, but I shrink away automatically, chills running down my arms.

He takes it the wrong way.

"Figures," he spits, eyes turning dark and eyebrows gathering into a scowl. He struggles violently to his feet.

"Psi, I don't touch—"

"Yeah, you and everyone else—"

"I don't touch *anyone!*" I snap, voice rising a few octaves, stopping him before he can take it too far. "I can't or, I... won't. After I first started seeing Aurora, it started bothering me to touch people. To touch anything living really. It comes with seeing her. I'm becoming like the *letyz*—taking on their traits."

Psi blinks at me vacantly, the cogs turning in the back of his mind. The fight drains out of him and eventually he sits. "Sorry. I'm just... sorry."

I nod, and he pulls on one of the feathers on his arm, our previous conversation forgotten.

I remind him, feeling timid, "You could come with me."

He snorts. "How?"

"You know something nice about having a friend that no one can see, hear, feel, or anything else? She makes a good thief."

I can see my idea click as his head snaps up. If Psi didn't like me before this moment, there's no doubt now. I'm his new favorite human. He doesn't speak, but his midnight eyes sparkle.

"After you're done studying me?"

"Yes, and Psi? You can't tell anyone about Aurora—the mages keep anything they can't understand. They can't find her, but I'm the next closest thing."

"I know. I won't," he says and rubs his covered wing.

Late that night, after returning from Psi's company, I pull up his brother's picture only to erase it again. I shouldn't be looking. Psi has not once mentioned his family; I know nothing about the life he had before all of this. It makes me curious. Does the brother know? Should he know? Maybe Psi told him. Did his brother look at him with disgust? What happened? What is happening?

A knock sounds on my door—a rhythmic, careful pounding of six that sends Aurora flying under the bed although no one can see her. Then, immediately after and without my permission, one of the mages steps in. Mariet. She greeted me when I first arrived at the City of Stone. Brown haired, brown eyed, and middle aged, she seemed friendly enough when I first met her. She seems friendly enough now.

When I see her, I see the faces of my parents as I'm pulled from their arms.

"Hello Elza," she says. "May I come in?"

I shrug, nudging the feather into a crack in the desk.

She takes a seat on the edge of my bed. "You're up late."

I nod, suspicious. What does she want? "I was talking with Psi."

"Your study subject?" Her head cocks to the side just the slightest bit, and I get the distinct feeling she's manipulating me.

Fine. "Oh yes, I find that the best way to study other living creatures with the capacity for complex emotion is to do it personally. There are plenty of techniques for putting people at ease, but none work better. It makes for a more rewarding experience for both me and the subject. Wouldn't you agree?"

She blinks, thunderstruck, but a split second later the mask slams back into place. "Well, that's fine. You're the expert after all. But I've just spoken to Psi and now I'd like to let you know. Just to make things go easier. Personal experiences should not be shared in the event of a study such as this one. As well as being unnecessary, they may become cause for emotional involvement, you see. I'm sure you understand."

I plaster on a smile. What does she not want me to know about Psi? "Of course."

Seeming satisfied, she rises, nods to me and says, "Have a pleasant evening."

Aurora reappears once the door has closed, humming curiously. I shudder, getting up to take a bath and go to bed.

"Apparently Psi's hiding a little more than we thought."

It is more knocking that wakes me from an exhausted sleep, violent this time, but soft enough so that no one will hear it down the halls. I stumble out of bed, pulling a robe around my shoulders and yanking open the door. Psi stands there, recognizable by the deep blue of his cloak, bouncing nervously on his toes.

"Please let me in," he whispers, desperate.

I step to the side, rubbing my eyes and temples to clear my head. Psi sits on the floor at the foot of my bed, tense. Aurora, curious, emerges from her nest of blankets at the end of my bed and begins to shimmer, making herself visible. He glances at her, stressed.

"What's wrong?" I ask.

He stares at me for a long moment, right into my eyes, daring me never to tell anyone as he pulls the cloak away from his right arm.

Unconsciously, I feel something tighten in my stomach. A patch of feathers, mostly downy but a few quills, litter the upper part of his right arm, accompanied by the rough, bluish skin.

That grew within the last five hours.

Fascination sets in, immediately followed by defeat. An unpleasant sensation slides down my chest to settle in my stomach. The conversation I had with Psi just a few hours ago rushes back—about never telling anyone of Aurora, and why. Psi is no longer just a boy with a wing that can be studied, understood, and released. He's growing slowly into something else. And as long as he continues to change, the mages will never let him leave.

It isn't maliciousness on their part. He would be treated well, but it isn't a life. Not really. The mages' greatest downfall is their curiosity, insatiable and violent until the sun collapses in the sky.

"Oh," I say, voicing my realization.

"Yeah," he says, panic lacing the undertones of his voice. "I don't want to stay here forever. I don't know what I am, but I don't want to stay here forever!"

"Shhh!" I wave my hand at him. The unusually high pitch in his voice might carry to the other rooms.

His chin trembles and he stares away, not wanting to cry in front of me. I try to form some sort of plan. "Okay, if Aurora can steal the papers to get us onto a ship to the skysea—"

"You have to pull them out," he mumbles.

My stomach turns with a new sort of fear. "What?"

He won't meet my eyes. "It's going to be daylight in a couple of hours, and they won't let us just sit in our rooms all day. If they see it, I'll never get out."

"Why don't you just do it?"

"I can't!" He holds up his other hand—talons don't exactly work wonders for fingers.

I grit my teeth. "Psi—"

"The skin will turn back to a normal color. I've tried it before. They'll grow back in a few days, but that's all we need, right?"

"Psi, I can't do that."

"*Why not?*"

"I can't touch you!"

"They're going to keep me here forever Elza! Earth and sky, I don't even know what I am!"

I glower at him. Tears are shining in his eyes, and I just can't touch him. But he's right. Earth and sky, why does he have to be right?

I yank on his cloak, and he fumbles to help me get it off. I grab ahold of his pajamas and pull him roughly forward onto his hands and knees. Aligning myself with his left arm, I secure one knee over his hand and, swallowing back nausea, grab under his right armpit. Cold and burning run up my arm all at once, emanating from his skin. It's painful, but at the same time, isn't. Unpleasant but bearable, and I didn't think it would be. It's more than I could have asked for.

Psi goes along with all my rough movements in the knowledge that I'm doing for him what he can't do for himself. I pinch some of the smaller pin feathers and pull them out swiftly. He hardly winces, like pulling out little splinters. When those are removed, I grasp the larger quill, yanking with force. This one bleeds, and he yelps and wrenches to the side under my grasp.

"Sorry," I breathe, but he doesn't try to move out of the way. There are three more of these size feathers, and one larger. One at a time, I free them from his skin until his right arm is featherless and the skin fades back to its original tan hue.

I release him and sit back. He stays still without looking up. "Thanks."

I punch him in the shoulder, lightheartedly. "Don't ever make me do that again."

He nods. "We'll be gone then, right?"

"Yes, I have an idea, but it has to wait until morning."

He returns to his room after that, and I stay still for a while, letting the burning cold seep from my arms and hands. I look at the pile of feathers on the floor.

The plan has to wait until tomorrow, but I have something I need to do tonight.

Psi's brother appears on the other side of the shimmering apparition I called up using a pin feather. The boy is sleepy—it's still the middle of the night—his hair ruffled and eyes half closed, but at least he doesn't seem too shocked by this kind of contact. He's a bit familiar with sydar. The only difference from his picture is the five pink and puckered claw-like marks still healing across his right eye.

"Um, hi?" he says, yawning widely. He has his brother's accent.

"Hi, sorry about this. Um, what's your name?"

He gives me a look that clearly says, *Are you kidding, you're contacting me and you don't know?*

"Sorry, I just know your brother, Psi."

I don't know what kind of reaction I was expecting, but every bit of sleepiness drains from his face—he looks as if he wants to leap through the shimmering connection and hug me. He looks as if he loves and misses his brother.

"Holy sky, you found him! Where is he? I'm gonna kill him!"

I can see by the excitement in his eyes that he means it playfully, and I smile.

"We're in the City of Stone... but, it's a little complicated—"

"The thing?" he asks, and I blink at him. He pokes his left arm. "His... thing?"

He looks hesitant, not wanting to let me in on the little secret if I don't already know. I smile at him again. "Yeah, that thing."

His face melts into a smile, but he touches the healing wounds on his face that will soon become scars. "I don't know what he told you, but he blames himself. This was an accident. It wasn't his fault."

Psi hadn't mentioned anything, but everything clicks into place all at once... Psi hiding his wing, he's turning into something he can't understand, something more than human, defensive and tight-lipped about his past, Mariet warning me not to discuss his past, the claw marks in the wall...

Oh.

"Please tell me where my brother is," the younger boy pleads with me.

I can't fix my own problems; I don't know if Aurora will come with me or I will ever be able to see the rest of the *letyz*. Earth and sky, I don't even know *what I am*.

But I can fix this.

I smile at the boy across the shimmering illusion. "I'll tell you everything."

Psi and I meet in the dawn-lit study room. It's early, but we must leave before the sun rises.

Aurora is playing with the stolen passes to the skysea.

Seconds after we enter, the shape-shifting twins, B and Z, appear. Each carries a dead chicken from the kitchen, grinning. I contacted them right after Psi's brother, who did eventually calm down and mention that his name is Simon. Once again, they are happy as clams.

"We're escaping from here," I tell them, and B wags his eyebrows. "And we need to you help us by pulling a huge prank on the mages."

The two mischief makers are immediately alert, their faces brightening further.

"We need you to hide in this room, and when the mages come in, make those two chickens look like our bodies."

Psi grins as he finally hears the plan. The twins nod to one another.

"And," I say, holding up my finger, "you can make it look like Psi here went crazy and killed me before he turned into something horrible and died."

"Yes!" B and Z both shout, ecstatic.

Psi shakes his head and chuckles. It's ridiculous, but it'll work.

I hold up the four largest feathers I pulled from Psi last night, their blue glittering in the pale morning light. "And I have treasures for each of you."

Less than a quarter of an hour later, just as the sun is beginning to peek over the shadowy horizon, Psi, Aurora, and I are safely in one of a caravan of coaches on our way over the mountains to the sea.

As it turned out, the twins were brilliant. They shape shifted us into two mammoth birds of prey—which Psi did not at all think was funny—and let us fly, with our belongings in our talons, out the window of the tower and down to the streets. It was the most exhilarating and wonderful experience of my life. The air felt sweet and cool through my feathers. Back as humans, we could see them waving to us as little specks so very high up. We waved back and fled the City of Stone forever.

Psi is despondent on the two-day journey to the sea where the skyships are docked until ready to depart. Once, he asks me if I have any family.

"My parents are in the lands of the skysea, waiting for me."

He nods without meeting my eyes, and I push down my excitement at the journey. I know he is thinking of Simon. Traveling to the skysea means leaving this world behind forever.

I have to hide my smile lest I give away my secret.

When we finally reach our destination, the port town of Larenth, I am overwhelmed with the sights and sounds. What a wonderful place to spend my last hour on this world. At the sight of the skyships, I can no longer contain my excitement—I'm finally going to be with my parents. Psi watches me skip down the streets, probably suspecting but too wrapped up in his own misery to ask. While waiting for our ship, we wander the aisles of food and bright clothing, life buzzing around us. We stick close to the sea when the time draws near, and nervousness begins to build in my chest as I look around for a familiar yet absent face. With five minutes left, I feel crushed.

Was he lying?

Psi notices the sudden change in mood. "Elza, what's wrong?"

"I—"

"Psi?" a familiar voice brings us spinning around.

Simon grins when he sees his older brother. "Psi!"

But Psi is horrified. He backs away, guilt swallowing up his emotions, bumping into one of the clothing stalls. He turns to me with pain etched into his face.

"Elza, what have you done?" he practically sobs.

Aurora hums and I feel my heart sink. I never meant to—

"Oh, for sky's sake!" Simon yells in exasperation, throwing his hands in the air. "She was trying to help you, stupid!"

Psi blinks at him, slack-jawed and at a loss. Simon shakes his head and grins again, dropping his pack and leaping at his older brother before he can escape. Psi stumbles back to maintain his balance, but Simon sticks to him like a barnacle. I can't see Psi's face around Simon's, but the older boy's human arm finally wraps around his brother, leaning into the embrace. Simon mumbles something into his ear, comforting him, the victorious smile never fading.

A horn sounds—the final call for our ship, and the two brothers separate.

"We should go," I say, and Psi's face falls. Simon just shoulders his pack. The glow in his whole expression seems to lessen the scars over his eye.

Psi looks blankly at the pack, then over to me. I fan myself with three passes to the skysea.

"You're coming with us?" he asks Simon, astonished.

"Earth and sky, you're slow today!" Simon laughs, grabbing his brother's hand and yanking him along as we sprint to make it to the skip.

Once on board, gasping for breath, the four of us watch the sails unfurl and the floating black and red skystone being raised into the ship's hull from the cool ocean water. Once warm, it will guide the captain and his ship to the skysea.

Psi rushes me, picking me clear up off the deck in a one-armed hug. I half laugh, half scream, "Still bad!"

"Oh, sorry." He drops me, grinning and rubbing his neck, tears glossing over his eyes.

Behind him, Simon watches the shimmering Aurora play with the hem of his coat. He looks at the two of us in awe, grinning for the countless time. The little creature scampers over and settles on my shoulder. I bear her touch for the joyous knowledge she's coming with me.

Water sucks at the undersides of the ship as it rises from the sea, beginning its journey up. After all these years, I'm finally going to be with my family. At the thought, Psi isn't the only one with tears in his eyes.

The four of us stumble to catch a last glimpse over the side, water droplets spraying down upon the city below. I look down at the world—it's a good last sight to have.

I beam at Psi. "Let's go home."

He returns my smile, gazing upwards into the clouds, at the shimmering lands and sea above.

And we fly.

Sequel to the author's story "Shattering the Spear"
in *Heroic Fantasy Quarterly*.

Redemption For Adanna

Phenderson Djèlí Clark

The shrill call of the crier bird pierced the morning of the dense forest. Ears perked to life and all went still, listening. When the cry came again, feathered wings quickly took flight. Feet scurried, sending small forms scampering deep into the mist-shrouded woods, or into tree holes and earthen burrows. The intense bustle of the morning was suddenly drowned in a hush. Dwellers of the forest knew well that the crier bird did not issue her call without reason. It was a warning: Flee! Hide! Take cover! Somewhere near, a hunter walks among us.

There in the tall grass, in a wide clearing that broke through the vast forest like a sea running between isles of green, the hunter of the morning lay in wait. She crept forward with silent steps, coming to the edge of where the thick stalks provided cover. There she she stopped, gazing out at what lay ahead.

Men—the children of men.

She counted three—two boys and a girl. They had likely come from one of the villages that dotted the western edges of the Jembe forest. Here, farmers planted fields and drew their sustenance from the abundant woodlands, named after the ceremonial wedge-shaped drums of their ancestors. Unaccompanied, none of the man-children looked to have counted many seasons. The only weapon amongst them was a knife, tucked away at waist of a sinewy boy on the cusp of young manhood. And its blade looked better suited for cutting figs, than flesh.

Adanna smiled, her heart drumming in anticipation as the fire behind her eyes danced with a fierce hunger. Flexing an arm covered in thick bands of gold and smaller bracelets of silver, copper and polished bone, she moved her fingers absently along the string of the great bow strapped to her back. These man-children were ripe for the taking, like bush boars that had strayed too far from their mother. She kept her eyes trained on her prey, ignoring the beads of perspiration that filtered between her braided rows of golden hair, trickling slowly upon her brow. Droplets gathered back, between her breasts, soaking through the tightly wrapped tunic in the humid morning and trapping it to her skin. Still she remained motionless, in a crouch, her muscles straining, poised more like a cat than a woman. She had been trained to ignore the discomfort, to push past the pain and embrace only the fire—that burned so bright within. She was a warrior, a hunter. And woe onto any she marked as prey.

Adanna emerged from her hiding place, a terrifying cry spilling from her lips as she bounded forward with a terrific burst of speed. Her feet barley touched the earthen ground, allowing her to move fast—faster than any woman should have been able. Such strength and swiftness was but one of the gifts of her new master. Pulling a curved knife from her waist, she uttered a word that set its dark blade alight with red flames. That too had been a gift.

The man-children turned as one, startled. Their laughter broken, they stared, made immobile by her approach. The markings painting her face, the weapons that adorned her, the burning knife—all were meant to fill her prey with fright. But Adanna knew well what stilled them than all else. It was her skin—so unlike theirs, pale and without color. It was what made her different. It always had.

She dealt with the sinewy boy first. Not breaking her stride, she pulled forth a bit of rope and iron, twirling it high and slinging it loose. It whistled through the air, catching him by the legs, wrapping about them and sending him to the ground. Finding his wits, his younger companion cried out in fright and launched into a run. A second throw ensnared him, bringing him down just as fast.

Adanna broke from her run, slowing to admire her handiwork. She slid her blade back into its sheath, the fires upon it dying out. The weapon was more show than of use here. She had no desire to damage her prey. Her master wanted captives in the best condition.

Turning, she stared down at the only remaining man-child. It was the young girl—thin and spindly as a newborn calf. Her small body shook uncontrollably, setting an assortment of beads about her neck to rattling. Her large eyes looked up at Adanna, into those dark pupils ringed with fire, as if gazing at a demon from the spirit world.

Adanna stared back, taking in the rich smoothness of the girl's ebon skin, becoming uncomfortably aware of the stark difference with her own.

"I only have bindings for two," she told the girl. "You will only be a burden upon me. And I have no use for one so young, not today. Run home to your people. Let them know what demons now stalk these woods."

The girl did not move.

Adanna scowled deeper.

"Go!" she growled. "Lest I hunger for the flesh of fool girls!"

The threat should have been enough to send most fleeing. Yet, the girl did not move. At her feet her bound companion—a sibling from the resemblance—pleaded with her to leave him. But the girl child refused, shaking her head as tears streamed down her face. Then, she did the unexpected.

Moving with surprising speed, the girl dropped down, picking up an object in the grass before returning to her feet. The elder boy's knife, Adanna realized. More shocking, this small girl now held it menacingly, standing over her elder sibling. In her eyes there was a determination to push past her fear, even in the face of an adversary she could not match.

Adanna barked a sharp laugh, unable to hide her astonishment. Here this small bit of girl was willing to stand and fight, when grown men had before dropped sword and spear to flee from her path. Placing a hand to her own knife, she pondered whether to cut down this impudent child or take her back. Perhaps such fire and courage could be harnessed for her master.

It was in the midst of the odd standoff that the sensation came. There were things a warrior could always attribute to past lessons—the way one parried a blow or swung a sword. Other things however, the way one's senses came alive at the feeling of being watched, was a rare gift shared only by a few.

Adanna spun about, pulling the great bow from her back and nocking an arrow in one motion. The large weapon had come from the famed archers of the stone cities far to the East. But she had long trained in its use, and could pierce the wings of the swiftest falcon in flight. Farmers that moved clumsily on two legs provided little challenge. To her surprise, however, what stood before her wasn't a man.

It was an antelope.

The majestic creature stood perhaps the size of a small horse, greater in height and width than any antelope she had ever laid eyes upon. Its coat was sable, near blue in the morning sun. Muscles rippled along its flank and down long, powerful legs, imbuing it with a sense of grace. Long curving and ridged horns adorned its head, like scimitars carved from black rock. It stared at her with dark eyes that seemed to shine, as if filled with small stars.

Adanna gaped at the creature's beauty, taken in by those eyes that seemed to gaze not simply at her, but through skin and flesh, perhaps even spirit. She had seen antelope enough in her time—from the small and slender kind that picked their way through the dense woodlands, to their swifter kin that bounded in great leaps across vast savannas. But never had she seen one such as this. If among the dwellers of this forest there were a king, this magnificent beast would bear the crown.

A new fire surged to life inside her. She had to possess this creature. Many beasts she had hunted in her life, but this would be a prize above all others, to make her sisters envious! Smiling at her seeming fortune, she leveled her bow and took aim. Fingers carefully pulled back on the weapon, ready to let a single arrow fly to fell this beast. Then, it would be hers for the taking.

But to her dismay, nothing happened.

Her fingers gripped the arrow, unwilling to let go. Her smile disappeared as she attempted to strike her target again, pulling back further on the string of the great bow. But once more, she was unable to complete the task.

Face contorting, Adanna clenched her teeth as she remained there poised to strike—yet unable to do so. She stood motionless, bow in hand, arrow nocked, the muscles on her arms and back tensed, her body trembling and straining to release. Perspiration formed on her brow from the exertion, trickling into her eyes with a blinding sting. She blinked, and whatever unnatural force stayed her hands, vanished.

There was a sharp twang, as her fingers released the bowstring. The arrow flew, embedding itself into the flesh of a tall sapling with a dull thunk. She stared in disbelief. Gone! The antelope was gone! The beast had vanished, in the blink of an eye. She was still working through this puzzle, when something else nagged at her. Turning, she looked for the man-children, only to find them gone as well. Only the ropes of her snares yet remained, the frayed ends showing where they'd been cut away.

The elder boy's knife, she recalled. The brazen girl child had done this. But she had only turned her back for a moment. How could the three have escaped in so short a time?

Adanna's question was stilled as her eyes caught the sky. The sun had moved. She had stalked the man-children when the sun yet dwelled just above the dawn horizon. Now it was higher, signaling it was at least mid-day. She had lost an entire morning, in what had seemed moments. How could such a thing be possible?

She glanced to where her arrow still lay buried. The antelope. There could be no other answer. It had worked some magic upon her, trapping her like a mosquito in tree sap. Yet what beast could do such a thing?

Fingers of uneasiness crept over Adanna then. She peered about at her surroundings, feeling suddenly very vulnerable in this unfamiliar forest. Lowering, she hid herself in the tall grass and began retracing her steps, wanting very much to be away from this odd place.

Adanna hurried through the forest, scowling in her frustration. She had risen long before dawn, setting out on her hunt. Her sisters would have long expected her back. Now here she was returning, late in the day and with nothing to show. What would she tell them? That three children had escaped her? That a great antelope that came and went like the wind had bewitched her? No, she could not speak of these strange events. Among those she called sisters there was little sympathy for failure.

She had been initiated into the caste of her people reserved only for daughters, charged with the protection of the king. He was their Leopard and they his royal guardians, his hunters who would fiercely defend him to the death.

Or, at least, that was how it had once been.

These were new times. The Leopard was dead. They had renounced their sacred caste. They now served a new master—the Witch Priest, who defied the spirits and the gods. He had remade them as his daughters, his Isat—from an ancient tongue in the East—his Fire. And they would in turn help him remake the world.

The flames behind Adanna's eyes danced at thoughts of her new life. The price had been steep—to renounce all that she had been. Let your past lives, your doubts and all your troubles burn away, the Witch Priest had instructed. Let them be like embers scattered on the wind. And they had. No more fear. No more doubts. No regrets. She let a hand stray absently to her side, feeling for her fire knife—the one gained upon swearing fealty to her master. Instead she touched upon something else—sharp, but decidedly different. She knew it instantly. The broken spear haft was her prized possession, won through blood and battle.

It had belonged to a warrior of the Southlands, known for their great decorative shields and spears. They had journeyed up from the plains, giving up their ceaseless cattle raids upon one another to make war upon the Witch Priest. Adanna had danced fire with the spear bearers many times. One had been a young man, who had likely counted no more than her twenty seasons. She had offered him the Witch Priest's blessing, but he refused. It had been a good fight, but she prevailed, shattering his spear and taking his life.

Adanna felt her brow furrowing at the recollection, as it did so often of late. In service to the Witch Priest she had slain many who dared oppose her master's will. Their faces shifted and disappeared like clouds in the sky. Yet this one, this young spear bearer, he remained. She could see his face clearly, strong, eyes unwavering in battle, and that final visage of death, as he lay shattered, much like his spear. Why it so moved her she did not know. But it was an unsettling memory, one she seemed unable to forget despite her best attempts. He was even there when she closed her eyes, in her dreams. And they were always the same.

She hunted a fleeting shadow—a frustrating chase that kept her prey close, yet always out of reach. Not until the end did she realize she was being baited, led to a dark place, where specks of crimson stained the tall grass. There on a windswept plain would lay the fallen warrior, his spear broken atop his shield. She would look at her hands then, only to find them stained in blood. Then, without warning, his lifeless mouth would fly open and, in a hoarse whisper, he would call out her name.

Adanna.

Adanna pushed away the image, troubled at the peculiar emotions it brought up. The fires of the Witch Priest should have filled her with certainty, clarity, and taken away her regrets. Yet here this warrior was, haunting her dreams. Her nights had been fitful of late, these visions sapping her will and wearing upon her mind. She had hoped this hunt would clear her thoughts, help her find her strength again. Instead, it only left her more troubled. She dared not confide such feelings in her sisters, who would think her mad—or worse, weak. And in the armies of the Witch Priest, those who showed weakness did not long survive.

A familiar sight greeted her upon clearing the dense forest—a great plume of black snaking its way into the sky. Smoke from a nearby village. It could only mean one thing. The armies of the Witch Priest were once again victorious, and new lands had fallen to his rule. Drawing herself up, Adanna put on her strongest face, and walked down towards the ruins.

It had taken half a day to journey back to this village, the same one she and her sisters had scouted just the night prior. She had thought the attack would come tomorrow, but it seemed plans had changed. Charred earth cracked beneath her feet while once elaborate dwellings of wood and mud brick still smoldered, sending fiery embers drifting through the air. That had been the Witch Priest's edict—put flame to any land, even a mere village such as this, which refused his blessings.

Bodies of the slaughtered had been stacked atop each other and burned, giving off an all too familiar stench. These simple farmers must have put up a strong fight, if so many had fallen in battle. She stared at the mass of burned and blackened flesh, fast being reduced to ash. In the past she had reveled in such a sight, the flames in her eyes raging in exhilaration at the mingling scent of fire and blood. But since these troubling night visions, such scenes no longer brought pleasure. Instead they made the fire within seem cold, empty.

A burst of cackling laughter pulled Adanna's eyes from the pyre. Most that called the Witch Priest master may have walked on two legs, but they were not men and women—they were something else.

She stared at the still laughing forms in the distance. Hyena-men. Golden hair with dark spots covered their human-like bodies that were adorned with little more than ragged pelts that hung from their waists. Most held crude short swords and jagged edged shields. How hyena-men had come to be, none truly knew. Some said they were the progeny of women seduced by sorcerers who could take the shape of hyenas. Others claimed they were once a beautiful people from the scorched plains, on the edges of the Desert Sea—struck down and cursed for their vanity. Yet, still, some said hyena-men were creations of the Witch Priest—willful men reduced to half-beasts by his power, now forever bound to his service.

Whatever the truth of it, the creatures now swelled the ranks of the Witch Priest's armies. Even now a pack of them bickered over a bit of meat, growls and barking cries mingled between their maniacal laughter. Adanna grimaced, trying not to think on where that flesh had come from. Drawing to full height, she walked towards the pack, a hand resting casually on her fire knife. The hyena-men looked up at she approached, their yellow eyes narrowing as they bared sharp teeth fitted into black muzzles. She met them with a look of her own, the flames in her eyes rising to a fierce glow. The show of force was enough. As one the they broke apart, whimpering their submission.

Walking through them, she kept a firm grip upon her knife, still feeling their baleful gazes on her back. Cowards these man-beasts may have been, but as a pack they would attack anything that looked weak. Besides, more than hyena-men marched beneath the banners of the Witch Priest and not all were so easily cowed.

Hordes of Eloko milled about, looting through the wreckage. Their strange speech filled the air, as they gnashed razor like teeth together in clicks and snarls. Their green dwarfish bodies made them look like small men, perhaps even children. But this belied their ferociousness, better gauged by the brutal weapons they carried. Normally found in the dark regions of the forests, they had answered the call to serve the Witch Priest—as did their more dangerous cousins.

Somewhat larger than their Eloko kin, fierce Mmoatia with blood red painted faces sat astride their steeds—great black bats larger than horses. The creatures stared out with eyes like burning coals, shifting under the reins of their masters, and stretching leathery wings in anticipation of flight. Both riders and beasts wore large hoops of gold strung through their noses and ears, as if to boast their bond.

Tall and muscular Bikolo were too gathered, looking like monstrous versions of men, and brandishing spiked swords with long spears. They argued over the spoils of victory, and bragged of their exploits. Adanna noticed one in particular, bigger than the rest, with skin like burnt rock and a single topknot of hair atop his shaved scalp. He proudly displayed a necklace, strung with the ears of men.

She turned from them, more repulsed than usual at their presence. Of late she had begun to wonder why the Witch Priest would employ such creatures in his service. He had come to free the land, from the tyranny of corrupt rulers and their gods. Yet what would any of these beasts know of freedom? She knew these doubts had come with the haunting night visions, causing her to question what she had so long accepted. But she knew of no way to stop it.

Caught up in her own thoughts, she almost did not see the greater danger that approached. Only the sharp barking alerted her ears. A giant hyena stalked past, covered in white fur and easily the size of an ox. Kept half-starved, it glared about with blood-red eyes as saliva dripped from a set of bone-crushing jaws that hung wide to reveal teeth long as daggers.

Adanna stepped back quickly, casting her gaze downward and not daring to look up. Though monstrous, it was not the ravenous hyena that caused her concern, but its rider. In the armies of the Witch Priest, there were more dark and dangerous creatures than hyena-men or Bikolo. Much worse.

It was a Kishi. She did not need to see the tall figure clad in dark robes that sat astride the giant hyena to name it. She could feel its presence—a creeping cold beneath her skin. It towered upon its steed, casting a shadow over those beneath. Kishi served as leaders in the Witch Priest's armies, whipping along the varied hordes that wisely feared them. At first glance they seemed like nothing more than extraordinarily handsome men, beautiful to the point of aberration. But that was but one face, a false one—for the Kishi had another that none dared look upon.

Some claimed the true face of a Kishi shifted continuously, a maddening display of horrid beasts. Others said it was a hollow emptiness, so dark it swallowed light. But in truth, only those that dared look at it could say for certain—and they now spoke to no one.

Adanna let her gaze follow the length of jagged chains that trailed behind the Kishi's mount. Each was attached to gaunt figures that stumbled along behind, half naked, with blank faces and milk-white eyes, rotting flesh reeking. This was the fate of those who had gazed into the true face of a Kishi, now neither living nor dead. Somewhere in those dark robes their master was said to keep a great black calabash that housed the souls of these unfortunates, forever enslaving them to this cursed existence.

And such monsters, Adanna thought, are who I now call allies.

"Yovo!" someone cried out.

Adanna turned at the call, eager to look away from the nightmare in her path. Her eyes fell on a familiar face. It was Nawi, one of her elder sisters. Tall and with the stride of a hunter, she wore a painted face and shaved scalp save for a strip of hair at its center. Skin like richly burnt wood covered her frame, causing Adanna to self-consciously run a hand across her own, which always seemed like fine ash in comparison.

"Where have you been little Yovo?" the woman asked, coming to stand before her. "Your sisters have worried over you."

"Hunting," Adanna answered. She hated being called Yovo, a name reserved for foreigners, and those born like her—different. It was meant only in jest, but still stung.

Nawi arched an eyebrow. "Hunting? Where then is your catch?"

"I found nothing," Adanna lied. She nodded at the destroyed village, eager to move from this talk. "I thought the attack was to wait?"

"As did we," the woman replied. "But a Kishi arrived this morning. It ordered we take the village at first light. You missed a glorious battle."

Adanna frowned. A glorious battle? Against farmers? She gazed to where a group of Eloko whipped along a lumbering Zimwi. Straps and chains covered its hulking body, several tons of muscle and flesh with legs that could trample a man, and fists that could pulverize rock. The slow witted gargantuan had been fitted and trained for battle, carrying a stone mace as thick as a tree trunk and a wooden shield the size of a door. It roared at its tormentors each time the lash stung its coarse hide, enraged at being dragged from the dank and lightless caves its kind preferred.

"So large a force to conquer mere farmers?" she asked.

Her sister smiled. "Ah, no Yovo. Our master has greater plans." A familiar burned fiercely behind her eyes. "We march on Agadu!"

Adanna gaped in disbelief.

"Agadu? But how? The Gold kingdom boasts thousands of warriors, horsemen with iron spears. Its walls are thick. Even this force cannot—"

"Ease yourself Yovo," Nawi chided. "A great army is being raised. Even now more hyena-men and Bikolo move to join us. Zimwi are brought up from the South. Kishi are being dispatched from our master. Let the warriors of Agadu stand to defend their kingdom. Take us before their mighty walls. They will bow before us, or break!"

Adanna fell silent. Agadu. The rich and powerful Gold kingdom. Once it fell, the other lands in the West were certain to follow. Their master's attention would turn east then, to the stone cities. The promised Great War had come at last, to drench the world in blood and fire.

"When you make that face you remind me of your mother," Nawi chuckled.

Adanna said nothing. Everyone said she resembled her mother—her fleshy nose, her full lips, the prominent bones of her cheeks, even the wide space between her eyes. It was her strange colorless skin and golden hair that marked her as different.

"Come Yovo," her sister beckoned. "No time to stand idle. There is work to be done."

Adanna nodded, following. When they reached the other side of the village, she found her sisters gathered—a sea of fierce and powerfully built women, with painted faces of eternal youth. Some carried bows or spears, others swords. They watched over the remaining villagers, those that had survived the onslaught, fitting them with heavy shackles. The unfortunates trembled before the fearsome warriors, likely wondering at their fate.

"New captured to march to the coast," Nawi said. "The ghost ships await."

Adanna hid a grimace. Ghost ships. The hulking vessels came mysteriously from across the sea, sailed by frightful wraiths that collected the living. What valuable riches they gave the Witch Priest in trade for their human cargo none knew, but those they took away never returned.

"Demons!" a voice cried. "Demons who walk on two legs!"

Adanna turned at the sound, eyes settling on an old woman amongst the shackled. Her tightly drawn skin covered her like a sheet of ebony, while white plaited hair fell to her shoulders. Wrapped in earth brown cloth, she wore amulets and other items of magic. A holy woman. She glowered at the warriors as a mother would an unruly child, hurling her contempt.

"What's this?" a sister sneered. "I did not know a tortoise so old could speak!" The other Isat laughed, more amused than put off at the priestess's rebuke.

The old woman spat derisively. "I know you! Servants of the Leopard!"

There were angry murmurs then. None here liked reminders of their past life. Adanna too frowned. The Leopard. It had been a long while since he crossed her mind. She could not even recall his face, more memories burned away by her master's will. Moving off a bit she sat down and brought forth the broken spear haft. Picking up a long shaft of wood—the ruined weapon or tool of one of these farmers—she began tying the two together.

"We are Isat," a sister retorted firmly. "Other names mean nothing to us now."

"You were servants of the Leopard!" the old woman accused. "I know well your tale, how you betrayed your king—killing him as he slept!"

Adanna felt a jolt to her body, as if someone had seized and shaken her from the inside. They had killed the Leopard. This she knew. So why did it make her tremble so?

"Watch your tongue old tortoise," another sister warned, twirling a blade deftly between her fingers. "Or I shall cut it out and feed it to one of our companions." She made a nod towards a group of nearby hyena-men, who were stripping the meat from the carcass of a slain bull.

The holy woman spat and laughed in the face of the threat.

"Brave warriors," she mocked, "who fear the simple words of old women. What were you offered for such betrayal? To make a pact with these dread beasts and the monster you serve?"

Adanna found herself trembling now. A rage was building inside, a fire that roared like a beast. Why these words so angered she did not know, but it was more than she could sit and bear. Moving quickly to her feet, she pushed past her sisters and came before the old priestess, staring the old woman down. The flames behind her eyes burned, as she toyed with the idea of grabbing onto that frail neck and snapping it like a fowl. It would be so easy, and she would enjoy it. But instead, she spoke, feeling a greater need to give answer to the question put forth.

"Freedom!" she declared. "Our master granted us power and promised eternal freedom! From the servitude of kings, of spirits, of gods, and from suffering beneath weak fools like you!"

The old woman paused in her tirade, looking Adanna over with interest. From the other villagers, frightful whispers came of the warrior with ashen skin. Some called her a ghost. Others named her a demon.

"Your treachery haunts you," the old priestess spoke finally, her voice unnaturally calm. "It stalks you in the tall grass, making over the hunter as the hunted. It fills your nights, and now your waking moments. Turn away now child. Turn away from this evil that burns away your very soul, while you still can."

Adanna's mouth went dry, and the fire that had held her died away. She almost reared back from the old woman in a moment of gripping fear. This mad priestess knew! Somehow she knew of the dreams! Of what had happened this past morning! But how?

Before she could complete her disordered thoughts, her sisters pushed past to form about the old woman, laughing and jeering.

"And where are you spirits now?" one cried out. "Do you see them here? Shall you call upon them to strike us down? To break your chains?" There was more mocking laughter. The warrior turned to the villagers, addressing them while pointing to the priestess.

"Look upon your holy woman! Her spirits have forsaken her! They have forsaken your village! They have forsaken you! Yet you still call to them? You still look to them to save you? I say save yourselves! Turn away from your weak religion and magics! The Witch Priest has come, to show us the way, to take us from our bondage! Embrace him! Bow to his power, that of a man, not a meddling spirit or an uncaring god! Do this, and you will truly know freedom! His hand is outstretched! You have only to take it!"

The shackled villagers stared at the warrior, contemplating the irreverent offer. Their gaze went to where their humiliated priestess stood, silent but defiant. Adanna watched, and for the first time something stirred within her. It was their faces, so full of despair, which called upon long buried emotions deep within her. Was it to be named... 'pity'? When, she wondered in amazement, had she last known pity? In silence she found herself urging that the villagers answer. Swear their fealty and escape the ghost ships. It was that simple. No more lives had to be sacrificed today. They needed only to take the chance offered to them.

A sudden cry issued forth from the shackled villagers. Yet to Adanna's surprise it was not in acceptance. They were not bowing down and pledging themselves to her master. Instead, they were praying!

As one, all those gathered—young and old, men and women—raised bound arms, chanting fervently, calling out to their spirits. Adanna glared at them. These elders had chosen enslavement. These mothers and fathers had condemned their sons and daughters. Each and every one had willingly given up their bodies to an unknown fate, rather than abandon their spirits. Such acts left her in confusion. Were these simple farmers to be pitied? Admired for their bravery? Or should they be damned as fools?

Her sisters however had no such dilemmas raging across their thoughts.

"Cry out to your dead spirits then!" one scoffed. She grabbed onto the priestess, pushing the old woman back amongst her people. "But they will not save you!"

Adanna moved back, returning to where she had sat. She could not look at the villagers that yet cried out. Instead, she cast her gaze away, hands gripping tight to the mended spear, her mind unable to understand their damning choice.

Chains rattled as bound feet pounded along the dusty trail. Adanna ran alongside the coffle, gazing at the setting sun. It would be night when they reached the coast, where the ghost ships would be waiting to ferry away this hapless lot. Hopefully her sisters would begin the trek to Agadu soon after, to join up with the main army they had parted ways from. To stop would mean sleep, which in these strange nights brought more torment than rest.

A sudden feeling stopped Adanna in her tracks. She spun about, eyes scanning through the forest. She was being watched. There was something out there, something familiar.

"Yovo!"

Adanna did not answer the call, though she knew it was a sister. Instead she gaped at the form that could now be seen between the dense greenery of the forest.

It was the antelope.

It stood there, ever majestic. Its powerful body rippled with muscles beneath a sable coat, while curving horns glistened even in the fading dusk. And those eyes... those beautiful eyes... they stared out like dark pools shining with light. The great beast was as fascinating now as it had been in the early morning.

"Yovo!" came the cry again from her sister. "What stills you so?"

"Do you not see it?" Adanna breathed.

"See what?"

"There!" Adanna lifted a hand to point towards the entrancing creature. "It stands there! So beautiful... where does such a thing come from?"

Two sisters stopped, staring in confusion to where she pointed.

"What do you mean, Yovo?" one of them asked. "Nothing stands there."

Adanna gaped at them in exasperation. "Are you blind? It is the antelope! The same one from morning! I must have this beast. It will not escape me again. I swear it!"

As if hearing her words, the great antelope turned suddenly—and dashed into the darkening forest. Adanna did not let the moment go unanswered. With a high cry, she leapt after it, the mended spear in hand and eyes aflame. The calls of her sisters went unheeded, her mind now consumed with the hunt.

Her prey proved as swift as it was elusive. It vanished often, only to reappear—sometimes stopping to flick its tail or give a taunting glance, before breaking into a run anew. Adanna followed her quarry, refusing to let it slip away. The forest raced past in a blur, becoming an elaborate and dense maze. Finding her way back out again would prove difficult. But such things did not concern her at present. Nor did the burning of strained muscles, or the threat of exhaustion. She would run until the last breath escaped her body, until heart and sinew collapsed. All that consumed her now was the hunt of this beast, trapping her in a void where time held no meaning.

Entering a clearing of tall grass, the antelope suddenly stopped, turning to stare at her. Adanna too halted, surprised at this move. The beast had made a fateful mistake. In this open space it was trapped, unable to hide between the bush and the brush. Its beautiful flank was exposed, laid out before her. Cautiously, she raised her spear and began her advance. She had to be careful, to not scare the beast away before the final blow could be struck. There would only be one chance. Her aim had to be precise, her throw without fault.

So intent was her focus, she almost did not see the form that lay in the tall grass.

It was a man, sprawled out upon the earthen ground, between the tall stalks. Had she continued on, she might have tread upon him. His body was still, with a quietness that could only be achieved in death. He wore golden fur on his shins, and a pelt at his waist. Atop his bare chest lay a broad, oval shield, richly decorated with markings. And upon his head was an elaborate bushy dress that partially concealed a hauntingly familiar face.

Adanna's heart nearly stopped and she faltered. She knew this man. She had seen his face before. He was the warrior from the Southlands—the very one that haunted her dreams. She had seen him die, slain by her own hands. Even now she held his spear. How then could he be here?

Without warning, the dead warrior's mouth flew open. Adanna reared back, fear clutching at her insides. A part of her almost turned and fled, but she summoned the courage to hold fast. For a moment the man laid there, eyes closed and mouth opened in silence. Breaking the quiet, a hoarse whisper escaped his lips, and he uttered one word.

Adanna.

"No! No! No!" Adanna screamed out in the panic that now seized her. She stumbled back, trembling, the grace of the hunter gone out of her. This was her dream! Her dream given flesh! But it couldn't be. Nightmares did not follow you into the waking world. She would not accept it! It simply could not be! She shut her eyes tight, closing out the terrifying vision, seeking to banish it away. When she dared open them again she steeled herself for what might await. But the apparition had gone, body and shield and all.

Confusion locked Adanna in momentary paralysis. Was she going mad? Had this strange day taken its toll on her mind? She looked up, still at a loss, only to find the antelope. The majestic beast had not moved from where it stood. Silent, it stared at her, the light in those dark eyes piercing.

"You!" she breathed in accusation. "You are the fleeting shadow! The one that haunts my dreams! This is all your doing!" Anger coursed through Adanna then, the fire of pure rage. This creature was toying with her, tormenting and taunting her with these maddening visions. This was the source of her newfound doubts, her confusion, her weakness! It dared play such games with her? Did it not know that she was Isat! Lifting her spear, she sounded a cry of blood and vengeance. "Cursed beast! I do not know from where you came! But on this day I will end you!"

Adanna took up a run, intent on plunging her spear deep until the blood flowed on her hands. But the fatal blow was stayed by and eruption of light, so powerful it seemed to come from everywhere, so bright it blinded. In a blur, the great antelope changed.

The limbs of a beast turned to arms and legs. Sable fur gave way to skin. From seemingly out of nothingness a golden sword flashed. It cut down, striking the spear, shattering the wood in a spray of splinters and breaking it in two. The force of the blow drove Adanna to her knees, hands held protectively over her eyes. Only when the stinging light died away did she dare look up in awe.

At first glance she would have named it a woman. But that did not begin to speak the full truth. This figure was tall, taller than any woman—or man for that matter. Her skin looked as if it were carved from the black of night itself. Golden cloth draped over her graceful body, while beads adorned her slender neck. In one hand she held a golden leaf-shaped sword, with an elaborate pattern carved into the blade, the very one that had shattered Adanna's spear.

Long black horns emerged from between thickly coiled hair wrapped behind an elaborate headdress. There was a stunning awe to her flawless countenance, which could only be described as beyond beauty, beyond perfection. And her dark eyes, familiar eyes, shined as if filled with an ageless wisdom. Adanna knew then what she truly gazed upon.

"You are a spirit," she stammered in whisper.

The being's voice was powerful.

"I am as you name me young warrior—a protector of these lands."

"But the spirits... they... you... are gone"

"We are eternal. Formed when the world was still young, and will be here when it is rendered to dust. How then can we be gone?"

"But why?" Adanna asked. "Why are you here? Why now?"

"You called me," the spirit replied.

Adanna clenched her teeth. "Never..."

"Yes, young warrior. You called to me. In your dreams."

"You haunt my dreams," she accused.

"I only lead. To that place your master has not yet corrupted."

Adanna frowned. "The Witch Priest...?"

"So the deceiver now names himself..."

"My master is no deceiver. We walk his path to free ourselves."

"A path of blood and war," the spirit scorned. "How can a world enslaved be free?"

Adanna bristled, finding some of her prior fire.

"You would rather us be slaves to your kind," she hissed.

The spirit shook her head, as one would to a child.

"You cannot see. You are enslaved—to one of my kind."

Adanna glared, staggered by the charge.

"What deceit is this? My master is no spirit! He is the Witch Priest. A man!"

"A man who controls Hyena men? A man who bends Kishi to his will? You yourself have questioned this. It is why you sought me out."

Adanna knelt there, momentarily dazed by the spirit's words. This being knew her, knew even her innermost doubts that she spoke to none. Could there be truth to these wild accusations? No! She shook her head to push out the poisonous thoughts. This was a spirit, she had to remember. They were deceitful, her master taught. They could not be trusted!

"You lie!" she screamed. "I name you a liar, spirit! Like all your treacherous kind!"

The spirit's face darkened at this outburst. Her dark eyes seemed to flash with lightening, and when she spoke it was a bellowing thunder.

"I do not lie! See your master! See your Witch Priest for what he is! See him with my eyes!"

Adanna clutched her head in pain as a vision pierced her mind like a hot knife. She saw a being sitting upon a throne. His face was hidden by a mask of sharp iron behind which raged a living inferno. He laughed, laughed at her, laughed at them all, as the world was set afire, and burned away to ash.

When the vision vanished Adanna found she was doubled over, trembling and in pain. She wanted to call what she had just seen a lie, a trick. But she could not. What she had glimpsed she had seen through this spirit's eyes. And she knew it to be truth. That terrible being behind the mask of iron, the living fire, that was her master—the Witch Priest to whom she had pledged her life. He was not a man. He was no man at all. He was... something else.

"There is a balance to all things," the spirit spoke. "We spirits are bound to this eternal dance." Her voice hardened. "But some seek to upset that balance. Your Witch Priest is one of our own, a spirit. He came to us some time ago, whispering deceit, imploring that we interfere not in the affairs of mortals, that we allow you your own path, pledging to do the same. We agreed, only to later watch this Witch Priest lead you to destruction, unable to break our oath. We did not know then that this was none other than the deceiver, taken a new form, breaking his own oath through treachery, blinding us as he blinded you."

Adanna listened, her mind adrift. She... her sisters... they had all pledged fealty, their lives, to a lie. Her eyes caught sight of her broken spear and suddenly the fallen warrior was there again, laid out in the tall grass. She reared back fearfully.

"You torment me, spirit? Why?"

The spirit's eyes took on a pitied look. "I am not your tormentor. The deceiver yet blinds you. Among your sisters, how are you called?"

Adanna stiffened, gazing down at the dead warrior.

"Yovo," she whispered.

"Why?"

"Do you not see my skin?" she asked ruefully. "I am cursed."

"Yet this is not why," the spirit pressed.

"No," Adanna admitted. It was a while before she spoke "My mother was... foreign-born."

"Yet you were not, daughter of the king."

Adanna glared upward. None but her sisters knew that. None.

"Daughter of the Leopard," the spirit went on. "Your father was a king, who took a foreign wife."

"He took a concubine!" Adanna spat, the fire within her rising. "And when I was born, they called me a curse and shunned her! He shunned her—even unto her death!"

"And you hated him," the spirit said knowingly.

"Yes," she hissed, the anger in her raging now.

"Yet still, you chose to protect him. You were not born into the caste of warriors, you sought it out, seeking his love. For you, for your mother."

"And he never gave it," she said bitterly. "Nothing I did could please him. He ignored me at every turn."

"Is that why you committed your deed?"

Adanna stared up in confusion. "I don't understand. What deed?"

The spirit shook her head sadly. "The deceiver has so corrupted you, you deceive yourself. But the heart is not so easily blinded. It is your heart that has sought me out. It is your heart that has haunted your own dreams." She raised her sword, pointing towards the slain warrior. "Lift the veil the deceiver has placed upon you. Remember"

Adanna looked upon the spear bearer, his once fierce face peaceful in death. Why, she asked. Why did he haunt her so? What kept him in her dreams, and now her waking world? It was as she pondered those thoughts that a transformation took place. The slain warrior changed. His body remained that of a man, but became older, and with a face that frightened her so greatly her body trembled.

"No!" she wailed. "No! No! No!"

"Who do you see?" the spirit asked.

Adanna shook her head, refusing to answer. In horror she watched as the man's mouth opened, releasing her name in a hoarse whisper.

Adanna.

"No!" she screamed, pushing back, heart pounding in terror.

"Who?" the spirit pressed.

It took all her strength to answer.

"It is the Leopard," she cried. "My father."

"The slain king," the spirit said. "How did he die?"

There was a gulf of silence before the answer came.

"I killed him," Adanna whispered hoarsely.

The pain of that admittance struck her with such a blow, she swooned. The world seemed to spin and she thought she might tumble away to darkness. It was the spirit that put out a steadying hand, keeping her conscious.

"He died at your hands. His own daughter."

The memories burned away with her past, returned now in a flood. The Witch Priest had come to her, promising to take away her grief and free her forever from pain. All she needed do was kill the man she so hated, who she had spent a lifetime attempting to please, in vain. She had done the deed with the very fire knife given her, plunging it deep into his heart as he slept, until the blood stained her hands. It had been easy then to convince her sisters, each of them, one by one, seduced by the Witch Priest.

"And when he lay there, dying," the spirit said, "gazing up at you, knowing the fatal blow had come by your hand, he uttered one word. What was it?"

Adanna closed her eyes, remembering the final visage of her father, as he struggled to release his last breath. "My name. He called my name."

"Adanna. Given to you by your mother. A name from her people."

"Father's gift." Adanna felt a sob escape her throat. "It means, Father's gift. He had never spoken it before. Not once. Why? Why then? Why did he wait until death?"

The spirit paused before answering.

"Perhaps because as king he believed he could not do so openly. Perhaps like men of power he was too vain, too foolish. Or perhaps, like so many, he knew not how to love. None can truly know."

"How could I have forgotten?" Adanna asked.

"The fire inside you, it is a living thing, a part of the deceiver," the spirit explained. "It blinds, drowning you in its dark flames. But your heart held the truth, though you did not want to see, so you masked away your father in the face of another."

Adanna looked down to the apparition of her father. She could still feel the warmth of his blood on her hands. And suddenly she felt sick. The fire within now repulsed her. She wanted to tear off her skin, gouge out her eyes until she could reach that vile darkness. She stared up at the spirit, pleading.

"Take it out of me!" she cried. "Take this evil out of me! Please! Please!"

"Are you certain?" the spirit asked, her voice edged with warning. "It will come with a price."

"I do not care! I cannot take his foul touch! Not one more moment! No more! No more! Take it out! Please!"

The spirit stared down, as if contemplating her plea, before nodding. In a brilliant flash the spirit seemed to grow taller still. Her eyes burned on a face that was now terrible to gaze upon, and her body glowed fierce, becoming bright as a star. The blinding light struck Adanna, piercing through her, filling her, lifting the fire from her heart, from her soul—banishing it away. And then it was done.

A long shudder wracked Adanna. Her skin no longer burned. The flames behind her eyes no longer ranged. The fire that had once consumed her was gone. So too had the apparition of her father. The night air felt cool upon her face. The sounds of the forest, the moon in the sky—all seemed more vivid than she could remember in a long time. She almost laughed aloud at these forgotten pleasures.

But there was something else. Images filled her thoughts. The faces of men, women and children, slain, or captured, sold into bondage or given death. All at her hands, her bloodied hands. Each of them flashed before her eyes.

"What sorcery is this?" she gasped.

The spirit fixed that piteous gaze upon her. "No sorcery, young warrior. Only your heart. In the service of your master, you committed grievous deeds. The fire of the deceiver left you without feeling, without care. But now, the memories return."

"No." Adanna tried to shut out the terrible images. "Make it stop... please."

"That is not in my power," the spirit replied.

"I cannot live like this!"

"No," the spirit agreed. "You can however, make penance. There is a path to redemption. It is long. Yet, it may offer you some of the absolution you seek—if you choose to accept it."

Adanna looked up hesitantly, gazing into the face of the being before her. She had spent so long now cursing the spirits, only to learn she had been deceived by one of their kind. Could she truly trust another?

"I do not want to be your slave," she said.

The spirit shook her head. "And you shall not be. We spirits are here to guide, to assure balance. The one you call the Witch Priest, who has deceived us all, has upset this. It falls upon us all, mortals and spirits, to restore that balance. To stop him from destroying this world. It is not your servitude I seek, but your help."

Adanna remained kneeling, overwhelmed by her grief.

"But I am cursed," she whispered. "Nothing can erase the mark on my skin. Or bring back those I have wronged."

The spirit stepped forward she placed a hand to Adanna's chin, nudging it upward. "You are not cursed child. You were born as you are, different but beautiful. You have only been deceived. It is true, the past cannot be undone. All that is in our power now is the time to come. How shall you use that gift?"

Adanna closed her eyes for a long moment, reliving a lifetime of terrible memories. She wrapped arms about the spirit who embraced her in turn. The touch was beautiful, like holding onto a star. Resting her head, she nodded in acceptance at the path that would help her heal the wound in her soul. She had found her redemption, and would not let go.

God-Daughter

Melissa Mead

As soon as the canoe drew close to the island, Naira started kicking the two warriors manning the paddles. With her hands bound and her mouth gagged, she didn't have many options in the way of protest.

"Stop it, Hex Girl," said one.

"Do you want to dump us all in the lake?" said the other.

Naira nodded savagely and rocked the canoe back and forth. It capsized in the shallow water. The men cursed and spluttered. Naira landed feet first on a sandy patch of lake bottom, barely wetting the fringes of her dress, and waited while her guards cut the bonds on her wrists. It took several tries. The men dropped their knives, stepped on sharp clamshells, and slipped on weed-covered rocks. Both men were bruised and bleeding by the time the last strand of rope parted. Naira ripped the gag from her mouth.

"You'll be sorry! The Storm God will curse you for exiling me. He'll sink your little boat before you're halfway home."

"Actually, we'll be safer now that you're not in it," said one man. The other heaved a cloth-wrapped bundle toward shore.

"Better catch that before it sinks," he said, grinning.

By the time Naira hauled the bundle ashore, the little canoe was far out into the main lake, making much better time without Naira in it. Not just from the loss of its disruptive passenger, either. The men weren't stopping every few lengths to bail, or to retrieve a dropped paddle.

"Cowards!" Naira shouted after them. "Such brave warriors, stranding a girl in the middle of nowhere just because she happens to be lucky!"

The men didn't even turn around.

"Father, don't let them get away with this!" Naira called. "Send the wind and waves to avenge me. Drench them with the waters of the storm. Hail on them!"

Somewhere in the cloudless sky, a hawk cried.

"Right. I shouldn't be surprised. It's not like you did anything to save Mother. You're a lousy model of parental responsibility, you know!"

"I know. But I am rather new to it all."

Naira spun around. She could see from one end to the other of this scrap of island, and she knew she'd been alone on it. Yet now she faced a short, squat man with tangled gray hair and a face like weathered moose leather. A menagerie of hides dangled from his belt. One appeared to be imperfectly-tanned skunk.

Naira moved upwind from the stranger. "Who or what are you? And how did you get here?"

"You called me." He took a step forward. The look in his eyes when Naira stepped backward reminded her of a wounded deer.

"I did not! I called upon Wayawo, the Storm God. My father." She expected the little man to look awed, but instead he looked even more hurt.

"Is that what Aylen told you?"

"Well, she said he was one of the gods, and I do have the most unusual luck. At least I did until she died. Wait—how did you know my mother's name?"

The stranger looked wistful. "I loved her, you know. Such a sweet, forgiving woman. I would have come sooner, but death is hardly a petty misfortune, so I had to take it up with the god of Tragedy, and he decided to be hardheaded, even though he's done this sort of thing for the Goddess of Spring at least once, and..."

Naira wasn't listening. The phrase "petty misfortune" had stuck in her memory.

"Oh no," she said.

The little man brightened. "You do recognize me! Ono, God of Petty Misfortune, at your service. Of course, you can call me Father. If you want to. Or Dad, or Papa... you wouldn't believe how many names the other gods' children have for their fathers. I don't know how they keep them all straight. There's an advantage to only having one, hey? Plus you'll get all the attention."

"Oh no, no, no." Naira backed up until the lake lapped around her ankles. "This can't be right. I have good luck, not bad. Incredibly good luck. Unbelievably good luck. Rest-Of-The-Clan-Gets-Jealous-And-Strands-Me-On-An-Island luck."

"Well, of course you do! I'm not about to let misfortunes happen to my only child, am I?"

"But they happen to everyone around me instead! The Skin Keeper claimed that I brought bad luck to the whole tribe."

"Well, it has to go somewhere." Ono frowned. "I thought Aylen was the tribe's Skin Keeper. Why didn't she pass the power on to you? How—how did she die?"

"Bad luck," said Naira, more harshly then she'd intended. She hadn't cried in front of her kidnappers, and she wouldn't cry in front of this strange little man.

Ono's face crumpled with fresh grief. "But death isn't a petty misfortune."

"No. In this case it's the result of some seriously annoyed neighbors deciding that they're sick of burnt fingers and spoiled food and skirts that come untied in the middle of a dance. So they threw her in the lake and held her under..." Naira trailed off.

"They drowned her?"

"No, the Chief stopped them. But she'd gotten water in her lungs, and she just got sicker and sicker." Naira glared at the heartbroken little god. "The Chief gave the skins to Nuka—who has no sense of drama and proper storytelling whatsoever—and while he was blessing the new Keeper, he stepped on a rotten spot on the ceremonial platform. While everyone else was trying to help him get his leg unstuck, Mother's killers decided that I must be the real source of the bad luck. They tied me up and dumped me here—and where the heck were *you*?"

She shouted the last word. Ono flinched.

"Doing... things. God-type things."

"What; giving someone pimples? Tangling fishing line? Prioritize! You say you loved Mother, but you weren't there!"

"But I'm here now! I'll make it up to you."

"You can't. Go away."

"I'll take you to the Island of the Gods. You'll love it. We'd be just in time for the Father-Daughter Picnic."

"I told you to leave me... Wait. You can get me off this island?"

"Of course! Basic godding skill, that is." His weathered face lit up. "So we are going to the picnic, then?"

"There really is a Father-Daughter Picnic? Just for the gods?"

"Of course! And a Mother-Son one, and Family Day. I've always wanted to go to Family Day."

"And all the gods will be there?"

"Every one! From Wayawo the Storm God himself down to... well, me."

"I'd love to go. I've dreamed about something like this my whole life."

Ono clasped her hand in his leathery one. Skunk-scented air swirled around them.

"Don't worry, I've got you!" he cried, and the island vanished.

Naira decided that she never, ever wanted to travel that way again. It felt like she'd swirled around with the air, spread out like smoke from one island to the other, before her body rebounded into place. It was sheer luck that she hadn't thrown up.

Oh. Right. Luck.

Beside her, Ono clutched at her arm, trying to steady her. "Are you all right? I'm so sorry. I really haven't interacted with mortals all that much. I forget about things like bones and digestion."

Naira straightened up and looked around. No one seemed to have noticed their abrupt entrance. The more she looked the more she realized that here, popping out of the air was more or less normal. It was like being in one of the wildest tales in the Skins.

That fellow over there, with the flaming hair, for instance. He had to be the Fire God.

"Those girls, they're the Fire God's daughters, right? They look human. I mean, their hair's red, but it's not actually burning, like his."

"Half mortal, like you. You see, gods and goddesses, well, we need a mortal partner if we want children."

"That's got to be awkward."

"That's an understatement. Wayawo's wife hasn't spoken to him in months."

"What about you?"

Ono looked mournful again. "There was only Aylen."

Naira turned away, uneasy, and studied the crowd more closely. There! A stormcloud hung over a gaggle of girls, all dressed in thundercloud grey shot with electric blue. Naira shook her arm free of Ono's grasp and ran to them. "Am I late?"

The tallest of the girls wrinkled her nose. Naira prayed that none of Ono's skunk had rubbed off on her. "Late for what?"

"The picnic, of course! Wayawo... I mean Father... sounded so excited about it."

The girls snickered.

"Father never gets excited about anything," the tall girl informed her. "If you were really his daughter, you'd know that. And you'd be dressed right."

"Well, he just found me. I've been held captive on a distant island."

"Really? Which one?"

"Uh... it's so distant it hasn't got a name."

"Right"

"Father does get around, Wikolia," put in another girl. "Besides, this is the first new thing that's happened at one of these picnics in ages."

"True." Wikolia gave Naira a look that made her feel like a hooked fish. "Go on, New Girl. Why were you being held captive?" She leaned closer and whispered "Father hates liars, you know. And he's got a temper. Amuse us, and we just might stand up for you."

The Skins were full of stories of the consequences of the Storm God's wrath. Some involved islands that weren't there any more. Naira shuddered.

"Well, my mother was a Skin Keeper, and her enemies were jealous of her power, so they drowned her." Real emotion choked Naira's voice.

"Politics. Happens all the time," said Wikolia. The smug, knowing look on her face made Naira's temples pound.

"It wasn't politics! It was my mother! And my no-good father didn't do anything to stop it. He wasn't even there, the coward!"

"What did you just call me?" rumbled a thunderous voice. Naira came out of her red rage to see Wayawo's daughters backing away slowly, slowly, from a vast column of thunderheads that had somehow sprung up behind her.

Naira looked up, and up. The livid face of the Storm God glared down.

"So, my newest daughter calls me a coward. In front of the entire Picnic."

Naira looked around in terror, and saw Ono trying in vain to shoulder his way toward her through the crowd that pressed around them, waiting to see this impertinent girl incinerated by lightning. Naira wished Ono wouldn't risk it. The Storm God wasn't the type to trip over a broken sandal strap.

"She says what she thinks. I like that in my offspring."

His actual offspring, and anyone within earshot, relaxed visibly. Except for Ono. The little god looked stricken.

"How about a game of Thunderball, girls?"

He held up a hand, and a crackling ball of darkness and lightning formed within it. The girls did the same. Naira held up her hand, trying to look confident. Nothing.

"Having a problem, girl?" Wayawo shook his massive head in mock concern. "How odd. All my other daughters knew how to play Thunderball since they could walk."

"She's been held captive," the girl who'd spoken up before offered. "Maybe she's traumatized."

Wayawo turned to face her, slowly. "Daughters of the Storm God are never traumatized, Lani. Give her your ball."

With an apologetic look, Lani handed over the crackling sphere. It stung Naira's hand, but she refused to wince.

"Choose your targets!" Wayawo bellowed, and everyone within earshot scattered. Except for Ono.

"What's that stinking wretch doing here?" the Storm God muttered. He looked from the God of Petty Misfortune to Naira, and smiled.

"Well, well! There's your target, kiddo. See that dried-up old furry fellow? I want you to hit him with that thunderball as hard as you can. Show the world you're the Storm God's daughter!"

Ono just stood there, watching her with his droopy doglike face. Naira raised the thunderball.

"Oh, I'll show the world, all right! I call upon the power of my father!"

Ono just stood there, heartbroken.

"I said: I call upon the power of my father!" Naira repeated.

The God of Petty Misfortune brightened. Naira tossed the ball—not at him, but to him. Ono caught it and threw it back. Naira hurled it to the ground.

For just a moment, lightning blinded her. Thunder deafened her. Then her ears stopped ringing, her vision cleared, and she could take in the chaos around her. Daughters of Wayawo were sucking burnt fingers, re-tying dropped skirts, hopping about from stubbed toes, and crying to Wayawo to make the ringing in their ears stop.

Wayawo, now half his former height, wasn't paying attention to them. His thunderheads had turned pale, and water soaked the ground around him.

"Stole your thunder, did I?" said Naira. "Bad luck for you." She put her arms around Ono. The deflated Storm God glared.

"So you're his brat. Of course."

"Isn't she something?" Ono beamed. "Did any of your girls ever stand up to you like that?"

Wayawo's eyes flashed lightning. Literally. Naira tugged Ono's arm. "Um, Dad, this might not be the smartest place for us to hang around right now."

"Did you hear that? She called me Dad. We can go anywhere you'd like, Sweetheart. Unless you'd like a cup of ambrosia first?"

"No, really. I think we ought to be going. Right now."

"So soon? If that's what you really want..."

The world lurched again. Sand crunched underfoot. Naira looked around. "This is the island I was stranded on."

"I know. I just wanted to say goodbye." He scuffed a toe in the sand. "I'll take you back to your island, and then I'll leave you alone. It was nice of you to be a good sport in front of the other gods and all, but I know I'm not what you really wanted."

Naira thought about Wayawo's sneering face. She imagined appearing on the ceremonial platform in a swirl of magic, and the Chief, overawed, handing her the sacred Skins.

Ono just stood there, waiting to grant her wish. He looked like he was drinking in the sight of her, trying to store up memories to last his immortal lifetime.

Maybe she wasn't what he'd wanted, either. But here they were.

"Where will you go?"

He shrugged. "Somewhere."

"I've always wanted to go somewhere. Could I come with you... Dad?" Ono blinked, then whooped and grabbed her in a loving, skunky embrace. "Of course! I'll take you to the Fire Falls, the Crystal Desert... I know! Have you ever seen snow?" She hadn't. No one in the Islands ever had. Even the Skin Keepers only hinted at the stuff in their oldest, most incredible stories. Maybe she'd inherit her mother's place some day after all.

"I'd love to!"

"Then off we go! We'll just pop in on the Snow God first, so we know where he's working this time of year."

Just as the island swirled out of existence, Naira heard her father mumble "of course, Wayawo *is* the Snow God's favorite brother. But word can't have gotten around that fast..."

Oh no.

About the Authors

Phenderson Djèlí Clark is an Afro-Caribbean-American writer of speculative fiction. Raised on genres of fantasy, sci fi, horror and the supernatural, he felt a need for more diverse tales with more diverse characters drawn from more diverse sources. To that end, he put pen to pad and fingers to keyboard, seeking to Imagine, Dream and Create new realms to explore.

Kelda Crich is a new born entity. She's been lurking in her creator's mind for a few years. Now she's out in the open. Find Kelda in London looking at strange things in London's medical museums. Kelda's work has appeared in *The Lovecraft eZine, Dreams from the Witch House* and in the Bram Stoker Award winning *After Death* anthology.

Mame Bougouma Diene is a French-Senegalese American humanitarian based in Aguascalientes, Mexico, with a fondness for tattoos, progressive metal and policy analysis. He is previously published in *Omenana, Brittlepaper, AfroSFv2,* and by *edilivres* (French).

Tom Fletcher studied Creative Writing at the University of Leeds. His first novel, *The Leaping*, was published by Quercus in 2010 and shortlisted for the 2011 British Fantasy Society Best Novel award. His first fantasy novel, *Gleam,* which is the setting for his story in this anthology, was published by Jo Fletcher Books in September 2014, and he is currently working on its sequel. He lives in Cumbria.

J. W. Hall currently resides in the suburbs of Boston with his wife and infant son. He tries with all his might to concentrate at his day job as a project manager for a healthcare technology company, but finds his mind drifting to others worlds with strange characters and creatures too often. Luckily his nightly writing time allows him to trap some of his disruptive imagination onto a page so he can at least pretend to pay attention at work. Outside of writing, working, and spending time with his family you'll find him playing basketball, sampling as many local restaurants as possible, and reading fantasy novels.

M. K. Hutchins studied archaeology at BYU, which gave her the opportunity to compile histories from Maya glyphs, excavate in Belize, and work as a faunal analyst. She often draws on her background in archaeology when writing. A long time Idahoan, she now live in Utah with her husband and four kiddos. Her YA fantasy novel *Drift* (Tu Books, 2014) is both a Junior Library Guild Selection and a VOYA Top Shelf Honoree.

Terry Jackman is a mild-mannered lady living in a quiet English village—who when her neighbours aren't looking turns into the coordinator of the British Science Fiction Association's 'Orbit' writers' groups, reads submissions for *Albedo One* magazine, edits both short story and novel length, oh and writes. Her cross genre novel *Ashamet* came out last year in the USA and is collecting great reviews.

Benjamin Jacobson is an author, father, teacher, fan and futurist. His fiction has appeared in print and online in dozens of venues. After completing his master's degree in genre fiction, he plans to continue to confound his own expectations and those of the audience.

Amy Power Jansen lives and works in Johannesburg, South Africa with her husband, Stephen. By day, she inhabits the prosaic world of finance in the guise of a behavioural economist, and by night, she explores worlds fantastic and science fictional and as many shades as possible in between. Her work has previously appeared in *Abyss & Apex* and *Perihelion SF*, and is forthcoming in *Futuristica 2*.

Tanith Lee was a British writer of science fiction, horror, and fantasy. She was the author of over 90 novels and 300 short stories. In the course of her long career she produced adult and young adult novels, science fiction, fantasy, horror, crime, spy fiction, erotica, a historical novel, radio plays and two episodes of the television space opera Blake's 7. She was the first woman to win the British Fantasy Award best novel award, for her book *Death's Master* (1980). She died of breast cancer on 24 May 2015.

Samuel Marzioli is an Italian/Filipino writer of mostly dark fiction. His stories have appeared or are forthcoming in *Apex Magazine*, *Intergalactic Medicine Show*, *Shock Totem*, *Penumbra eMag*, *Ares Magazine*, *Stupefying Stories*, and more.

Emily McCosh is a student living in sunny California. Her love (possibly obsession) for writing books and short stories occupies her everyday daydreams, and she is working on her debut novel in the SF genre. She also writes and publishes poetry through AllPoetry, an online self-publishing website for poets. When not writing you can find her wrestling two crazy dogs or listening to music for inspiration.

Melissa Mead lives in Upstate NY. Her stories have appeared in *Daily Science Fiction*, *IGMS*, and other fine places. She is a part of the Carpe Libris Writers Group.

Lev Mirov is a disabled mixed race Filipino-American who lives with his wife, fellow writer India Valentin, and their two cats in rural Maryland, where he feeds the ghosts of Antietam when it rains. Read more of his fictional magical worlds, his medieval research, or his Rhysling-nominated fantastical poetry, at Wordpress.

Nitai Poddar lives in Florida and writes game manuals for Ubisoft. He has no previous fiction publications, but has been a life-long fan of fantasy and science fiction.

Katherine Quevedo was born and raised just outside of Portland, Oregon, where she works as an analyst and lives with her husband and two sons. She graduated from Santa Clara University with degrees in English and Business Economics. Her speculative fiction and poetry have appeared in the *Santa Clara Review*. When she isn't writing, she enjoys watching movies, singing, playing old-school video games, belly dancing, and making spreadsheets.

Alter S. Reiss is an archaeologist and writer who lives in Jerusalem with his wife Naomi and their son Uriel. He likes good books, bad movies, and old time radio shows.

Adrian Tchaikovsky is the author of the acclaimed Shadows of the Apt fantasy series. More recently he has authored the science fiction novel *Children of Time* and started a new fantasy series starting with *The Tiger and the Wolf*. He has been nominated for the David Gemmell Legend Award and a British Fantasy Society Award. In civilian life he is a lawyer, gamer, and amateur entomologist.

Neil Williamson is a writer and musician, based in Glasgow, Scotland. His first short story was published in *Territories* magazine, edited by the inestimable Erich Zahn, in 1994, and he has been lucky enough to keep the fiction thing rolling ever since. His debut novel, *The Moon King*, which is the setting for his story in this anthology, was a BSFA award and British Fantasy award 2015 nominee.

Likhain is a queer Filipina artist working in traditional media to create fantastical worlds. She has illustrated for publications such as *Lackington's Magazine, Editions Jentayu,* and the anthology *AN ALPHABET OF EMBERS,* and has created art for stories by Kate Elliott, Zen Cho, Cindy Pon, Roshani Chokshi, and others.

Enjoy more stories
of unique fantasy, adventure, and magic in

Myriad Lands
Volume 1: Around the World

Volume 1 contains stories based on real cultures (or their magical analogues) traditionally under-represented in fantasy literature from all over our world.

Stories by: Tade Thompson, Mary Anne Mohanraj, Lyn McConchie, Daniel Heath Justice, Dilman Dila, and more.

- A Chinese ex-soldier is confronted by the ghost of a young man he killed in battle.
- Two sisters disagree on how to deal with the African gods who followed their family to modern Britain.
- A blind Japanese girl journeys through the woods to tend her grandparents' grave and encounters a nefarious fox spirit.
- A Nigerian boy catches a magical fish the local magicians would love to eat. But is it worth more to him alive?
- A girl from the Caucasus mountains is set to marry a young man from the valley, when an invasion of Cyclopses interrupts the wedding.

Available from Guardbridge Books.